Also by Lucy Gilmore

FOREVER HOME
Puppy Love
Puppy Christmas
Puppy Kisses

Ruff
and
Tumble

LUCY GILMORE

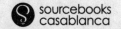

sourcebooks
casablanca

Published by Sourcebooks Casablanca, an imprint of Sourcebooks
P.O. Box 4410, Naperville, Illinois 60567-4410
(630) 961-3900
sourcebooks.com

Printed and bound in Canada.
MBP 10 9 8 7 6 5 4 3 2 1

chapter

1

IF THERE WAS A WAY TO HIDE A HEAVILY PREGNANT GOLDEN retriever under a desk, Hailey had yet to discover it.

"Bess, love. This would be so much easier if you'd just sit." She paused and watched as the dog panted, squirmed, and licked the top of her favorite red Converse shoes. There was no sitting of any kind. "Okay, then stay. Lie down. Heel. Didn't your previous owners teach you any commands?"

Bess wriggled out from between Hailey's legs and began pacing the length of the office. It was a small room, a windowless hole that held the floor's air-conditioning unit in addition to Hailey's desk, so the dog didn't have far to go. Her swollen belly swayed and undulated with each step.

"Jasmine is going to eat you alive if she sees that dog." A smiling face appeared at the office door. As usual, Penny looked perfectly put together and amused to find Hailey in what could only be described as *a mess*. Which, to be fair, was daily. "Quick... Give her a football to play with. Maybe Jasmine will think she's here for a photo shoot."

It wasn't, as her coworker's irreverent tone suggested, the worst idea in the world. They—along with a dozen other people currently staffing this office—often performed photo shoots. With dogs. And footballs. In fact, one might argue that was *all* they did.

As the official offices of the Puppy Cup, the canine counterpart to the professional football game held every February, making dogs look adorable for the camera was Hailey's stock-in-trade.

Well, she was technically just a production assistant on the show, so her stock-in-trade had more to do with grabbing coffees and running errands than anything else, but the idea held true. Someone had to help wrangle the fifty different puppies that appeared on-screen every year to play with stuffed balls, chase one another, and otherwise adorably simulate the game of football during the Kickoff Cup's halftime.

Hailey Lincoln was that someone. In fact, Hailey Lincoln had been that someone for six years. While other people were promoted and celebrated and otherwise applauded for their professional choices, she remained exactly where she was.

On the floor. With a dog.

Hailey sighed as she dropped to Bess's level. "I know how Jasmine feels about having animals in the office, but I didn't have a choice." She put out a soothing hand, but the dog had no intention of being soothed—which was fair, considering the half-dozen puppies taking up the space where her intestines were supposed to go. "I couldn't leave her at home. Not this close to her due date."

"You should have called me for help," Penny said. "I know people."

As was almost always the case when Penny made an offer like that, Hailey wasn't sure how to take it. On the surface, it seemed legit, and Lord knew she could use the help. Bess wasn't Hailey's dog, but she was her responsibility. As her foster placement until the puppies were born and could be found good homes, Hailey had signed on to keep the animal safe and happy—and the more hands on board with that, the better. But Penny was nice to *everyone*, and always with that same friendly smile and air of unconcern, regardless of how obnoxious they were. She was even nice to the guy who delivered sandwiches from the deli down the street, and he'd once followed Penny home and keyed her car because she wouldn't go on a date with him.

"Thanks, but I don't want to be a bother." Hailey forced a note of cheer into her voice and added, "Besides, it's more exciting to live on the edge like this. Will Jasmine fire me? Will I be thrown out without a reference? Tune in at eleven for the update."

Penny chuckled obligingly, but like the friendly overtures, it could just as easily be a sympathy laugh. Hailey was about to let her coworker off the hook with a smile and a wave, but Bess began panting anew. From her vantage point on the floor, Hailey could detect the light scent of acetone assailing her nostrils—a warning sign the dog wasn't getting all the nutrients she needed.

"Uh-oh," Hailey said. "Before you go, would you mind smelling her breath? I hope she's not developing toxemia."

Penny's response to this was a gasp. "Don't move," she warned from her position in the doorway. "Scratch that. Don't blink. Don't even breathe."

Assuming Jasmine was heading their way, Hailey cast a panicked look around the small rectangle of her office. There was nowhere to hide—not herself and not Bess, whose breath was really starting to worry her.

But then Penny spoke again, this time with a slight squeal. "You'll never guess who's walking down the hall. Hailey, I told you not to blink. You're blinking."

It was true. She *was* blinking. She was also breathing and moving, but only because she enjoyed her life on this earth, however little it might appear to someone as glamorous as Penny.

"Cole Bennett," Penny said. "It's Cole Bennett. My heart is leaving my chest. My blood is on fire. I might die."

At the mention of the quarterback of the Seattle Lumberjacks, local celebrity and football god, Hailey's body underwent a similar change. Her pulse leaped and a hot thrumming filled her veins, but she fixed her attention on the dog instead. She wasn't going to fall for that trick again. Her coworkers liked to pull it out at lunches and meetings and pretty much anywhere Hailey could make a fool out of herself—which, to be fair, was a lot of places. The last time one of them had faked a Cole Bennett sighting, Hailey had actually stood up so fast she'd nearly fainted.

"Well, maybe *he* can get down here and smell Bess's breath," Hailey said. The dog panted in agreement, sending another hot blast of that worrisome smell her way. "Do you think anyone would notice if I slipped out for an hour or so?"

A body lowered itself to the gray carpeted floor next to her. Much to her surprise, it wasn't the long, lean figure of her coworker. In a former life, Penny had been a ballerina, and she had both the posture and the waistline to prove it. This figure, however, was much bigger. Broader. Built like the kind of man who—

"What are we smelling for?" he asked.

All the air left Hailey's lungs at the sound of that voice. Lots of men were big and broad, but only one of them spoke with that low, dulcet richness. She barely had time to register what was happening—or, more to the point, *who* was happening—when a pair of impossibly large hands came up to cup either side of Bess's head and pull her muzzle close.

"No, don't…" Hailey began, but it was too late. Cole Bennett's face—that gorgeous, flawless, famous face—was pressed against the nose of an unknown golden retriever in the final days of her pregnancy. Bess was an absolute darling of an animal, and her sweet disposition made her about as easygoing as they came, but there were certain rules to this sort of thing.

The most important rule was that when it came to mothers and their babies, all rules were off. Bess was 100 percent within her rights to view this oversized stranger as a threat and act accordingly.

Fortunately for them all, Bess took one look at him and began to enthusiastically lick.

"Well, hello there," Cole said, laughing as the dog's tongue explored his cheeks and chin. "I normally like to buy a lady dinner before things get this far, but I appreciate your enthusiasm."

Hailey doubted he'd appreciate the same level of enthusiasm from a lady like *her*, so it was a good thing she'd long ago memorized the exact angles of his face. His cheeks were wide-set and well sculpted, his chin a perfectly chiseled square. Sometimes, when he stood in profile, it was like looking at a statue of a man rather than the real thing.

"Ohmygod," Penny said as Cole gave the dog one last pat and rose to a standing position. Both she and Hailey had to step back—not because of Cole's size, which was substantial, but because his presence expanded to fill the tiny office. "It's really you."

The comment wasn't as silly as it sounded. Even if Cole Bennett hadn't been the most famous quarterback in the entire American Football Club, he was a man to admire based on pure physicality alone. In addition to his perfect facial bone structure, he had piercing blue eyes, a swoop of luxurious brown hair, and a dimple in his right cheek that flashed every time he smiled. And that wasn't even counting the body attached to it all.

"I can't believe it," Penny added breathlessly. "This is even better than the dream I had where you flew me to Spain in your private jet."

Cole paused in his acceptance of Bess's adoration to bask in Penny's. It took him all of five seconds to appraise her, but it was obvious he was pleased with what he saw. Most people were. In addition to her former ballerina physique, Penny had a rich copper skin tone that matched her name and a smile so natural that it was impossible not to return it.

"I don't have a private jet, but if I did, you'd be the first person I'd invite to Spain with me," he said with a wink. "Ibiza is beautiful this time of year."

Penny sighed her pleasure at this piece of nonsense, but Hailey only felt more out of her depth than before. Cole Bennett had never been to Ibiza in January—she'd bet her life on it. With the Kickoff Cup looming on the horizon, Cole's life was a blur of practices and playoff games. This time of year, he probably didn't have time to sleep, let alone whisk women away to glamorous international getaways.

If Cole sensed her confusion, he didn't show it. He nodded down at Bess. "What's her breath supposed to smell like? It seems kind of fruity, but in a chemical way."

That confirmation of Hailey's diagnosis was all she needed to hear, if only because it gave her something concrete to focus on. Penny and Bess might be able to get away with slavish adoration of the man, but Hailey wasn't about to prostrate herself at his feet. Which, she knew, were size twelve. She also knew he preferred to wear Nike cleats when he was on the field, but ever since he signed a sponsorship deal with Ball Zone, he'd been running around emblazoned in their logo instead.

Not that she was obsessed or anything. Everyone was aware of Cole Bennett's footwear habits. They were impossible to ignore. If you ever watched a commercial or picked up a trashy magazine, he was right there, shoving his feet in your face. The rest of him was usually there, too. Arms and legs and those million-dollar hands...

"Well, Bess." Hailey allowed her curtain of mousy hair to cover the side of her face so she wouldn't be tempted to stare at him. She scratched the dog's chin. "If he thinks your breath smells like chemicals, then it's probably toxemia. You and I are going to the veterinarian—but first, we're eating second breakfast."

"Second breakfast?" Cole echoed.

Hailey flushed at the way he phrased it, full of equal parts curiosity and judgment. "The meal between breakfast and lunch?" she offered. "Beloved of farm folk and Hobbits alike?"

Her first breakfast had been one sad, solitary English muffin consumed over the sink at five o'clock that morning between gulps of scalding coffee. Football players weren't the only ones who had a lot of work to do this time of year. *Puppy* football players had their fair share, too.

"That sounds good," Cole said as though she'd issued an invitation instead of an explanation. "I could eat."

Looking at Cole Bennett head-on was like staring at the sun during an eclipse, but Hailey forced herself to straighten her stance and meet his eyes. Yes, the man had a 72 percent completion percentage over the course of his career. Sure, he earned twelve million dollars a year in base salary alone. And okay, he was wearing a well-fitted blazer that made the most of an impressive pair of shoulders. But this was her domain. Four partitioned walls covered from top to bottom in puppy photographs might not seem like much to an outsider, but it was all she had.

Unfortunately, Cole didn't seem to have any problems returning her gaze. If he found anything impressive about a twenty-eight-year-old production assistant of average height and weight, with freckles covering every inch of her exposed skin, he didn't show it. Nor did he appear to move, blink, or—in a way that would do Penny proud—even breathe.

"I really should get Bess looked at," Hailey said, hoping to move things along before she made a fool of herself—a *bigger* one, anyway. "She's been worrying me all morning."

Cole didn't take the hint. He tilted his head and, with the bland disregard of a man used to being in command of the room, asked, "What does it mean? The way her breath smells?"

Since he was blocking the door, Hailey had no choice but to answer. "She's pregnant, and I've been struggling to keep her calories up. That smell could mean she's not getting enough nutrients. She's got six babies in there that are demanding a lot of her resources."

"What can I do to help?"

It was on the tip of Hailey's tongue to disclaim any right to Cole's time or energy. They didn't normally get such high-profile visitors in their little corner of the football world—and by normally, she meant ever. The most she could claim was once sharing an Uber pool with the announcer from the stadium. For the quarterback of the Lumberjacks to show up unannounced and in person at the Puppy Cup production offices was nothing short of bizarre.

Then again, this was an emergency. She wasn't in a position to look a gift quarterback in the mouth.

"Do you have a car?" she asked, moved by desperation to ask for the one thing she needed most. "Bess could use a ride to the vet."

Penny squeaked. "Hailey, you can't ask him that!"

"I know, but they won't let me on the bus with Bess anymore. They said she's not a service animal, so she's not allowed." Hailey turned to Cole and, realizing what she'd just done, added, "Unless you're busy, of course. I understand if—"

He interrupted her with the flash of his signature smile, complete with the dimple. "I'm not busy. Does this mean you want to stop for food on the way, or should we eat after?"

Hailey could only blink up at him. She had no idea what was going on here—if this really was a prank or if she was going to suddenly find herself standing naked in front of her elementary school classroom—but she wasn't sure she could handle it right now. Bess needed food and veterinary care, and the sooner, the better. If this ended up being some elaborate joke that Penny and the rest of the office had put together, Hailey was never going to forgive them.

"Did you make an appointment to see me?" she asked suspiciously. "Or am I just supposed to know what this is about?"

Instead of taking offense at this line of questioning, Cole chuckled and held out his hand. It seemed almost too good to be true—to actually touch him, to shake hands as equals—but Hailey managed to slip her palm against his.

"I did this all wrong, didn't I?" he said, giving her hand a squeeze. He didn't let go right away, his massive palm engulfing hers. "Bursting in here without an invitation or an introduction. I always forget about that part. I might know who *you* are, but you don't know me from Adam. Let me start again. You're Hailey Lincoln, production assistant for the Puppy Cup. I'm Cole Bennett. I play football for the Lumberjacks."

There was so much about this speech to unpack that Hailey had no idea where to start. *Of course* she knew who he was. The idea that she could live in Seattle and be ignorant of the man who pretty much dominated sports and news headlines for six months out of every year was ludicrous. Even more ludicrous was the idea that he knew who she was.

She was nothing. A nobody. A blip on the cosmic human radar.

"Um, okay?" Not her most articulate response, but at least she was making all the right sounds. "It's nice to meet you?"

He gave her hand one last squeeze before finally letting go. With another of those dazzling, dimpled smiles—this one for Penny's benefit—he said, "I'll have her back by second lunch, I promise. She and the dog both."

Penny waved her hand. "Keep her all day if you want to. All week. No one around here will miss her, I promise."

That wasn't true, but not because Hailey was particularly beloved. There were only about five more weeks until the Puppy Cup aired, which meant the number of things she had to do were enough to make a grown woman cry. In fact, she *had* cried. Several times. If things today kept moving along these lines, she might even do it again.

"Thanks for the show of support, Penny, but I doubt it'll take much more than an hour."

Hailey took a moment to turn off her computer before grabbing her oversized bag and Bess's leash. The golden retriever was so overburdened with her pregnancy that she wasn't likely to make a break for it, but Hailey needed to feel like she was in control of *something*. This wasn't how her life was supposed to work. She showed up to her job on time every single day. She went home and took care of whatever foster dogs were living with her at the time. Sometimes, she broke tradition and ordered take-out on the way.

Men like Cole Bennett—*people* like Cole Bennett—didn't seek her out for anything unless they needed someone to pick up their mother from the airport or book an appointment for a massage.

"Now that I'm thinking about it, I *have* heard of second breakfast," Cole said as they made their way past the reception desk. He seemed indifferent to the fact that everyone from the television production office was watching them, but Hailey felt like she was drowning in thoughts and emotions.

Foremost among them was that she'd never be able to live this moment down. Everyone she worked with knew how she felt about Cole Bennett—how closely she followed his career, how many of his jerseys she owned, how he was her first pick every year in the office fantasy league. For the rest of her working life, she'd be asked about everything he'd said and done, the way he smelled at close proximity.

Like clean sheets sprinkled with evergreen. Like a warm bed in the forest at dawn.

Hailey had to shake her head to clear it. This was neither the time nor the place to start thinking about this man in association with a bed. She needed to focus on the regular movements of her feet and the elevator in the distance. As long as she could make it to the elevator, she'd be fine. It was all downhill from there. Or downstairs, at the very least.

She chuckled at her own terrible pun.

"Did I say something funny?" Cole asked as they reached the elevator doors. He pushed the button and leaned against the wall as they waited for it to arrive, heedless of the receptionist pretending to water a plant behind him.

Since it was obvious he was doing his best to strike up a conversation, Hailey tried to think of something—anything—to say, but her mouth seemed to have grown temporarily detached from her brain.

"Something in my teeth, maybe?" he prodded.

The idea of something so ordinary happening to this man only increased her surreal sensation. "You're all clear," she said, the words wavering slightly. "Not that I would mention it if you weren't."

"That's not very nice. What if my shirt was on inside out?"

"Um." She did her best not to stare at the shirt he wore under his blazer. It was artfully faded and tight across his chest. She could even make out the faint line of his nipples underneath. "It's not."

"Or there was toilet paper stuck to my shoe?"

"I'm sure someone else would point it out."

He studied her for a long moment. The building's elevator always ran slow, but this was becoming interminable. "You're a very odd woman," he eventually said.

The words themselves bordered on an insult, but the way he said them didn't. Hailey didn't know if it was her heightened awareness of him that did it or if there really was something caressing about the way he spoke, but she felt a warm glow overtaking her. This was happening. She was having a conversation—an admittedly strange one, but *still*—with Cole Bennett. Who was about to drive her to the veterinarian. With her pregnant foster dog. In his own car.

"I'm not odd," she protested, feeling faint. "I'm not anything, really."

It was closer to the truth than he would ever know. Hailey had always walked a carefully mediocre line. She was never the most beautiful woman in any room. She'd always gotten average grades in school. She was good at her job, it was true, but should she disappear tomorrow, Jasmine would find a replacement and forget she existed within the week.

She was so busy ruminating on how mortifying it was to be so wholly without appeal that she didn't realize—until Cole cleared his throat—that they'd been standing in silence for well over a minute.

She glanced up to find him smiling at her in a way that made her heart stop.

"I don't think anyone will care if we chat while we wait for the elevator," he said, a teasing lift to his perfectly molded lips. "We can talk about anything you want."

"Um…." She willed the elevator to arrive, but she could hear it crunching to a halt several stories away. The stairs would have been a faster route, but Bess was in no condition to drag her six babies down all that concrete.

"The weather?" he prodded. "The fall of the Romans? You've got to give me something, or this is going to be a long drive."

Hailey began tapping her foot. Maybe this was part of the prank. Maybe they were going to record her asking Cole Bennett his thoughts on fading democracies and then play it back to her for the rest of her working life.

"It's too bad you aren't a football fan, or we could always fall back on that," he mused, running a hand along his jaw. When she *still* couldn't manage to dislodge the lump in her throat far enough to form a coherent sentence, he gave in with a nod. "I always abide by lady's choice. Complete silence it is, then."

She could hear the receptionist clucking his disapproval in the distance, but she didn't take offense at it. Truth be told, she was disappointed in herself. This was probably the only opportunity she'd ever have to talk to a professional football player face-to-face. It was the sort of thing that she and her father had once only dreamed of, and she was wasting it.

She managed to uncleave her tongue long enough to say, "If it's *really* lady's choice…"

Cole nodded his encouragement, his smile so friendly and warm and real that something in Hailey unhinged.

"If you don't mind shop talk, then what I'd like to know is why you've been taking so many unnecessary hits this season," she said. "I'm not sure if it's an issue with your confidence or your arm, but you're never going to break the Kickoff Cup Curse if you don't do something about it."

She realized, too late, what she'd said—and who she'd said it to.

She slapped her hand over her mouth, but a look of shock had already caused Cole's unnaturally blue eyes to open wide. Even Bess sensed that Hailey had flung herself headfirst over a line, because the dog gave a small whine and tried to hide her head.

"I'm so sorry," Hailey said from behind her hand. "I can't believe I said that."

"Don't apologize," Cole said, his voice slightly strangled. "You're absolutely right."

She was, but that didn't make it okay. Especially since she'd said the name of the curse out loud. You weren't even supposed to mention it in private, in *secret*. To say it to the face of the one man who had the power to break it was downright dangerous. Her dad had probably rolled over in his grave.

"To be honest, I'm just glad you know who I am," Cole added. The strangled note was still there, but Hailey could have sworn it was verging on laughter. Not outrage. Not incredulity. *Laughter*. "I was beginning to fear you'd never heard of me."

Hailey was deciding whether to carry Bess down the stairs as a means of escape when the elevator gave a cheerful ding. She prepared to jump in and hide herself in the corner as fast as humanly possible, but the doors slid open to reveal the slightly harassed face of her boss.

Jasmine Jones was, without a doubt, an exceptional person to work for. The woman produced no fewer than two dozen television shows every year, most of which won awards and were watched by millions of viewers. She was always immaculate, always precise, and always polite. Hailey sometimes dreamed of what it would be like to be her—to know what to say in every situation, to issue a command with so much confidence that no one dared do anything but their best to carry it out.

It also would have been nice to look that much like Kerry Washington and to wear white pantsuits that never got a speck of dirt on them, but Hailey had never been one to wish for what she couldn't have.

"Hailey, thank goodness." Jasmine put a hand up to prevent the elevator doors from closing. Her voice was cool and rich, and Hailey could feel her spine straightening under the power of it. "I need you to pick up my blue dress from the dry cleaners and take it to the tailor on Third. They should have a copy of my measurements on hand, but if they don't, you'll have to get them from the tailor on First. You know the one."

Hailey could only nod. The rest of her was frozen in place, trying hard not to look as though there was a dog panting heavily at her feet and a football player looming just as heavily over her shoulder.

"Good. After that, if you could pick up the lunch order I put in at Thai Garden and set it up for the meeting at the main office, I'd really appreciate it. The head honchos always approve my changes faster if I feed them. You'll need to be back here for the light test at three, but that shouldn't be a problem if you hurry." Jasmine noticed the first of Hailey's two companions and blinked. "Oh. You brought the dog with you to work. Again."

"I hope you don't mind," Hailey said, wincing. She knew very well that Jasmine minded, but her boss would never stoop to say so. To do so would be unprofessional, and that was the one thing Jasmine was incapable of. "It's just that she's been really restless the past couple of nights, and I was worried—"

"It's my fault."

The elevator doors had begun buzzing a protest by this time, so Cole stepped forward and took Jasmine by the hand. He some-how managed to pull her out and perform a handshake at the same time and without giving the appearance of doing anything more than politely introducing himself.

"You're Jasmine Jones," he added with a smile that brought his dimple out full force. It was the same move he'd made with Hailey—the smile and the foreknowledge of her name, a built-in friendliness that was almost overpowering in its design. "I can't tell you what a fan I am of your work. That miniseries you did last year highlighting the corruption of college sports was phenomenal."

"Oh my." For the first time in the six years that Hailey had been working for Jasmine, her boss showed signs of being in a flutter. She blinked several times in rapid succession before lifting her hand to her chest. Toying with the top button of her blouse, she said, "Mr. Bennett. I can hardly believe it. To what do we owe the honor?"

Cole's smile deepened, and he caught Hailey's eye just long enough to wink. "This girl right here," he said. Before Hailey could protest at being referred to as anything less than a woman, he added, "The dog, I mean. I hope you don't mind me stealing her away like this, but we'd like to get her looked at. We're worried about toxemia."

"Toxemia?" Jasmine echoed blankly.

"I didn't know dogs could get it, either," Cole admitted. "But as soon as Hailey mentioned it, I could see she was right. I'm taking them both to the vet."

Jasmine accepted this explanation for Cole's presence with aplomb. Hailey could tell her boss was burning with questions—most of which Hailey shared—but nothing would prevail upon Jasmine to admit it. Instead, she directed a perfectly arched brow at Hailey.

"If you were worried about the dog's health, you should have said something earlier."

Hailey shrugged, knowing the line was just for show. Despite producing the Puppy Cup every year—their company's most profitable show by a large margin—Jasmine wasn't a dog person. Fostering an animal was a foreign concept to her. Fostering a *pregnant* animal was even stranger. Hailey still shuddered when she remembered what had happened when she'd tried to apply for a few days of maternity leave.

"That's my fault, too," Cole said. "I asked her not to. The less alarm we show, the better. We wouldn't want this leaking out to the press before we're ready. Isn't that right, Hailey?"

Hailey nodded her agreement. There was nothing else she *could* do. Even if she was able to stand up to her boss—which she wasn't—she could hardly contradict Cole Bennett after what she'd said to him.

"It's a hell of a story," Cole added with a soft laugh. He paused and started to play with Bess's ears. Bess showed no shame in turning toward his touch. Like the rest of them, she was wholly under his spell. "A shelter animal in need. The Puppy Cup PA who provides it. What's the term they use for that sort of thing? Human interest?"

Jasmine nodded along as though all of that made perfect sense, but Hailey felt a tingling along her spine. How could Cole know about any of that? Granted, she made no secret of her fostering work, but it was hardly the kind of thing to interest a man like this one.

"We'll hash out the details when we get back," he said with a decisive nod. "I think you'll like what I have in mind."

Hailey didn't know what Jasmine's thoughts on the subject were, but she was starting to develop plenty of her own—most of which revolved around the certain, irrevocable feeling that she was about to be asked for a kidney. There was no other explanation for any of this—for why Cole Bennett would even deign to look at her, let alone save her in front of her boss.

True, she admired him. She idolized him. She was, okay, a little bit obsessed with him. But *he* didn't know any of that.

"She seems nice," he said in a low, amused voice as Jasmine disappeared from view and the click of her heels trailed off in the distance. "And she didn't say one word against my game play. To tell you the truth, I'm a little disappointed. It seems I could use the pointers."

The last of Hailey's ability to maintain rational thought fled. She was already so far out of her depth—floundering, flailing, her mouth seemingly unattached to her brain—that for Cole Bennett to laugh at her, *with* her, was too much.

"You want pointers?" She started regretting the words before they left her lips, but she could no more stop them than she could the Sounder train. "Then it's not just your unnecessary hits that are a problem. I think your game has been off all season. It's probably your worst one yet, and that includes the year you were recovering from shoulder surgery. If you didn't have Garrett Smith to catch all your Hail Mary passes, the Lumberjacks would have no chance at making it into the Kickoff Cup this year. He's saved you at least half a dozen times."

"Probably more," Cole murmured. "Is there something wrong with this elevator? Why does it take so long to get anywhere?"

Hailey could only stare. Everything she'd just said was true, but he should have been insulted to hear it—outraged, even. Did he want *both* her kidneys?

"It's old," she managed. "Old things don't work very well."

"Oh, I'm well aware of that. Why do you think I'm having such a bad season?"

The elevator finally opened its sluggish doors again—and a good thing, too, because Hailey had no idea how to respond. Cole Bennett *wasn't* old. At least he wasn't old in quarterback years. At thirty-two, he was a young buck compared to many of the more veteran players who graced the annals of sports history. If he played his cards right, he could last another decade on the field, delighting the masses and reaping his millions.

"Well?" he asked as he stepped inside. "Are you coming, or am I going to have to call Garrett and ask him to carry you down? I'm happy to do it, but I should warn you that he doesn't take criticism as well as I do. You'll probably make him cry."

Hailey opened her mouth and closed it again, her whole body flushing with embarrassment. There was nothing she could say—and even less she could do—to redeem herself after this. When faced with the most beautiful and talented man in the world, she didn't swoon or faint or even grow weak in the knees.

Apparently, she critiqued—and she critiqued hard.

Which was why, as she gave Bess's leash a gentle tug, she was both horrified and surprised to hear herself say, "Garrett has nothing to fear from me. His ability to find an opening in a packed end zone is nothing short of miraculous. He should be very proud of himself."

Cole's whole body stilled. He didn't make any sort of sound, either, but she was pretty sure he was laughing at her. *Again.*

"Is there anyone on my team you don't have a strong opinion about?" He shook his head before she could say anything. "No, don't answer that. I don't think my ego could take another blow."

"I don't think you have to worry about your ego," she shot back. "I doubt there's much it couldn't survive."

And there it was. She'd done the unthinkable. She'd lost control of her mind and her mouth, and now she was going to have to suffer through the entire elevator ride with the personal hero she'd just insulted to his face.

"There," Cole said as he pressed the parking level button and the doors closed in on them. "That wasn't so difficult, was it? Now we're well on our way to becoming friends."

Not only was the elevator old, but it had been constructed at a time when it was de rigueur to panel every wall in mirrors. There was nowhere Hailey could look—nowhere she could turn—that didn't contain hundreds of tiny images of the three of them. One man, godlike and laughing. One dog, panting quietly. And one woman, red from the roots of her hair to the tips of her toes. She wouldn't have gone so far as to call this the worst day of her life, but it was definitely in the top ten.

When the elevator gave a shudder and lurched to a sudden stop somewhere between the third and fourth sublevels, she hastily amended that ranking.

This was top-five territory; she was sure of it. Especially when Bess whimpered and turned around three times before her water broke.

chapter 2

I CAN'T GET CELL PHONE RECEPTION." COLE HELD HIS PHONE up to the corner of the elevator and shook it a few times. The concrete block that supported them prevented any signals from getting through. "No internet, either. You weren't kidding when you said this elevator is old."

"I told you not to bother," Hailey said. "We just have to wait for help to arrive. With any luck, Bess will be able to hold on long enough."

Cole glanced down at the dog panting laboriously on the aged linoleum of the elevator floor and found himself sharing that wish. As he was also of a practical turn of mind, he shrugged himself out of his blazer and dangled it from one finger. The bespoke wool would never get clean again, but it would make a semicomfortable bed. He was no veterinary expert, but that animal didn't look like she was going to hold on to anything.

"Are you kidding?" Hailey blinked at the offering. "I can't take that. It must have cost hundreds of dollars."

Thousands of dollars, actually, but it didn't seem like a good time to point that out. He shook it at her. "It's comfortable. You can't leave the dog on the floor like that."

Hailey bit her lower lip in consternation, her every feeling flitting across delicate features. Cole had always heard that expression about wearing your heart on your sleeve, but he'd never seen it put into action before. Although this woman's heart might not be in literal view, he could still count each beat of her pulse. It was in the pink flush behind her multitudes of freckles and the gently throbbing vein on her temple. It was in the short breaths she took and the small moan at the back of her throat.

She didn't like him. She didn't like him, and she *definitely* didn't like being trapped in an elevator with him.

"The only other options are my shirt or my pants," he said. "You choose."

To his complete lack of surprise, this remark caused the blush of pink across her cheeks to deepen into vibrant red.

"I'm not ruining your jacket," she said.

"You'll forgive me for pointing out the obvious, but you're in a dress. Unless you've got another one on under there, I don't see what other choice we have."

She glanced down at her gray sweater dress and gave another of those back-of-the-throat moans. He wanted to point out that it was a *nice* gray sweater dress and that he liked that she'd paired it with a pair of bright-red Converse shoes, but he didn't dare. She didn't seem as though she'd appreciate his sentiments—that she looked exactly like what she was. A woman who ran other people's errands and took care of other people's dogs.

She was also his best chance of breaking the stupid curse that had held his team back from making it into the Kickoff Cup for the past two decades, but she didn't know that yet. Asking that particular favor from a woman who was as impressed by him as she would be a piece of burned toast was proving more difficult than he'd anticipated.

"You'd better get my bag," she said, sighing.

"You *do* have another dress."

"Not exactly."

Cole handed her the oversized black purse and watched as she

began rummaging around, his mind running over the possible articles of clothing that might be contained within it. *Something* had
to be turning her that particular shade of red. He'd just decided
that it must be a piece of scandalous lingerie when the dog gave a
whimper.

"I know, Bess girl." Hailey clucked sympathetically. "It's not
how I'd have chosen to do this either, but nature has her own way
of deciding things. Don't say anything."

It took Cole a moment to realize that the second half of that
was for him. "Why would I?" he asked. "I think it's nice that you're
talking to her. Your voice is calming her down. See? She likes it."

"Not about that," Hailey muttered as she drew her hands out
from her bag. It took much less than a moment for Cole to make
the connection this time around. He tried to fight his laugh—he
really did—but one look at that teal jersey, and he was done for.

"Is that…number eight?" he asked, his voice wobbling as he
caught sight of the back of the jersey. Hailey did her best to hide it
from his view, but she wasn't fast enough.

"I told you not to say anything."

"And is that…my name above it?"

"This is an emergency situation. You could show more tact."

He could have shown more tact. He *should* have shown more
tact. But it was too much. This woman—a complete stranger who
was able to sum up everything that was wrong with his game in
two painfully succinct sentences—carried his jersey in her purse.
Not only that, but she was mortified about it.

"I could sign it for you," he said, unable to help himself. "After
Bess is done with it, I mean."

"No, thank you," she said. Her words were prim, but the red
flush was starting to creep down her neck, and she was careful not
to look at him. "I wouldn't want to put you to the bother."

"Oh, it's no bother. I'm always happy to meet a fan."

Her gaze snapped up, her eyes blazing. In the office, they had seemed a sort of murky, indeterminate gray, but in the bright lights and mirrored walls of the elevator, they flashed with sparks of silver. "I'm not a fan."

"Obviously."

"Your name and game play come up in my regular line of work, that's all. It's my job to know who's going to be in the Kickoff Cup so we can leverage that information for our puppy version. Advertisers like the tie-ins."

"Oh, I believe you." He paused and watched as she arranged the jersey in a neat pile around the golden retriever. He had no idea how many puppy births she'd presided over, but there was an efficiency to her movements he couldn't help but admire. "But does that mean you think the Lumberjacks are going to break the curse and make it to the final game this year? Even with my terrible arm?"

She didn't answer him. At first, he thought it was because he'd finally gotten the better of her. A pleasant—if shameful—feeling of triumph flooded through him, and he allowed a grin to form. But then the dog gave a heave and a whine, and his grin dropped.

So did he. He fell into a crouch next to Hailey and Bess, suddenly feeling as anxious as he had the day his niece was born. At least he'd been semiprepared for that event. He'd read dozens of books on pregnancy and childbirth ahead of time and even attended a few of the Lamaze classes that his sister, Regina, had insisted on until she decided it was a waste of her time.

Somehow, he didn't think that slow, careful breaths and soothing Chopin in the background were going to do the dog any good.

"Uh-oh," he said as what looked like the hind end of a tiny, glistening golden puppy started to emerge inside its iridescent sac. "Doesn't that mean the puppies are breech?"

Hailey knelt next to him and adjusted the jersey to clear her view of the puppy being born. She was careful to ensure that no part of her body touched his, even though he could feel the warm pulse of her skin next to his. It was such a rare thing in his world—this innate respect for his personal space—that it took him aback. People normally did whatever they could to find a reason to touch him. A hug, a pat on the back, a clandestine foot sneaking up his leg under the table... In most social situations, he was considered fair game. Some days, he felt more like a llama at a petting zoo than a man.

"A lot of puppies are born this way," she said, her voice dropped to a low whisper. "So I don't think we need to worry. Bess knows what to do."

"That makes one of us," Cole whispered back. "Are we supposed to...catch or something?"

"Sorry, but I don't think catching is your strong suit."

"More notes on my technique?"

She ignored him, but the stiff way she held herself indicated that his barb hadn't missed its mark. "Oh, look. It's out. It's so tiny."

She wasn't wrong. The puppy *was* tiny. It was also incapable of breathing while inside that sac. Acting more on instinct than reason, Cole reached out to try to clear it away, but Hailey smacked his hand. *Hard.*

"Don't," she hissed. "Bess will do that."

She wasn't wrong in that regard, either. Now that the first of her six puppies had been born, the dog took a moment to relax and gently lick her baby. Within seconds, the puppy was free and breathing. It looked more like a mole rat than a dog, but Cole wasn't going to mention it. He didn't dare.

"The last time I witnessed the miracle of birth, it was in the same room as a six-foot midwife who told me that she wouldn't hesitate to kick me out if I got in the way." Cole shifted his position so the dog had more space to do her thing. He also used Hailey's distracted state to slip his jacket into the goo-covered fray. Long experience had taught him that those jerseys weren't made of the most absorbent material in the world. The whole doggy family would be much more comfortable on Italian wool.

"Your beautiful jacket!" Hailey cried. "What's the matter with you? It's ruined."

"I repeat…a six-foot midwife," Cole said with painstaking deliberation. "She was a grandmother thirteen times over, had buried two husbands, and told me point-blank that she considers football to be the most barbaric physical display in the history of humankind."

"Shh. The second baby is coming."

"And she was still a much less strict birthing-room attendant than you are."

Once again, he got no response, but it was difficult to care as they both watched the second puppy being born. It came with such ease and fluidity that Cole was able to relax. *He* might not know what he was doing, but Hailey had obviously read up on the subject, and Bess had Mother Nature on her side. His Italian wool came in handy as the two shivering pups crowded around their mom for warmth, but he wished he had more to offer them. The stick of gum in his pocket wasn't going to do them much good, and it wasn't so cold in the elevator that he needed to resort to burning the cash in his wallet. Yet.

"Is there a reason it's taking them so long to get to us?" he asked as he stood and began pushing elevator buttons at random. He pressed the alarm button longer than the others, but the jangling seemed to distress the dog, so he gave it up. "They *do* know we're trapped in here, right?"

Hailey didn't answer him. He was already growing so used to her lack of interest in him that he didn't think anything of it. Instead, he started searching for a ceiling panel or some other kind of emergency access point. There always seemed to be one in the movies, but it was difficult to see where they'd put one among all these stupid mirrors.

"I've always thought elevators should stock emergency kits," he mused, more to entertain himself than because he expected a reply. "Just the basics—granola bars and water and Xanax. I bet people get easily panicked in these types of situations."

Normal people would get panicked, anyway. This particular woman was so caught up in the dog that he doubted she'd notice if he stripped himself naked and started doing the Charleston. The internet would think it the greatest thing in the history of viral videos, but he suspected Hailey would probably point out that he wasn't doing it correctly.

She'd be right, too. Dancing had never been his strong suit. He'd spent so much of his childhood throwing a football through a tire that he'd somehow missed out on that chapter of his life.

He'd missed most of the important chapters, actually. He could throw a ball and smile for a camera, but that was about the extent of his worldly knowledge.

"Something's wrong." Hailey reached out and tugged at Cole's pant leg. Her hand left some kind of slimy residue behind, but he barely noticed. The fact that she'd touched him—voluntarily, no less—was more alarming than the fact that she was struggling to keep her voice level. "I don't know what's happening. The third puppy isn't coming as quickly as it should. I think it might be stuck."

Physiologically speaking, Cole had no idea what he was looking at. He'd already maxed out on his knowledge of the birthing process after the first puppy made its appearance, and he wasn't likely to expand on it anytime soon. However, one glance in the dog's fretful, pleading eyes, and he realized he didn't need a veterinary degree to understand what was happening.

She's in pain.

It was a feeling he knew far too well—not just the bone-searing, soul-deep agony of physical pain but the equally bone-searing and soul-deep determination not to let it show.

"That's it," he announced.

"What is?" Hailey asked. She angled her body over the dog, forming a protective curl around Bess's panting form. "Don't come any closer. You can't just reach in there and start yanking puppies out. It's not a clogged drain."

He grinned. It wasn't the most appropriate response, but he couldn't help it now any more than he could when Hailey had criticized his football technique. No one, with the exception of his sister, talked to him with such a complete absence of flattery.

"Thank you for that visual. I'll carry it with me to the grave." He tilted his head toward the elevator doors. "What am I going to find if I pry those open?"

Hailey followed the line of his gaze with knit brows. They were a few shades darker than her hair and just as expressive as the rest of her.

"An elevator shaft?" she ventured.

"Thank you. I gathered as much. But it says we're between subfloors, so I'm assuming this is all parking?"

"Yes, but I don't think you should—"

"Stay down there with Bess," he said. Hailey made a motion to get to her feet, but he stopped her. "Talk to her like you were before. Keep her calm. If my knowledge of parking garages is any good, there's not much surrounding us but the occasional concrete pillar. If I can get the doors open, there should be a way to shimmy out."

"But you can't," she protested again. "It's not safe."

"I'll be fine."

"I know, but if anything should happen to you…" She trailed off and glanced at him, concern flooding her eyes. To both his surprise and his amusement, it wasn't concern for his well-being that made them sparkle like that. "They'll never forgive me. Not if I break you this close to the Kickoff Cup. Not when you guys are almost there."

He strove to keep from laughing out loud. Hailey obviously subscribed to the same ridiculous superstitions that everyone else did. If you asked him, the Kickoff Cup Curse was more of a personal torment than a supernatural one. He couldn't go anywhere these days without people crossing their fingers or throwing salt at him or doing God-knew-what-else they thought would help him get a ball into the end zone and the Lumberjacks into the final game.

He had a much better answer for them. It took hard work, lots of practice, enough painkillers to take down a horse, and the total subjugation of every nonfootball desire he'd had in his lifetime. Unfortunately, none of that made for a good story. People wanted mysticism and pizzazz. People wanted a token good-luck charm.

Behold. He was doing his best to deliver one. Unfortunately, *she* was too busy delivering puppies for him to broach the subject.

"And who, if you don't mind my asking, are 'they'?"

"Your fans. Your sponsors. The world." As if just realizing that the world was only the start of her problems, Hailey groaned. "*Jasmine.*"

"As touching as it is to find that you're more worried about your boss than the possibility of irreparable harm to my health, you don't have a choice. I'm doing it anyway."

He didn't wait for her to argue further. For one thing, he wanted to get them out of the elevator before the dog's situation became any more dangerous than it already was. For another, he honestly didn't know if he could get the doors open anyway. Like the escape panels that *didn't* exist anywhere inside this elevator, he'd only seen this next bit done in the movies.

"I just need something to pry it open," he said, mostly to himself. A quick survey of his surroundings revealed nothing that might work...unless he counted the items currently on his person. "I hate to do this to you, Hailey Lincoln, but you might want to avert your eyes for this next part."

"For what next part?"

He began unbuckling his belt with an efficiency that would have done a gigolo proud. "I'm about to damage another article of clothing, and there's nothing you can say to stop me."

"I'm not even going to ask how much that cost," she said,

moaning slightly. "Actually, I am… Was it more or less than the jacket?"

"Less," he said. Unable to help himself, he added, "But not by much. I'll have my manager send you the bill."

She moaned again, but he ignored it. He was too busy trying to figure out how to shimmy the buckle into the small space between the doors. To his relief and—he was ashamed to admit—his pride, it turned out to be a much easier task than he'd reckoned on. The metal bent a little, but he managed to create a big enough space to slip his fingers in. From there, nothing was needed but brute force.

Brute force and the leverage of his right shoulder. He realized his mistake about thirty seconds in. The burning sear was a familiar sensation in so many ways. He knew well the strain and tug of overtaxation—knew even better the determination to push through in hopes of reaching the other side.

He also knew that there *was* no other side. After years of physical therapy and miraculous surgery that had turned out to be not so miraculous, he could attest to that. Sometimes, the pain just was.

"Thank God. It's working." Hailey's voice reached him just as he was about to give up. "Please hurry. Her breathing is becoming awfully shallow."

Nothing could have been more calculated to keep him intent on his goal. With a reserve of strength he didn't know he had, he continued pulling at the doors until they hit an automated system and slid the rest of the way open.

As he expected, there was plenty of room for a man of his size to slip out between the garage levels and go for help. They could probably even lift the dog out and rush her to the vet.

Rather, they *could* have done those things, had there not been a crowd of feet and flashing lights awaiting them on the other side of those open doors.

"It's him. It's Cole Bennett."

"He pulled the doors open. Did you see that? He's like Superman."

"Cole, how does it feel to save the day? How does this compare to the possibility of finally making it to the Kickoff Cup?"

Cole didn't bother answering either of these questions. With a jump and a crawl that caused his shoulder to burn even hotter, he pulled himself out of the elevator. "I need someone to get me some water, blankets, and a veterinarian," he said. "And step on it. We've got some newborn puppies and a pregnant dog in distress."

"Oh wow. He delivers babies too. Is it your dog? Did you pull the puppies out by yourself?"

Cole forced his lips into the smile that had earned him so much in this lifetime: money, women, a following of determined photographers. Hopefully, it would also get him the thing he wanted most right now: a way out of football for good.

"Are you kidding?" he asked. Unable to help himself, he smiled wider and added, "You can't just reach in there and start yanking puppies out. It's not a clogged drain."

chapter
3

"So you didn't actually get her to agree to the plan."

Cole winced as his sister wound a bandage around his shoulder. It was heavy and thick and had frozen bags of vegetables interspersed throughout. The peas and the corn were fine, but the okra was starting to poke in several places.

"It's not my fault. We were busy with other things." He paused and lifted his arm so she could wind the bandage around his rib cage. Regina wasn't the most qualified person to provide first aid, but she was the most discreet. "Besides, I did the important part."

"Which is?"

"I laid the groundwork. Greased the wheels. Wooed her with my strength and ability to single-handedly pull open elevator doors."

Regina snorted and secured the bandage. She stepped back to view her handiwork, if you could call it that. He looked—and felt—like he'd been run over by a Jolly Green Giant delivery truck. "I thought you said she gave you football pointers."

"She did. *Very* detailed ones...the kind you couldn't give unless you've been paying close attention. Besides, she was carrying my jersey in her bag. I think she might have a crush on me."

His sister sighed and started to roll up the remaining bandages. Ever since his surgery two years ago, she'd been buying the things in bulk. "I don't know why you won't just let me go to the network directly. They'd be all over it. Cole Bennett takes on the Puppy Cup. An attractive, single man dedicates his free time to the welfare and adoption of animals. I can almost smell the hormones from here."

Yes, he was well aware of that. A man didn't reach his level of success in a professional football career without learning a little bit about the way the world worked. If he sent Regina into the television network in full sports-manager mode, she'd emerge with a huge contract and all the puppies he could ask for.

That was the problem. He didn't want a huge contract. He didn't want *any* contracts—not television ones, not Puppy Cup ones, and definitely not football ones. To admit as much out loud, however, would be to ruin any and all chances the Lumberjacks had of breaking the curse. An announcement of Cole Bennett's retirement would hit his team hard enough as it was. If he did it while the curse lingered overhead—while the mystical hands of fate or fairies or whatever nonsense was responsible for keeping the Lumberjacks from the Kickoff Cup held sway—there was a good chance the team would give up hope altogether.

"It'll be better this way," he said, striving for nonchalance. Remembering what he'd said to Jasmine yesterday, he added, "A real human-interest story."

Regina wasn't buying it. She lifted one of her perfectly arched brows. "Since when does the world consider you *human*?"

"Since the day I was born one?" Cole gave his shoulder a few tentative rotations. It hurt, but not nearly as much as it had after the elevator stunt yesterday. He met his sister's bright-blue eyes—so much like his own—and sighed. "I know you don't like this, Reggie, but it's the best way. If something happens to me—"

"It won't."

"If something happens to me," he repeated with careful deliberation, "the entire team is going to lose their shit—and their momentum. You know how much stock they put in this stupid curse."

"It's not stupid."

"It's pretty stupid." Cole knew it went against all the rules of sports history and fandoms to say so, but *come on*. "If I can get this Hailey woman to rub some of her puppy luck off on me— publicly, I mean—then the guys will feel more secure going into the final few games. Who knows? We might even have an actual shot at winning this year. It won't matter as much if I'm sidelined then."

Or if I leave the team.

His sister struggled to find an appropriate response. Even though she wouldn't admit it, this whole thing had been her idea to begin with. No one was more connected when it came to all things Seattle and football. If there was someone within a five-hundred-mile radius who could give Cole the competitive advantage, Regina had already found them, cataloged them, and run a full background check. Hailey Lincoln was no exception. She might not seem like the most obvious choice to break a twenty-year superstition, but she'd been working on the Puppy Cup for the exact same number of years that he'd been playing for the Lumberjacks.

Only *her* team never lost.

"Your shoulder is fine, Cole. I know it is. You just have to stop forcing open elevator doors."

He smiled at Regina's naive optimism. To the outside world, his sister was a ruthless sports manager, a woman who painted her fingernails bloodred to hide the stains of battle whenever she emerged from a contract negotiation. Cole knew better. If anyone realized how much she worried over things—over *him*—they'd destroy her. She might be older than him by two years and forged of steel, but she wasn't unbreakable.

Neither of them was.

"I promise to never force open another elevator door for as long as I live." He held out his pinkie but yanked it back just as his sister was about to seal his vow in their time-honored tradition. "Unless there's a dog trapped inside and giving birth."

"Cole…"

"You're right. If there's a woman trapped inside and giving birth, I should probably save her, too."

Although Regina was laughing as she hooked her finger against his, there were etched lines of worry on either side of her mouth. They seemed to be getting deeper and more pronounced with every passing day, a thing he knew full well was his fault. He was her only client, which meant that the day he gave up football was likely to be the end of the line for her, too.

"Uncle Cole!" A squeal from the kitchen doorway prevented them both from saying more. Even though he knew it was a terrible idea and that Regina wouldn't approve, he swooped down and lifted his four-year-old niece into his arms.

"Just the person I came to see," he announced. Mia's face was sticky with some unknown red substance, but that didn't stop him from dropping a hearty kiss on her cheek. Strawberry jam was his guess—and not the cheap kind, either. "You'll never guess what I did yesterday."

"I wanna see the puppies."

"Hmm. Maybe you *can* guess." He glanced at his sister over the top of the girl's head. She had the same dark-brown hair that both he and Regina sported, but hers was done up in a pair of tufty pigtails. "Please tell me you didn't show her that YouTube clip. It's embarrassing enough as it is."

"*I* didn't show her anything." Regina tsked and lifted Mia out of his clasp. She frowned at the stiff way he moved his shoulder but didn't comment on it. "It was You-know-who. She was watching Mia yesterday, and she keeps the television on the Cole Bennett Channel at all hours of the day and night."

Cole laughed. "Weird. I don't get that one with my cable package."

"You laugh now, but it's becoming an obsession. No one should love you that much. It's obscene."

"I think my own mother is allowed to love me that much."

"Sure thing, Norman Bates. It's totally normal."

Mia was unwilling to let the conversation veer so far off course. "I wanna see the puppies," she said again, this time with a wobbling undertone to her voice. "Please, Uncle Cole?"

"Of course you can," he promised. "But you'll have to wait a few weeks until they're old enough. Right now, they're too little to do much of anything. They can't even open their eyes yet."

"But I want to see them," Mia insisted. Her face screwed up into a tight ball. It was a cute face—all round cheeks and long lashes— and she knew how to work its assets to the fullest. "I won't touch, I promise. I just want to see. I just want to love."

"Don't do it," Regina warned. "Don't you dare give in."

"I don't have a puppy to love." Mia allowed a single tear to fall from her eye. Cole had no idea how she did it—manufactured tears one at a time, each drop designed to wrench his heart from his chest—but he was powerless against it.

She clinched matters by wiping the tear away and looking woefully up into his face. "I on'y have you."

It was so far from the truth—this child with a loving mother, doting grandparents, a full-time nanny, and who knew how many other adults wrapped around her little finger—that Cole could only laugh and give in.

"I'm sorry, Reggie, but there's nothing I can do. She only has me." With a fond smile for his niece, he said, "Of course I'll take you to see them. I'm sure Miss Lincoln would be more than happy to show them off."

In all honesty, he wasn't sure that Miss Lincoln was eager to see him so soon after their last parting, but it was as good an excuse as any. If he was going to run a successful puppy football campaign to break a "curse" and provide himself with a foolproof exit strategy, then he needed to get things moving.

"In fact, I think we should go over there right now," he said. "And if she tries to shut the door in my face, you have to cry *exactly* like that, got it?"

"You are not using my child as a passport to some poor woman's private residence," Regina protested.

"But she has the puppies," Mia said, her lower lip quivering.

Cole forced his lip to do the same. "But she has the puppies."

Regina stared at them both for a total of three seconds before heaving an exasperated sigh. "Fine. You can take her. But only because the nanny has the morning off and I need to make sure the optics on yesterday's stunt are where we want them."

"A glorified babysitter, that's me. Oh, how the mighty have fallen."

Regina treated his commentary exactly the same way that Hailey had—by ignoring it.

"You will not promise that Mia gets to keep any of the puppies," she said, pointing one of her bloodred fingernails at him. "You will not take her to the pet store afterward and buy her a consolation puppy. There will be no puppy acquisition of any kind."

"I wouldn't dare," he promised but with a wink at Mia. Regina saw it, of course, but there was little she could do by this time. Mia had wriggled her way down, all thoughts of tears and despair forgotten.

"She didn't say anything about *me* not getting a puppy," he said in a low voice that was clearly audible to all. "Come on, Mia. You can help me pick the cutest one."

"Promising to adopt that woman's litter isn't going to make her like you," Regina warned.

"Probably not," Cole allowed. "But dangling this cute face at her will. I'm sure of it."

"You can't come in."

Hailey slipped through the crack in her front door before pulling it shut behind her. There wasn't enough room on the small wooden platform that served as her front porch for her *and* Cole Bennett *and* the young girl he'd brought with him, but she had no other choice. Under no circumstances could she let this man inside her house.

"Good morning to you, too," Cole said, his low voice brimming with laughter. If she dared to look into his eyes, she was sure they'd be equally brimming—and equally laughing.

So she didn't.

"I'm sorry if that came out wrong." She stared at a space a few feet to the right of his head. "You took me by surprise, that's all. What do you want?"

"That's not a very nice question. How do you know we're not selling Girl Scout cookies?"

"Oh dear. *Are* you selling Girl Scout cookies?" She allowed her gaze to fall on the little girl, who shared Cole's gorgeous bone structure and deep-blue eyes. *His niece.* She knew Cole's manager was also his sister and that the sister was a single mother, so it all checked out.

Not that she was going to admit as much out loud. Knowing a man's detailed family history wasn't the sort of thing one liked to roll out and shine a light on.

"I'll take two of everything," she said. "Except the coconut ones, please. I'm allergic."

"I'm not a Girl Scout!" The little girl crossed her arms and stared up at Hailey. "Are you the lady with the puppies?"

"Oh. Um. Yes."

There was no choice but to meet Cole's eyes. As expected, they danced with amusement. Also as expected, that amusement was directed at her. It was too much. She was at *her* house, on *her* own time, and somehow she was the one who felt like the ground had been pulled out from underneath her. What kind of a man lied about selling door-to-door cookies?

"Two of everything, huh?" he asked. "Someone's ready for second breakfast."

"I was being polite."

"Do you buy that many from every girl who stops by, or just the ones who come attached to football players?"

"I'm a strong supporter of young female entrepreneurs."

Cole leaned on the porch rail as if he hadn't a care in the world. He was dressed much as he had been yesterday, in a way that screamed casual but obscenely rich. She wasn't sure how it worked. They were both in jeans and flannel, Seattle chic at its finest. But while she looked like she'd just rolled out of a discount clothing store, everything about him was elegant and put together.

And attractive. There was no denying it. Even without the bright lights of the football field overhead, he walked around in a haze of gilded glory. The muscles were what accounted for it. Even though she couldn't technically see them, they were everywhere—in the powerful way his thighs strained against his jeans, in the way his shoulders extended much more broadly than any human being's should. *I am perfect,* those muscles said. *I am strong.*

They didn't need to be so obvious about it. She already knew.

"If we come back with cookies, will you let us in to see the puppies?" Cole asked.

"*No.*" Hailey didn't mean for the word to come out like that, but it was issuing from a deep, dark place that she couldn't control. The idea of Cole Bennett inside her house—this tiny, storybook cottage that was all she had left of her dad—was overwhelming enough on its own. Add in the fact that her decor was somewhat... questionable, and this was the result.

A strong, visceral negative.

Cole straightened and frowned, obviously taken aback by the force of her reply. "Oh, God. I'm so sorry. Are we interrupting something?" He ran a hand through his hair and cast an anxious look around. "My sister said I should probably call first, but I thought…"

"Who gave you my phone number?"

His frown deepened. It shamed Hailey to be so inhospitable to anyone, let alone a football legend like Cole Bennett, but she didn't know what else to do. On a good day, she was one social misstep away from burying her head in the sand. In about ten seconds, she was going to have no choice but to bury her whole body. No matter who he was or how heroically he'd rescued her yesterday, she was determined to stand her ground, to be firm, to…

A small hand slipped into hers.

"Please, can I see the puppies?" The girl blinked up at her. "I don't have a puppy."

"It's not… I can't…" Hailey didn't know where to look. Cole wasn't a choice for a variety of obvious reasons, and this little girl with his eyes didn't seem like a safe idea, either. She drew a deep breath. "They're sleeping right now, and their mom is resting. They don't feel up to visitors."

"I'm very quiet," the girl promised solemnly.

"I'm sure you are. But they're so little and are recovering from yesterday, and—"

Hailey could have gone on like that for hours. There were dozens of reasons why it wasn't a good idea to expose the six squirming puppies and their exhausted mother to new faces, most of which were grounded in science and a hearty dose of common sense. Unfortunately, none of those excuses seemed to matter the moment a lone tear began to trickle down the girl's face. She made no move to wipe it away—just kept holding Hailey's hand and looking as through her tiny heart were breaking.

"Oh dear," Hailey murmured. "It's really that important to you?"

The girl nodded. The action caused the tear to loosen and drip to the top of her shiny black Mary Jane. "My mommy says dogs are messy. And I don't have a daddy."

"Er, I should probably mention that Mia here is my niece. And if you really would like us to go—"

Hailey squatted down to the girl's level and took her other hand, clasping both of them in front of her. "I don't have a daddy either," she said. "He passed away a long time ago."

Mia blinked at her. "That's sad."

"It *is* sad."

"Do you have a mommy?"

Hailey shook her head.

"But you have puppies?"

Hailey couldn't help but smile at the child's naivete. The pain of her father's death was no longer the sharp agony it had been at nineteen, but she still felt the effects of it every day of her life. All the puppies in the world couldn't fill that aching hole.

She knew. She'd tried.

"I do have those," she agreed. "For the time being, anyway. There's no more room at the animal shelter, so I'm taking care of them until they find a real home."

From the way Mia's face lit up, Hailey could guess the trend of her thoughts.

"Do you want one?" she asked. "Is that why you came by? You can't take one home today, obviously, but you can pick out your favorite and I'll save it for you."

Mia screamed so loud that it was a wonder the entire neighborhood didn't come running. The area where she lived in West Seattle was more like a beach town than a big metropolis, which meant people actually cared when someone was being murdered next door. In fact, it looked an awful lot like the pink calico curtains belonging to Mrs. Magda across the street were starting to twitch. Mrs. Magda's sight wasn't what it used to be, but if word got out that Cole Bennett was hanging out on Hailey's doorstep...

"They're in the kitchen right now, since that's the warmest room in the house," she said to Mia. She turned the knob to let the girl inside. "But I should warn you—"

Mia darted in before Hailey could issue a warning, which was just as well, since she wasn't sure what she would have said. That her house was a one-woman shrine to the Seattle Lumberjacks? That the afterbirth-covered jersey Cole had laughed at was just one small part of her massive, mortifying collection?

"That was a low blow," Cole said as he held open the door and waited for her to walk through. His words were more of a sensation than an actual sound, his mouth closer to her ear than she realized. His breath was warm and his lips dry, though how she could tell, she had no idea. She just knew. "Her mother is going to kill me."

"You're not here for a puppy, are you?" she asked. Since she was struggling to breathe, the words came out strangled.

"No, Hailey. I'm not here for a puppy." Although he had every right to be upset with her, his tone was light. "And don't worry if your house is a mess. I promise not to judge. If I didn't have a fleet of housekeepers who came by every week, my place would be…"

Hailey would never learn the extent of Cole's slovenliness. The moment he followed her into the living room, the words died on his lips. And who could blame him? To call her house a museum would have been pushing things too far, but it could very easily be mistaken for a museum gift shop. Hailey's only consolation was that the football jerseys, framed posters, and team photographs weren't only of him; the entire Seattle Lumberjack franchise was included. Some of the items were old and quite valuable. In fact, the hand-stitched football on the mantel was from the very first season the Lumberjacks played. It was older than she was, but you wouldn't know it to look at it. Her father had gotten it signed by every player and then immediately put it under glass. He'd always said it was his most valuable possession—with the exception of her.

"You mentioned the kitchen?" Cole asked, a strange thickness to his voice.

"Yes." Her cheeks burned, and she could only be grateful that her face was turned away so he couldn't tell. "It's through there. I gated it off so Bess and her babies could have some privacy."

For a moment, she thought he wasn't going to say anything—that she was going to be gifted an unprecedented show of kindness. She was wrong. Cole brushed past her and got as far as the arched doorway that led out of the living room before he said, "I love what you've done with the place."

Her cheeks burned hotter. "It's not what it looks like."

"I especially like the team photo next to the couch. I don't remember posing for that one."

"You didn't."

"No?" he said, but with such a mischievous air that her heart sank. "Remind me before we leave, and I'll have my sister send you another."

Hailey could only follow him into the next room and be grateful that the worst was over. The living room was the most decorated of the lot; her kitchen was basically normal, with the exception of a few hand towels and a helmet decal mounted above the fridge, and the bathroom was too small for anything but a Lumberjacks shower curtain.

It wasn't, as Cole most likely presumed, as obsessive as it seemed. Very few of the items in the house had been purchased with her own money; in fact, anything dated before the twenty-first century had been bought and installed long before she'd come to live with the man who had become her father. Most of her memories of those early days—when she'd been twelve years old and certain that this foster home, like all her others, wouldn't last—were of the two of them sitting in front of the television, decked out from head to toe in their matching teal jerseys. At the time, it had seemed a strange way to acclimate a scared, lonely child to a new environment, but it had worked.

Oh, how it had worked. Bruce—*Dad*—had breathed football, ate it, slept it. Draft day had been more important to him than Christmas, and Hailey remembered with fondness how jealous her classmates had been when he pulled her out of school every year to celebrate.

As for the items collected since then, well, that wasn't her fault. For as long as she could remember, people had been giving her Lumberjacks paraphernalia for presents. Work birthday parties, secret Santa exchanges—you name it, and she was gifted a poster to celebrate it. Other people got jewelry or books or thoughtful items chosen by the people who knew and loved them.

She got...collectibles.

"One, two, three, four, five." Mia twisted to look up at them as they approached. The kitchen was closed off with a child- and dog-resistant gate, which she was straining to peer over. There wasn't much to see, since Bess was sleeping like a long bar of fur toward the back, but at least the squirming puppies crowding around her midsection were cute. "Where's six?"

"That's very good counting," Hailey said, surprised.

"I can on'y go to ten," Mia admitted. "Is one dead?"

"Of course not," Hailey said, though not without a spike of fear. She'd spent most of last night curled up on the floor exactly where Mia stood, doing exactly what Mia was doing—counting puppies. They weren't very mobile yet, but the darkness had brought terrifying thoughts about straggling babies getting trapped inside a cupboard. "Oh, blast. It's Rufus again, isn't it?"

She lifted a leg to climb over the gate, surprised to find a strong, steady hand extended to help her. Although she would have preferred to keep her contact with Cole to a minimum, she couldn't resist placing her palm against his and accepting his help.

It was such a small, silly thing—Hailey had climbed over that gate on her own several dozen times already—but her heart still fluttered up from her chest to her throat. His hand was so strong. She could only imagine what the rest of him was like.

If she were being honest, she *had* imagined what the rest of him was like. In embarrassing detail.

She transformed her sigh to a cluck of concern as she approached the resting family. So far, Bess trusted her not to puppy-nap or damage her darlings, but Hailey didn't want to push the mother's patience too much.

"Where's he gone this time?" she asked, her voice low and calm. "I swear, he's going to be the death of me."

"Which one is Rufus?" Cole asked.

"The one who caused us all that trouble in the elevator," she said without looking at him. "He's darker than the others, all brown except the tips of his toes. He's not acclimating well. He keeps rolling away."

"Let me help."

Hailey was about to protest, but there was no stopping a six-foot-two, two-hundred-and-twenty-pound man on a mission. To his credit, he didn't mention the decal above the fridge or the hand towels, but Hailey was sure he saw them.

"Be careful about approaching Bess," she warned. "She's protective."

"Oh, Bess won't hurt me," he said as he reached a hand out and allowed the golden retriever to lick it. "We have an understanding. Isn't that right, girl?"

"You can't have an understanding with a dog you've known less than twenty-four hours."

"Sure I can."

Something about his arrogance—and his certainty—struck her hard. In all her lifetime, Hailey had never felt that sure about *anything*, let alone a relationship with another living being. "You don't know that. Some animals take longer to warm up than others."

"So do some people, it seems," he said with a sideways look at her.

She colored deeply but resumed her search for the wayward pup. Her fears led her to first check inside every cupboard, but those were empty. She didn't *think* he'd fit under the fridge or behind the stove, but—

"Ah, here he is." Before Hailey could protest, Cole swooped down to pull the puppy from a corner near the back door, where her ancient-but-functional stacked washer and dryer were wedged. Rufus had somehow made it all the way across the linoleum and taken up residence in one of her oversized wool sweaters. "All nestled up inside your clothes."

"Rufus, you wretch." She was tempted to take the puppy from Cole, but the less the animal was handled, the better. Besides, Rufus decided that he was exactly where he wanted to be. He sighed, wriggled, and made a home inside Cole's cupped hands. "There's no food in that sweater. Or heat. What's the point?"

"Maybe he likes your scent," Cole said. He paused a beat before adding, "I like it, too. You smell like lavender."

It was all Hailey could do not to lift her arm and do a sniff test. She'd been allowed to work from home today—reluctantly—to take care of the puppies. Even Jasmine, the workaholic that she was, knew that losing one of Cole Bennett's famous puppies would result in a public relations nightmare from which none of them would ever recover. Hailey was ashamed to admit that she'd used the day off to *not* shower and *not* wash her hair. If she smelled like lavender, it was only because of the laundry detergent she used.

"Is that the one I get to keep?" Mia asked from her position by the gate. She stood on tiptoe, her small face peering over the top.

"Er…remember what your mother said." Cole coughed. "If I come home with a puppy, she'll never forgive me."

"You're not a'scared of her."

"I'm a little bit a'scared of her."

"You're not a'scared of anybody."

"I'm a'scared of Miss Lincoln." Cole lifted the puppy to his cheek and nuzzled it. His eyes met Hailey's, but they weren't—as she'd expected—mocking. "She has no idea how much power she has over me right now."

The power dynamic in her tiny kitchen swayed so wholly in Cole's direction that his remark was laughable. Hailey was physically, financially, and socially his inferior, and she couldn't meet his gaze without falling into a mortified blush. Even the puppy he was cradling was more his than hers; now that the news had picked up the story of his daring rescue, there was nothing she could do to stop him from claiming paternal rights to the entire pack.

"Mia, could you do a very important job for me?" Hailey asked. Mia's nod was solemn. "If I put a chair right there, could you sit and watch the puppies to make sure Rufus doesn't wriggle off again? He's such a little worm that he refuses to stay in one place for long."

"Yes, please."

"Good call," Cole said in a voice low enough that Mia couldn't hear. "That'll keep her busy while we talk. You must have nieces and nephews."

It was an innocent remark, but it hurt more than Cole realized. She didn't have nieces or nephews. She didn't have anyone.

"Try to be gentle when you put the puppy down," she told him by way of answer. "He's even more breakable than he looks."

With Mia stationed and alert on her chair and the puppies momentarily settled, Hailey went to the living room to await Cole. It would have been nice to have a few minutes to whisk away some of the more embarrassing of her Lumberjacks paraphernalia and run a brush through her hair, but he'd already seen the worst she had to offer.

And the best, unfortunately. Most of the time, those two things were one and the same.

"I have a proposal for you," Cole said as he walked into the living room and lowered himself onto the couch. It was an old couch, and the cushions were well worn, so he sank back. Most people looked ridiculous when they fell into the seats like that, but he only looked relaxed and at ease.

Hailey, on the other hand, was neither relaxed nor easy. "A proposal?" she squeaked. "Me?"

"I wanted to ask you yesterday, but things got a little out of hand." He grinned up at her, his dimple peeping. "It's not every day that I get to be present at a birth. Thank you for that."

He was thanking her? And proposing to her? She needed to sit down.

She did, but shakily, careful to station herself at the end of a faded recliner.

"You're welcome?" she said carefully. When he didn't respond right away, she rushed to fill the conversational gap. There was no way she was giving herself an opening to repeat yesterday's disaster. "Technically, I should be the one thanking you. Things moved so fast after you got the elevator doors open… I didn't have an opportunity to say anything, but that was amazing, what you did. You probably saved Rufus's life. Bess's too. I don't how I'll ever be able to repay you."

His smile deepened. "Don't worry. I do."

She swallowed, unable to look away from that smile. It was the same one he brought out every time a camera was rolling, every time he threw a winning pass or won a big game. Knowing that he pulled it out so easily *should* have made it less effective, but it wasn't. If anything, seeing that smile in person only made it worse. On TV and in interviews, Cole always sold himself as a good guy, a strong leader, a team player—and now Hailey was discovering for herself that he was all those things in real life, too. His niece adored him. He was good with puppies. And most surprising of all, he took her awkwardness and weirdly obsessive decor with good humor.

"I imagine you're wondering what brought me to your office yesterday," he said.

"A little."

"And what brings me to your house today."

"I thought it was because your niece wants to see the puppies."

His smile dimmed. "You don't make things easy on a man, do you?" He sat up, his elbows propped on his knees and an earnest expression on his face. "No, don't apologize. I'm the one who should be sorry, bursting in on you two times in as many days. The truth is, I need a favor."

"From *me*?"

"Of course. You're the person in charge of the Puppy Cup."

"Well…" As much as she would have liked to claim credit for the entire production, honesty compelled her to shake her head. "Not really. My job seems fancier than it is. There's a lot to do now that we're getting ready for filming, but the rest of the year, I mostly just run errands and answer phones."

"But you pick the teams, right? Train them and coach them and all that?"

"There's not a whole lot of training you can do for puppies of that age, but yes. I'm also the one who finds them homes afterward."

"Finds them homes?"

She waved a hand. Here, at least, she knew herself to be on solid ground. Puppies were something she could talk about. With the exception of football, they were *all* she could talk about. "It's why the project was started in the first place. It's an adoption ploy. This time of year is always tough for animals, so we take unwanted puppies from shelters in the area and make them football famous. People can't take them home fast enough after that."

He eyed her askance. "Why do you say 'football famous' like it's one step above emptying portable toilets?"

A giggle escaped before she could stop it. "I mean, it's not like you're out saving the world. You're playing a game."

He cast a slow and very obvious look around the living room. There was no mistaking his meaning—that this was not the residence of someone who would call football *a game*. In here, it was a passion, a way of life. In a lot of ways, that was how Hailey saw it… but not for the reasons Cole thought. Sitting in front of that television, surrounded by the familiar faces of the Lumberjacks and their fans, was the closest thing to family she had.

"Can I ask where this is going?" she said by way of changing the subject. "I'm assuming it has to do with all that stuff you said to Jasmine yesterday?"

He hitched his jeans and leaned forward. "It does. I'd like to know your secret."

"My secret?" she echoed. Instinct urged her to sit up, but she forced herself to remain seated. To move in that direction would only bring her closer to Cole, and that was the one thing she was determined to avoid. "My secret to what?"

"Winning."

Hailey had to pause a moment to digest this remark. She might be a painfully obsessive watcher of football, but she was just that—a watcher. For as long as she could remember, her sports skills ranked right up there with her social skills. Which was to say very, *very* low. In fact, the only time she did anything remotely athletic was when she ran after puppies to try to keep them on camera.

"Wait… Are you talking about the show?" she asked. "*My* show? Football-playing puppies?"

He nodded.

It was happening again—that sensation of feeling as though there were cameras parked at every angle, that the world was just waiting for an opportunity to jump out at her and yell *gotcha*. This time, however, she didn't let it win.

Instead, she laughed.

Hailey had spent so many years working behind the television scenes that she forgot people believed whatever they saw. The story the producers liked to tell the public about the Puppy Cup was just that—a story. They pretended to separate the animals into two teams and spent weeks taping them "in training" as preparation for the big game. It took hours of footage and tons of poop cleanup to get what they needed, but it worked. Viewers bought into the idea that the two teams were in fierce competition, and only one could come out victorious.

"You know it's not real, right?" she asked. "They're dogs. They don't know how to play football."

"Yes, thank you. Even my slow athlete's intellect is able to figure that much out."

She blushed. She hadn't meant to make it sound so condescending, but how was she supposed to know if he understood the magic of television? "I'm sorry. It's just that I don't know what you're asking for. I don't actually win the Puppy Cup. No one does."

"Sure you do. Your team wins every year. You're six and oh. I watched the behind-the-scenes footage."

"There's behind-the-scenes footage?"

He chuckled. "Tons. I'm surprised you don't go through it. Coach Taylor makes us go through every second of every game so many times, I see them in my sleep. It might improve your performance."

"But you just said I'm six and oh. What is there to improve?"

Cole's eyes acknowledged a hit. "There she is. I knew she couldn't be gone for long." With a grin to show he meant no harm, he added, "I didn't watch *all* of the footage, but I've seen enough. From what I can gather, you usually take half the puppies, and some other poor PA grunt takes the other half. And then you and your puppies proceed to demolish them."

She ignored the part where he belittled her job as a "poor PA grunt" and stared at him. That tingly sensation in her spine was sending her yet another warning, but this one came with a pleasant aftershock.

"I think you can tell where I'm heading with this," he said.

She had an idea, but she wasn't going to put it into words. She didn't dare.

"Ms. Lincoln, with your permission, I'd like to be that other poor PA grunt." When she didn't respond right away, he laughed, obviously mistaking her silence for something other than what it was: shock, disbelief. *Delight.* "Cole Bennett takes on the Puppy Cup against longtime champion Hailey Lincoln. Imagine how the press would eat it up. Imagine how your *boss* would."

He wasn't wrong. All Hailey had to do was call Jasmine and even hint that Cole wanted to participate in their show, and she'd have a helicopter sent over to collect him within minutes. And they didn't even own a helicopter.

"I don't understand," she said—and she really didn't. Cole Bennett wanted to play puppy football? With *her*, of all people? "You want my job? What's wrong with the one you have?"

"I know it'll mean more work for you in the long run, but I think you'll like what I have to offer." He pulled out the dimple once again. "Please? I don't have a lot of experience with dogs, and it'll require quite a bit of coordination with my manager and my team, but it would mean a lot to me."

Hailey could only blink at him. It would mean a lot to *him*? He was asking to lend his cachet and influence to the Puppy Cup, wanted to make their show the highlight of this year's football season, and he was phrasing it as a personal favor?

Every one of Hailey's protective instincts rose in an instant. It wasn't the appropriate reaction to a request like this one—and Jasmine would fire her on the spot if she knew—but Hailey could no more help it than she could stop breathing. Nothing in life came without strings attached, especially where she was concerned.

She'd had to fight for every opportunity, every kind word, sometimes for the very roof over her head.

"Why?" she asked, unable to keep the sharp note of suspicion out of her voice.

"Uh, for the good of the world?"

She was unable and unwilling to accept such an easy explanation. "If you wanted to do good in the world, you could donate your salary to the charity of your choosing and keep them operational for the next thousand years. What else?"

"Because I like puppies?"

"Lots of people like puppies," she countered. "You're going to have to do better than that."

"Because I like you?"

She *definitely* wasn't buying that one. She wasn't the sort of person who dazzled and awed upon first glance. She rarely even dazzled and awed after twelve glances. Most of her relationships— professional and otherwise—were the result of forced and repeated interaction.

She shook her head. "You want something else, something you're not divulging. What is it?"

Instead of answering, he flung a question back at her. "How can you tell?"

The same way she knew that Penny didn't really want to receive a call every time she had a puppy-related favor to ask and that Cole Bennett hadn't shown up in her office or her home out of the blue. When it came to people worth knowing, Hailey Lincoln wasn't the answer. She never was.

"Call it a hunch," she said. "What do you really want?"

He watched her for a long, drawn-out moment. She fought the urge to burrow herself in the chair and succeeded only by reciting the alphabet inside her head.

"Okay, you win. There might be a *slight* ulterior motive to my plans." Her heart sank just as she reached the letter J. Of course there was. If this had been as good as it seemed, he would have gone through the usual channels, wooed Jasmine with an upscale restaurant and an expense account. Not sought out a low-level employee whose name most people couldn't remember.

"What kind of ulterior motive?" she asked.

"The truth is, there's a news story that may or may not break sometime here in the next few weeks, and it would be great if I could get ahead of it."

Every muscle in her body tensed. "Define what you mean by *news story*."

"It's not what you're thinking."

"You don't know what I'm thinking."

His brow came up. "Yes, I do. You have the most expressive face of any woman I've ever met—none of whom, by the way, I've taken sexual advantage of."

A wave of heat overtook her, making it even easier for him to read what she was thinking.

"The puppy is gone again," a small voice interrupted. Hailey's first reaction upon hearing that Rufus had once again wriggled away shouldn't have been relief, but it was. She wasn't sure how much longer she could sit there without breathing into a paper bag.

"Did you see where he went?" She wasted no time in leaping to her feet and rushing over the kitchen gate. "I don't know what I'm going to do with that creature."

"He rolled away. What's the matter with him?"

Hailey was too busy lifting the warm, squirming bundle to reply, which was just as well, since Cole had an answer ready. "Nothing's wrong with him. He's probably trying to find Ms. Lincoln—or at least something that smells as good as she does."

"Don't—" Hailey began.

"And who can blame him? Being near her is like traipsing through a field in springtime."

"Oh dear."

"Or taking a long, hot bubble bath with someone else's grandmother."

Hailey couldn't decide whether to laugh or cry. She was leaning strongly toward the latter when Cole scooped up his niece and held her under his left arm like a football. He swung them both to face her. "Thank Ms. Lincoln for letting you see the puppies."

"Aw, Uncle Cole."

"Don't even try it. I have to meet with my trainer in an hour, and if your nanny is to be believed, you have an appointment with a tub of finger paints this afternoon."

"Please can I stay?" Mia tried wriggling out of his grip, but if there was one thing Cole Bennett knew how to do, it was protect that hold. "I can help."

"I'm sure you could, but we've taken up too much of Ms. Lincoln's time already." He gave the girl a playful shake. "What do you say?"

Mia's face scrunched up, but she smoothed it out before it had a chance to turn into a sob. "Thank you for the puppies."

Hailey was tempted to screw her own face up into a sob, but she didn't go through with it, either. "You're very welcome. You did a good job watching them."

"I can come back," Mia offered.

"Oh, um. I don't know—"

Cole laughed before she was forced to come up with an excuse that wouldn't break the girl's heart. "You're too late. I've already lodged a request. We don't want to flood her with demands until she knows us better." His gaze caught Hailey's and held it. "You'll let me know what you decide? The timing is a little sensitive, so the sooner, the better."

It was on the tip of her tongue to tell him that she'd already decided—that having his name even remotely attached to the Puppy Cup was something she couldn't pass up, even with her personal reservations—but there was no opportunity. Cole hoisted his niece more firmly under his arm and made for the front door. He paused at the threshold, looking back over his shoulder with an unmistakably charming grin.

"Oh, and I'll have my sister send over a new jersey this afternoon," he said and winked. "To replace the one that was ruined yesterday. I wouldn't want you to go without."

chapter
4

"IT'S LOOKING REALLY GOOD TODAY, COLE! AMAZING, ACTUALLY! Never better!" Cole's companion, an enthusiastic sports trainer who only spoke in exclamation points when she was lying, stood back and examined her handiwork. In this instance, her handiwork had involved a rotation through the hot and cold tubs, an intensive shoulder massage, and weight training that had lasted about an hour too long. *To strengthen his ligaments,* she'd said. "How does it feel to you?"

"Like I've just spent the afternoon in a torture chamber, thanks," he said. "What's the one where they tie your limbs to four different horses and drive them off?"

"Drawn and quartered." Garrett Smith popped into the weight room just in time to witness the end of Cole's agony. "There's also the rack, which I've always found to be a much neater approach. Same limb-rending pain, much less mess. Horses are unpredictable bastards."

"If it doesn't hurt, I'm not doing my job right!" Aiko replied brightly. "Pain is gain! You can have results or excuses but not both!"

Considering that all three of these sayings were posted above Aiko's head, neither man paid much heed to them. Like the exclamation points, motivational platitudes were another of her go-tos when she didn't know what else to say.

"I'll just, ah, write up my report and hand it off to Dr. Hampton, shall I?" she said as she bounced toward the door. From what Cole could gather, she arrived at work every day around five in the morning and didn't leave until damn near midnight. Where her perkiness came from, he had no idea. "All good things, of course! I'll leave you to it!"

"Leave us to what?" Garrett asked as Aiko's form retreated in the distance.

"Hell if I know." Cole gingerly tested his shoulder. Excruciating pain notwithstanding, there was no denying that Aiko knew what she was doing. His range of movement had already improved. "She probably thinks I'm going to curl up in the corner and cry."

Garrett looked him over. "Are you?"

Cole didn't answer right away. Garrett was in the peak of health, all six feet, four inches of him in perfect working order. As Hailey had oh-so-helpfully pointed out, he was also having the season of his life. The man was light on his feet, nimble as fuck, and rarely showed signs of being winded. He was also Cole's best and oldest friend.

"I'm thinking about it," he admitted. "Will you hold me if I do?"

"Only if you promise I can be the big spoon," Garrett joked, but the mood didn't last. He knew too much about Cole's struggles with his recovery to pretend otherwise. He'd been there when Cole took the hit that tore his labrum, visited in the hospital when Cole had his surgery, and pushed him through every physical therapy session that got him back to full fighting form.

The thing Garrett didn't know, however—the thing that *no one* knew—was that Cole's physical struggles were only part of the problem. A shoulder was a tangible thing, a thing that could be worked on, a thing that could be fixed.

His *heart*, however…

"Do you think they're going to put you on limited participation for the rest of the week?" Garrett asked.

Cole grimaced. "No."

"*Should* you be on limited participation for the rest of the week?"

He shrugged. The fact that he could make that motion in the first place was a good sign that he was on the mend. If he pushed, he could probably ease up on the training and practice routines, but it wouldn't go over well. Not with the curse looming overhead, and not when everyone was working so hard to keep him in fighting form.

The pain you feel today will be the strength you feel tomorrow. If you believe it, the body can achieve it. End zones, not comfort zones. Everywhere Cole turned, there were more of those stupid posters.

Where were the ones that would really help him out right now? *Life doesn't begin and end with football. You're more than just an athlete. People won't hate you if you decide you've had enough.*

"No one else seems to think so. Who am I to question the authority of a team of doctors and therapists whose sole job it is to determine my physical viability?" It was a rhetorical question, and they both knew it. The amount of money that had been funneled into making sure Cole was operating at his best was enough to keep a small country running for several years. It would be an insult to the men and women who worked so hard to throw it away.

Not to mention the fans. *Most* of the fans, anyway. One—who would remain nameless—wouldn't have batted one of her long, sweeping eyelashes to hear that Cole Bennett was no longer operating at full capacity. She'd blush, yes. And stammer. And maybe even release one of those back-of-the-throat moans.

But that wouldn't stop her from saying exactly what was on her mind.

"Let me ask you something… What do you think about my unnecessary hits lately?" Cole asked.

"Is this a trick question?"

"They're bad, right?"

"I feel like this is a trick question."

Garrett was rarely able to sit still for long. He was the kind of man who was always moving, always pushing, always strong. As if to prove his physical superiority, he motioned for Cole to join him at the squat rack and didn't resume the conversation until the weights were in place.

"Does this have anything to do with that stunt you pulled in the elevator yesterday?" Garrett asked as he prepared to heft three hundred pounds. "I saw Reggie in the office earlier, and she didn't seem too happy about it. She said you're losing your focus."

"Don't listen to my sister. She has nothing but focus. She's like a laser beam on top of a shark, and all her energy is pointed at me."

"I wish *my* manager were a laser-beam shark."

Cole sighed and put himself in the spotter position. "No, you don't. Trust me. At least you can turn off your phone and pretend you have a life. Reggie knows I have nothing of the sort. You can lie to your manager or your sister, but you can't lie to a woman who's both."

For the next few minutes, Garrett didn't say anything. He was too caught up in his repetitions, which he pushed out with the ease of a man who had never seen the sharp edge of a surgeon's scalpel. As he hoisted the weights back on the rack, Cole broached the subject of his game play once again.

"You'd say something if you thought I was doing more harm than good out there, right?" Cole asked.

"Of course."

"You wouldn't hide the truth from me?"

"Never."

"You'd put this old, broken-down horse to pasture?"

Garrett put his hand over his chest. "I'd lock the gate myself."

Cole wished he could believe his friend. Once upon a time, they'd been college ball players together, both so full of themselves and their God-given right to dominate the field that no one else could stand being around them. Probably not the most auspicious way to begin a friendship, but it had worked for them. They'd gone through so many football rites of passage together that Garrett knew exactly what Cole was feeling on any given day—the highs and lows, the euphoria and exhaustion.

Cole didn't know when things had started to shift—when *he* had started to shift—but it wasn't the sack that had caused his stupid injury in the first place. He suspected it had more to do with Mia's birth than anything else. It had been a bloody, messy, terrifying affair...and the happiest day of his life.

All the things he'd accomplished in his career, the heights to which he had risen, paled in comparison to holding that perfect, squirming bundle in his arms. Mia had been so tiny and had wailed so loudly that the nurses were forced to put in earplugs before they came into the room. Just a few minutes into life on this planet, and she'd been making herself heard.

That was a real accomplishment. *That* was real life.

He'd felt the same way on the elevator yesterday. Dogs gave birth to puppies every day, obviously, but there was something extraordinary about witnessing it firsthand. Even in the company of a woman who would have preferred being trapped with anyone else.

"With *you*, for example," he said, seeing his friend as if for the first time.

Garrett must have sensed something in Cole's voice, because his hands came up in a gesture of surrender. "I didn't do it."

"Not yet, you haven't. But you will." For the first time since he'd walked into the weight room, Cole felt a genuine smile cross his face. He didn't know why he hadn't thought of it earlier. Nothing could be better calculated to get Hailey to agree to his plan—or to make her turn pink with embarrassment. At this point, he wasn't sure which motivation was stronger. All he knew was he wanted to be part of the Puppy Cup.

And bizarrely, he wanted to see her again.

"What are your plans tomorrow morning?" Cole asked.

"The same plans I have every morning" came Garrett's prompt reply. "This. Why do you want to know? And why are you looking at me like I'm a Christmas ham?"

"She likes you," Cole repeated, a smile creeping across his face. "She might be able to resist me, but *you're* Garrett Smith. She'll let you right in, and you won't even have to shed tears to do it."

chapter
5

I BROUGHT YOU A LATTE. ALMOND MILK, TWO SPLENDAS, AND A dash of cinnamon, right?" Jasmine pushed the door to Hailey's office open with her hip, a steaming paper cup in each hand. Without waiting for Hailey to respond, she slid the larger of the two cups across the desk. "Where's your dog today? And her babies?"

Hailey stared first at the cup and then at her boss. Instead of Jasmine's usual white pantsuit, she was in one that looked an awful lot like Lumberjacks teal.

"I left her at home," Hailey said, still warily eyeing the latte. Jasmine didn't bring coffee. Jasmine never brought coffee. In fact, nine mornings out of ten, Hailey was the one who got sent on an office-wide caffeine run. Apparently, they all liked the way she organized the cups.

"And those little darlings of hers?"

"They're too little and too darling to haul around just yet," Hailey replied, her heart thumping. She might not be the smartest person in this office, but she was no fool. The coffee, the teal pantsuit, the unprecedented show of concern for her foster pups... they could only mean one thing.

"That's a shame. I was hoping we could get the photographer in to snap a few shots. I thought you might be able to get Mr. Bennett to come in for some quick promo."

And there it was. Hailey knew it had been a bad idea to tell Penny about yesterday's visit from Cole and Mia before she got any of the details confirmed, but she'd had to talk to *someone* about it. The only other option was Mrs. Magda, and she was even less discreet.

Jasmine further unbent to take a seat on the edge of Hailey's desk. "You *were* going to tell me about his offer, right?"

Hailey plastered a smile on her face and nodded, using the coffee as an excuse for not answering right away. The latte was delicious and exactly the way she liked it. Jasmine must have either asked around or gone to the place on the corner where they knew her order by heart.

"Of course," Hailey said. "I was just waiting for you to get in."

"You must have made quite an impression on him."

Hailey almost choked on her mouthful of coffee. If by *impression* Jasmine meant a complete and utter fool of herself, then yes, she'd done an admirable job.

"Hiya!" Penny breezed through the open door with yet another latte. "Do you know what kind of coffee Cole likes? I was going to grab him a cup, too, but… Oh, Jasmine. Good morning. You beat me to her."

"Yes, I did. It's one of the benefits of getting to work on time." Jasmine looked pointedly at the clock. Penny barely had time to do more than stammer an apology before Jasmine waved her off and returned her attention to Hailey. "*Do* you know what kind of coffee he likes?"

She did, actually, but not for the reasons her boss supposed. She'd read an article a few years ago about the dangerous amounts of caffeine that some football players consumed, and it had mentioned Cole's preference for extra-dry cappuccinos. So it was a totally normal thing to know about a stranger.

"It doesn't matter, because he's not here," she said. "They started training and practice at six this morning and go all day."

"Oh. Right." Jasmine's lips formed a moue of disappointment. "We'll have to get a copy of his schedule so we can work around it. Can you get on that, Penny, and have it forwarded to Hailey and me?"

Hailey could only stare at her. When it came to doling out menial tasks, Jasmine never looked to Penny. For six long years, that had been Hailey's role. Making coffee, sending faxes, calling the IT guy and listening to him condescendingly tell her to turn the computer off and back on again... At this point, she was the only person in the office who actually knew how to use the copier.

"I want this to be your entire focus," Jasmine said with a warm smile. "We've doubled the budget and pulled a few guys from the animal cops show—they're yours to order about as you see fit. From what Penny tells me, you'll need access to all the old footage to pull together the promo materials, so here's the key to the archives. And I'll see what I can do about getting you producer credits. I can't promise there will be much of a raise, but—"

"Are you sure you don't want to wait a few days first?" Hailey asked. As thrilled as she was at the prospect of all this professional glory, she couldn't remember actually agreeing to anything. Cole had just smiled and promised to be in touch before whisking his niece off, like a fairy godmother who couldn't get out the door fast enough. "Maybe he was only being polite. Maybe all he wanted was to check up on Bess, and I misunderstood—"

A knock sounded. Hailey had no idea who else could possibly be stopping by—or who else could fit inside her small office—but the bouquet of flowers that appeared in the doorway offered a few clues.

"Oh dear," she murmured, her heart leaping to her throat. That wasn't just any bouquet. It was a ridiculously oversized bunch of lavender. And it wasn't just any delivery boy. It was—

"Is one of you Hailey Lincoln?" The flowers were pushed aside to reveal yet another football famous face. Like the last one that had appeared unannounced in her office, his was just as handsome in profile and as easily recognizable to anyone who lived and breathed in the city of Seattle. "I was told to deliver these in person to Hailey—and only to Hailey. Upon pain of death."

"Ohmygod." Penny's voice practically bounced from the corners of the room. "This can't be happening. Not again. My heart can't take it."

Hailey's heart was holding up, but her body temperature wasn't doing so well. She dropped her head to her hands to hide the sudden rush of heat to her cheeks. "Garrett Smith," she moaned. "I can't believe he sent me Garrett Smith."

Luckily for them all, Jasmine took one look at the six-foot-four frame, rich chestnut skin, and shoulder-length locs of the second most famous Lumberjack and rose to the occasion. She slid off the desk and took the flowers, nothing but polite interest on her face. "Wasn't that thoughtful? We were just discussing the changes to our program. I'm sorry Mr. Bennett couldn't come himself."

"Mr. Bennett sends his regrets and apologies," Garrett said, equally precise. Through her fingers, Hailey thought she could detect a smile playing about the corners of his mouth. "But he had a hot date with a cold tub. Coach's orders."

That got Hailey to look up.

"I *knew* pulling those elevator doors open couldn't be good for him. I warned him not to do it."

Garrett's smile deepened. He didn't have Cole's signature dimple, but that didn't make it any less effective. There was something about these football players—these huge, brawny men— giving in to something as simple as amusement that made her heart stutter. "He said you'd say that."

Her cheeks burned hotter. "I need to know for my fantasy league, that's all. If he's going to be nursing an injury, it would be nice to know so I can unload him before the weekend."

"He said you'd probably say that too." Garrett reached into his coat pocket and pulled out a slip of paper. Hailey couldn't think of any way of refusing it without appearing rude, so she gave in.

"What's this?"

"The address to his sister's house. You're invited to go over there to watch the game on Sunday. They're expecting you."

Hailey dropped the paper and watched as it fluttered to the floor. She might have left it there, but Penny was quick to snatch it up and smooth out the wrinkles. For all the wonder and delight on her face, she might have been reading a proposal of marriage.

"What a wonderful idea," Jasmine said, once again stepping into the breach. "Put that in Hailey's calendar for her, would you, Penny? And, Hailey, if you need one of the company cars, clear it with Charles, and he'll have one sent over to collect you."

Penny showed no signs of dismay at being reduced to Hailey's assistant—or jealousy at her access to one of the town cars. They'd spent many a bitch session lamenting the injustice of a system that gave the wealthiest company employees free transportation while the rest of them had to fork over toll fees and bus fare on a meager pittance.

"Sure thing, boss." Penny paused long enough to mouth another *ohmygod* at Hailey before whisking herself out the door. She didn't bother to hide it, either, which meant Garrett got a clear view.

"Oh, and if you're worried about leaving the puppies at home, you can put a pet sitter on an expense account," Jasmine added. "I'll head down to accounting now and open one for you."

Hailey was momentarily bereft of words. Since she couldn't find it in her to breathe, either, she was also momentarily bereft of oxygen. The world started to get a little wavy around the edges before she finally remembered how to function as a living organism, but by then, it was too late. Garrett had already nudged her into a chair by the door and gently pushed her head between her legs.

"Breathe in," he urged. "Breathe out. There you go."

"I'm fine," she said through the wall of hair that surrounded her downturned face.

Either Garrett didn't hear her or he didn't heed her, because he held her in place. "A few more—in and out, in and out."

To be fair, Hailey did feel a lot better once she took a few deep breaths and paused a moment to collect herself. It would have been better if the air hadn't been scented *quite* so strongly with lavender, but that couldn't be helped.

It seemed that Cole had been serious about the offer to help her with the Puppy Cup—and about the offer to work by her side. She'd lain in bed last night replaying the entire conversation in mortifying detail, but it hadn't made any more sense at two o'clock in the morning than it had at noon.

Yet here she was. Breathing on Garrett Smith's command. About to change the lives of thousands of dogs across the country.

That was the thing she needed to focus on, to remember despite her personal fears that the rug was going to be pulled out from under her at any moment. She hadn't been kidding yesterday when she told Cole that the Puppy Cup had been started as an adoption ploy. After Christmas, when families unloaded the puppies they'd bought as gifts and subsequently regretted, when the cold and wet weather made it difficult for strays to stay warm, the shelters were flooded with unwanted animals—most of them destined for a life behind bars. All it took was a few minutes of screen time, and the bulk of America jumped to open their doors and their homes. For the fifty puppies they showed during halftime, it was a chance at a new life, a *real* life.

For the thousands of abandoned animals across the country, the story was a similar one. People adopted more pets after the Puppy Cup aired. They donated more money to their local shelters. The unwanted stragglers, the twelve-year-olds who'd been cycled through so many homes they no longer held out hope of anything more, found someone to love.

Something in Hailey's chest lurched and clamped. They *would* find someone to love. She'd make sure of that.

"Send Mr. Bennett my thanks but also my regrets," she said with genuine feeling. "I'm more than happy to accept his help with the Puppy Cup, but I have plans this weekend."

Garrett's brow went up, but his expression remained otherwise neutral. "Plans? During a Lumberjacks playoff game?"

The heat that had been starting to dissipate flushed up to her cheeks again. Clearly, Cole had prepped his teammate about her slight fixation. No one with an original Lumberjacks football on display would miss a game this close to the Kickoff Cup.

"It's a party," she lied, thinking fast. "A bunch of people are coming over to watch with me. I can't just abandon them."

"That would complicate things," Garrett agreed. "Hang on."

Hailey had no idea what she was supposed to hang on to, so she made a valiant attempt at holding on to her sanity. It was difficult when Garrett pulled out her office chair and seated himself in it as though that were an everyday occurrence.

"Mind if I use your phone?" he asked.

Hailey shook her head and watched as he picked up the receiver and punched a series of numbers. It was like flipping through the pages of a trashy magazine. *They're just like us!* Making phone calls from stranger's desks. *They're just like us!* Swiveling around in circles because a bolt is loose.

"Hey, Cole. It's me."

"Wait… You're calling *Cole*?" Hailey dived for the phone, but there was a reason Garrett was one of the highest-paid wide receivers in the American Football Club. His reflexes were like lightning.

"Yeah, I'm here. Yeah, I found her." Garrett ducked and weaved, making it impossible for Hailey to reach the button that would end the call. "But she doesn't like me nearly as much as you said she would. She's trying to wrestle the phone from my hands."

Hailey bit back a moan. This was it. This was the end. She was going to go down as the only woman in the world to literally die of mortification.

"Well, obviously not. She barely comes up to my shoulders. I think I can handle her." Before she could fully absorb this remark, Garrett held the phone out to her. "He wants to talk to you."

"I can't," Hailey said.

"You'll hurt his feelings."

"He'll get over it."

Garrett paused and held the phone against his chest. Like Cole, he sported the same classic, dressed-down style that professional football players made look so easy, but Hailey noticed that his shirt wasn't *nearly* as tight as Cole's. "You'd better talk to him and get it over with. I don't know if you've noticed, but he can be a bit of a drama queen when he doesn't get his way."

Hailey pulled her lower lip between her teeth, something perilously like a giggle threatening to escape.

Seeing it, Garrett pushed harder. "You'd be doing me a real favor if you just played along. Please? Seattle is counting on you."

With a shaking hand, Hailey accepted the phone. She was being manipulated, obviously, and by a pair of men who only had to smile and flex to have the world falling at their feet, but what else could she do? *Think of the puppies.*

She spoke without preamble. "I can't believe you told Garrett what I said about him."

"Hailey! What a delightful surprise."

"You know what? I *can* believe it." A man who could fake that much excitement at the sound of her voice was obviously capable of anything. "What's next? Is the mayor going to come pick me up for lunch? Are you buying the production office and taking over operations from here on out?"

"That's not a bad idea, actually. Is it for sale?"

Aware that Garrett was watching her much more closely than she liked, Hailey turned her back to him and leaned against the desk. Not for the first time in her life, she wished she was better at hiding her emotions—not just because it was embarrassing for her every feeling to flit across her face, but because it rarely ended well for her. As a young kid living in group homes, her tendency to blush had been painfully and relentlessly used against her. Those who fared best in the system were the ones who learned to embrace stoicism early on, who didn't cry every time someone hurt their feelings. They may have felt the same loneliness and despair that she had, but by God, nothing would have prevailed upon them to let it show.

Hailey had let it show. She'd shown it every moment of her life. And until the day she'd been placed with the man who would eventually become her father, she'd paid a heavy price for it.

"It wasn't necessary to send reinforcements," she said, determined to do this part right. "The Puppy Cup team is delighted to accept your offer of assistance."

"The *entire* Puppy Cup team?" Cole tsked. "It's not polite to lie."

She swallowed and forced herself to keep going. "And thank you for the invitation to your sister's, but I already have plans to watch the game at my house. Send her my apologies."

"Hey, Reg... She says she can't come over on Sunday."

"Wait. She's there? *Now?*"

"She's throwing her own party, apparently. I didn't know."

"It's not really a party," Hailey was quick to say. "Just a small gathering. For my family and friends."

"Yeah, I'll tell her." Cole's voice grew a little louder as he returned his attention to the phone conversation. "Reggie says you're welcome to bring them along. She has more than enough space."

For a long moment, Hailey was afraid she was going to have to ask Garrett to shove her head between her legs again. In another lifetime, this would have been a dream come true. She was invited to watch a Lumberjacks game at the home of Cole Bennett's manager and sister—and she was allowed to bring witnesses with her. She could hobnob and talk shop and indulge in her love of football with the one woman in the world who probably knew more about Cole than she did.

Except…she didn't have any family or friends to bring along. Oh, she could rustle up Penny and a few other coworkers, of course, but it wasn't the same. Deep friendships—*lasting* friendships—had always eluded her, a sort of what-if dream that came easily to other people, the same way they had things like extended families and social safety nets and someone to call when they needed a hug. And the only other person she could imagine sharing this with, her father, was long gone.

But oh, how Dad would have loved to go.

She could almost hear his deep laugh, smell the sharp tang of his favorite IPA and the burning cheese of the pizza they always cooked—and forgot about—on game day. She could also imagine exactly what he'd say if he knew she was acting so silly about all this.

If you want something, Hailstorm, go after it. You only get one chance at this life. You might as well throw the ball.

"Sure," she said before she was even aware that her lips were moving. As was the case the first time she'd lost her mind—and her verbal filter—around Cole, something about this man caused every logical reaction she had to fly out the window. "That's very generous of her. I'll be there."

"Really?" Cole sounded as surprised as she felt at her sudden turnabout. "You aren't going to fight me over it? Not even a little?"

She couldn't help but laugh. Until Cole had waltzed into her office, she'd never fought anyone over anything. Just last week, she'd watched as the receptionist had walked up to the break-room refrigerator, pulled out the yogurt with *Hailey* written on it in permanent ink, and proceeded to have a midafternoon snack.

"No. I mean, I think it's pretty cowardly that you had to send your wide receiver to do your dirty work, but considering how often you rely on his catch radius to get the job done, I shouldn't be surprised."

Behind her, Garrett choked on a laugh.

"I just spent the past hour going over all my shortcomings with Coach Taylor," Cole said. "Nothing you say can hurt me."

"Then you won't mind if I tell you to work on putting more realism into your pump fakes. A down-on-his-luck magician could sell it better than you do." As soon as the words escaped, Hailey wished them unsaid. Not—as might be supposed—because they were unpardonably rude, but because both Garrett and Cole roared with laughter.

"Oh, man." Garrett got up from the chair and shook his head, a grin splitting his face. "What I wouldn't give to watch the game with you and Reggie on Sunday. You two are going to get along great."

"We are?" Hailey asked, suddenly wary. "Why?"

Cole must have overheard his teammate, because he answered for him. "Reggie says you don't have any choice now. If you don't show up, she'll come to your house and drag you by force."

The thought of yet another Bennett viewing the spectacle of her home was more than Hailey could bear. "That won't be necessary," she said quickly.

"Good," Cole said and paused. Hailey could almost swear there was hesitation—uncertainty, even—in that pause, but that was ridiculous. What could Cole Bennett have to feel uncertain about? "Thank you, Hailey. This means a lot more to me than you know."

chapter
6

"I WASN'T SURE WHAT TO BRING, SO I MADE THIS." HAILEY shoved a plate at the woman standing on the other side of a colorfully paned wooden door. The door matched the rest of the house—a huge, historic residence located near the top of Seattle's Queen Anne Hill. "Sorry."

"What for? It's perfect." The woman accepted the cheese log and parted her bright-red lips in a smile. Even if Hailey hadn't already assumed that this tall, wide-shouldered woman was Cole's sister, that smile confirmed it. The dimple in her right cheek was identical. "Let me guess…a log for the Lumberjacks?"

Hailey blushed. She'd downed several bottles of water on the way over in hopes of controlling the inevitable flush of heat, but it didn't appear to be working. Plus she really had to pee.

"I'm Reggie, but you probably already guessed that, didn't you?" The woman stepped aside to allow her into the paneled foyer, pausing a moment to peek over Hailey's shoulder. "Where's the rest of your party?"

"Oh, um. It's just me, I'm afraid," she said. And a good thing, too. Penny would have started screaming before they even made it up the driveway. "I thought it would be better if—"

"It's the puppy lady! The puppy lady is here!" A small figure darted around the corner and hurled itself at Hailey's legs. It was fortunate that she'd already handed off the plate, because Mia hit her with such force that she almost toppled over. "Where's Rufus?"

Hailey couldn't find it in her to meet Regina's eyes. Offering this child a puppy was all well and good when she'd thought it was the reason for Cole's interest in her, but it took on new meaning now that she was meeting Mia's mother face-to-face.

"He's at home with his brothers and sisters," Hailey said as Mia disentangled herself from her legs.

"Oh." Mia's face fell. "So it's just…you?"

Hailey was struggling to come up with an appropriate response when Regina laughed. Like the smile, there was something unsettlingly familiar about it. "Listen to the two of us. You'd think we'd never had company before. We're delighted you're here, Hailey, and don't require anyone else—human or canine."

It was such a nice thing to say, coming from such a nice woman in such a nice house, that Hailey wished she'd never come. She should have channeled her inner Jasmine while she'd had a chance and maintained a strict professional veneer over the rest of her interactions with Cole instead of gallivanting about with his sister.

"If it helps, I do have this." Hailey pulled out her phone and pushed a few buttons. A gray, grainy image of her kitchen popped up. The camera was focused on Bess and her puppies, most of whom were contentedly napping on her stomach. Even with the pet sitter thoughtfully provided by Jasmine's deep company pockets, Hailey had some qualms about leaving them alone any longer than she had to. Bess was starting to show signs of neglecting poor Rufus. "See? So I can check on them while I'm gone."

"Gimme!" Mia didn't wait for permission before she yanked the phone out of Hailey's grasp. Regina admonished her for it and began to apologize for the girl's behavior, but Hailey was too grateful for the change of topic to care.

"I don't mind," she said. "It's not a very exciting thing to watch, but I remember doing the same thing when I was little. There was this channel on public access that showed nothing but an eagle's nest and a bunch of eggs that were getting ready to hatch. I used to watch it for hours."

"Hours" was an understatement. She'd actually spent weeks sleeping in front of the group home's television, fearful of missing even one minute of the big event. The anticipation of those eggs cracking open, of the babies being welcomed into the world by two loving parents who took turns carefully watching over them, had been her everything.

In the end, they'd hatched while she was at school.

"Well, isn't that the sweetest thing," said a low-pitched female voice. They were in a formal living room daintily decorated to match the historic characteristics of the home, but the woman who stepped in didn't match. For one, she was six feet tall. For another, the first thing she did upon sight of Hailey was whisk her into a hug that was incredibly strong and just as strongly scented with rose. "You must be Cole's friend from that TV show. Aren't you lovely? And so darling to offer Mia one of your puppies. Isn't that darling, Reggie?"

"The darlingest," Regina agreed but with a wink that showed Hailey she knew where to assign the blame. "Hailey, if you haven't guessed, this is our mother, Paula. Dad is already parked in his favorite chair in front of the game, so don't expect anything out of him but monosyllables until the final whistle. He takes his football very seriously."

"We *all* take our football seriously," Paula said. She released Hailey from the hug, but only enough to wind an arm through hers and start leading her through a pair of double doors. "My mother-in-law is pottering around here somewhere, too, but don't pay any heed to her. She uses game day as an excuse to hit the gin a little harder than usual, if you catch my meaning. She loves a prelunch tipple. Sam is coming, too, isn't she, Reggie? With her family?"

Hailey's head was starting to spin.

"I think they're already here. The Wegmores too." Regina quirked a rueful smile at Hailey. "I'm sorry. I should have warned you that Sundays are a kind of family reunion around here. You've entered the official home of the Cole Bennett fan club."

The cheese log was starting to seem woefully inadequate in face of all these new revelations. So was Hailey. She'd had the foresight to google the address before she came, so she knew she would be entering a neighborhood where million-dollar properties were on the low end of the price value scale. She'd expected wealth and abundance. She'd expected to find herself a weed among gilded lilies.

She hadn't expected every branch and twig on Cole's family tree.

"Sam and her wife are lovely, but don't sit near the Wegmores unless you want to be bored to death hearing about their recent trip to Italy." Paula gave Hailey's hand a warm pat. "If I have to hear one more word about the correct pronunciation of *vermicelli*, I'm going to swear off pasta forever."

As it turned out, Sam and her wife *were* lovely. Sam was some sort of cousin who worked in a high-powered financial firm downtown, but who always—always—took football Sundays off to watch the game. The Wegmores weren't half bad either, even if they did wax poetic about the health benefits of hand-pressed olive oil. From all that Hailey could gather, they were related to Cole in a vague, nebulous way that no one was willing to define.

Apparently, no definitions were needed. They were here to watch the game and support Cole, and that was enough.

"Shove off, Gertie," said a frowning, powerful bear of a man seated in a deep leather recliner in the center of the television room—which, as far as Hailey could tell, was a modest descriptor for a room that contained at least twenty thousand dollars' worth of audiovisual equipment. "Let the new girl sit next to me. She looks sensible. She can help me break down the plays."

His words had the effect of causing the woman seated to his

right—Gertie Wegmore—to slap him playfully on the arm. As she also got up to leave, Hailey could only assume she was used to being treated so cavalierly.

"What's your name again?" Cole's father asked as Hailey approached his chair. "I can never remember all of Cole's girlfriends."

"Oh, um." Hailey felt the blush mount to her cheeks. Even though everyone in the room was politely pretending they hadn't heard the remark, Cole's father spoke much too loudly not to be overheard. "I'm Hailey. Hailey Lincoln. And I'm not Cole's girlfriend. I'm—"

"She's the woman who's going to help with the you-know-what, Dad." Regina swooped in and planted a kiss on her father's cheek. She lowered her voice in an attempt at discretion, but Hailey was still close enough to hear. "So be nice."

"What?" Cole's dad turned to stare at Hailey. "That's bullshit."

"Dad!"

"Julian!"

"Uncle Jules!"

"Grandpa said a bad word!"

Hailey was oddly grateful to the older man for drawing the room's attention away from her. He reminded her a lot of her own father—gruff and rough and a little bit cranky, but with a twinkle in his eye that made it difficult to take offense.

"Well, it *is* bullshit," he said, repeating the word much more clearly this time. He also patted the seat until Hailey lowered herself into it. "No offense, but I never went in for any of that hocus-pocus nonsense. Get her a beer, would you, Sam? Get her two. She's going to need them."

"One is fine, thanks," Hailey managed.

"I know, but they've got me on a strict watch. You can pretend it's yours, and I'll sip when no one is looking." Cole's dad thumped his chest. "The ol' ticker isn't what it used to be."

Since everyone in the room also overheard *that*, Hailey wasn't surprised to find just one bottle placed in her hands.

"Keep it out of his reach," Sam said with a wink. Like the rest of the family, she was built on generous lines, her eyes that same preternatural blue. "He's a liar and a thief, but we love him anyway."

Hailey's chest felt tight as she lifted the bottle to her lips and drank. She wasn't a huge fan of beer—and she definitely wasn't used to drinking at ten o'clock in the morning—but it seemed rude to refuse when everyone was being so nice. Besides, she felt the need for liquid courage. Especially when she turned toward the older man to ask the question that was burning on her lips.

"What hocus-pocus are you talking about?" she asked in what she hoped was a casual voice.

"Eh?" Cole's dad asked before reaching up and adjusting his hearing aid. Everyone in the room jumped as the feedback screeched through the air. "What's that?"

"You said you don't go in for *that hocus-pocus nonsense*," she repeated. "You don't mean the Kickoff Cup Curse, do you?"

From the gasp her use of the phrase elicited, Hailey realized her error almost at once. This was a room full of die-hard Lumberjack fans—Cole Bennett's family, in fact. She couldn't have picked a worse audience to say the name of the curse out loud to. His mother made the motion of a cross over her chest. Gertie Wegmore muttered something under her breath. And Sam's wife, a slight woman whose chunky hair was worn in spikes colored in Lumberjacks teal, actually covered her ears in an attempt to keep the words at bay.

"I'm so sorry," Hailey said, flushing with mortification. Just once, it would have been nice to be the kind of person who could think before she spoke, who had at least a *little* bit of a verbal filter in place. "I don't know what came over me."

"As long as you break the darn thing, you can say whatever you want." Sam laughed and pulled her wife's hands down. "Do you really think you can do it?"

All heads in the room—even those belonging to Sam's two young children and Mia—turned her way. Hailey blinked, dazed by the intensity of all the attention. She might have remained that way for quite some time, but she was starting to realize what was going on.

A hell of a story, Cole had told Jasmine that first day. *Real human interest.* He'd also admitted that he had an ulterior motive in asking for Hailey's help and that her six-and-oh winning streak was part of it. All that footage of her "winning" at puppy football, throwing her into the pit of his family without warning...

Why on earth hadn't she realized it before? This wasn't about Cole wanting to do good in the world. He was going to ride her coattails in hopes of breaking the curse. He was making her responsible for the outcome of the most anticipated sporting event of the year.

Of all the sensations she could have felt in this moment—anger at being manipulated, annoyance at not seeing it earlier, fear of what Jasmine would say if she found out—one in particular stood out: relief.

At least now I know what he wants with me. At least now I know what I'm doing here.

"Cole tells us that you haven't lost a single game since you started playing puppy football," his mom prompted, smiling kindly. "You must have extraordinary luck."

"Extraordinary luck," Hailey echoed, her mouth dry. "Yes. Yes, that's it. I was born with it."

She didn't know what compelled her to say such a thing, unless it was the entire room of strangers staring at her with hopeful expectancy. *Extraordinary luck* was the last way anyone would describe her entrance into the world. She'd been born the usual way, she presumed, but someone had dropped her off at a fire station when she'd been eight months old, leaving no trace of her birth or origins. From there, she'd lived in a succession of foster homes and group facilities. None of them had been terrible, and she hadn't been abused in any way that could be quantified, but her early years had been marked by a kind of indifference that was difficult to overcome. The places she'd lived had been full to capacity and struggling to do their best, accomplishing what they could with what little resources they had.

She'd gotten by. She'd survived. But she hadn't been loved.

There was nothing extraordinary or lucky about that.

"Thank goodness!" Cole's mom rushed over and grabbed Hailey's face between her hands. She squeezed until Hailey's lips were forced into a pucker, at which point she planted a loud smack on them. "What a doll you are for helping out like this. Cole never says so, but it gets him down, always coming so close only to lose at the last minute. Anything you need from us—anything at all— and it's yours for the asking. Isn't that right, Julian?"

Cole's mom kicked a leg sideways, hitting the recliner with a thud. In addition to being a tall woman, she was a strong one, and Cole's father grunted as his footrest came crashing down.

"Well, of course she can have anything she wants," he said, as though it were the most obvious thing in the world. "But that doesn't make your woo-woo magic any more real."

The entire family seemed as though they'd like to protest this remark, but Cole's father was blissfully inured to their scathing looks.

"Oh, look. They're getting ready to flip the coin," he said as he pulled his footrest back up. "It's going to be heads. I always guess it right. Tell her, Paula."

Cole's mom threw up her hands, obviously giving up on the other conversation. "It's true," she said. "He has a gift."

"What he has is a selective memory," Regina said in a laughing undervoice. "He also thinks he invented DVDs and wine bottles with screw caps. Don't listen to a word he says."

The sudden image of Cole's face on the oversized television screen drew Hailey's attention. It was a familiar sight in so many ways. She'd been seeing it for years—that dimple and those cheekbones, the way he seemed to ooze confidence as he led his team out onto the field—but it had never felt quite like this before.

In the past, he'd always been a legendary figurehead, like Alexander the Great or Hercules, a man revered by the masses. To be near him was to be near greatness, to bask in the presence of a god. Now that she'd met his family and discovered them to be the nicest, most welcoming, most truly *lucky* people in the world, Hailey could marvel at how foolish she'd been.

His powers weren't mythical. His strength wasn't pretend. This was his actual existence, the life he got to live every single day.

"It's not going to be heads," Hailey said as the camera moved past Cole to the coin toss taking place in the middle of the field. She took a large swig of her beer—too large, considering how close she came to choking on it—and pointed at the screen. "It's going to be tails, and the Lumberjacks are going to defer."

It was nothing more than an educated guess. The team often made the choice to defer when playing an away game, especially one as important as this, and her odds were fifty-fifty about the coin.

That didn't seem to matter as her prediction played out word for word on the screen. Cole's mother and the Wegmores gasped. Sam and her wife cackled with glee. Regina looked at Hailey sideways. Even Cole's dad turned to her with renewed respect.

"Well, shit," he said, ignoring the repeated outcries on his language. "Maybe we do have a chance at making it to the Kickoff Cup this year. I think I'm starting to like this girl."

chapter
7

COLE STEPPED THROUGH THE BACK DOOR OF THE DOG shelter onto a patch of damp lawn littered with toys. Most of them were well used and well loved, with frayed ropes and chewed ends. One of them—a football—appeared to have been ravaged more than the rest. The faux leather was almost completely torn apart.

"In my world, this is sacrilege," he said, picking up the ball and spinning it lightly in the air.

"Oh. You're here." Hailey had been playing tug-of-war with a compact, muscular puppy whose gray fur was so thin that his skin showed through. She turned toward Cole, no sign of surprise on her face. The rope—with the puppy attached—dangled from one of her hands. "Your plane was supposed to get in hours ago."

"It did."

He angled the ball and threw it, allowing it to skim past the puppy. It was close enough to draw the animal's interest but not so close it made contact. As he'd hoped, the puppy pounced off after it.

Hailey's gaze followed the line of the ball. "That was a good throw."

He knew it was. He could feel it burning in his ligaments. Yesterday's game had been a success, but like most of his successes, it had come with a cost. Not even Regina and an entire freezer full of produce could touch the pain. This was a grin-and-bear-it day.

Weirdly enough, the grinning part was easier now that he'd seen Hailey.

"I would have come straight here, but I had to wade through my family's extravagant praise of you first." Cole shifted his weight to one leg and stood watching her. "I have no idea what you did to them, but you have some serious explaining to do. My dad is ready to divorce my mom and make you an offer in her place."

This speech was calculated to get a blush out of Hailey—and blush she did. She was already flushed with exercise and the cold, but the blossoming pink across her cheeks indicated that she had plenty more where that came from. Wisps of her hair played about her face, not unlike the puppy frolicking in the grass around her feet. Her freckles were especially visible in the outdoors, and her eyes matched the heavy gray clouds overhead. Whether to counteract the gloom and doom of a Seattle January sky or because it was the only pair of shoes she owned, she was once again wearing the bright-red Converse.

Cute. She's cute.

Cole was almost startled to realize it. The women in his life had a tendency to boast much more dramatic adjectives than that. They were graceful. They were gorgeous. They were glamorous. Even his own sister, who he rarely saw as anything but the playmate and protector of his youth, was always well put together. He couldn't remember the last time he'd seen her in anything but full body armor.

In a pair of faded jeans and a clunky fisherman's sweater, her hair in a loose braid over one shoulder, Hailey looked, well, cute. There was no other word for it.

"That was some game you played yesterday," she said. She was still blushing furiously, but her discomfort—if that was what it could be called—did nothing to deter her. "My ears are still ringing from the sound of your family's cheers."

"I should have warned you," he apologized. "They can be a bit...effusive."

She pushed the wayward strands from her face. Her hands were dirty from playing with the puppy, leaving a streak of mud along one cheekbone. "That's one way to put it. I would have said they were nice."

Nice? Puppies were nice. Hailey was nice. His family was a behemoth of enthusiasm and aggression. He couldn't remember a time in his life, even as a kid, when they just stood quietly and let the world unfold around them. They pushed and pulled and demanded, and there was no escaping their reach.

"They liked you," he said.

"Yes, because you told them they had to."

It was true. He *had* told them to be on their best behavior, and—if it was at all possible—to tone down their glory-be-to-Cole routine, but that didn't account for the plate of snickerdoodles currently sitting on the front seat of his Lexus. His mom only baked cookies for people she genuinely liked.

"Sam wanted me to thank you for sending her the link to that website of Cole Bennett GIFs," he said by way of answer.

Hailey's blush deepened. "She didn't believe it existed."

"And the Wegmores have the recipe for spaghetti Bolognese you asked for."

"They were very enthusiastic. I didn't know how to say no."

"Also, my mom managed to find the scrapbook of all my high school football injuries, and she left a standing invitation for you to come over and see it whenever you want."

That one gave Hailey pause. "Wait... That's a real thing? She wasn't just making it up?"

Cole only *wished* his mom had made that up. Thirty-four pages of stitches, scrapes, and black eyes, all of them carefully cataloged and colorfully highlighted. She put it out every Christmas to remind them all of how far he'd come—of the years of pain he'd had to go through to get where he was today.

"Oh, it's real," he said. "She's very proud of her project."

"People who scrapbook generally are."

"No, you misunderstand. The book isn't her project. *I* am."

It was the first time he'd ever said the words out loud, and he was surprisingly nervous to see how they'd be received. A lot of the men on his team had families who played a big role in helping them succeed. Fathers who spent every afternoon throwing balls in the backyard, mothers who worked double shifts to pay for equipment, sisters and brothers asked to put their own dreams aside so weekends could be dedicated to travel teams…his story wasn't the only one.

That was what made this all so difficult. Cole wasn't unique. He hadn't sacrificed anything extraordinary. His pain wasn't greater than that of anyone else.

So why did he feel so damnably alone in it?

Hailey was watching him with a slight tilt to her head, her eyes scanning his face as though reading the pages of a book. In this, as in most things, he could see what she was thinking. She was deciding whether or not to believe him, whether he was worthy of her pity or her scorn.

He'd never know which one she'd been leaning toward. As if sensing that Cole was feeling much less stable on his feet than he appeared, the gray puppy came bounding up and shoved his head under Cole's hand.

"Hello there," he said, giving the animal's head an obliging scratch. Like Hailey, the puppy was covered in swipes of mud, his paws caked in it. The kennel yard attached to the shelter was obviously well used, that hard-packed earth showing signs of regular canine wear. "Aren't you a lucky dog?"

"Not really." Hailey squatted down to the puppy's level and

grazed his cheek with a kiss. "This is Philip. He's a pit bull mix, five months old. He was left tied to a tree out in front of the shelter right after Christmas."

"Oh." Cole wasn't sure how to respond to this. That anyone would tie a cute little puppy like this to a tree and drive away was bad, obviously, but Hailey was kissing the dog's face with unself-conscious abandon. A life like that couldn't be too bad. She'd shown no signs of wanting to comfort *him* with kisses.

"He's not taking well to life in the shelter," she said as she rose to her feet. "He picks at his food, cries all night long, and starts shaking anytime they shut the gate to his pen."

"Oh," Cole said again, this time with more sympathy. He looked at the puppy again, this time noting how visible the ribs were under the thin coating of fur. The animal did look as though he could use a good meal. Or ten. "Are we going to make him football famous so he can find a new home?"

"That's the plan, yes. He's one of the fifty puppies in the area I've selected for the show."

"Then why are you looking at me like that?"

Her answer was to clip a leash to the dog's collar and hand it to Cole. "Until the show airs and someone steps up to adopt him, Philip is going to live with you."

"Uh…" He glanced at the leash in his hand and then down at the puppy. As if sensing that something exciting was happening, Philip planted his hind end in the dirt and lolled an oversized tongue out the side of his mouth. "Is this retribution for me promising Mia a puppy? Did Reggie put you up to it?"

"No. You did."

He transferred his gaze to Hailey. She squirmed under the directness of his stare, but she held herself firm, unable to hide the sudden spark of silver in her eyes.

"Consider it a payment of sorts," she said. "If you're going to use me to try and break the Kickoff Cup Curse, then giving Philip somewhere comfortable to live for the next month is the least you can do."

If Cole had been a decent man, his first reaction upon hearing these words would have been embarrassment. It was wrong to leverage Hailey's puppy luck for personal gain, not to mention roping her into this project without telling her what he wanted out of it. He owed her the benefit of truth and full disclosure. He owed her at least a little shame.

Instead, he laughed. "They told you, huh? I was afraid something like that might happen."

"You aren't even going to try and deny it?"

Not a chance. Not when she was drawing closer to him, her lower lip pulled between her teeth.

"So this whole thing," she said. "The puppies, the show, *me*... It's about the curse? About you trying to break it? That's the ulterior motive?"

Cole nodded, even though she was only partially right. He wasn't about to get into a detailed medical history—pull out the charts and projections, discuss his complicated relationship with the sport, ask her opinion about his viability as a human being without football to prop him up. Not because he didn't want to hear her thoughts but because she already acted like he was on the bottom rung of a ladder that descended far, far below the earth's surface.

He was well aware that he wasn't out curing cancer or reversing climate change—that his value to the world lay in his ability to throw a ball with unerring accuracy. He didn't need Hailey to remind him.

For some reason, hearing it from her seemed so much worse.

"You caught me," he said. "It's ridiculous, I know, but we can't spend another year getting so close only to lose at the last minute. As the last six years have proven, you've got luck on your side—and even better, you have the *appearance* of luck. When it comes to my team, that's just as valuable as the real deal. A few smiles, a few photo ops, and they can break this thing. I know it."

And then maybe, just maybe, he could sit down and have a serious conversation about retiring. A Kickoff Cup win wouldn't change anything fundamental, but it would give him leverage. He could depart on a career high, leave his team with something to carry them through the years ahead.

Give his parents something to be proud of.

"Couldn't you, like, sacrifice a goat or something?" Hailey asked.

His laugh escaped before he could stop it. "I'd rather sacrifice something a little less bloody, if that's all right with you."

He took a step toward her, careful not to jostle the puppy that sat panting at his feet. Unable to fight the sudden impulse, he reached out and tucked a wayward strand of hair behind her ear. He even went so far as to allow his hand to linger, the silky-smooth strands sliding through his touch, the warm and rapid beat of her pulse evident under his fingertips.

"There must be something I can do for you in return," he said, his voice low. "Something you want. Something only I can provide."

Hailey's breath hitched and her whole body trembled, but she didn't take the bait. "I already told you what you have to do," she said with a nod toward their feet. "Take Philip home. Feed him. Love him. It's only a month, and it will make a huge difference to his quality of life. It's why I asked you to come all this way."

Cole glanced down at the animal in question, trying to decide whether he was insulted or intrigued by Hailey's determination to make him take this dog home. There were hundreds of things she might have asked him for instead: money, fame, success, *sex*.

She asked for none of them. She hadn't even taken home the signed photo he'd had Regina set aside for her yesterday. He couldn't understand it. There was no denying that Hailey was a fan of the Lumberjacks or of him. From the things his family had said, she knew her shit when it came to his team—better, probably, than anyone who didn't share his blood. And this thing he was offering her, free publicity for the Puppy Cup, was obviously something she was willing to accept on behalf of her career.

But that was it. That was where the exchange stopped, where Hailey's admiration came to an end. Cole had the sinking feeling that although she appreciated him as an athlete, she didn't think much of him as a man.

"Take Philip home," he repeated carefully.

She nodded.

"Feed him."

She nodded again.

"Love him."

He didn't wait for her nod this time. Instead, he reached down and tucked the puppy under one arm in the same football hold he'd used to carry Mia. It took a lot more of his strength than he cared to admit to keep Philip there, but he managed the same way he always did.

With grit and determination and a desperate wish that he could just once admit he didn't have nearly as much of his shit together as the world believed.

"Okay," he said. "I'll do it. *And* I'll take this little guy for my team. Look at him wriggle. He's got fight in him. He'll make an excellent offensive tackle."

An exasperated sigh escaped her. "For the last time, we don't pick teams. Or assign positions, for that matter. They're *puppies*. We just let them run around for a while."

"As long as we let them run in my favor, I don't care how we play it," he said. "But for the record, you never want to lead your pick with an OT. Or a kicker, but don't tell Johnson I said that. He got us six points yesterday. He's feeling a little smug."

"Cole!" Hailey released a shaky laugh. "It's not real football. It's literally a patch of Astroturf with puppies and chew toys. We film them for like forty hours in hopes of whittling it down to thirty minutes of play time. You've seen the Puppy Cup before, right?"

"Well, no," he admitted. "I'm usually busy during the game. Sorry."

Cole took advantage of Hailey's momentary discomfiture to set Philip on the ground and watch as the puppy took off after a bird that landed on the edge of the yard, his leash dragging behind him. If history planned on repeating itself, Cole had about ten seconds before Hailey recovered and gave him his own back again, and he didn't intend to waste them.

"That dog has good speed," he said with a nod. "Not to mention good form and lots of energy, but I feel like he could be easily distracted. Are you writing this down?"

"Of course I'm not writing it down."

"Fine." Cole made a big show of reaching for his phone and pulling it out. He snapped a quick photo of Philip, who was barking excitedly at the bird, before turning on the record function.

"Philip the pit bull," he said in a loud, careful voice. "Five months old and—what was it you said?—abandoned next to a tree. Good speed and strength, but he can't even scare that bird on the fence away. Final assessment: All bark. No bite."

He turned to Hailey with the phone held out. "Anything you'd like to add?"

"What are you doing?"

"Building a roster. It's only fair. You've spent the past few months assessing and getting to know the animals. If I'm going to have a chance at picking a winning team, I need basic stats from all of them. Philip has promise, but I'd like to see who else there is to choose from."

As he hoped, this focus on football and puppies—the only two things that didn't seem to fluster Hailey—worked in breaking down any of the barriers that remained between them. Stalking forward, she yanked the phone out of Cole's hand and held it to her lips. "Cole the football player. Thirty-two years old and *not* in charge of this project. Despite his years of being the center of attention, this is supposed to be about the animals, not him."

Cole felt a laugh well up from somewhere deep within him. He also took his phone back and kept the recorder going. "Hailey the puppy lady. Twentysomething and adorable as all get-out. Doesn't play well with others, but that's okay. I've always liked a challenge."

Somewhere in the middle of his assessment, Hailey's eyes had grown wide. If Cole had to guess, he'd say the cause was that bit about being adorable, but he didn't regret his words. She *was* adorable. Flushed with pleasure, squaring up for battle, more belligerent than his sister's birth-room attendant—there was something seriously wrong with him to find the combination of those three things appealing, but that was no surprise. He'd been saying he was broken for years, and no one believed him.

Since he was holding the phone out of Hailey's reach, she couldn't snatch it back to list more of his faults, but that didn't stop her. She drew so close that he could feel the heat radiating off her and got up on her tiptoes. As before, she didn't take advantage of their proximity to touch him in any way, but that didn't seem to matter in the slightest. The almost-but-not-quite touching, the way he could sense the shape of her body rather than feel it, was working much more powerfully on his blood flow than he could have anticipated.

"Cole the liar," Hailey said, her voice carrying up to his phone. "Not going to get his way with empty compliments. Some of us have work to do today."

"Hailey the disbelieving. Should probably back down, or she's going to get kissed. Immediately."

Her mouth fell open and stayed there, a look of surprise warring with something more—something that looked a lot like invitation.

Which was why he made good on his threat—not quite immediately but after a few more intoxicating seconds. The rules of fair play that had been instilled in him since he'd first touched a football meant he would give her an opportunity to decline. There was ample time for her to back down or relinquish her ground.

She did none of those things. With a defiant toss of her head, she tilted her lips so they were within easy reaching distance.

I dare you, she seemed to be saying. *You don't have the nerve.*

He almost didn't, but there was something about the soft part of her mouth that he couldn't resist. Her full lower lip, the curve of a mocking smile, the quick, panting breath that escaped before he made contact—it would have taken a much stronger man than him to pull away at that juncture.

In terms of kisses, it wasn't Cole's most impressive performance. Over the years, he'd come to learn that women had certain expectations when it came to being kissed by a professional quarterback with a reputation like his. They wanted mastery and confidence—a man as powerful and in control as the one they saw every week on the TV. In this, as in all things, expectation weighed heavily on his shoulders.

But with Hailey, all he did was brush his mouth lightly against hers. It was a whisper of a kiss, more suggestion than reality, and all the more powerful because of it. He had just enough time to make out the outline of her lips and the taste of her breath, to enjoy a warm rush of anticipation that crept up from his toes, before he felt the sharp stab of teeth on his pinkie finger.

"What the—" He reared back and snatched his hand to his chest in a move that was mostly instinct. Glancing down, he found Philip smiling up at him, his tongue lolling out of the side of his mouth. "Your puppy just bit me!"

It took Hailey a moment to respond. Out of the corner of his eye, Cole could see that she'd gone pink with embarrassment—that his kiss had, for all its brevity, unsettled her. One look at Cole standing there with his hand clutched against him, and that sentiment fled.

"Don't be such a baby," she scolded with a cluck of her tongue. She knelt next to the puppy, heedless of her knees on the soggy ground. "He was just trying to get your attention. Weren't you, Philip? You haven't had nearly enough love in your life."

Now that the initial shock had worn off, Cole realized his reaction had been more surprise at those razor-sharp puppy teeth than actual pain. Instead of admitting as much, however, he doubled down.

"My finger will have to be surgically reattached," he protested. "I'll never throw a football again. What'll your boss say now?"

"That you're being dramatic." Hailey nodded up at his hand, which was, to be fair, perfectly fine. "He didn't even break the skin."

"Not all trauma is visible on the outside," he said.

Hailey's eyes narrowed, and a look of steely determination took over. Once again, she was making it very easy for Cole to read her thoughts. Whatever positive feelings she'd been harboring toward him in the aftermath of that kiss were gone.

"You have no idea what trauma is," she said. "Not the great Cole Bennett. Not a man with a contract like yours and a mom who carries around a scrapbook of his childhood injuries. Not a man who could buy a hundred of these shelters and give homes to every unwanted dog in the city."

So that was the game they were going to play, was it? He held out a hand—his uninjured one—and pulled Hailey to her feet. In a move of pure perversity, he didn't let go, either. He kept her warm, slightly muddied palm next to his, his grip strong and his determination stronger.

"You think I don't know what trauma is?" he asked. "You think I haven't felt pain?"

She faltered but didn't lose her ground. "Physical pain, yes. But everyone's felt that at some point in their lives—and most of them don't have twelve doctors and physical therapists to help them get over it."

"What about the sting of rejection?" he returned.

She released a disbelieving chuff of air. "Please. When have you ever been rejected?" It must have been a rhetorical question, because she yanked her hand away and put it on Philip's head before Cole could answer. "This puppy was abandoned before he even knew the meaning of home. He was dropped off here, unwanted and neglected, with the assumption that someone else would make him their problem. But he's not a popular breed, and the shelter doesn't have the resources to give him the attention he requires, so he spends most of his nights curled in a ball on a concrete floor, crying for someone to love him. *That's* rejection. *That's* what it feels like to have nothing."

Although Cole's chest gave a lurch at the picture she'd conjured up, he held himself firm. He was no monster; he already knew there was no way he was leaving this place without Philip. He wasn't the dog Cole would have chosen to break his thirty-two-year stint of not having a pet, but there was something about the puppy's fierce vulnerability that appealed to him.

That dog needs me. Not because Cole was a good quarterback and not because he could sell magazines and sportswear but because he had a heart in his chest and blood in his veins.

"He's welcome to spend the next twenty-eight nights with me, but only on one condition." Putting stipulations on his care of the dog wasn't Cole's best move, but it was all he could think of. If Hailey only cared about football and puppies, he'd have to leverage them. A man could only work with what he was given. "Well, two conditions."

"You already tricked me into being your curse-breaker. It's not a very magnanimous offer if there are more conditions."

Cole couldn't help laughing. Hailey obviously had no idea just how unmagnanimous he was about to get. "The first condition is that you and your team pull together a puppy roster—a *real* roster, with stats and bios and pictures so we can do our draft the right way. We have to make it look like a real competition, or it'll never work."

"For the last time, they're—"

"Not football players," he finished for her. "I know. But you have to admit there's a certain charm to it. Draft day. Puppy against puppy. A battle for the best and brightest. The press will eat it up."

She *did* have to admit it—and if the way she pulled her lower lip between her teeth was any indication, she wasn't happy to do so. "What's the other condition?"

"Have dinner with me."

Like the kiss, the invitation wasn't the most sophisticated he'd made in his lifetime. He was too rushed and too eager, too uncertain of the outcome—a feeling that didn't go away when Hailey's eyes widened and she took a step back. Cole was no expert, but he was pretty sure a woman physically balking at an offer of a date was a bad sign.

"With me *and* my sister," he amended hastily.

Hailey was no longer trying to ward him off like an evil spirit, but she didn't bear the look of a woman who was excited at the prospect of sharing a meal with the Bennett siblings, either.

"Why?" she asked, a wary expression pinching her brows. "What's in it for her?"

Cole had no idea how to answer that question. In all his years as a professional football player—and as a normal, human man— he'd never had to work so hard to get someone to spend time with him. The idea that there had to be an underlying reason before Hailey would even consider saying yes was new and, frankly, a little lowering.

So he answered the only way he knew how. Honestly.

"Nothing's in it for her," he said, shrugging. "She likes you, that's all."

And so, he thought, *do I.*

It was a good thing Philip was still at his feet, because petting the puppy gave Cole something to do with his hands while Hailey deliberated with herself. He knew that was what she was doing because her thoughts flitted across her face like words across a page. She wasn't pleased at the offer of a date, but she was even less pleased at the prospect of leaving this puppy at the shelter for one more night.

"Fine. We'll do this your way." She nodded at the puppy. "If you take that little guy home with you right now, I'll set up your draft and work with your press team so you can smile pretty for the cameras. I'll make sure you're on the front page of every newspaper in America, encouraging people to fall in love with these puppies."

Cole felt strangely disappointed at this capitulation. It made him an ass to admit it, but he didn't want this to be about the puppy draft—or about the publicity. He wanted it to be about having dinner with him.

"*And* I'll have dinner with you and your sister," she said. She added, almost defiantly, "But it will be at my house. My house, my food, my terms."

"Agreed." He extended a hand and held it out to her. She didn't take it right away, eyeing his fingers like they were snakes. "If you don't want to shake on it, we can always seal the deal with a kiss. You know I'm good for it."

Her hand slipped into his with a speed that would have done his coaches proud. She shook and released his grip just as quickly, as if afraid lingering would lead to something more.

"It wasn't *that* bad, was it?" he asked, only half joking. "I won't do it again if you don't want me to, but I've never had any complaints before."

She released a chuff of air that bordered on a snort. "Of course you haven't. Who would critique the great Cole Bennett to his face?"

A week ago, he might not have known how to respond to that question, but he knew the answer now. Especially since she hadn't forbidden him from trying again. "You."

The oh-so-familiar color started to mount to her cheeks, but something stopped her telltale blush before it reached all the way. With a toss of her head, she said, "You may have a tendency to lose too many yards behind the line of scrimmage, but I will say this for you, Cole Bennett. You know your way around a kiss."

chapter
8

"D ON'T ASK."

Garrett and Regina looked up from the table where they sat, their heads bent close together. As soon as they noticed Cole, they jumped as far away from each other as two people *could* jump when seated in separate chairs, shared expressions of guilt and annoyance on their faces.

They'd been acting like this for a few months now. Cole wished they'd just come out and admit they were seeing each other. His sister had always vehemently declared she'd rather die than date a football player, but Cole assumed that was just her way of showing she cared.

Football players made the *best* boyfriends. Sure, they were moody and self-involved and had a tendency to devolve into twelve-year-olds whenever they were together, but everyone had their faults.

"Don't ask about what?" Garrett asked.

Cole's answer was the tentative poke of Philip's head inside the front door to his condo.

"It's okay, buddy," Cole urged the puppy. Philip had been fine on the way over here, his head hanging out the window as he basked in the damn-near freezing-cold wind off the freeway, but the moment Cole had lifted him out of the car, he'd started showing a marked tendency to shake in fear. "You can come in. No one here is going to hurt you."

Regina heaved a sigh. "What did I tell you about adopting that woman's puppies?"

"This isn't an attempt to get her to like me," Cole protested. He gave up trying to urge the puppy through the door and scooped him into his arms instead. Philip seemed to enjoy being held, so Cole didn't put him down right away. "This is strategy, plain and simple. I'm taking care of this little guy for a few weeks. In exchange, she's setting up a puppy draft."

"A puppy draft?" Regina echoed.

"It'll make more sense once you read the proposal. Which, ah, she's probably faxing over to you as we speak."

"Goddammit, Cole."

"I know." He gave her a rueful grin—the one he knew from long experience would get him exactly what he wanted. Even as kids, Regina had been susceptible to it. He'd gotten way more than his fair share of Halloween candy that way, not that he'd been allowed to eat it. "But you don't have to be there. You just have to work your public relations magic a little. You love that stuff."

Regina's look of reproach spoke volumes, but Cole ignored it and started to fill a bowl with water instead.

"You might also have to come with me to dinner at Hailey's house afterward, but it's better if you don't ask about that part, either," he said.

"What's the matter with you?"

Other than his exhaustion and his fears for the future and the fact that he couldn't stop thinking about the warm rush of Hailey's breath?

"Oh, you know. The usual." He glanced over his shoulder at his sister. "And don't worry. Philip won't be here forever. I'm his caretaker until the Puppy Cup is over, that's all. Like Mary Poppins, but for a dog."

"Then under no circumstances will you introduce him to Mia. I don't want her getting attached only to have you disappear up a chimney." Regina drew closer and eyed the puppy in his arms. "Huh. He's not much to look at, is he?"

"He has deep internal trauma," Cole said, thinking of his conversation with Hailey. "So be gentle."

"I'll have to be gentle later. Apparently, my least favorite client just dumped a ton of work onto my lap." Regina gave his shoulder—his bad one—a light squeeze. It might have been a sisterly gesture of affection, but it also could have been a test.

"Your most favorite client appreciates it," he returned without so much as a wince. "It's for the good of the Lumberjacks, Reg. The good of *Seattle*."

"Save the golden-boy routine. No one here has bought it in years." Regina released his shoulder and turned to Garrett. "And you'll think about what I said, Garrett? *Really* think about it?"

"I'll walk you out," Garrett said by way of answer. Cole did his best to give them privacy, but he couldn't help from peeking around the corner once or twice. He could just make out the dark tailoring of Regina's suit and hear the indiscriminate murmuring of Garrett's low-rumbling voice, but that was only to be expected. They were hardly going to start making out in the hallway while he was standing within earshot.

"You and Reggie seem to have made yourselves at home," he said as soon as Garrett returned to the kitchen. He placed both the bowl and the puppy on the floor, but Philip had no interest in liquids. He adhered himself to Cole's leg instead. "It's nice you could both make use of the emergency keys I gave you. For this *emergency*."

"It is, isn't it?" Garrett replied, nothing but goodwill in his voice.

"You're not going to tell me what you two were doing here?"

"Nope." Garrett opened the fridge and pulled out an energy

drink. He pointed both it and his finger at Cole. "Not unless you plan on telling me what you're doing with that Hailey woman."

Fair enough. In a different frame of mind, Cole might have sacrificed his emotional well-being to hear Garrett admit the truth, but not right now. Not when he wasn't sure what he was doing—or why. Part of it, he knew, was a perverse determination to get the better of a woman who showed no real signs of succumbing to his charm, but that didn't explain everything. He'd faced challenging women before without resorting to puppy adoption.

He didn't have time for a dog; at this point in his life, he didn't even have time for a goldfish. He *wanted* one, the same way he wanted to spend Sundays eating brunch with his friends and for a woman like Hailey to look at him and think "there's a highly interesting man," but none of that was likely anytime soon.

Yet here he stood, a dog bone in his pocket and a woman on his mind.

As if aware of what Cole was thinking, Philip lifted his head. He caught sight of one of Mia's stuffed footballs on the couch and began inching bravely toward it.

"Go for it, buddy," he urged the dog. "She never uses it. These days, she prefers ninja fairies."

Philip took him at his word and pounced toward the couch. It was on the tip of Cole's tongue to order him to stay on the floor, to avoid the curved white leather that his interior designer had insisted was the only way to sit in comfort, but he didn't have the heart to crush Philip's spirit.

Garrett lifted a brow but didn't speak. He took a long, slow drink from the can in his hand instead. That deliberate action said everything his friend was thinking and more—especially when Philip turned once, pawed twice, and began liberally licking himself on the ten-thousand-dollar couch.

"Don't you have your own house to go to?" Cole grumbled.

"I do, but Dr. Hampton wanted me to come over and check on you. And to drop off this."

The *this* in question was a refill of prescription painkillers. Garrett pulled the orange bottle out of his pocket and set it on the kitchen counter, but Cole made no move to grab it.

"I don't need that," he said, eyeing it with distaste. "I still have some left from the last batch."

"Maybe it's a hint that you should start taking them."

"Maybe Dr. Hampton needs a new hobby."

Garrett nodded and slipped the bottle back into his pocket. "Reggie thought you might react that way."

Cole couldn't decide which was worse—his best friend and his sister sneaking into his house for a secret love affair, or his best friend and his sister sneaking into his house to discuss the state of his health, but he was leaning toward the latter.

With a sigh, he lowered himself on the couch next to Philip, who lost no time in pulling the football onto his lap and chewing it there. There was something soothing about running his hand up and down the puppy's short fur, at how the warm body planted itself in place and stayed there.

He leaned his head on the back of the couch and closed his eyes. That felt good, too, until he felt Garrett sink onto the seat next to him.

"We won the game," Cole said, the words coming out more gruffly than he intended. "What more do you want?"

"Me? Not much. I mean, you *could* offer to feed me lunch now that I've come all this way, but…"

Cole laughed. "Feed your damn self. I'm not running a hotel over here." He opened one eye and rolled it toward his friend. "Am I?"

Garrett shook his head. "Nah. It's not like that with me and Reggie."

Cole released a disbelieving chuff of air. There had been a time, before Mia was born, when Garrett would have given both his thumbs for a shot with Regina. "You're adults. What happens between the two of you is no concern of mine."

The moment stretched a few seconds too long. Although Cole tried to distract himself with the puppy, he felt a compulsive need to fill the silence. "It doesn't hurt as much as it used to," he said, rolling his shoulder in a slight shrug. It wasn't a complete lie—the regular work with Aiko was building up his strength, and he really only needed the painkillers to get through game day.

That was another thing that didn't make him unique within the world of professional football. Lots of guys were being held together by sports tape and opiates, by their determination to win no matter what the cost. For Cole, with his one tiny labral tear, to bitch and moan and act like he was the only man in the world who was suffering was ridiculous. Even the little puppy in his lap had gone through more in his short lifetime.

Hailey had been right about that, too. *Real* trauma, the kind that dug deep and imprinted hard, was something Cole had never known. There were too many people who cared about him, too many places he could go to seek shelter when things got rough. He had no right to whine when he had so much—when he'd been *given* so much.

"If I leave, are you going to sit here all day, petting your puppy and looking depressed?" Garrett asked as if reading his mind.

"Yes."

"Do you want me to leave anyway?"

"*Yes.*"

Garrett laughed. "Don't worry. I can take a hint when it's being shoved down my throat. I don't know why you have to be such a fucking drama queen all the time, Bennett. It's only football."

Cole grunted a noncommittal reply, glad but not glad to see his friend go. The thing Garrett didn't understand—the thing that no one could understand—was that *only football* wasn't a term that belonged in his vocabulary. Not when it supported his grandmother and parents and sister and niece, keeping them in comfortable homes and financial security. Not when they'd spent their whole lives sacrificing everything so he could have a chance at greatness.

"What if I don't want to be great?" he asked Philip, whose only response was a happy loll of his tongue. Cole made sure the door had closed and clicked behind Garrett before adding, more softly this time, "What if all I want is to be me?"

chapter
9

IT WAS JUST LIKE A FOOTBALL PLAYER WITH THE WHOLE WORLD at his feet to underestimate the amount of work required in critiquing, cataloging, and ranking fifty puppies located in different shelters across the Pacific Northwest.

"I think that's the last one." Penny rubbed a hand blearily over her eyes. Her perfectly winged eyeliner didn't smudge, so Hailey could only assume she'd either made a pact with the devil or resorted to permanent marker. They'd been hard at work since six that morning. "What time is it?"

Hailey looked at the clock above her desk and groaned. "We have ten minutes until he shows up. How's my hair?"

Penny's grimace said it all.

"Oh dear." Hailey sighed and lifted a hand to her head. "It looked fine this morning, but my hair is too thin to hold its shape for long, and—"

"I've got you." Penny whisked the ponytail holder from her own long, perfectly shaped coiffure and reached for Hailey's oversized bag. Hailey was about to protest this breach of privacy, but Penny was a woman on a mission. "Sit down and close your eyes. Do you have any dry shampoo in here?"

Hailey wordlessly shook her head. Ever since Cole had caught her carrying around one of his jerseys, she'd been packing light.

There wasn't even an old Lumberjacks ticket stub to give her away.

"Never mind. I'll just use your brush. This might hurt a little."

In reality, it hurt *a lot*. Hailey had no idea what Penny was doing to her head, but it involved wrenching her neck into strange positions, teasing every strand until it stood on end, and otherwise yanking her hair this way and that. Penny snapped the elastic band with a flourish and stood back to survey her handiwork.

"I'm a genius," she murmured before reaching for the nearest desk drawer. After rummaging for a few seconds, she pulled out...a permanent marker.

"I *knew* your eyeliner couldn't look that good on its own," Hailey muttered, shrinking back as Penny loomed close. "Is this hygienic?"

"Not even a little," Penny replied cheerfully. "But desperate times call for desperate measures. Hold still."

Under normal circumstances, Hailey would have fought this attack on her eyelids, but these were strange times. Any minute now, Cole Bennett was going to walk through that door so they could pick puppy teams in front of an audience of twelve different newspaper outlets. The reporters were excited about it. His people were excited about it. Her people were excited about it. At this point, she was one small step away from being carried through the city on a golden litter.

So yeah. It might be nice to look a bit more like Penny. Just this once.

As if in agreement, Penny capped the marker and started to undo the tie at the waist of her casually elegant black jumpsuit. When Hailey didn't make a move to strip off her own outfit—a carefully selected floral wrap dress that was the same color as Bess so it wouldn't show any dog hair—Penny nudged her with her foot.

"Come on, slowpoke. Off with it. You can't be nationally syndicated in a dress that looks like my grandmother's couch."

Hailey ignored the slight on her dress to focus on the more immediate problem. "Uh, Penny?" She gestured first at Penny's hips and then at her own. "Are you sure about this?"

Penny slipped out of the pantsuit with the unselfconsciousness of a woman who'd come of age in a ballet dressing room. Even her underwear was perfect, a matching set with black lace that wouldn't have lasted one cycle in Hailey's ancient washing machine.

"Oh, I'm sure. Your waist is the size of a kitten. This will look so much better on you than it does on me."

Hailey had no choice but to believe her. Well, she *did* have a choice, but it seemed cruel to leave Penny standing in the middle of the office in her underwear. With a quick look to make sure the door was firmly shut, she stepped out of her dress and handed it over.

"I think I hear someone coming," Hailey hissed as the sound of voices in the hallway started to pick up.

Penny had already cinched the wrap dress at her waist and lost no time in helping Hailey navigate the jumpsuit. It was made of some kind of stretchy, forgiving material, so it *technically* fit, but Hailey would have preferred a moment to check herself in a mirror. The waist might have been the right size, but she was acutely aware that the bust and the butt areas were stretched to their limit.

"Damn," Penny said, taking her in with a blink. "You can thank me for this by inviting me over for drinks sometime, okay?"

"Drinks?" Hailey echoed blankly.

"Yes, it's that thing normal friends share after a long day of work. Alcohol and relaxation and maybe even a few laughs." Penny gave her one more appraising look before nodding once. "Now switch me shoes and get out there."

Hailey did as she was told, trading her beige flats for a pair of strappy sandals that were wholly inappropriate for the weather.

She wished there was more time to unpack Penny's statement—
They were friends? She wanted to hang out outside work?—but
she'd just managed to secure the final buckle before the door was
pushed open.

"Welcome to draft day," Cole said, sweeping inside just as
Penny kicked Hailey's half-open purse underneath her desk. "Are
you ready for this?"

Nothing could have been more calculated to make Hailey *less*
ready than the way he looked as he stood in the doorway, his chest
and arms straining at a button-down shirt that looked as though
it had been woven with strands of moonlight, his face relaxed
and gorgeous. The sight of such a perfect specimen of manhood
should have made her swoon—and from the way her blood was
pounding, that was a likely possibility—but it also made her
acutely aware of the differences between them.

Even in this, he was her master. It didn't matter that this was *her*
workplace and that today's event was *her* doing—every instinct
she possessed was warning her to run and hide, to cast this job
onto Penny's more capable shoulders and salvage what remained
of her ability to protect herself.

But Penny nodded at her from the doorway with a smile and a
wink. And the binder in front of her fell open to a puppy that had
been living in an overcrowded dog shelter for seven of the eight
months he'd been on this earth.

Some things were more important than her weak, stupid pride.

"Don't worry. I'm ready." Hailey drew a deep breath and tossed
the binder at him. "You have half an hour to go over these, and
then we'll make our picks in the conference room. Use your time
wisely. I already have my dream lineup picked out."

He caught the notebook easily, but something in his expression
shifted as he stood there looking at her. Hailey fought the urge
to squirm and tug at Penny's jumpsuit, wanting to put distance
between her skin and the tight cling of the fabric.

"Well?" she asked, her tone more abrupt than she intended. She couldn't help it—that look on his face was doing strange things to her, wreaking havoc on a circulatory system that was already prone to causing her the maximum amount of embarrassment in the shortest amount of time. "Do you want to look those over in here, or should we head to—?"

She was prevented from finishing by the enthusiastic entrance of Philip, who showed no hesitation in recognizing Hailey despite her recent makeover. Sometime in the past twenty-four hours, the puppy had been washed and dressed in a teal bow tie. She didn't know if it was the bath or the natural outcome of a day spent in a palatial mansion, but he looked, well, *good*.

"Hello, Sir Philip," she said as she squatted down to the puppy's level. He was a body in motion, squirming and wriggling as though he had no choice but to wear his happiness on the outside. "Yes, I'm very pleased to see you, too. Yes, I know you want to lick my face, but I'd rather you didn't."

"Is that something you don't enjoy?" Cole asked. "Interesting."

Hailey glanced up to find that Cole had returned to his former state—which was to say in complete mastery of himself and the room. His smile was back, though a little lopsided this time, his eyes twinkling as they took in the sight of her trying to prevent Philip from burrowing in her neck.

"I hope you didn't let Jasmine see you come into her precious office with a puppy," she said by way of answer. She didn't trust herself to address the other part—the *flirtatious* part—until she had a better handle on herself.

"Don't worry. We snuck in through the back," Cole promised. He held out his hand and hoisted Hailey to her feet. A decent man would have let her go right away, but he was no such thing. He used his hold to tug her close and transfer his grip to her waist. He spanned a good portion of it, his thumb grazing her belly. "Do I dare hope this is for me, or did you dress for the cameras?"

She tried not to fall for it. She took a deep breath and willed her heart rate to maintain a steady beat. She imagined herself inside an ice castle. She pictured the deepest, darkest cave in Norway.

It was no use. Her blush spread like wildfire across her cheeks.

"I don't know what you're talking about," she said, her voice prim. "But on the subject of cameras, might I suggest you start looking through that binder sooner rather than later? The photographers will be here any minute."

Her tactics failed. If anything, they had the reverse effect of what she intended. Cole's grip tightened, his fingers pressing into her waist so much that a shiver moved up and down her spine. There was something deliciously possessive about his hold. Even Philip pouncing playfully around their feet and Penny standing a few feet away didn't seem to weaken him.

"You look good," he said. And, more forcefully this time, "*Really* good."

As was rapidly becoming the case whenever she interacted with this man for longer than five minutes, Hailey felt all her verbal filters strip away and her raised hackles take their place. Okay, so she was rarely the best-dressed woman in the room. And there wasn't always time to do her makeup and hair as nicely as she wanted. And yes, she'd have never chosen this particular outfit by herself.

But it wasn't as if she'd just stepped out of a pumpkin carriage. Her transformation hadn't occurred by magic. All that had changed was some permanent marker on her eyelids and hair that felt about three times taller than it normally was. He could show a *little* less surprise.

"I know I do," she said and stepped back. That small bit of distance between the hard planes of Cole's body and the heated planes of her own wasn't much, but it was enough. "And I'm going to look a hundred times better when my team of puppies demolishes yours. Wouldn't it be awful if you lost both the Puppy Cup and the Kickoff Cup this year? What would your parents say?"

He looked as though he wanted to argue further—maybe even pull her into his arms again—but he allowed the moment to pass. With a chuckle and a shake of his head, he said, "Yet another low blow, Hailey Lincoln. You know very well what they would say."

He was right. She did know. She might have only been in their presence for one day, but that had been more than enough to tell her everything she needed to know. One of the least helpful skills she'd developed in her lifetime was the ability to dissect a family at a glance. She could sense financial strain as soon as she walked in the door. She knew when a couple was on the brink of divorce and hoping to stall it by becoming foster parents. She felt their disappointment when the child who'd been placed with them was shy and awkward and not at all what they'd been expecting.

She also knew genuine love and affection—felt how it radiated in everything a family said and did, joined it in front of the television to watch a game of football.

Cole didn't know how lucky he was to have that in his life—to *always* have had that in his life. This man, with his twelve-million-dollar arm and his good looks, his easy charm and loving family, had no idea what it was like to have to fight for every scrap of affection.

Philip did, though. Along with the hundreds of other puppies desperately waiting to find their forever homes.

"They'd tell you to get off your ass and get to work," she said. She nodded at the expensive and wholly unnecessary gold watch on Cole's wrist. "You're not so far ahead that you can afford to run out the clock, Cole Bennett. But then, I don't have to tell you that, do I?"

———

Cole was doing his best to concentrate on the roster of puppies spread out in front of him, but it was no use.

He'd been tricked. Duped. Lured into this project with false promises of easy, friendly competition.

There was nothing easy or friendly about the way Hailey looked right now. As she bent and twisted, tacking photos and stats and other useful bits of information on the wall that was to serve as their draft board, the only thing he could seem to focus on was her ass. In the clothes she'd worn every other time they'd met, she'd seemed attractively curvy—a warm collection of round parts that fit her personality.

Today, however...

He shook his head to clear it and forced himself to focus on the task at hand. Today, she'd revealed more than just the small curve of her waist and the way her body swelled above and below it in perfect proportions. Today, she'd revealed her hand.

She was going to do her best to win, and if he allowed himself to be mesmerized by the way the fabric of her jumpsuit clung to her hourglass shape, she was going to demolish him.

This is a game I know how to play.

Cole waited until Hailey finished with the board and turned toward him, a question in the arch of her brow. It matched the rest of the look she'd pulled together for the day—a sort of tousled, tumbled pinup who knew exactly what she was doing to him.

"Well?" she asked. "Have you finished looking everything over? Can I call in your adoring hordes?"

He didn't answer her—at least not in words. Without losing eye contact, he began to unbutton the cuffs of his shirt. His sister had once told him, back in the days when his enthusiasm far outstripped his charm, that women were more attracted to forearms than to any other part of a man. He'd suspected Regina of saying that to make him feel better—as a gangly teen who hadn't yet grown into his body, his arms had been the only impressive thing about him—but he'd quickly realized she was right. A slow, careful rolling of his shirtsleeves did more to attract the ladies than any other display he put on.

He halfway feared Hailey would prove herself as immune to this as everything else, but he only made it to one elbow before her eyes flashed silver. He might have felt triumphant at having so easily overset her, if not for the fact that those silver sparks had a way of setting off a fire in his veins—especially when they were matched by that telltale pink flush on her cheeks.

Damn. He was supposed to be the one driving her out of her mind with desire, not the other way around.

"Hiya!" Penny burst through the door before he could make the mistake of doing anything more than finish rolling his sleeves. She dragged a pair of photo lights behind her. "I'm just going to set these up in the corner. Are we ready to go in here?"

"I'm good," Cole said with a pointed look at Hailey. "You might as well release the hounds. Metaphorically speaking, that is."

Penny laughed and obliged him, popping her head out of the conference room just long enough to call the press in.

"I can tell what you're trying to do," Hailey hissed as they watched the half-dozen photographers crowd into the room. They were already liberally snapping pictures, taking in the draft board and the pit bull puppy curled up with his stuffed football in the corner like they'd never seen a PR puff piece before. "And it won't work. I'm not so easily distracted."

"It's warm in here, don't you think?" he asked. He didn't bother lowering his own voice, which had the benefit of drawing the rest of the room's inhabitants into the conversation. "I'm feeling awfully warm."

"I can adjust the temperature—" Penny began but stopped as soon as Cole undid the top button of his shirt. "Oh. Okay. That works too."

He grinned. "How about you, Hailey? Are you feeling the heat?"

She narrowed her eyes at him. "Penny, did you bring the coin for the toss?"

"Oh, there's no need for such formality," Cole said with a smile that was mostly for the cameras. "Ladies first—I insist."

He expected Hailey to argue or demur, but she hesitated all of half a second before announcing, "I'll take Ursula. She's the six-month-old rescue from the shelter in Sequim."

Cole was startled by both the promptness and the quality of her first pick. "Isn't that the Chihuahua with only one eye?"

Hailey turned on him with a look that contained equal parts disgust and challenge. "Yes. She's small but mighty. A fighter. A top draft if ever I met one."

Penny took the photo from the board and moved it over to Hailey's side, pausing only to cast a look over her shoulder at Cole. "You'd better be careful. Hailey is crazy good at this. She wins our office fantasy league every year. It's like she can see into the future."

Nothing could have been more calculated to fit in with Cole's plans. Announcing Hailey's ability to win in front of the press was exactly what this was supposed to be about. She was a fan, a believer, a good-luck charm. They might have to fudge the footage a little to make him look like the winner, but the harder she played, the better their chances of helping his team break the curse.

Nothing could have been more calculated to get his competitive juices flowing, too. Crazy good, his ass. How hard could it be to pick a team of football puppies when he'd been playing the real game his whole life?

"I'm not psychic," Hailey protested. "Well, Cole? Who's your top pick?"

"Cleopatra," he announced, not missing a beat. "The one that's half Great Dane and half Rottweiler. From Bellevue."

Hailey snorted. "I knew you'd pick her."

Cole didn't want to ask. Not in front of an audience. Not when the proverbial cameras were rolling.

He did anyway. "Why? What's wrong with her?"

Hailey rolled her shoulder. It caused the strap of her jumpsuit to slip oh-so-slightly, exposing the thin line of her clavicle, which was just as spattered with light freckles as the rest of her. As if aware that he was staring at it—at her—she didn't make a move to put the strap back. "Nothing. She's just the showiest one of the lot, that's all. Let me guess… You have the gray-and-white bulldog for pick number two, don't you?"

He did, actually. He liked its angry little face. He didn't think it would take a tackle easily.

"Penny, slide Jerry over to my side, if you please. Jerry," she said to the journalists, "is a three-legged mixed breed with the most beautiful brindle coloring. He was found on the side of the freeway just south of Everett. The vets weren't sure he'd make it after they had to amputate his leg, but his spirit is strong."

All of Hailey's puppy picks followed along the same lines. Cole got his bulldog and a pair of twin black Labs, as well as Philip—though he picked his puppy more out of loyalty than because he'd be any good at football. In the short time he and Philip had spent together, he'd learned that in addition to being scared of solitude, Philip was scared of can openers. Not to mention the front door, the balcony door, windows that were even the slightest bit open, and cheese.

Hailey's choices were much less illustrious. She chose the small dogs and the dogs with the most traumatic pasts. She went for personality over muscle, a cute pair of eyes over a solid pair of legs. In other words, she picked all the animals Cole had put on the bottom of his wish list, and she picked them without hesitation.

"Okay, I'll bite," he said after she snagged a curly poodle-looking thing whose weight was listed at all of four pounds. "What do you know that I don't?"

She didn't miss a beat. "How to win."

Behind them, the cameras flashed. They had to have more than enough photos by now, but the spirit of the competition was infectious. He didn't blame them for sticking around. Watching a beautiful woman confidently and unceasingly put Cole in his place had to be the most fun they'd had in ages.

He grinned his appreciation but didn't allow himself to be distracted. "I'm serious." He reached across the table and plucked the sheet of paper out of her hand. A quick scan told him nothing—she'd listed the puppies in numerical order and had so far gotten all the ones she wanted. "Did you pick these at random?"

She yanked the sheet back. "Of course not. I know what qualities to look for in an athlete, that's all."

"I warned you," Penny said from her position at the drafting board. "You should see her fantasy lineup. She always seems to make her picks without any rhyme or reason. The guys in accounting have been trying to figure out her formula for years, but they can't crack it. The only player she always gets for her first draw, no matter what, is—"

At a warning glance from Hailey, Penny stopped herself short, but it was too late. The color was mounting to Hailey's cheeks, her conscience-stricken expression stripping away all the trappings of hair and makeup and that damnably appealing black outfit.

Cole leaned back in his chair and steepled his fingers. "I like where this is going. Proceed."

"Don't," Hailey told her coworker.

Penny laughed. "No offense, but I think he already knows."

"I want to hear her say it," Cole said. Thinking of the list in her hand, he added, "Or else I'm going to pick that lolly-tongued hairless puppy you plan to take after my turn."

She sat up in her seat, the silver in her eyes sparking. "That's cheating. You peeked at my list."

"Admit it."

"I won't."

"Say the words."

"You can't make me."

"Fine." Cole crossed her arms and nodded at Penny. "Lolly-tongued no-hair for me."

Penny made a move to pin the picture of the puppy in question onto his side of the board, but Hailey stopped her with an exasperated sigh. "I can't believe you're making me do this," she muttered. With a smile for the cameras, she adopted a syrupy voice and said, "I always pick Cole Bennett first for my fantasy team. In fact, I refuse to play without him. He's my favorite Lumberjack, and he always has been. You might even call him my good-luck charm."

Cole acknowledged the concession with a shout of laughter. Hailey had neatly—and sweetly—turned the tables on him. It was no more than he deserved and everything he'd been hoping to hear.

"There you have it," he said. "I'm her favorite. Garrett is going to be so pissed."

Mentioning Garrett was a mistake. The moment the wide receiver entered the conversation, the focus moved from puppies playing football to men playing football. Cole realized his error when a journalist from the local paper asked a question about one of the past weekend's trickier plays. It would have been rude not to answer, but that was followed up with a few more about the starting lineup and strategies for this weekend's game against Texas. Cole could practically see the situation slipping away from him.

Not that he was the least bit surprised. This sort of thing *always* happened. It didn't matter if he was out for dinner with a friend or shopping for furniture with his mom or even just going out to pick up a cup of coffee.

Football. Lumberjacks. He could spend the next fifty years living like a hermit on top of a mountain, and the first thing people would ask when he reentered society would be his opinion on the upcoming playoffs.

"Well, I think we've got all the puppies covered," Hailey said the moment the barrage of questions had slowed to a trickle. She clapped her hands to prevent anyone from speaking out of turn. "I don't mean to be rude, but we're getting kicked out of this conference room in about five minutes. You can email any follow-up questions about the Puppy Cup directly to me, but all other media inquiries will have to go through the regular American Football Club channels."

Cole watched as Hailey proceeded to clear the room with admirable efficiency. So far, his interactions with this woman had been more social than professional, usually with him doing his best to wheedle or charm something he wanted out of her. This thing he was witnessing now was of an entirely different composition. He wasn't watching Hailey Lincoln blush her way out of a tight spot; he was watching a television production assistant with six years of experience handling the press. He was watching a woman on a deadline doing what was necessary to finish a project.

She looked capable and in control and, well, a lot like his sister.

"You're really good at that," Cole said as Hailey closed the door behind Penny and the rabble of journalists she was escorting to the elevators. "I had no idea."

"What? That I can do my job?"

"No. That you aren't just straightforward and mean to me. You put those journalists in their place in less time than it takes most people to blink."

Her eyes narrowed in the way he was coming to recognize. "I'm not mean."

"I also said 'straightforward.'"

"I don't have a mean bone in my body."

Cole was unable to resist a good, hard look at the bones under deliberation. Right now, with her hip jutting out to one side and her torso twisted to face him, Hailey looked as though she was poised to attack. But the longer he stood there, his appraisal slow and unblinking, the more she seemed to melt. Her stance became less rigid, her posture a squirming, liquid discomfort.

This was not a woman who was used to having an audience—especially not an appreciative one.

"Stop it," she snapped, a flush of color starting to creep down her neck. She'd never worn anything this low-cut before, so this was the first time Cole realized that her tendency to blush wasn't restricted to her face. It started there before blossoming outward, traveling into her neckline and toward her chest.

He felt a profound and sudden urge to know the precise location where it ended. He wanted to see it. He wanted to study it. He wanted to *touch* it.

"I mean it." Hailey darted to the other side of the room, positioning herself behind the table, both of her hands gripping the edge as though it was the only thing keeping her standing. "Don't look at me like that."

"Like what?"

"Like…that." She waved a hand in his general direction. "Like you can see through my clothes. I've had that nightmare before. It never ends well."

Cole chuckled and drew closer to the other side of the table. There was an expanse of wood grain between them, an interminable distance when all he wanted to do was examine every inch of her skin, but he also needed to grip the edges. Not to stay standing but to keep himself from launching across the room at her.

"Oh really? I'd like to hear more about these nocturnal habits of yours."

She bit down on her lower lip and shook her head. "Nuh-uh. No way. Not on my life. Not even on yours."

"That good, huh?" he asked. "Are you actually naked in this dream, or is it just that your clothes are invisible?"

Even from this distance, he could hear Hailey's low, back-of-the-throat moan. "Nightmare," she said. "It wasn't a dream… It was a *nightmare*. Kind of like this, actually."

"Naked, then," he said, nodding. "I like it."

"I never said I was naked!"

He shifted his position so he half sat on the table's surface. It brought him close enough to smell the light lavender that always seemed to envelop Hailey but not so close that he lost all reason and accountability.

"So you're standing in front of a room, presumably naked as the day you were born." Cole had to force himself to breath before he continued. "Who else is in the room? Is it one of those generic, walk-into-the-classroom sort of deals? Oh! I know… It's football-related, isn't it? Everything in your life is football-related."

"Cole, *please*."

The sound in her voice—desperation and desire mingled as one—caused something inside him to click. "Oh shit. It's me-related, isn't it?"

She lifted her hands from the table's edge and buried her face in them.

"So wait," he said. "If these dreams—oh, I'm sorry—*nightmares* of yours never end well, what happens? Do I publicly shame you? Boo and hiss? Or do I just fail to deliver?"

Hailey's whole body began shaking, her head still in her hands. Cole's general response time was slower than usual—understandable considering how much of his blood flow had been diverted southward—but he recognized the signs almost immediately.

"Hailey, I'm sorry." He slid off the table and rushed over to her side, careful not to touch her. "Please don't be upset. I didn't mean to make you uncomfortable. I'll stop, see? Not another word."

She continued shaking. Cole had to use every ounce of strength he had not to reach out and pull her into his arms—and even then, it was a struggle. All the strength in the world didn't mean much when he'd made a woman cry.

"I'm an idiot," he confessed. "I always have been. Just ask Reggie."

At the mention of his sister, Hailey glanced up. Her face wasn't, as he'd feared, streaked with tears or rimmed with red around the eyes. Her makeup was untouched, her color delightfully diffused. In fact, from this angle, it looked as though she hadn't been crying at all.

It almost looked as though she'd been...laughing.

"Oh, crap!" she cried. "Your sister is going to be at my house in less than an hour."

"Wait... You're not upset?"

Hailey glanced at the clock above the door and released a soft curse. "Traffic is going to be awful. We'll never beat her there."

"Hailey." Cole finally gave in to the urge to reach for her. He gripped her shoulders and whirled her so that she faced him. With her face upturned toward his, the light of laughter still on her lips, she was irresistible.

"Were you just laughing?" he demanded. "At me?"

She nodded. A slight giggle escaped. "I'm sorry. It's just... This is all so surreal. You. Me. This ridiculous outfit."

He slid his hands down her arms, her skin soft and temptingly warm. "What's ridiculous about it? I think you look nice."

She giggled again, this time quelling it with a hand slapped over her mouth. "Ignore me," she said between her fingers. "I can't react to situations like a normal person. I speak my mind at the worst possible moments and turn to stone for everything else."

"Does this mean the dreams *were* about me?"

Her eyes snapped up to his. Despite this direct approach, her long lashes fluttered shyly, and her voice dropped to an embarrassed choke. "Don't be stupid, Cole," she said. "Of course they were about you."

His grip on her arms tightened. He didn't want to hurt her, but it was an automatic response, the curl of his fingers tied to the jolt that rocketed his groin. "I lied before. You don't look nice. You look—"

He didn't have a chance to finish his remark—which was for the best, since he didn't have adequate words to describe how he was feeling. She looked tempting and beautiful and *cute*. She also looked as though those things meant as little to her as a football player who was rapidly passing his prime.

As if to prove it, she glanced at the wall of draft picks and sighed. "I'll have to beg Penny to clean all this up for us," she said. "It's the only way we'll make it on time."

"Forget my sister," Cole said—begged, really, his voice strained and his hold on Hailey remaining firm. He knew that letting her go would mean letting this moment go, and he wasn't ready to do that yet. "Forget all things football-related. Let's go find an office-supply closet instead. Isn't that how it works in places like this?"

She laughed, and just like that, he lost her. He could have tried his usual tricks—a knowing smile, a low-voiced innuendo, a hand placed low on her back—but it didn't feel right. Those were seduction tools, ways to show his interest and stake his claim.

He *was* interested, and he *did* want to stake a claim, but he wanted a lot more than that, too.

"I've never had a fling with anyone at work before, so I can't answer that," Hailey said, stepping away. Cole felt the gap between them like a blast of cold air, but all she did was shake her head and sigh. "I don't have flings at all, actually. Did you want me to call down and have them bring your car around?"

"Fuck the car," Cole said with more heat than the situation warranted. He couldn't help it. How she could stand there, looking prim and untouchable and so appealing at the same time, was beyond him.

She stood her ground. "I'd rather not, thanks. *You* might be able to get away with showing up late to social engagements, but I'm not so lucky." She smiled ruefully. "Just be sure not to tell anyone, okay? My luck is supposed to be the reason behind all this in the first place."

This time, he took the rebuff as it was intended. Hailey was obviously unwilling to take their flirtation any further than it had already gone. She'd been more than happy to laugh and challenge him while the cameras were rolling—and while the puppies were the main event—but now that it was just the two of them, he was back at the starting line.

Alone. Uncertain. *Useless.*

"Hailey Lincoln is no luckier than your average three-leaf clover," he said and made the sign of an X over his chest. "Your secret is safe with me."

She sighed. "If you guys don't make it into the Kickoff Cup after all this, the city is going to demand my head on a platter. I hope you know what you're doing."

He didn't. Not even a little. He woke up every day wondering if this would be the one that broke him.

"You're the one who watches every game with the eye of a detective and the soul of a critic," he said. "You tell me."

"Oh, you'll make it, all right," she said with such confidence that Cole couldn't help but believe her. "*And* you'll win once you get there. They'll renew your contract for double the pay, and you'll spend the next decade of your life showing everyone how the game of football was meant to be played."

Cole reared back, the speech that had started so promisingly dashing over his head like cold water. *The next decade? Ten more years?*

"Don't look so worried," she said, but even the warm smile she bestowed on him wasn't enough to stop the chill from seeping into his spine. "If there's one thing I know in this world, it's football. And you, my friend, have a long and prosperous career ahead of you."

chapter
10

IF COLE HAD POSSESSED ANY DECENCY, HE WOULD HAVE made up an errand to give Hailey a chance to gather herself before he descended upon her house in all his six-foot-two glory. Since they'd spent the better part of the day together, she'd had no time to do more than glance at herself in the rearview mirror—and what she'd found had horrified her.

She looked like a rebellious teenager trying out a noir phase for the first time. Worse than that, she looked like a woman who was trying way too hard to impress a man.

"Thank you for driving me home," Hailey said as she stepped out of Cole's car. He owned several, but the hybrid Lexus was one of his favorites. She liked to think it was because he was worried about the environment, but mostly she suspected he liked how shiny it was.

Rather, it *had* been shiny. Philip and his thin, gray hairs left quite a trail on that glossy black interior.

"To be honest, I thought about following behind the city bus while you got home that way, but I don't think Philip is enough to allow me in the car-pool lanes."

Recognizing his name, the puppy poked his nose out of the car door and began tentatively sniffing the environment, his stuffed football clutched protectively in his mouth. Most puppies would have happily bounded out and started exploring, but not Philip. For every fun new smell her yard afforded, he cast an equally anxious look back up at Cole.

Hailey understood his sentiments perfectly. Philip had been shuffled around so many times that he viewed each new place—and each new person—as an opportunity to be left behind.

From the looks of it, Cole understood, too. He put a reassuring hand on the puppy's head and nodded down at him. "Go for it," he told the animal. "This is a happy place."

Hailey wasn't sure how happy her house had been in recent years, but the epithet had once held true. She'd learned to throw a football exactly where Cole stood. She'd learned to ride a bike there, too, though she'd never mastered either skill. Moving around on two rickety wheels seemed to be *asking* for trouble.

"You're sure he won't be a bother?" Cole asked, watching the puppy as he sniffed at the damp grass and half-frozen ferns. "Bess won't get upset if there's an intruder threatening her family?"

"There's one way to find out," Hailey said as she trotted up her front steps to unlock the door. Over her shoulder, she added, "And don't worry—if they don't get along, I have lots of ways to keep them separated. I often have multiple dogs living here, and no matter how hard I try, not all of them end up as best friends."

Cole didn't respond right away. Hailey assumed he was once again acclimating to the bizarre decor of her home, but he had paused on the threshold, watching as Philip began sniffing his way around the living room. The animal's nose was pressed to the floor as though on an important hunt, though he had yet to relinquish his grip on the football in the slightest.

"Don't you ever want to adopt one?" Cole asked as Philip picked up on the scent of the entire pack living in her kitchen. "Doesn't it hurt to keep giving them away?"

Hailey's chest gave a sudden, lurching pang. She'd said so many goodbyes in her lifetime that she should have grown accustomed to it by now, but that clench came every time she got the call.

"Of course it hurts," she admitted. "I cry every time—usually for days. It's embarrassing. They've had to buy so many tissues for the supply closet at work that they get a bulk discount now."

Since she didn't want Philip to frighten Bess into a defensive position, she rushed to head the animal off at the gate.

She needn't have worried. Bess lifted her head at the intrusion of another dog into her sphere and might have even growled a warning, but she caught sight of Cole standing behind Hailey and gave her tail an eager thump.

"Good girl," Cole said, his mouth so close to Hailey's ear that it caused a wave of goose bumps to move over her. "You know a friend when you see one, don't you? Such a smart dog."

"She got knocked up by the first handsome scoundrel to come her way," Hailey retorted as she lifted a leg to step over the gate. "I wouldn't put my faith in her abilities as a judge of character."

As was the case the last time the pair of them stood in this position, Cole's hand was ready and waiting to assist her into the kitchen. And as was the case the last time he did it, Hailey felt her whole body flutter into uselessness. Matters weren't helped any when he held her hand much longer than a step over a gate necessitated.

"Maybe their affair was brief but passionate. Maybe it was worth it. Maybe she'd do it again in a heartbeat." He gave her fingers a meaningful squeeze. "Something smells delicious, by the way. When did you have time to cook?"

It was on the tip of her tongue to tell him that she'd been up at four in the morning—that her entire day had been spent catering to his schedule—but something in her held back. She was trying to look *less* like a woman who had nothing in her life except work and football, not more.

"It's just some stuff in the slow cooker," she said, blushing when he still refused to let her fingers go. "I thought it would be easiest."

She busied herself by checking on Bess and the puppies, counting the little heads to ensure that Rufus hadn't wandered off again. He was huddled close to Bess's hind legs, but it wasn't a cause for celebration.

"Oh, you poor honey," she said, scooping up the tiny bundle and examining him closely. "I was afraid of this."

"What is it? What's the matter with him?" Cole remained on the other side of the gate—mostly to keep Philip from barging in after him—but there was a sharp note of worry in his voice.

Hailey nestled Rufus closer to her neck so he could absorb some of her body warmth. His small body was so delicate, his skin so much like paper, that she could feel each of his bones. "He's not taking well to the family dynamic," she said. "He's always the last to eat and the first to wander away."

"Bess is rejecting him?"

Hailey nuzzled the puppy closer, fearful of him overhearing the words and taking them to heart. Which was ridiculous for a lot of reasons, but she couldn't help it. Rufus needed all the love he could get his tiny paws on.

"Not rejecting, exactly," she said. "She seems to like him just fine when he's around, but with so many other, stronger, more insistent puppies to look after, he kind of gets lost."

Overlooked. *Forgotten.* It was no one's fault, but that didn't make it any less awful. Sometimes, puppies—even sweet, beautiful ones like Rufus—slipped through the cracks. There just weren't enough people in the world to care for them all.

Despite her determination not to cry, Hailey felt emotion thickening in her throat.

"What can I do to help?" Cole asked.

It was the same thing he'd asked that day in her office, when he'd shown up uninvited and unannounced. There was the same matter-of-fact quality to it, but also the same authenticity. Unlike so many people, when Cole offered his help, he meant it. The fact that he was standing outside her kitchen, gently massaging Philip's ears, was clear proof of that.

"How are you at bottle feeding?" Hailey asked.

"Phenomenal," Cole said. When he saw her wide-eyed look of surprise, he laughed. "I mean it. I used to feed Mia all the time."

"You did?"

He gave Philip a command to sit—which the animal ignored in favor of whimpering anxiously—and stepped over the gate to join her in the kitchen. "Of course. I changed diapers, too, so you can stop looking at me like that. All evidence to the contrary, I'm not a *complete* waste of space."

Hailey doubted that anyone could accuse Cole Bennett of wasting space. Everything he touched and everything he did was extraordinary. Even this, pulling open her cupboards and searching for the puppy milk replacement and bottles she kept on hand, was like something out of a movie.

"I assume this stuff is similar to the human variety?" Cole read the label on the can of milk replacement and nodded. "Huh. It looks identical to baby formula, actually. Don't tell Reggie. She used to spend a fortune on the name-brand stuff."

Hailey watched as if in a dream as Cole efficiently and cheerfully went to work. He hadn't been kidding about being an old hand at this. There was something about the deft way he handled the bottle's nipple that indicated long experience.

"You never answered my question, by the way," Cole said as he tested the temperature on his wrist. He must have found it satisfactory, because he lifted the puppy from Hailey's arms and cradled him in his own.

"Which question?" she asked, the words on autopilot. She thought she'd already experienced every kind of physical and emotional reaction possible to having this man in her kitchen and in her life, but she was wrong.

So. Very. Wrong.

Cole Bennett was holding Rufus like a baby. He was holding Rufus like a baby and coaxing a bottle into his mouth. Every part of her body gave one heaving, yearning pang—for all the things she would never be and for all the things she could never have.

It's not fair. She might have been able to stand up to Cole's charms if he'd been a jerk or if his confidence was accompanied by cockiness, but it wasn't. His confidence had been ingrained in him since birth and was as much a part of him as his dimples. He was an exceptional athlete. He was genuinely kind to people. He had a large family who cared about him and who showed up whenever he needed them to.

Of course he acted like a man who had it all. He *was* a man who had it all.

While she, on the other hand, was a woman with nothing except a house full of football paraphernalia and far more puppies than she knew what to do with.

"About whether or not you ever want to adopt one." He gave the puppy in his arms a gentle shake. Rufus had found the nipple and was greedily gulping at it, his eyes closed and his body undulating with the in-and-out movements of his sucking. The animal looked so comfortable—so natural, so *happy*—that Hailey found that her throat had constricted to half its size.

"No," she snapped.

Cole shifted his gaze from the puppy to Hailey, an inquiring lift to one brow. "You sound awfully sure of that. Why not?"

There were several different answers to that question. Her yard was too small. She spent too many hours at work. She was just one woman living all by herself. She could have defended any one of those responses and come out sounding perfectly rational, but they weren't the truth.

I can't risk getting attached.

It was difficult enough to say goodbye to the puppies after a few weeks—a sort of ripping-the-bandage pain that stung for a few days before settling to a more comfortable numbness. She relished that feeling, enjoyed it, even, because it was predictable. Reliable.

The other sort of pain was the kind she couldn't bear. Permanent loss. Death. Saying goodbye to the only person who'd ever loved her and knowing that she'd never find that kind of acceptance again. If she let herself fall in love with Bess or Rufus or Philip or any of the dozens of puppies who came through her home each year, that would be the end of it for her.

She wasn't strong enough to recover from that kind of thing again. She'd barely made it through the last time.

"I can help more of them this way," she said. It was only a part of the truth, but at least it was a large part. "Adoption is the best outcome, obviously, and the goal is for every animal to have somewhere safe and stable to live. But fostering somewhere safe and stable is important, too. It gives the dogs a place to go when their whole world feels dark and out of control. It helps them recognize what home looks like when they finally find their own."

She'd said too much, as usual, but at least she'd had the sense to stop there. She could tell Cole all kinds of horror stories about the damages done by foster homes that were too crowded or poorly run, by people who let the dogs wrangle by themselves outside instead of providing the order and comfort the animals so desperately needed.

When Cole didn't say anything—just kept watching her with a strangely intent look in his eyes—she nodded down at Philip and added, "We'll never know what Philip went through before he was abandoned, but we do know that it wasn't good. He's too skinny and too unsure of himself, too fearful of new situations. Although we can fix the skinny part, those other qualities may never leave him."

Unable to help herself, she reached out and ran a finger along the side of Rufus's contentedly suckling mouth. "These guys, however, will know nothing but love. That's six puppies that will have a good start in life, six puppies that will be able to attach to their future families with no baggage. Would I like to keep this little guy forever? Of course. But I can do a lot more good by passing him on and opening my house to the next litter of puppies that no one else wants to take care of."

Cole was still looking at her as though she were some kind of freak specimen at a child's science fair, so she forced herself to step back and take a deep breath.

"Sorry," she said, opening the refrigerator and welcoming the blast of cool air. "I sometimes get a little soapboxy when I start talking about dogs. It's why they usually keep me on animal duty at work. Everyone is tired of listening to my speeches."

"Don't apologize," he said. "It was something, wasn't it? Watching them be born?"

She could only nod. She'd assumed he'd been more horrified than delighted to be trapped in that elevator with her, but the way he was looking down at the puppy in his arms seemed to indicate otherwise.

"I haven't felt anything like that since Reggie had Mia. It's the most alive I've ever been."

"Cole—" she began, but the sound of the front door clicking open stopped her. Which was probably for the best, because she didn't know what she would have said. That he came to life every time he touched a football? That *she* came to life every time he touched her?

"Knock-knock!" came a singsong voice. "Are you two decent? I rang the doorbell, but no one answered."

"We're in the kitchen," Hailey called back, her voice unsteady. When Regina appeared behind the dog gate, she added, "I turned the doorbell off so it wouldn't wake the puppies while they're sleeping."

"No need to tell me." Regina leaned forward and dropped a light kiss on her brother's cheek. "I used to disconnect every electronic device I owned when Mia was a baby. I'd have fought a duel to the death to protect her sleep—and mine. What smells so good?"

For the second time, Hailey found herself flustered by the question. "It's just a sweet potato and chicken thing I threw into the slow cooker." She cast an apologetic look at Cole and added, "There's a quinoa and kale salad in the fridge to go with it. I hope you don't mind, but I had your nutritionist send over a copy of your diet and calorie guidelines. He was very helpful."

Cole blinked down at her. "You emailed Piers?"

"Technically, I called him, but yes. He thought I was just some crazy stalker at first, but we got to talking about your mom, and I convinced him I'm the real deal." She paused and added, "Well, he might still think I'm a crazy stalker, but even he had to admit that I could hardly try to kill you with kale."

Regina laughed. "You say that now, but you should have seen his face the first time Mom served it to him. He was—what?— sixteen at the time. He told us it looked like something that food eats."

"Oh no." Hailey had been so careful to stick to the caloric and ingredient guidelines that she'd forgotten to ask about his personal tastes. "You don't like it?"

"I love it," Cole said firmly.

"Do you?" Regina asked, an arch lift to her brow. "Do you really?"

"It's my favorite thing."

He spoke with such resolve that Hailey knew it for a lie. But it was a polite lie, and one he seemed determined to uphold as they sat at the table to eat. It was an interesting dynamic, what with Cole holding a napping Rufus in the crook of his arm, Philip panting anxiously at his feet, and a framed Lumberjacks jersey mounted above Regina's head, but Hailey had no one to blame for it but herself. She'd wanted to do this on her own terms, even if her terms were unorthodox and slightly pathetic.

It helped that Cole must have warned Regina ahead of time what to expect inside the house. Other than a slightly lifted brow at the decor, she hadn't said anything about it.

"By the way, that Penny woman sent me a list of the two puppy teams you guys picked," Regina said between mouthfuls of the kale—which she, at least, seemed to appreciate. "We should get some good press out of it, but I'm curious about what happens next."

"Filming, mostly," Hailey replied. "The crew is going to start putting up the set next week, and then we'll introduce the puppies a few at a time until we're ready to start. It takes us a while to get enough footage. Puppies rarely do what they're told."

"Football players are the same," Regina said, dimpling at her brother. "And preschoolers, come to think of it. Cole and Mia have a lot in common."

Cole pointed his fork at his sister. "The joke's on you. Mia is the best person in the whole world."

"Mia throws tantrums when I make her wear shoes that match."

"She's a woman who knows her own mind. I can respect that."

Hailey sat back and watched as the two siblings continued their conversation, which was half argument and half love letter to the child they both adored. She doubted they had any idea how much it revealed, how deeply it showed the bond between them. These two had grown up side by side and, now that they were functioning adults, chose to continue that relationship by working together every day of their lives.

"What?" Cole demanded when he realized Hailey had stopped eating to watch them. "Why are you looking at us like that?"

She shook her head. There was no way she could explain that their relationship—so effortless, so natural, so *real*—was everything she'd ever wanted and nothing she would have an opportunity to know.

Cole looked as though he was going to demand an explanation, but both his and Regina's phones chimed at the same time. Since Cole was still balancing Rufus, Regina got to hers first.

"Oh shit." Regina cast a stricken glance at her brother.

"What?" He pushed back in his chair, jolting both the table and the puppy. "What happened? Is it Mia?"

"No. It's Dad." Regina held her phone up so Cole could read the message. It took him a moment to absorb the contents, his eyes moving anxiously back and forth across the screen. It was as though he needed to read it a few times before he was able to believe what he was seeing.

"I knew this was going to happen," Regina muttered. "I knew he wasn't taking care of himself."

Hailey rose to her feet at once. She might not know much about having siblings, but she knew that look of shock and self-reproach.

"Let me take Rufus," she said as she lifted the puppy from Cole's arms. Although Rufus was quick to whimper his protest, Cole didn't appear to notice. "You guys probably want to get going."

Regina transferred her look of anxiety to Hailey. "I'm so sorry to do this. Everything has been so lovely and delicious, but…" She gulped. "It's our dad. He's—"

Hailey mentally crossed her fingers and called on all the fake powers of luck that she'd been granted, but it was no use.

"He had a heart attack." Cole blinked, his gaze not focused on anything at all. "They're taking him to the hospital now."

"Then you'll want to meet him there." Hailey spoke with a calm authority she was far from feeling. She knew all too well the overwhelming sensations that were filling them right now, the disbelief that this could be real life. She'd gotten a similar call while studying for an economics test in her University of Washington dorm room during freshman year, and the only thing that had gotten her out the door had been her roommate's steady voice walking her through the steps needed to board the correct bus. "You can leave Philip with me. He's getting along well with

Bess, so he won't be any trouble for a night or two. We'll have a sleepover. Mia—?"

"Is with her nanny." Regina was the first to recover. She reached out and gripped Hailey's hand with so much strength that Hailey felt her fingers crack. "But thank you for thinking of her."

"Of course."

Cole still bore the dazed look of a man who'd been hit with a surprise sack and wasn't sure if he'd be able to get up again, but as Regina grabbed her purse and started nudging him toward the door, he regained a hold on himself.

"Thank you for today, Hailey. All of it—the puppy draft and the food and the..." He waved his hand over her in a vague, slightly feminine-shaped gesture. "*You* know."

She didn't, actually, but she recognized his comment for what it was—the bewildered outburst of a man who'd just felt his world turn upside down.

"Go," she said as she placed a hand on his back and gave him a gentle push. The ripple of his muscles underneath her touch was undeniable. So was his tension. "Philip and I will be here when—and if—you're ready to resume our project. Don't worry about us."

They didn't. As Hailey saw them out the front door, the pair of them walking side by side down the short walkway to Regina's car, they didn't once look back or remember her existence.

Which was only to be expected, really. She wasn't their friend, and she wasn't a member of their family; at this juncture, she barely even qualified as an acquaintance. Philip joined her at the screen door, dropping his football as he watched his beloved master go.

Hailey put her free hand on his head, but it didn't seem to bring him much comfort. "I know, little buddy," she said. "But you and I are on our own, I'm afraid. Well, you and me and Rufus."

That didn't do much to boost the pit bull's mood, either. Nor, if she was being honest, did Rufus take as much comfort from her arms as he had from Cole's.

"All I need is for Bess to start howling that she misses him, and this whole house will have reached maximum absurdity," she said. "We've known him less than two weeks, you guys. Don't start acting like fools. He was never going to be ours to keep."

Hailey didn't wait to watch them drive away, but it didn't seem to matter. As she shut the door and turned to face the ruins of their quarterback-friendly dinner, she only felt worse. She should probably start cleaning up, but she suddenly felt the full weight of the long day.

"The sleepover starts right now," she said as she sank into her couch and basked in the two warm bodies pressed in her arms and against her side. They weren't human bodies, but they were puppy bodies, and—as Mia would be the first to point out—a reasonable alternative.

Almost.

chapter

11

"T HE NEXT PERSON WHO WALKS IN HERE LOOKING LIKE HE'S attending my funeral is getting a swift kick to the head."

Regina turned to the nurse who'd appeared in the doorway with an apologetic grimace. "I'm sorry. If it's any consolation, he said the same thing to the last three doctors who came in. And one of them has been a friend of the family for over twenty years."

The nurse must have been accustomed to irascible old men making feeble threats from their hospital beds, because all he did was chuckle and make his way inside, his head bent over the chart in his hand. "If you can manage to reach my head from your current position, then I'll start the discharge papers myself. How's that?"

The nurse's cheerful voice did little to improve their dad's mood. "Get a little closer, and we'll see what I can do."

"I'm not falling for that one so easily. This isn't my first rodeo." The nurse checked as soon as he looked up and noticed Cole standing over his father's bedside. He blinked and swallowed and said the inevitable. "Holy shit. You're Cole Bennett."

Cole resisted the urge to deny this claim and stuck out his hand instead, taking note of the man's name tag as he did. "It's a pleasure to meet you, ah, Kenny, is it? You have my permission to treat this bitter old man the same way you would any patient who doesn't do what he's told. I hear restraints are an option."

As Cole had hoped, this remark helped the nurse regain some of his composure. Kenny laughed slightly and managed, "Oh, I'm sure he'll be no trouble once we get him comfortable."

Cole grimaced. "I'm not."

Of the two of them, Cole ended up being correct. His dad didn't go so far as to physically assault the nurse, but he grumbled and complained and otherwise made it difficult for the man to do his job. It would have been embarrassing if Cole and Regina hadn't already had a lifetime in which to accustom themselves to it. Julian Bennett wasn't a man who took the act of lying down, well, lying down.

"What a lovely young man," their mom said as soon as the nurse left them with promises that yet another specialist would be by to see them in a few hours. She smoothed the blankets over her husband's legs. "How are you feeling, dear?"

"Hungry," came the prompt reply. "What does a man have to do to get a cheeseburger around here?"

Cole and Regina shared a look of exasperation. They'd arrived at the hospital prepared to find their father unconscious, in surgery, or—as their deepest fears wanted them to believe—dead. Their relief at finding him already in bed and recovering from what the doctors called "a minor attack" had been quickly replaced by...this. He looked pale and frail and much older than they'd ever seen him.

He was also seriously starting to piss them off.

"You can't have cheese," Regina said, her voice sharp. "Or burgers. Or mayonnaise or the spicy jalapeños you like on top. And don't even get us started on the beer you'd be sure to demand to wash it all down."

"That's right," Cole said, both verbally and physically backing his sister up. From the way their dad was glowering up at them, it looked as though his sister might be the one in danger of that kick to the head. "From now on, it's nothing but kale as far as the eye can see."

"Kale?" his dad demanded. "What the hell am I supposed to do with kale?"

Cole laughed. He imagined his dad would take the same approach he did with the stuff, which revolved mostly around throwing it into the nearest garbage. Unless, of course, it was being served by a woman who'd taken the time to hunt down his nutritional guidelines and painstakingly prepared a meal she knew would fit in with them.

Not even Julian Bennett at his most belligerent could refuse it after that. His son certainly couldn't.

He could feel Regina looking at him, the same amusement in her expression that had been there at Hailey's house, but he ignored her. He didn't have to explain himself. It was only kale.

"We should probably figure out who's going to stay with Dad tonight," Cole said with a meaningful glance at his sister. Their mother would most likely demand the first shift, but she looked exhausted, as well she might. Getting their father into an ambulance in this mood couldn't have been an easy task. "You'll have to work your magic tomorrow and get me out of this week's game, Reg, but—"

"The devil she will!"

"Cole, love, you don't mean that."

"I'm not going to do any such thing."

Of the three responses, Regina's was the most alarming—and not just because she was Cole's manager and therefore the one in a position to actually *do* something. She spoke with the calm, damnable authority of an older sister who believed herself wise, infallible, and always, always right.

"Mom and I will work something out between us," Regina said, still in that same tone. "You're going home and going straight to bed. You have to be up and at practice at six."

"Are you kidding me?" Cole asked. He could hardly believe he was being forced to say the words out loud. "I'm not going to play football while Dad's lying in a hospital bed."

"It wasn't even a real heart attack," his dad said as he struggled into a sitting position. He made it only halfway before Regina and their mom shoved him back down again. He accepted this with a meekness that said more about his current condition than all the charts and blipping monitors could. "You heard the doctor. It was a partial blockage, that's all. I'll be back on my feet in a week."

"The doctor said you can get discharged from the hospital in a week, barring any additional complications," he countered. "That's not the same thing."

"I'm fine."

"You could have died."

"I'm *fine*."

He wasn't fine. Not by a long shot, and not—if the doctor was to be believed—unless he drastically changed his way of life. Apparently, the chances of a repeat and more catastrophic attack were high in this sort of situation.

Cole knew better than to push the issue, however. For as long as he could remember, he'd been taught that Bennett men didn't show weakness or acknowledge pain. It was a large part of the reason his mom kept that scrapbook of his high school injuries: not for sympathy or for posterity but as proof.

Proof that a Bennett didn't let things like physical pain get in the way of success. Proof that results were more important than all the things that had to be sacrificed to get there. What was a personal life when football was on the line? What were feelings when there were reps to get in?

"You guys can't be serious," he said, his gaze skimming from face to face, his entire family staring at him with the same stony resolve. "You're kicking me out?"

His mom rose and put a hand on his arm. The exhaustion that had lined her face was still there, but it was matched by a determination he knew better than to fight. "There's not much for you to do here, and you know it. The doctors have everything under control, and your father will rest better if he knows you're focused on the game against Texas."

"You know their spread defense always throws you off," his dad said.

Cole made one last effort. He turned to his sister, who should have been the one person in the room most on his side. "Reggie, you don't mean it."

"You'll only be in the way here." She smiled in an attempt to show she meant no harm, but the damage had already been done. "Go do what you do best, Brother dear. Win. Make it to the divisional championship. Give him something to live for. You'll only be a distraction if you linger around here. I've seen six nurses tiptoe past the door in the last two minutes alone."

There was nothing Cole could say or do after that to convince his family to let him do his part. It was no use telling them that he wasn't likely to get any sleep after a scare like this one or that he wasn't going to be any good at practice if he was worrying about his dad the whole time. As a collective, they'd already decided the role he would play. He was the football star, the hero, the son whose only value was the glory he brought to the family name.

And that, if they had anything to say about it, was all he'd ever be.

———

"Cole!"

Hailey peeked through the narrow opening in the door, her chain in place against the late-night visitor who'd seen fit to stop by just as the clock chimed one in the morning. It would take a daring intruder to break into a house that often had several large, angry dogs living under its roof, but she knew better than to take chances. A single woman living alone was open to all kinds of dangers.

Including, apparently, nocturnal visits from football players.

"I'm sorry." From the other side of the opening, a tired-looking Cole winced. "I shouldn't have knocked, but I came back to get my car and your lights were on, so—"

She shut the door and slid the chain out before opening it all the way again. "Don't be silly. I'm glad you did. I haven't gone to bed yet."

That wasn't strictly the truth. She *had* gone to bed—and was wearing her favorite Lumberjacks pajama set to prove it—but sleep hadn't been forthcoming. She'd tossed and turned and contemplated calling the hospital half a dozen times for an update before giving up and making herself some hot chocolate.

"How did it go?" she asked.

"Well, my dad is awake and stable, and he threatened to have me forcibly removed from his hospital room if I didn't go home and get some sleep for tomorrow's practice, so you tell me."

The amount of relief Hailey felt at those words was hugely disproportionate to her relationship with a man she'd met only once, but she didn't care. She'd been so worried—for Cole and for Reggie, for Paula and Mia—that she'd take anything she could get. A man making threats and worrying about his son's future could only be a good sign.

"That sounds like good news," she said. Catching sight of Cole's expression, she added, "Also like you didn't much care for the suggestion."

His laugh was short and bitter, but at least it was a laugh. "Is it that obvious?"

To her, it was, but she knew enough about fathers in hospitals to recognize that Cole wouldn't have been sent home if there was any chance of danger in the immediate future. In this, as in all things, luck had been on the Bennett family's side.

"He's not wrong," she said. "You probably don't want to miss practice this week. I don't know why it is, but Texas's defense always has a way of making you—"

This time, Cole's laugh was much more natural. "I should have known better than to come here to get cheered up."

"Yes, you should have. But now that you're here, do you want some hot chocolate?" She felt a little ridiculous at making the offer, since brawny, football-playing millionaires were supposed to drink things like hundred-year-old scotch when they wanted to drown their sorrows, but Swiss Miss with stale marshmallows was all she had. "I know it's not on your nutritionist-approved list, but—"

"Hot chocolate would be perfect," Cole said, and so quickly that she believed him. "Thank you."

Hailey ducked her head and went to the kitchen to prepare a second mug, careful not to jostle Bess or her sleeping puppies as she did. By this time, Philip had realized that his savior had come to claim him and ran wriggling to greet him. She could hear the enthusiastic sounds of their reunion in the background and felt a pang of guilt. She'd meant to do Philip a favor by placing him under Cole's temporary guardianship, but she was starting to wonder if that had been a mistake. He was getting awfully attached in an awfully short time. Like Hailey, that puppy had no problems showing what he felt, opening his heart at the worst possible times and to the worst possible people. He was going to be devastated once he learned that he didn't get to live with Cole forever.

She returned to the living room to find Cole making himself comfortable on the faded recliner and held out the steaming mug, complete with blobs of white marshmallow on top. Naturally, it was a teal mug with a football emblazoned on the side. Just as naturally, Cole noticed it.

"I know," she said, feeling irritable at being caught, once again, Lumberjack-handed. "But you can't tell me you're the least bit surprised."

"Not surprised, no. Just curious. Are we ever going to talk about what's happening inside this house?" Cole took a long, careful sip from the mug, his eyes never leaving hers. "Because I have questions."

"You can ask all the questions you want, but I can't promise I'm going to answer them."

Instead of accepting this rebuff as it was intended, Cole laughed. "Touchy subject? I can't imagine why." He paused a beat before adding, "I like your pajamas, by the way. I have the exact same pair."

"You do not."

"I do, too. They wanted pictures of us modeling them for a charity calendar." He cast a sweeping glance around her living room as if searching for the calendar in question—which she knew for a fact didn't exist. If that were the case, someone definitely would have purchased it for her by now. "I'm Mr. April, in case you were wondering."

She lowered herself to the couch opposite Cole, watching as he sipped hot chocolate and ran his hand over his puppy as though both of these things were perfectly ordinary. It didn't seem to occur to him that it was the middle of the night or that it was highly unorthodox to sit chatting about pajamas and sexy football-player calendars following the hospitalization of one's father, but she suspected that was the point. He obviously wasn't ready to go home yet—and just as obviously needed a friend.

As intimidating and unreal as it might be to have this man in her life, she knew that feeling well enough to give in.

"This was my dad's house," she said, nodding at the walls around them. "Most of the stuff in here—including the mug you're drinking from—belonged to him. It's sentimental and silly, I know, but I don't have the heart to throw any of it away."

"Oh."

He said just that—*oh*—and she realized that if she was ever going to get this out, now was the time to do it.

"He loved football in general and the Lumberjacks in particular.

He was the first in line to buy season tickets every year, and we never missed a home game—not even one year when we both had the flu. We ate Lumberjacks pancakes for breakfast on Sundays. We put up a Lumberjacks-themed Christmas tree during the holidays. He would even mow the logo into a pattern on our front lawn when the grass got too long. Believe me, it would have been much weirder for me *not* to become a fan after the childhood I had."

There. She'd said it. She'd laid out all her crazy for him to see, and he could decide what he wanted to do with it.

"He died, didn't he?" Cole asked. "That's what you told Mia the day I brought her over."

She turned to stare at him, but he was looking at the glass-encased football on the mantel. She had no idea he'd been paying that much attention.

"Yes, he did," she said softly. "He had a heart attack about nine years ago. Unfortunately, his was fatal."

"You must have been really young. I'm sorry."

And that was all Cole said. He didn't attempt to probe any deeper into her past, and he didn't use the moment to talk about his own father's condition. She should have tried to redirect the conversation, to mention the lateness of the hour and Philip's need for a warm bed, but something about his gentle sympathy caused her to keep going.

"I know how it looks," she said. "A single woman living alone inside a Lumberjacks shrine, all these pictures and collector's items and knickknacks, but it's not what you think. I like football. I probably love it. But if my dad had been a fan of cricket or building those tiny ships inside bottles, I could have just as easily become obsessed with them instead. It doesn't have anything to do with you specifically."

"I believe you."

Although he spoke sincerely enough, Hailey felt it was important to drive her point home.

"He never even heard the name Cole Bennett. You were still playing college ball when he died, not yet a twinkle in the Lumberjacks franchise's eye." She paused, and honesty compelled her to add, "He would have liked you, though. You're calm under pressure, and you're really good at anticipating your team's movements. It's easy to tell that you *know* them—what their habits are, what they're capable of. You never play down their strengths in an attempt to highlight your own."

Hailey felt rather than saw Cole come toward her. One second, he was sitting opposite her, hiding behind his mug of hot chocolate, and the next, he was grabbing her by the hands and yanking her to her feet.

"What did I say—?" she began, but there was no time for her to finish. With a speed that could only belong to a man who spent as much time in the gym as this one, he had one strong arm around her waist. His free hand came up to cup her cheek.

"I'm about to kiss you," he said. "Very deeply and very thoroughly."

It was the same weirdly chivalrous declaration of intent that he'd made at the dog shelter, and it had the same effect on her as before. She was surprised and confused and *eager*, unable to do much more than lift her lips toward his and wait.

Most of the men Hailey had kissed in her lifetime either came bumbling in at the end of a date or waited until there was a clear sign from her that things were about to progress to the next level. Both of which were fine, but nothing at all compared to this. Cole wasn't asking, but he wasn't not-asking either. He was *taking*, but only once she'd given her implicit consent.

Heady stuff, that.

His lips touched hers with the same gentleness as before, a direct counter to his claim that she was going to be taken deeply and thoroughly. Oddly enough, she didn't feel disappointed. There was something about that light graze and flutter of his mouth that felt more intimate than an immediate tangle of tongues.

He was tasting her, sampling her, enjoying her—*her*, Hailey Lincoln, clad in men's pajamas bearing the logo of his professional sports team. A woman who had watched and admired him from afar for years. A woman who wasn't particularly beautiful or interesting and whose main claim to fame was that she cleaned up dog poop on television for a living.

It was the last thought that made her lose control. Well, that and the fact that Cole's right hand had moved from cupping the side of her face to bury itself in the tangled coils of her half-braided hair. He was holding her head in place in order to move from that light, soft, playful nibbling to...

Yep, there it was. Cole Bennett's tongue. Inside her mouth.

"I'm sorry. Are you *laughing* right now?" He pulled back just enough to separate his mouth from hers, but she could still taste the light chocolate of his breath and feel the vibration of his words. "At me?"

She giggled harder. She also did her best to move away so that she wasn't literally laughing in his face, but his grip on her hair was too strong for that.

"Not at *you*," she managed, gasping. "At the situation."

"And what situation is that?" he demanded.

"Oh, you know..." She let her voice trail off, hoping he would realize the futility of trying to kiss a woman who didn't know a good thing when it planted itself on her lips. It was no use. He showed no sign of wanting to save himself. "I always thought I had weird reactions to situations, but I've obviously got nothing on you. What was it that moved you to such passionate heights? The sad stories about our fathers or the way these pajamas have a toothpaste stain on the cuff?"

His eyes narrowed slightly, but he didn't move from his position.

"I didn't notice it until right before you got here," she said, showing him the white spot on her wrist.

"I don't care about your damned pajamas," he said, grumbling in a way that only made her want to start laughing again. She didn't think she'd ever heard him that irritated before—not even in those postgame interviews where they asked deeply offensive questions about why he lost. "This is the second time I've been interrupted in the middle of kissing you, and I don't like it now any more than I did the last time."

She pulled her lower lip between her teeth and did her best to look solemn. "I'm sorry?"

His laugh came out in a chuff of warm air. "You are not. If you were sorry, you'd kiss me back instead of treating me like the guy who guesses people's weight at the fair." When she didn't say anything right away, he added, "No one likes the guy who guesses people's weight at the fair."

"His mother probably does," she pointed out.

Something she said must have pushed him over the edge again, because he once again fixed his gaze on hers, the laughter mingling with something more—something that caught in her chest and tugged. *Hard.*

"Hailey Lincoln, for the third time, I am going to kiss you. Not—as you are about to incorrectly guess—because of your pajamas or because I have inappropriate reactions to things but because I find you adorably and irresistibly charming. It was bad enough when you stood in front of me and told me all the ways my game is lacking. When you sit there and tell me all the ways it's not, I cannot and will not be held accountable for my actions."

Hailey's eyes opened wide, the tugging in her chest now more of a hammering.

"And if you dare—*dare*—to laugh at me this time, I will continue kissing you until neither one of us can stand on our own two feet. We'll roll to the carpet, a mess of our former selves, and not get up again for hours."

This was such a nonsensical thing to say that Hailey was in

perilous danger of laughing again. She might have done it, too, except one of Cole's hands moved down the side of her neck, his fingers trailing along her skin in a way that left nothing but shivers and sensation behind.

"Understood?" he asked, his eyes boring into hers.

She swallowed and nodded. It would have been so much better to give him back his own again, to call his bluff and see how far he'd take his threat, but words were beyond her. No one had called her adorably and irresistibly charming before. No one had looked at her quite like that before, either.

"Good," he said and kissed her.

This kiss wasn't at all like the other two. There was nothing tentative or gentle about it, no light exploration of his lips against hers. There was heat and there was pressure, and then Hailey stopped being able to think about much of anything at all.

Feelings, however, were everywhere.

She felt the glide of his tongue along hers, playful at first and then increasingly demanding. She felt his hand tangle deeper in her hair, his fingers winding through the strands until their separation wouldn't be an easy thing. She felt him shift so he hovered more possessively over her, felt the heat and the strength in every part of his musculature.

She also felt her own response to the kiss, mortifyingly passive as she struggled to accept that this was really happening. Fortunately, she felt no desire to laugh this time around. A woman didn't laugh when a man was kissing her as though he'd never felt anything as good as her mouth opening up to his. A woman didn't laugh when her entire body had turned to hot, throbbing gelatin, apparently unable to lift a hand but more than capable of emitting a soft moan that he captured with an even deeper kiss.

"That's the exact same sound you make when you're embarrassed," he murmured, the words pressed against her lips and then the side of her mouth and then—dear God—along the curve of her jaw toward the sensitive prickle on the side of her neck. "I like it."

She gasped as he pressed a kiss just below her earlobe—hot and wet and impossibly soft. Her whole body jerked in reaction to it, the intimacy and the unabashed pleasure, the way it set off a series of sparks that traveled insistently toward her belly.

Hailey had never been more grateful for anything than that kiss. Something about the thrill moving up and down her spine finally brought movement back to her limbs.

The first thing she did was twine her arms around his neck, latching around and pulling him down so he had no chance of escape. The second thing she did was draw him close for another round. She paused just before she touched her mouth to his.

"You like it when I'm embarrassed?" she asked.

"I like it when you're *you*."

And there it was. She was done for. Any chance she might have had of making it out of this moment—out of this entire situation—in one piece was gone. She wasn't foolish enough to believe that Cole Bennett saw her in a seriously romantic light, but it didn't matter. Her heart had always been like that. Too soft and too unprotected, too eager for love and acceptance to care that it was being used. She couldn't count how many men she'd scared away by the strength and immediacy of her feelings, how many just plain *friends* she'd scared away the same way.

Life would have been so much easier if she'd just learned to wall up her stupid heart when she'd had the chance.

It was a good kiss, their tongues meeting in the middle and their bodies pressing with equal urgency against each other. The hot sweep of his mouth over hers was matched by the willing press of her own. His low groan of approval had nothing on the increasing sighs and moans that she was unable to hold back. Just when Hailey couldn't remember the last time she'd breathed, her whole body awhirl with sensation and pleasure, Cole yanked himself upright.

"Holy mother of God," he said, staring at her. His hair was slightly messed up and his eyes a deeper blue than they'd been before, but other than that, he showed no signs of exertion.

He wouldn't, of course. He was a trained athlete, a man who could spend three hours running up and down a field without growing fatigued. A hot five-minute make-out session wouldn't have the same effect on him as it did her.

Which, if she was being honest, seemed to be the physical equivalent of running a marathon. Twice.

"What?" she retorted, breathless and so flushed that she could feel the heat throbbing in her cheeks. "You started it."

"You didn't laugh that time."

She blushed deeper, but that didn't stop her from replying in kind. "Neither did you."

He chuckled now, pausing just long enough to run a hand through his hair and return it to its former glory. Hailey didn't dare do the same. She could feel how loose her braid had become and knew the color wouldn't leave her face for another few minutes. To attempt repairs without a mirror would only make her look worse.

"For a minute there, I think I might have forgotten how," Cole said. He reached over and tucked her hair behind her ear. It wouldn't do anything to improve her appearance, she knew, especially since it caused the heat to flare up inside her all over again. "Consider this fair warning, Hailey. If you compliment me like that again, you're going to get soundly kissed."

He paused and stared, as if expecting her to urge him into a repeat performance. As if *hoping* for it.

It would be so easy to comply. Compliments on his appearance and muscle tone, on what a good brother and uncle and son he was, on how all he had to do was smile to light up an entire stadium full of people… Hailey had no shortage of options available to her.

But "You're not staying here tonight" is what she said. It was the only thing she could think of, and it didn't even begin to capture everything she was feeling. "You're getting in your car and going home. If you leave now, you can get a few hours of sleep in before practice tomorrow."

He seemed to find this highly amusing. "Yes, yes. I know. I can't crack a spread defense without it."

"I'm not worried about *that*," she replied. She blamed the fact that she was still so rattled for what she said next. "It wouldn't be right for me to take advantage of you in your current situation, that's all."

He blinked down at her, the flutter of his eyelashes the only movement he made. "My *what*?"

She made a vague gesture over him—at the wrinkles in his once-crisp white button-down, the lines of exhaustion on either side of his mouth, the way his shoulders were oh-so-slightly sagging from their usual granite position. "It's been a long day, and you just spent the last five hours at the hospital. You're feeling emotional and vulnerable and in need of human comfort—totally understandably, by the way—but it wouldn't be right for me to take advantage of you."

He still wasn't moving, but something in his gaze shifted. "You're afraid of taking advantage of me," he said, his tone flat.

"Yes."

"Because I'm in a vulnerable state."

"I know it might not feel like it right now, but the classic signs of shock—"

He didn't let her finish. "You'll kiss me and make me hot chocolate and open up to me about your own father's death, but you won't sleep with me."

She could feel the heat starting to fast-track to her face. Okay, so it was a little presumptuous of her to assume he wanted to stay the night, but after a kiss like that one, she figured the thought had crossed his mind. It had certainly taken up residence in her own.

"I'm sorry," she said, feeling flushed. "It's just that you said if I complimented you again—"

He swooped in and kissed her again, but this time, it was a quick, loud smack of his lips against hers. He put his hands on either side of her face and held them there, his eyes twinkling down at hers with unmistakable warmth.

"I don't know what I did to deserve you in my life, but it must have been something amazing," he said.

"Wait. So you *do* want to sleep with me?"

His chuckle was so deep and so rich that it sent her whole body quaking. "The things I want to do to you don't have anything to do with sleep."

Hailey had no idea if her cheeks were still flaming, because at those words, her whole body caught on fire.

"Don't worry. I'll go," he said, his voice low, his hands still holding her face like it was the most precious thing in the world. "Not because you told me to, and not because I'm in an emotionally vulnerable state, but because there isn't nearly enough time tonight for me to do things properly."

She opened her mouth and closed it again, unable to think of a single thing to say. Which was probably for the best, because she doubted she could manage much in the way of coherence right now.

As if sensing this, Cole leaned down and pressed a quick, light kiss on the end of her nose. "Thank you, Hailey. I knew that seeing you again tonight would cheer me up. I just didn't realize how much."

He stepped back and snapped his fingers. The sound did little to bring Philip to attention, but it did have the benefit of bringing Hailey to hers. She managed to walk Cole and his puppy to the door, saying all the right things and wishing him a safe journey home. She even got the door shut and locked behind them, but that was about as much as her limbs would comply.

Cole Bennett wanted to not-sleep with her. Cole Bennett wanted the time to do things properly.

Even if he woke up tomorrow and changed his mind, if he realized that Hailey had been right about the emotional upheaval that a beloved father's heart attack could wreak—and that she was the last person on earth he wanted to entangle himself with—she still had this moment.

And she'd always have that kiss.

chapter
12

THE MATCHUP AGAINST TEXAS WAS THE FIRST HOME GAME in the entirety of Cole's career that his parents weren't there to watch. Even though he couldn't see their usual seats from the field, he felt their absence the entire time.

It was ridiculous. He was a grown-ass man with a stadium full of fans. There were twenty television cameras pointed on him at any given moment. Two hundred people were working hard to ensure that every pass he made and every play he called were broadcast around the world in real time.

None of that made the least bit of difference. He still felt weird, like he was playing the game with only half of his heart.

"Would someone please tell Bennett to come get his damn dog?" The irate voice of one of the assistant coaches hailed him before he even made it all the way to the locker rooms. The team was euphoric, having secured a place in the championship game and now only one win away from the Kickoff Cup, but the assistant coach looked less than pleased to see him. "There you are. What the hell is wrong with this animal?"

The animal in question came bounding toward Cole as though they'd been parted for days instead of hours. Heedless of the fact that Cole was fully geared up and sweaty as all get-out, Philip launched himself into his arms. He wriggled and licked and otherwise made the pair of them look like lovesick fools.

"Yes, Philip. I know." He did his best to control the puppy's gyrating movements. "I missed you, too, buddy."

"How come Bennett gets to bring his dog to games, and I don't?" complained Johnson. "My kids would love to see Napoleon getting a little airtime."

"This isn't any dog." Cole pointed the puppy at the kicker. "This is my Puppy-Cup-winning lucky charm. Kiss him for seven years of good fortune."

Johnson, who was six feet of long, lanky foot power, eyed him askance. "I thought it was the woman who was the lucky charm."

"She is."

"Then what good is it going to do me to kiss the puppy? I'd be better off kissing her."

Cole couldn't argue with that. Kissing Hailey seemed to have done him a world of good. Not only had they won the game, but his arm wasn't giving him any more trouble than the usual grueling ache. Each pass had gone more or less where he'd wanted it to, his strength holding out for as long as the team had needed him. He liked to think that even Hailey's father would have been proud of his performance today.

"I'd kiss a frog if it meant we could get another win like that one," Garrett said, jogging up to join them.

"I'd kiss your mom for it," Johnson returned. "Hell, if it means breaking the curse, I'd kiss *you*."

Garrett responded to this by planting a loud, smacking kiss on top of the kicker's helmet. This kind of high-adrenaline camaraderie was common after a win as important as this one, and Cole would have normally jumped right in to join them. But he caught sight of Regina standing off to one side of the hallway, her cell phone pressed to one ear while she plugged the other with her finger, and moved to join her. He only had a few minutes before he'd be needed for the postgame interviews, and he wanted a word with her before she switched into full manager mode.

"Uh-huh. I'll tell him. I know. I *know*, Mom." Regina caught sight of Cole and rolled her eyes in an exaggerated gesture of annoyance. "Give Daddy our love and tell him we'll see him later, yeah? I have to go now. And please make sure Mia goes to bed at a relatively normal time tonight. I don't care how many tears she manages to squeeze out at you first."

Cole chuckled as Regina finished up the call. "You know she's going to be up until midnight now, right?"

"How is that my fault? I'm the only adult in her life who refuses to fall for that sob story of hers. She's all alone. No one loves her." Regina sighed. "Bullshit. You're turning her into a monster, the whole lot of you."

"Speaking of monsters..." Cole began with a glance at the phone clutched in Regina's hand.

She didn't miss his meaning. "He's alive and kicking, but just barely. It would have been nice if you could have won that game by a few more points. Mom says they were discussing sedating him until the game was over to keep him from having another heart attack, but he threatened to walk out if anyone came near him with a needle."

Cole assumed his sister was joking, doing her best to make light of a bad situation, but that didn't stop him from saying, "Our father's life is entirely in my hands. Got it. Win the Kickoff Cup or be held liable for patricide."

"Hey." Regina frowned and gave his foot a light kick. "I was kidding."

"Were you?" he asked. He heaved a sigh before she could answer. "I take it I'm not invited for visiting hours tonight?"

Regina winced. So far, he hadn't been invited for *any* visiting hours. Every time he'd expressed a wish to swing by the hospital, he'd been fed another story about how his dad was sleeping or he shouldn't leave practice early or it would be better if he focused on football so his dad could recover in peace.

"He'll just worry more if you're there," his mom kept saying. "You can do more for him by working with your team than by visiting."

"Stay *away*" had been Regina's less tactful approach. "It's not as if there's anything you can do for him, anyway."

"No need to come up with an excuse," Cole said as Regina prepared to hit him with a fresh wave of reasons why it was best for him to celebrate with the team instead of his family tonight. He curled a protective hand around Philip's head. "Message received."

"It's not personal, Cole," Regina said, glancing down at where he was clutching the puppy. "We're just trying to manage his stress levels, that's all. You know how he gets this time of year."

Yes, he knew. From what Regina had told him, his dad had cried last year when the Lumberjacks lost to their longtime rivals in Arizona. He hadn't shed a single tear when his own father—Cole's grandfather—had died, but that 21–18 loss so near to the Kickoff Cup had almost broken him. The same thing used to happen when the stakes were much lower, when becoming a pro player was the pot of gold at the end of an endless, laborious rainbow. Weddings, birthdays, *funerals*…they could easily be dispensed with, just so long as Cole got the ball in the end zone.

So he did. Then he did it again. Then he did it again.

And all the while, the people around him got married and aged and died. They *lived*.

"I'm sure the guys have something fun planned," Regina said with a smile for Cole and a friendly pat for Philip. "Go out. Celebrate. Lord knows you're going to feel like you got hit by a bag of rocks tomorrow. You might as well enjoy the adrenaline while it lasts."

"He's my dad, too, Reg."

Regina's expression softened. "Not during Kickoff Cup season he's not. You know that better than anyone. This time of year, he's Julian Bennett, the quarterback who never was. And you're the only chance he has at redemption." She looked as though she might say more—remind him, perhaps, that neither of them had really asked for this life—but Garrett popped his head into the hallway before she had a chance.

"Coach wants to know if he can borrow his quarterback for a few minutes," he said. "And by 'borrow,' he means if he doesn't see your ass in here immediately, he's going to do something drastic like ban puppies from the locker room from here on out."

"The horror," Regina said with a laugh. She put her hands on Cole's shoulders and spun him around, losing no time in pushing him down the hall. "Go. Be brilliant. And don't forget that we promised Hailey's people you'd mention the Puppy Cup at least twice during the interviews."

Cole went, mostly because he was contractually obligated to, but also because that mention of Hailey instantly perked him up. He might be banned from visiting his dad, but there was one place both he and Philip were always welcome.

Okay, so *always* was a bit of an exaggeration, and there was a good chance Hailey would decide that the euphoria of a win was yet another emotional vulnerability that prevented him from whisking her into his arms and his bed, but that was all the more reason to stop by.

No one had ever accused him of having emotional vulnerability before, but he was starting to like the way it sounded.

Emotional. Vulnerable. Human.

Real.

Hailey had never thrown such a successful party before.

Okay, so unless you counted the wrap party she helped organize every year for the Puppy Cup cast and crew, she'd never really thrown any kind of party before, but she didn't care. Multiple people had come over to her house. They'd eaten food. They'd consumed alcohol. They'd watched football. She wasn't saying she was the root cause of the Lumberjacks' win over Texas, but she *was* supposed to be the token lucky charm. There could totally be a correlation.

"You don't have to stay and help me clean up," Hailey said as Penny started stacking plates and carrying them to the kitchen. "I can get all this later."

"Are you kidding?" Penny stepped neatly over the gate and around Bess's puppies, who were growing larger and more mobile with each passing day. Only Rufus remained stunted, but Hailey had set up a box with a heated blanket for him to sleep in at night, so at least he was keeping warm. "I've been waiting for everyone else to leave so I can snoop through your house in peace. You never told me that you have your own little garden out back. And two closets in your bedroom. *And* a real bathtub. I haven't taken a bath in ages. My apartment is only big enough for one of those all-in-one wet rooms."

Hailey had a hard time picturing glamorous, elegant Penny washing her hair while seated on a toilet, but she could see the hint that was being dropped easily enough. "Do you want to take a bath?" she offered.

Penny laughed as she stacked the plates in the sink. "I do, actually, but even I'm not that pushy. I'll wait until you invite me over a second time."

Hailey felt a warm flush of pleasure at these words. She hadn't been entirely sure that anyone from the office would come if she threw a party, but she'd given it a try anyway. After watching the last game with Cole's family, sitting in front of the television screen alone had seemed pathetic, even for her.

"I'm sorry I haven't asked you over before this," Hailey said. "To be honest, I didn't know you wanted to come."

Penny stared at her for a moment before shaking her head, her long, dark hair breaking around the Lumberjacks jersey she wore.

She'd arrived in a tasteful boatneck sweater, but that hadn't lasted long. By halftime, she'd pulled one of the signed jerseys down from the wall and put it on in the sweater's place. The jersey had probably depreciated about five hundred dollars the moment it came down, but Hailey didn't mind. It was about time someone got some actual use out of the thing.

"Your problem, Hailstorm, is that you underestimate yourself." Penny clucked her tongue. "You've *always* underestimated yourself."

Hailey's whole body jerked at the sound of that nickname, which she hadn't heard in over nine years. "What did you just call me?"

Penny arched her brow. "Hailstorm? It's what we decided to call you after you landed both Cole Bennett and Garrett Smith in the same week. No one sees you coming, and then—BAM! You're pouring down hard everywhere." She paused when Hailey could do little more than blink at her. "You don't mind, do you?"

No, she didn't. She didn't mind at all. To hear her dad tell the tale, that was exactly why he'd chosen the same nickname for her— because she hit as if from out of nowhere. It had never been his intention to be a foster parent, even less to be an adoptive parent, but a coworker at the manufacturing plant where he'd worked convinced him to give temporary guardianship a try. Then Hailey had shown up on his doorstep, clutching a backpack of all her worldly possessions, looking lost and terrified out of her mind.

"And I fell in love," he'd said, as though that was all there was to it. "You changed everything."

Hailey felt her eyes flooding as she remembered the day he'd said those words for the first time, standing in front of a judge and making the appeal to become her legal parent and guardian.

So you never have to be alone again. So you always have somewhere to come home to.

It had been such a beautiful promise, and Dad had kept it as faithfully as he could. In addition to teaching her everything he knew about football, he'd also taught her everything he knew about life. It wasn't much, as he was always the first to point out, but it was more than Hailey had ever hoped for.

He'd taught her how to cook and also how to avoid the dishes for as long as possible. He'd taught her how to change a tire and fix a leaky faucet. He'd pushed her to go to college even though neither one of them could afford it and had cried harder than all the other parents when she graduated from high school.

He'd taught her how to love. And then he'd died.

"Hey, why are you getting all weepy?" Penny asked. "It's not anything bad, I promise."

Hailey shook her head, afraid that speaking would only loosen the lump in her throat and the tears in her eyes.

"You're like our goddess now, you know. You have the city's most eligible bachelor eating out of the palm of your hand."

Hailey finally found the strength to issue a protest. "It's not like that."

"Oh, it's like that. I was at the puppy draft. I saw the way he was looking at you."

At this, Hailey could feel herself starting to color up. Penny only had half the story. If she knew how Cole had looked at her the other night—the way he'd *kissed* her...

"That was because you made me wear your jumpsuit," she said.

"Nuh-uh. No way. I've worn that jumpsuit around plenty of men who didn't want to rip it off my body with their teeth. He *likes* you, Hailey." Penny paused a moment before adding, "I know you don't believe me, but everyone at the office does."

"Jasmine doesn't."

Penny laughed. "Okay, maybe not Jasmine, but she doesn't count. She doesn't like anyone except her hairstylist."

A knock sounded at the front door before Hailey could respond. It was loud enough that all six puppies jumped to their feet in excitement, and even Bess lifted her head in inquiry. Hailey could hardly blame them for their enthusiasm—the last batch of visitors had spent hours lavishing them with cuddles and affection. They were starting to get spoiled.

"Is that Charles?" Penny asked. "I told him I was going to stick around and hit you up for a dip in your sweet, luxurious bathtub, but I don't think he believed me. Men will never understand the appeal of two hours spent in a haze of bubbles and candlelight."

It seemed likely that her visitor was either Charles or one of their other coworkers who had left something behind, so Hailey didn't bother looking through the peephole before she pulled the door open. She regretted her mistake about two seconds later.

"Cole!" she cried, delight flooding over her. She tried to subdue that feeling, to resist the magnetic pull of him, but it was no use. She was a gangly, awkward twelve-year-old standing on that front porch all over again. "What are you doing here?"

"Ha!" Penny appeared behind her. "I *told* you so."

"Uh-oh." Cole looked back and forth between them. "Am I interrupting something?"

"No. I mean, yes. I mean, we were cleaning up, but—"

"I told her so." Penny nudged Hailey out of the way with her hip and pulled the door open farther. The extra space allowed Philip to dart through. Without paying the least heed to Hailey or her guest, he made a beeline for the kitchen gate. "Come on in. I was just getting ready to leave. Pretend I'm not here."

Cole seemed amused but not surprised to find Penny playing hostess. He also showed zero remorse at leaning down and dropping a kiss on Hailey's cheek. Under any other circumstances, it might have been taken as a greeting between friends, but his hand pressed against the small of her back, and he sighed heavily. "God, you always smell so good. Like puppies frolicking in a meadow."

This seemed like a polite way of saying she smelled like a dog, but there was no mistaking the way his body leaned against hers or the way his breath moved over her ear and down her neck. Or, truth be told, Penny's exhalation of delight at the sight of it, which bordered on a squeal there toward the end.

"That doesn't sound like someone who's not here," Cole pointed out.

Penny laughed. "Sorry. I'll swoon quieter next time. You two need anything before I head out?"

Hailey felt a strange impulse to beg Penny to stay. Cole's hand was still on the small of her back, his fingers exerting a gentle yet unmistakable pressure. The thin fabric of her logo-emblazoned T-shirt did little to prevent the heat of his hand from working through to the skin below. She could practically feel each ridge of his fingerprints leaving an impression behind.

There was something possessive about it—something promising. Something *terrifying*.

The last time he was here, Cole had made his intentions pretty clear. This time, his intentions were practically emblazoned in neon above his head.

"I think we can figure things out from here," Hailey said, blushing as the words escaped her lips. "But thank you for coming over today, Penny. I mean it."

She *did* mean it, and she sincerely hoped Penny would take advantage of her offer of the bath whenever she wanted, but her coworker waved her off as though the day had been perfectly ordinary. Hailey didn't know how to explain that *any* of this—the football parties and the football player, the easy friendship that Penny was offering without strings—were so far out of the realm of normal for her that she was starting to suspect this was some kind of out-of-body lucid dream.

It was a *good* dream, yes, and Hailey intended to enjoy it while it lasted, but she knew enough about life to accept that she'd have to wake up to cold reality eventually.

Penny waited only long enough to gather up her purse and her sweater before heading out the door, a laugh on her lips and her friendly smile in place. Hailey's first impulse was to check and make sure the puppies were behaving themselves, but Cole stood watching Penny walk away with a puzzled expression on his face.

"What?" Hailey asked. "What's wrong?"

"I could have sworn… But that's not…" He walked over to the couch and stabbed a finger at the wall, where a blank square of plastic loomed ominously. "Hailey, is Penny *wearing* your signed 1995 Lumberjacks jersey?"

Her laugh escaped before she could stop it. "Oops. You noticed that?"

He whirled on her. "Do you have any idea what that thing must be worth? That was the year Maitland scored six touchdowns in a single game."

"I know."

"And the year Arnsdale won Best AFC Defensive Player for the second time in a row."

"It was the best of times," Hailey agreed blandly. "They just don't make football players like they used to, do they?"

"Hailey, you *wretch*." Cole came toward her in two long strides. His hands gripped her shoulders, his look one of pure intensity. "You can't just let people go around wearing thousands of dollars' worth of your father's memorabilia."

"Why not?" Hailey did her best not to squirm under that intense gaze, but it was difficult. Cole wasn't angry with her, and she doubted that he cared much about the money, but he seemed to feel honest outrage at her actions. "Penny got more use out of it today than I have in the entire twenty-five years it's been sitting there."

"But you love this stuff."

"It's only stuff."

"Four days ago, you said you hadn't touched any of it in nine years in honor of your father's memory. What's happened since then?"

Cole was proving himself to be a good listener. *Too* good, if he was going to start keeping track of everything that came out of her mouth. She was far too indiscreet a person under pressure for that.

Her next words proved it. "*You* happened."

The grip on her shoulders tightened. "Me?"

"Yes, you."

Didn't he understand what it meant for him to be at her house right now? For him to be looking at her with that light in his eyes? He might be used to people throwing themselves at him, introducing him to their families and kissing him without abandon, but this was all very new for her.

"You just finished winning a game watched by thirty million people, Cole," she said. "You could go anywhere you want, do anything you want. But instead of showering in Cristal or having dinner on top of Mount Rainier, you're here. With me and my seven dogs. Yelling at me for letting a friend wear an old football jersey of my dad's."

"I wasn't yelling."

Emboldened by the boyish petulance on his face, she got up on her tiptoes to press a kiss on his lips. "There was a little bit of yelling."

"Hailey—"

"Don't worry," she was quick to add. "I'm not upset. It's just that a month ago, I considered all things Lumberjacks—and all things Cole Bennett—to be some kind of magical, untouchable dream. But now I've met you and your family and your fancy football-playing friends, and I realize you're not really that special."

He blinked, his lower lip falling slightly open.

"Sorry, but it's true. You're probably the most beautiful man I've ever met, and you'll go down in football history as one of the most precise and controlled quarterbacks of all time, but you're kind of a pain in the ass, too." A smile curved Hailey's lips as she stood staring up at this man—at the godlike creation who looked, for the first time, as overwhelmed as she felt every time he walked into a room. "Those were compliments, by the way. In case you're wondering where I'm trying to go with this."

He didn't wonder for very long.

One second, Hailey was holding herself warily, wondering if that bit about him being beautiful was pushing things too far, and the next, she was in Cole's arms. Literally. Even though he had to be ten different kinds of exhausted, he somehow managed to hitch his arms underneath her thighs and hoist her to his level in less time than it took her to blink. Her legs spread to encompass his hips, and her arms twined around his neck, all of her straining to be as close to him as humanly possible.

He seemed to feel the same sense of urgency, because he didn't even wait until she was fully settled before he started kissing her. Nor did he bother with any of that sweet, gentle nibbling to set the mood. His hands were cupping her ass and his mouth was open against hers, the full, hot promise of his tongue making it impossible for her to do much more than let him in.

Which was exactly what she did. She lowered her guard and stopped fighting. There was no use pretending she didn't want this man—near her, on her, *in* her. She wasn't sure how any of this had happened, but it was happening all the same.

"I'm still mad about the jersey thing," he said as he pressed her up against the nearest wall. There was a framed poster behind her, but Cole didn't seem to be aware of the irony as it banged and bent under the pressure of both their bodies hitting it at once. "And we're going to have a talk later about which one of us is the real pain in the ass."

"Does this mean you're not going to argue with me about the beautiful part?"

Hailey felt his smile curve against her lips. It was a wicked smile, slow and sensual, and it sent shivers of pleasure down her spine. "No, Hailey. I'm going to make you regret that in other ways."

If she'd thought it was strange to have this man's tongue inside her mouth, it was nothing compared to having the full, hard press of him between her legs. He used the grinding leverage of his hips to pin her against the wall, which freed one of his hands to explore her body at will.

The first thing that hand did was whip her shirt away and fling it into the nearest corner. She hadn't been expecting company of this variety, so her bra was just a basic comfortable beige, the sort of thing one wore when jumping and shouting at the television for hours on end. If Cole noticed it, he found nothing strange about its bland functionality. He was much too busy taking advantage of her suddenly bare skin. His hand ran up and down her side, reveling in the shape of her, memorizing each dip and curve.

"I've been dying to find out where your blushes end," he murmured as he began pressing kisses over the line of her jaw and down her neck. "They usually follow this path right here, but then your clothes get in the way."

The path he highlighted went past her neck to the line of her shoulder and then down, down, so close to the upper swell of her breast that she gasped. Cole had yet to remove her bra or explore its contents, but the gentle kiss he dropped on the softly rounded curve was all the more powerful because of it.

"Hmm." He pulled back, eyes narrowed as they scanned her chest. "I thought for sure that would make you blush."

He was wrong. In social situations, Hailey's blood was quick to rise to the surface and betray her—a thing Cole knew and used to his advantage all the time. In sexual situations, her blood was usually too busy elsewhere to bother. If this man knew how hot and pulsing the sensation between her thighs was right now, he'd realize that getting her to blush wouldn't be the easy task it had been before.

"Sorry," she said, arching her back so that her breasts thrust more enticingly toward him. "You'll have to try harder."

He lost no time in doing just that. With the same look of concentration she'd seen on his face hundreds of times on the football field and the other day as they drafted their puppy teams, he tested the various parts of her body. A deep, penetrating kiss only caused her to moan. The flat of his palm brushing over her breasts merely caused her to gasp. And the quick, effortless way he flicked her bra off did no more than kindle a fire low in her belly.

"I'll be damned," he said, gazing at her bare, upturned nipples. She might not be blushing right now, but there was no mistaking the havoc his kisses were wreaking on those body parts. He flicked his thumb over one tightened peak—yet another action that made her body ache for more. "I thought for sure having you half-naked in front of me would do it."

He loosened his hold on her hips, allowing her legs to slide down so she was once again standing on her own two feet. They weren't very stable feet, and the way he looked at her bare torso wasn't helping matters, so it was a good thing there was a wall at her back.

"Actions don't affect me nearly as much as words," Hailey admitted. "I don't know why, but it's always been like that. I'm like the opposite of that famous saying. Sticks and stones can't break my bones, but words will always hurt me."

"*Really?*" Cole sounded far too excited about this new development for Hailey's peace of mind. He took a deliberate step back and placed his hands behind his back, touching her with nothing but his gaze. "So if I were to describe your body in explicit detail, you'd start squirming?"

Yes, actually. Even discussing the *act* of discussing was starting to make her flame up. If he started using X-rated terminology, she was going to be done for.

"The first time I ever saw you, I thought you were cute," he said, his head tilted slightly. "In a gray sweater dress and red tennis shoes, looking like a woman who'd just rolled out of bed and went to work without a care in the world."

Some of the heat died. Was he forgetting the part where she was naked from the waist up? "Um, this isn't exactly what I had in mind…"

"Quiet." He held up a warning finger. "I'm getting to the good part."

She clamped her lips shut and waited. If nothing else, this would be one more thing she could add to her Cole Bennett knowledge base. Size twelve shoes. Dry cappuccinos. A propensity to talk when a woman was basically throwing herself at him.

"You almost always look like that," he said and drew closer. It was just one step, and he wasn't touching her, but she could feel the air between them start to move. "Cute. Comfortable. Quiet."

Again, this wasn't exactly what she'd been thinking—

"Now I know that's just how you lull a man into thinking he's safe. A friendly face, a Lumberjacks T-shirt, a puppy in your arms." He shook his head and took another step forward. Nothing he was saying was causing her to blush, but she was definitely feeling something warm spreading up from her stomach. "But you, Hailey Lincoln, are fucking *dangerous*."

Oh yes. That something warm was definitely starting to take over. He reached out and grabbed the waistband of her jeans, giving it a strong enough tug to pull her hips toward his. He also expertly flicked the button open to reveal the top line of her panties. Like the bra, they were boring and functional, but Hailey couldn't find it in her to care. With any luck, she wouldn't be wearing them long enough to matter.

"You've been hiding the body of a pinup and the soul of a warrior," he said, dropping his lips to her ear. Her whole body quivered in response. "You make every part of me ache to be inside you. I never saw you coming, and now I'm completely under your spell."

Hailey had never felt less like blushing in her entire life. He'd done it—Cole Bennett had done it—found the one thing in the world that wouldn't send her into a spiral of mortification. He'd taken the heat from the surface of her skin and turned it inward, lighting a fire that scorched in the best possible way.

She placed her hands on his chest and used all the strength she had to shove him. It wasn't much when compared to a man of his size and stature, but she took him enough by surprise to force him to take a step back.

"What are you—?" he began, but she didn't give him a chance to finish. He'd kindled this thing inside her, and now he was going to have to do something about it.

She pushed again, this time keeping her hands in place long enough to guide him toward the couch. He must have realized what was happening, because he took a few willing steps backward before falling to the cushions in a whoosh of air and laughter.

"Uh-oh," he murmured, his smile deepening into that charming, dimpled expression she knew so well. "Was it something I said?"

"Shirt. Off." She nodded at him once before kicking her shoes away and tugging her jeans over her hips. Later, she'd realize how odd it was that she didn't stop to think about how she looked with the full lights of the living room behind her or regret that it had been a few days since she'd last bothered to shave her legs. In this moment, with Cole Bennett obediently stripping off his clothes on her couch, she could only think of how powerful she felt.

He thought she had the soul of a warrior, and for the first time in her life, she absolutely agreed.

"Jesus." She hesitated at the sight of Cole's bare torso, which was so freakishly perfect it felt almost surreal. His shoulders were impossibly broad, his chest a massive swell of strength and superiority. It was as if someone had taken the marbled ideal of a man sculpted hundreds of years ago and breathed life into him.

Fully aware of the effect he was having on her, Cole placed his arms behind his head and grinned. The pose was designed to make the most of his powerful biceps, but flexing only drew attention to the round scars on his right shoulder from the surgery he'd had two years ago. Seeing them—this visible proof that he, too, was human—gave her the resolve she needed to strip her panties away.

"Jesus," he echoed, dropping his arms.

It was all the invitation she needed. She lowered herself to his lap, sitting astride, her entirely naked body pressed against his half-clothed one. Even this inequality didn't disconcert her. She liked the way his jeans felt against her, the hard ridge of his groin pressing and pushing against her body with a need that neither one of them could deny.

Taking his face between her hands, she lowered her lips to his and kissed him. He was expecting it, his mouth ready and willing to accept hers the moment their lips touched. She was too hungry and too eager, small moans escaping every time his tongue slid along hers, but it didn't seem to matter. He matched her sense of urgency beat for beat and bite for bite.

"What the hell else are you hiding from me?" he asked when she pulled away to adjust her position. Her legs, already spread much farther than decorum allowed, widened until she could feel every part of his erection. He seemed to like this, wrapping his arms around her waist and holding her down so that she couldn't move in any direction but against him. "Secret tattoos? Sexy piercings? Deep, dirty kinks I'll have no choice but to play along with?"

Hailey felt a pang of regret starting to take over the hot, liquid yearning between her legs. If that was the kind of excitement Cole craved in the bedroom, he was going to be disappointed with anything she had to offer.

"Sorry to be the bearer of bad news, but I don't have any tattoos or piercings," she said, more serious than the moment required but unable to prevent the words from escaping. "I'm scared of needles. And infection."

"Noted."

He still seemed inclined to be amused, so she added, "And to be perfectly honest, I don't have any kinks. None that I know of, anyway. I'm not experienced enough for that. There are a few that seem like they might be fun, but I've never met anyone I'd want to try them out with."

This foray into the truth was having its inevitable effect on her—which was to say, the fire that burned in her blood was starting to rise to the surface. Of course. *This* was the thing to make her blush. *This* was the thing to make her feel as though she was, well, squirming and naked on a man's lap.

It was also the thing that kept her mouth moving long after a wise woman would have glued it shut.

"I wouldn't mind trying some of them out with you."

Naturally, Cole didn't have a response to this. How could he? In one breath, she'd admitted her lack of sexual experience, revealed her risk-averse tendencies, and thrown herself at him in ways she would regret for the rest of her life. It was one thing to offer sex to a man who clearly wanted it; it was quite another to open the door to boundary-pushing deeds enacted in the name of lust.

"Well, I'll be damned," Cole said after a pause that felt interminable.

She was almost afraid to ask. "What?"

"I should have known." He lifted a hand and trailed the back of his fingers down her cheek, his touch cool against the flame of her mortification. He skimmed over her jaw and along the pulse in her neck, danced over her clavicle and down the naked peaks of her breasts. She thought he might keep going until he reached the softest, wettest parts of her, but he stopped when he reached her sternum.

There, he placed his palm flat against the thrum-thrumming of her chest. "It doesn't stop until it reaches your heart."

At that, something inside Hailey cried out—not verbally but in a burst of energy and emotion that tingled in all of her fingers and each of her toes. She swung a leg off Cole's lap and made a move to dash away, but he caught her by encircling her wrist.

"Don't," he said—begged, almost, his voice low and hoarse. "Stay with me."

She shook her head, the loose strands of her hair tumbling around her face. Although she could feel some of her blush abating, she still felt hot and exposed.

Then again, she'd felt hot and exposed since the moment this man first walked into her office. It would be a far stranger thing to change the state of affairs now.

"I'll be right back," she said. "I'm just going to grab protection. Stay exactly where you are."

She didn't wait to hear his reaction this time around. There were so many things about this moment that felt fantastic, but that was pretty much her life in a nutshell. Every day was a new adventure in stepping outside her comfort zone, in revealing all her soft, squishy inner parts to virtual strangers. For whatever reason, Cole Bennett had taken one look at her soft, squishy inner parts and decided he wanted to stick around long enough to enjoy her soft, squishy *outer* ones.

And she, Lord help her, was going to let him.

It didn't take her long to find what she was looking for. She paused on her way back to peek at the puppies. Bess and her babies were all contentedly napping in their usual positions in the kitchen, but Rufus's box had shifted and the heated blanket was askew. Not, as might be supposed, because Rufus was once again trying to escape, but because Philip had somehow managed to sneak past the gate and make his way into the kitchen. He'd found Rufus's box and pushed the blanket aside. Their heads rested together, eyes shut and dreamy expressions on their sweet little faces.

"Good boy," Hailey whispered as she tiptoed away, fearful lest she disturb their rest. It was nice for Rufus to finally have a friend. Philip, too. Life was far too difficult when you had to go it alone.

"Sorry," she apologized as she returned to the living room. In accordance with her command, Cole hadn't moved—he was still on the couch, still gloriously shirtless, still a vision to behold. And if her quick peek at his groin was any indication, still fully committed to this act. "I had to check on the puppies."

"Of course you did."

"Their comfort is important to me."

"Of course it is."

She narrowed her eyes. "Are you just going to sit there and blandly agree with everything I say?"

"Of course I am."

She laughed and took her lower lip between her teeth. She wasn't fool enough to think that this conciliatory mood of Cole's was going to last—he was far too accustomed to having things his own way for that—but she might as well get some use out of it while it lasted.

"Then put this on." She tossed the condom at him.

He raised an eyebrow but did as she asked. He made a show of it too, slowly peeling off his jeans, tugging at the waistband of his boxer briefs, taking himself out like a man enamored of his own anatomy. Which, to be fair, he had every right to be.

She'd imagined this man naked before, had seen the pictures of him on a beach and in the locker room, but nothing could have prepared her for the real deal. His size was everywhere in proportion, his strength so much a part of him that even his muscles had muscles.

"Well?" he asked. "What now?"

Now she blushed, obviously. This was a moment of words, not actions, and therefore highly uncomfortable. She approached the couch somewhat cautiously, pleased when he took the initiative of once again encircling her wrist and tugging her close, his free hand gripping her bare hip to hold her in place. The breadth of his hand, always impressive, seemed to span much more of her than seemed possible.

"I guess it depends on what you like," she said, swallowing as his fingers pressed deep imprints into her skin.

His own swallow seemed to match hers, his throat bobbing hungrily. "What I like?" he asked. "You're standing there, gorgeous and naked and offering yourself to me, and you want to know *my* sexual preferences?"

She would have squirmed, but his hold on her was so complete that there was nowhere for her to go. "I'm not a mind reader," she said. "I usually prefer to be on top, but if you want—"

He pulled her onto his lap with so much force that she could only squeal and give in. It felt good to be back there, to have her thighs parted above his, this time with no barrier between them but a thin sheath of latex.

"I want *you*, Hailey," he said, his voice raspy. "Any way, anywhere, and anytime you'll have me. You have no idea what a gift you are."

She'd never been called a gift before, but that was exactly what she felt like as Cole dragged her mouth down to his and kissed her. There were no clothes left for him to remove, but that didn't stop him from unwrapping her, layer by layer.

The first thing he removed was any lingering embarrassment she might have felt at being naked and on top of the world's most gorgeous man. The way he kissed, deeply and intensely, as though he couldn't taste enough of her, left no room for any such thoughts. He might be sculpted like a god and forged of stone, but he was still just a man—and one who wanted her as much as she wanted him.

The second thing he removed was any shyness she might have felt at making her preferences so clear. He used his vantage point underneath her to explore her body at will, those million-dollar hands living up to their potential in all the best ways. He roamed over her breasts and along the tight pucker of her nipples, down the curve of her waist to the open splay of her thighs. His journey didn't stop until his hands were clutching either side of her hips.

"Can I—" he asked, waiting only until she moaned her agreement before lifting her up and guiding her over his length. He used his strength to enter her slowly, bringing her down inch by tantalizing inch until their bodies were one. It had been a while since Hailey had done this, so the fit felt tight and pleasant, a gentle stretch that almost sent her over the edge right then and there.

The last thing he removed were her inhibitions. They didn't go slowly, as they sometimes did, and she knew there was no chance she'd ever get them back again once this was over. The second she started moving against Cole, nothing mattered but the way their bodies fit together. His hands didn't move from their position low on her hips, holding but not controlling her, ensuring that their bodies stayed in full contact. He kissed and accepted, groaned and enjoyed, but in no way made any demands.

The demands were left up to her, and she couldn't have been more delighted about it. She moved and rocked against him, taking her pleasure as she saw fit. She hadn't been kidding when she said she preferred to be on top, to move at her own speed, but never before had she been given quite this much license. Cole let her ride him as fast or as slow as she wanted, arching her back when the mood dictated and stopping to kiss him whenever she felt the urge. He didn't rush her to climax and didn't take anything more than what she offered.

He did, however, warn her that there was a limit to just how godlike and made of stone he could be.

"I should probably tell you that I have about thirty more seconds of self-control, and then we're going to need to reassess the situation," he said, his words gruff with holding himself back.

She released a gasp as he slid one of his hands between them, expertly finding her clitoris and pressing against it. "I can work with that," she said. "Especially if you move your thumb about a centimeter to the right."

He laughed and obliged, his dimple so irresistibly charming that Hailey leaned down and dropped a kiss on it. Of all the things she'd done today—stripping naked in front of Cole Bennett, climbing on top of him, and taking her pleasure as she saw fit—that was the most surreal. She could kiss any part of him she wanted right now—lips or dimple or chest or cock. He was hers for the taking, wholly at her mercy and, if the dark desire in his eyes was any indication, more than happy to be there.

That thought was what pushed her over the edge. Well, that and the fact that he was doing something with his thumb that was rapidly whipping her into a frenzy. In that moment, she didn't care that he was a millionaire or a professional football player or that she could recite his entire career's worth of highlights without pausing for a breath. He was just a man who was enjoying her company and her body, who didn't ask for anything more than what she was willing to give.

Her orgasm came swiftly and explosively, brought on by the light drop of Cole's lips on the upper swell of her naked breast. There was nothing erotic about that particular kiss, but that was the power of it. It was sweet and spontaneous, the light touch of a lover of long standing rather than a man she'd met three weeks ago.

That was when he peeled away her final and last layer. Instead of taking his own pleasure as quickly as he could get it, he waited until the last of the rocketing sensation abated. And then, with painstaking deliberation, he lifted his hand to the back of her head and pulled her down for yet another kiss.

"We're not done yet, Hailey," he murmured. "Not even close."

This kiss was nothing like all the others. It was slow and careful and deep. It was a tangle of tongues and souls. It was so much more intimate than the joining of their two bodies, and that was reason enough for her body to explode in a second whirl of sensation.

She cried out, equally surprised and delighted at her body's response, only to have the sound swallowed by Cole's low chuckle.

"Well, that was easier than I expected," he said.

Hailey gasped, still full of so many sensations—and of *him*— that she had to force herself to breathe. "You're telling me. How many more times can you do that?"

"I don't know. I've never counted before."

She had no way of knowing if he counted this time, but she did. The answer was four. Four orgasms, each one building on the other and taking her more by surprise than the last. After three, when she was starting to feel a little light-headed, she was pretty sure he was just showing off, but she didn't have the energy to call him out on it. She could only cling to his neck as he took over, his hands gripping her hips and moving them in time to his own thrusts. These became much deeper as he neared his own release, instinct taking over reason and turning them both into nothing but skin and sensation.

Her heater was on way too high for this kind of athleticism, but the puppies needed the warmth. Besides, there was something intoxicating about her sweat mingling with Cole's. He was a man who spent literal hours refining and honing his body, pushing himself beyond endurance. Yet even he was spent by the time he was, well, *spent*.

She slithered off his lap and laid herself out on the couch, her legs propped on his, too exhausted to feel embarrassed at her cat-like stupor.

"I hope you don't expect me to move anytime soon," she murmured, eyes closed.

He chuckled and began stroking a hand up and down the length of her thigh with a light, negligent touch. Hailey imagined this must be what it felt like to be a puppy, to receive affection without cause or reason, and basked in it.

"You're a very odd woman," he said after a slight pause. They were the same words he'd said the day they'd met, and they carried the same caressing undertone. "Every time I think I have you figured out, you throw me a curveball."

She opened one eye. "Baseball metaphors? For shame. What would your coach say?"

"Fine. You throw me a long curl." He stopped stroking and laid his hand flat on her belly. It was warm and strong and made her wonder if five orgasms were out of the realm of possibility. "I came here expecting to have my wicked way with you, but there was nothing wicked about what we just did."

"Speak for yourself. I'm the one who sauntered around the house without any clothes on."

He laughed but refused to be derailed. "You always do that, Hailey—metaphorically, I mean. That's the thing I can't quite figure out. You don't pretend to be anything you're not, even when it embarrasses you. Even when it's hard."

"That's because *everything* embarrasses me. If I hid under a rock every time I said or did something I regret, I'd never see the light of day. Or have sex, probably."

She meant the words to be light and breezy, a conversational gloss over her very real discomfort with the world, but Cole wasn't done.

"You have no idea how lucky you are," he said without irony. If he noticed his use of that word—*lucky*—he didn't show it. "Not everyone has things so easy."

It was on the tip of her tongue to utter a sharp protest, to point out that when it came to easy living, he had the market cornered, but something about his expression gave her pause. He genuinely meant it. He genuinely believed that she had some kind of mystical good fortune that other people lacked.

If only he knew just how much she longed for what he had. Not fame and fortune and not millions of dollars in the bank, but a family. A safety net. A group of people with so much love for one another that it never occurred to them to question it.

"I thought my luck was what you came here for," she said, keeping things light.

"It was," he admitted and started to move his hand over her body again. It served as a distraction for them both. "But *this* is why I'm staying."

chapter
13

I GOT YOU ONE STEP CLOSER TO PROFESSIONAL AND PERSONAL glory. It's the least you can do." Cole stood in front of his friend, arms crossed and a firm set to his mouth. "Just come meet her— that's all I'm asking."

Garrett waved off Javier, a merciless massage therapist known to them all as Javi the Hammer, and propped his head on his hand. Spending the past forty-five minutes getting his muscles pounded hadn't put him in a conciliatory mood. "I got *myself* one step closer to professional and personal glory," he returned. "Did you forget the part where I scored two back-to-back touchdowns?"

"Only because I threw the ball directly into your hands."

Garrett snorted and turned his head toward the massage therapist. "Javi, of the two of us, who do you think carried the team last Sunday?"

Javier held up his hands—those instruments of so much torture—and backed away. "I'm not getting dragged into this one. The last time you guys started a friendly debate, I ended up with three extra patients. I like keeping busy, but…"

Cole whipped the towel from Garrett's naked and prone body. "Get up and put some clothes on," he commanded his friend. "You're coming with me, and I won't take no for an answer."

Garrett rolled over to expose every nook and cranny of his body and put his hands behind his head. "What's in it for me?"

Cole sighed. There wasn't much room for modesty in professional sports, but Garrett didn't have to be *quite* so comfortable flopping his junk around. There were only so many ways you could look at a man's testicles before they started to get old. And wrinkled.

"You mean, other than doing your best friend a favor?" He threw the towel at Garrett's head. "Reggie will be there."

Garrett bolted up and swung his legs off the table. "Why the hell didn't you lead with that?"

Cole didn't respond as Garrett reached for his clothes and shoved his limbs through them. He'd peeked at Garrett's schedule and knew his friend had a full day ahead of him—a meeting with the coaches before lunch and a full session with Aiko this afternoon—but mention of Regina apparently had him consigning all that to flames.

Not that he was judging Garrett for it. Cole was blowing off most of his day for the sake of a woman, too. He was *technically* doing it for the Puppy Cup, but that cover story was starting to wear thin. Hailey said she needed him for a few hours during filming next week, but that was it. He was only window dressing, a prop, a recognizable face that had long ago learned which angles worked best for the camera.

Well, that was too bad. She was getting his help whether she wanted it or not. Not only did he have a team of puppies to coach, but he'd gotten word that his prize Great Dane was causing all kinds of problems at the shelter that was housing her. Apparently, she'd become something of an escape artist, and they were at their wits' end trying to contain her.

Good thing he had a solution ready to go. One that, yes, gave him an excuse to see Hailey again, but that was only part of his motivation. He wanted to do something for her, give her a gift that mattered.

He wanted to matter, too, but he had a feeling that part wasn't going to be as easy.

"Tell me more about this favor you want from me," Garrett said as he slipped on his shoes and began doing up the laces. "You said something about a woman needing my help?"

"Not a woman, I'm afraid," Cole said. "A female, yes. A lady, maybe. A bitch, for sure."

"Fuck me." Garrett groaned. "You're talking about a dog, aren't you?"

Cole answered with a grin. "I could always call Javier back in here instead. It's your choice."

"At least I always know what kind of pain Javi is going to bring," Garrett promptly replied. "It's sneaky bastards like you I have to watch out for."

Cole wasn't sure what he'd been expecting from the Puppy Cup studio, but an abandoned warehouse transformed into a miniature football field, surrounded by bright lights, expensive equipment, and a crew of several dozen people wasn't it.

"Well, shit." Garrett summed up Cole's feelings in two easy words. They stood on the threshold, taking it all in with a bewildered air. "This is some production. Where are the puppies?"

Cole wasn't sure about the rest of the animals, but Philip came bounding across the fake grass that had been rolled out in the center of the warehouse. His teal bow tie was close to falling off, and his tongue was lolling out of the side of his mouth as though he'd just run laps around the building.

"Hey, buddy." Cole scooped up the animal and allowed him to wriggle into a comfortable position in his arms. "What have they been doing to you, huh? They told me today was just supposed to be an introduce-you-to-the-environment situation, not full-blown battle."

"What are you two doing here?" Hailey ducked underneath a

long pole being carried by two men in black lifting belts. "As if I don't have enough to do today already."

"Hello to you, too," Cole said, leaning forward and pressing a kiss on her indignantly parted lips. He could have blamed his impetuosity on the fact that she was once again wearing her favorite red Converse sneakers, this time paired with well-worn jeans and a men's button-down shirt that she'd tied in a knot at the waist, but that was just silly. Now that he'd seen this woman without any clothes on, nothing she covered her body with could move him.

Although that was a really cute way to wear her shirt. It emphasized the way her curves—

"It's nice of you to stop by and to, um…" Hailey trailed off with a stammer and a blush and a flustered gesture at her freshly kissed lips. Cole was tempted to do it again, but she pushed him backward with a hand against his chest and a deep, resolute breath. Not to mention the light of battle in her eyes. "But I thought I told you to stay away. We don't need you yet."

Next to him, Garrett coughed something that sounded like *Not my fault*, but Cole ignored him.

"It didn't seem fair that Philip gets to come but I don't," he said, heaving what he hoped was a pathetic sigh.

It didn't work.

"Philip needs to get used to the scents and sounds of this place—not to mention all the other puppies. We don't want them to be overwhelmed when we start shooting next week."

"What if *I* get overwhelmed?" Cole countered, undeterred. "I've never been on a miniature football field before. The yardage lines might confuse me."

"That's not new. You always start overthrowing when you're out by more than sixty yards anyway."

Hailey clamped her mouth shut as soon as she realized what she'd said, but it was too late. Garrett's guffaw of laughter was unmistakable, and Cole felt his own lips starting to twitch in response. Someday, he was going to sit Hailey down and make her list every criticism she had. His coaches could learn a thing or two from her.

Before he could come up with a suitable retort, they were interrupted by a twentysomething man in a headset. Cole recognized him as one of the PA grunts from the footage he'd watched—one of the many PA grunts whose teams Hailey had quickly and easily defeated in years past.

"Hey, Hailey? What do you want me to do with Cleopatra? She's already eaten through two of her leashes." He paused when he noticed who she was talking to, his mouth dropping open for a good ten seconds before he remembered himself and closed it again. "Oh. Wow. Penny wasn't kidding. You really are friends with them, aren't you?"

Hailey grimaced. "'Friends' is pushing it right now." She passed a hand over her eyes. "What happened to Fitz? I thought he was going to keep Cleopatra distracted until we were ready to bring her out."

"He was. But he's one of the only union technicians here today, so they asked him to set up the rigging."

"This is just what I need," she said in the same exasperated tone she'd used when she'd seen Cole and Garrett walk through the warehouse doors. "That puppy is going to be the death of me. Next year, we're not getting any animal who's bigger than a breadbox."

"Hey, now," Cole protested. "That's my *winning* puppy you're talking about. I told you she was top draft material."

Hailey's gaze snapped toward his, the steely glint impossible to ignore. "You're absolutely right," she said.

"I know I am."

"She's your problem, not mine."

"You say problem, I say secret weapon."

"Which means *you* should be the one to take care of her today.

I'd like to see how many leashes she can get through before you manage to quiet her down."

"I'm one step ahead of you." Cole laughed and darted out a hand to prevent Garrett from making good his escape. "In fact, it's why I'm here. Garrett offered to foster Cleopatra until the Puppy Cup airs. He wants to do his part to bring comfort and healing to the canine world."

"The devil I do." Garrett pinched Cole's hand until he was forced to let go. Garrett didn't leave, though, which was the most important thing. "What's wrong with her?"

Hailey narrowed her eyes at Garrett. Cole had been on the receiving end of that look so many times that he could only laugh to see it. For once, someone else was going to feel what happened when Hailey put on her full puppy armor.

"Nothing is wrong with her," she said, her voice clipped. "She's a large-breed, active puppy who needs exercise, that's all, and she's not getting it while confined in an eight-by-four kennel. Imagine if you had to live inside a concrete cage for most of the day, only allowed out when someone else decides they have the time and inclination. How would you like it?"

"Um."

It was probably the first time Cole had ever seen Garrett at a loss for words, and he was enjoying every second of it.

"You run every day as part of your training, right?" Hailey continued.

Garrett swallowed. "Why do I get the feeling there's no right answer to that question?"

Cole relaxed and stood scratching Philip while he watched the exchange, confident that things would turn out exactly the way he'd hoped. Other people might quail at the thought of asking favors of a man whose size and running capabilities had earned him the nickname of "Refrigerator," but not Hailey. Not when it came to this.

"I wouldn't ask you to do anything you're not comfortable with, and I know it's a big responsibility," she began, her voice a perfect blend of innocence and iron will. "But it would mean so much if you housed her until she gets adopted. It's only for a few weeks, and you and Cole could have playdates. So the puppies get comfortable being on the same team."

Garrett physically balked. "*Playdates?*"

"I meant man dates. Bro time." Hailey took her lower lip between her teeth and tried again. "Hypermasculine bonding rituals?"

Cole couldn't contain his laughter after that last one. "Just agree to the plan, Gar, and save us all the trouble. She'll win in the end. She always does."

"Nelson, could you go ahead and bring Cleopatra out so they can get acquainted?" Hailey asked the PA who was still standing with them. The poor guy looked torn between wanting to return to his work and awed at the opportunity to watch his coworker reduce Garrett Smith and Cole Bennett to putty. Cole didn't blame him. A few weeks ago, he'd have paid good money to watch such a spectacle himself.

"You aren't obligated to take her home with you afterward, of course," Hailey added to Garrett. "It's just an introduction. To see if you get along."

It wasn't just an introduction, and everyone standing there knew it. Garrett took the time to cast one last accusing glance at Cole before agreeing to be introduced to the Great Dane who was shortly to become his boon companion.

"I can't believe I bought that garbage you sold me about Reggie being here," he muttered. "Fucking Bennett."

Cole was about to hotly defend himself, but Hailey stepped up and did it for him. "He wasn't lying," she said, casting a quick look around the warehouse. "She's around here somewhere. She's been really helpful coordinating all the publicity between our people and yours. Honestly, I don't know if we'd have been able to do it without her. She's good."

Cole felt a surge of pride for his sister, who was, in fact, very good at her job, as his million-dollar contracts with various retail sponsors could attest. His pride, however, had nothing on Garrett's, who perked to a ridiculous degree.

"She *is* good, isn't she?" Garrett asked in a purely rhetorical spirit. "Maybe she'll have some ideas about what I can do with Cleopatra."

And just like that, Cole got his way, everything falling neatly where he wanted it. Garrett was the proud and temporary owner of a Great Dane mix. Hailey got another home for one of her precious darlings. And best of all, Cole finally had her to himself.

Well, except for Philip, but that could only be considered a point in Cole's favor. No woman—especially not one as enamored of dogs as this one—could reject a man holding a pit bull puppy in a lopsided bow tie. He was sure of it.

"Okay, now that you've proven your point, go away."

Or…maybe not.

"Is that any way to talk to the man who just rescued your run-away Great Dane?" he asked, setting Philip lightly on the floor. He used his free hand to grab Hailey around the waist and pull her close. As he'd hoped, the press of her body against his was warm and full of the curves so carefully hidden under the masculine cut of her shirt. "After all the work it took me to get Garrett here, I expected a hero's welcome."

"What do you think you're doing?" she said in the exact opposite of a hero's welcome. It was also the exact opposite of a woman-he'd-recently-slept-with welcome, but he was trying not to dwell on that part. "You're supposed to be at practice."

"I *am* at practice," he protested. "Puppies need to be trained, too. If they're all like Cleopatra, a lot more than I expected. I should probably have Reggie pencil me in for a few hours tomorrow, too."

"Cole."

The way she said his name was familiar in all the worst ways. It wasn't the sound of a woman who was happy to see him or even one who was playfully pushing him away. It sounded an awful lot like his mom whenever he'd begged to get out of peewee football practice so he could go ride his bike.

"Besides," he said, doing his best to ignore the condemnation he read in her face, "I wanted to stop by and see you. I haven't been able to stop thinking about Sunday night."

"Cole." This time, she said his name more as a plea, and the way her body melted against his proved that she was thinking about Sunday night, too. He responded automatically, tangling his hand in the hair at the nape of her neck and straining to pull her close. There were too many watchful eyes on them for him to do what he *really* wanted, but he was happy enough to have her in his arms.

Let everyone know. Let everyone see. He liked this woman, and he didn't give a damn who knew it.

"I *am* happy to see you," she said, her voice low. "And I'd be happy to continue this, uh, discussion at any other time. But you can't be here. I know your schedule. This isn't part of the plan."

Of course it wasn't part of the plan—the plan revolved around one thing and one thing only. *Football.* It was supposed to be the first thing he thought of when he woke up in the morning and the last thing he pictured before he went to sleep. It was supposed to drive him, shape him, *please* him.

Well, that was too bad. Yes, football had driven him for thirty-two years. And yes, it was so much a part of him that he wasn't sure where the sport ended and he began. But it didn't make him light up when it walked into a room. It didn't shyly ask him what his preferences were in the bedroom and then proceed to rock his world in ways he'd never imagined.

It didn't make him feel like an actual goddamn person for the first time in his life.

"The plan sucks," he said, inadequately summarizing his feelings. "I hate the plan."

Hailey smiled, but he could tell it wasn't enough. "The plan exists for a reason. You can't hang out here all day. Not only will your coaches call up Jasmine and demand my immediate termination but you're a distraction."

Cole was so used to drawing stares and double takes when he walked down the street that he barely noticed them anymore, but he paused long enough now to glance around him. There were, in fact, an awful lot of people in this part of the warehouse, their arms full of equipment and their eyes equally full of curiosity. Somehow, he didn't think it was the spectacle of a quarterback and his pit bull puppy they'd come over here to see.

"*I'm* not the distracting one right now," he said. "They're staring at you."

Hailey's whole body jerked, but he didn't relinquish his hold. If he was going to be banished to football practice for the rest of the day, he was going to enjoy this moment while it lasted.

"Only because you have your arms around me," she hissed, her cheeks starting to diffuse with color. "This is tempting fate—and luck—too far. They're probably waiting for lightning to strike me dead where I stand."

"Actually, I think they're waiting for this."

He dropped his mouth to hers for a kiss. Public displays of affection weren't something he indulged in very often, since the likelihood of it being captured on someone's phone and posted online was high. He didn't mind the *world* watching him kiss a beautiful woman, but he did mind his parents watching it. They had far too many Google alerts set up for his name to make him comfortable whisking random dates into his arms and putting on a show.

He felt no such qualms now—and even if he had, they would have disappeared the moment Hailey parted her lips to let him in, her own reservations equally null and void. She was always doing that, and it took him by surprise every time. It didn't matter if he was asking for entrance into her home or her body or even her heart. She opened the door every time.

He'd never known anyone so unguarded, so honest. So *real*.

She tasted like coffee and sugar, both perfectly ordinary and somehow the most intoxicating thing in the world. So, too, was the way her arms wound naturally around his neck and pulled him close. She was all heat and curves, and he could have stood there falling into those sensations for hours.

Unfortunately, the moment he dropped a hand to her lower back, his fingers unable to resist the downward journey toward her ass, a burst of catcalling and applause broke out around them.

That sound might not bother him, but Hailey reared back, her color heightened so much that he could practically count every freckle on her cheeks and across her nose.

"Oh my god." She dropped her arms from around his neck and released a low moan. "I can't believe I just let you do that. What's the matter with you? Don't you have any decency?"

He chuckled and dropped a quick kiss on the end of her nose. "Not a scrap. Besides, I don't think you have anything to worry about. From the sound of things, they liked it."

"They're a bunch of shameless wastrels who need to get back to work," she said, unable to meet his eyes. "And so are you."

"Actually, I'm going to agree with Hailey on that one." Regina's sharp voice hailed him from behind. He did his best to bite back a groan, but Regina either heard or sensed it. Given how well she knew him, it was probably the latter. "And don't give me that bullshit. I have four missed calls from the team offices, and I'm guessing you have twice as many."

"It was Garrett's idea," he protested, turning to face his sister. "He was desperate to foster one of Cole Bennett's famous Puppy Cup puppies."

Since Garrett could be seen in the background, wrestling with an enormous black puppy that appeared to be making a run for the nearest exit, this was an obvious lie.

"Garrett has already heard everything I have to say on this subject, so don't try putting the blame on him." Regina stood with her arms crossed, her foot tapping a staccato beat on the concrete floor. "Go *away*, Cole."

"All in good time."

"Go *away*, Cole," Hailey echoed, ranging herself on the side of his sister. She was still flushed and looking decidedly kissable, but Cole knew better than to make the attempt.

"Fine," he said, acknowledging defeat. He picked up Philip and pointed the puppy at his sister. "But I'm taking Philip with me. I want him to watch the replay of the Texas game with the rest of the team. It'll help with his own strategy. I don't know if you noticed, but I kind of killed it on Sunday."

Hailey muffled a laugh, but Regina only sighed. "I don't care what you do as long as you get back to work."

She meant it, which was the worst part of this whole thing. She didn't care if he publicly kissed Hailey or played puppy football or adopted twenty-seven different animals in the name of compassion—just so long as his game play didn't suffer for it. She was indulging him in this puppy plan, playing along in hopes that he'd work it out of his system, without recognizing it for what it was.

His parting gift. His way out. His goodbye.

"Oops." Regina glanced over Cole's shoulder and gave a sudden start. "I think Garrett just lost the battle with Cleopatra. She's heading for one of the side doors."

"Oh good," Hailey said with a complete absence of irony. "Hopefully, he won't catch her until she gets a few of her fidgets out. Try to distract him so she gets some exercise in."

Regina didn't find anything odd in this request. With a nod, she went off to assist and/or hinder Garrett's attempts to corral his new ward. Either way, Cole knew she'd be back—and sooner than he wanted—so he wasted no time.

"What are you doing after work?" he asked, grabbing hold of Hailey's hand and pressing it.

She stared down at the clasp of his fingers against hers. "The usual. Taking care of the puppies. Laundry. Maybe I'll go all out and rent a movie." She became suddenly suspicious. "Why? What are you doing?"

"I was hoping to visit my dad at the hospital."

All her suspicions melted away at once. "Good for you. He'll like that. Did you need me to puppy-sit Philip while you're there?"

"No," he said. "I was hoping you'd come with me."

She gave a slight jolt, but his grip on her hand was strong enough that she couldn't pull away. "What? Me? Why?"

He saw no reason to lie. "Because I can't get in the doors otherwise. My parents are afraid it's too distracting in these important Kickoff Cup times, so they've had me banned."

"They have not. You're just saying that to get me to agree."

He wished that were the case. Legally, he didn't think they could prevent him from entering the hospital and standing outside his dad's room, but he wouldn't put it past them to try.

"Please? They like you. They respect you." He gave a slight smile. "They fear you."

"They do not!"

He cocked an eyebrow. "Are you kidding? The woman with the power to break the curse? You could saunter in there and demand the keys to the city, and they'd move heaven and earth to make you a set. They're at your mercy, Hailey. We all are."

She didn't want to believe him. He could see it in the way she distracted herself by petting Philip, in the way she held her body at arm's length.

"You could just ask me as a friend, you know," she said. "Not everything has to be a curse-breaking, back-alley deal."

That was a matter of opinion. Curse-breaking, back-alley deals were what had brought Hailey into his life in the first place. He could swagger and preen all he wanted in an attempt to keep her, but he doubted it would work for very long. Hailey was a woman of substance, a woman who accomplished things that actually meant something. Strip away the trappings of football, and what did he have to offer in exchange?

Nothing. Nada. An underaccomplished and overhyped man with more money than was good for him, who'd spent his entire life in pursuit of someone else's dreams. Some deal that would be.

"Hailey Lincoln," he said, as one issuing a formal proposal, "will you please accompany me to the hospital after work tonight?"

"Why?" she asked again.

"Because I'm scared," he admitted. "Because you have experience with this kind of thing. Because it would mean a lot to me to have you there, and I don't think I can face it alone."

She didn't hesitate. "Of course, Cole. I'd be happy to go with you."

The tight feeling that had been mounting in his chest loosened. He hadn't realized until that moment how much he'd needed Hailey to agree—not just because it would make it easier for him to get in the door but because he genuinely wanted her by his side.

"Thank you," he said and meant it.

He might have added more, but he caught sight of Regina leading both Garrett and his reluctant new puppy back in the side door they'd escaped through. If Cole knew his sister—and he did—he had about two seconds before she came over and dragged both him and Garrett back to practice by the ear.

She was a woman of substance who accomplished things that mattered, too.

chapter
14

"YOU BOUGHT MY DAD *FLOWERS*?"

Hailey glanced down at the bouquet in her hand and blushed. She'd had to dash out on her lunch break to grab something, so the bouquet was a somewhat paltry assortment of gas-station carnations dyed in a variety of neon colors, but it had seemed better than showing up empty-handed.

"Doesn't he like flowers?" she asked. They were standing in a highly visible location outside the front doors to the hospital, and she couldn't help but be in awe of how easily Cole could ignore the reactions he elicited from the general public. She'd already heard several people comment on the likelihood of his identity—and even more disconcertingly, one man who seemed to know who *she* was.

"That's his good-luck charm," the man hissed as he'd pushed his heavily pregnant wife up the ramp in a wheelchair. "The one who's going to get them to the final game."

Either Cole had long since inured himself to the stares and comments, or he genuinely didn't care, because he leaned down and kissed her as though they were the only two people in the world.

"If a kiss like that doesn't get us in, I don't know what will," the wife hissed back.

Not surprisingly, Hailey was hot enough to melt the dusting

of frost on the ground by the time Cole let her go. She'd have liked to blame it on the embarrassment of being recognized, but that would have been a lie. Cole kissed the same way he played football—all in. This was no salutary peck on the lips. There was tongue and teeth and a warm hand on the back of her neck holding her in place.

She was being handled like, well, a football. And Cole *definitely* knew what to do with one of those.

How he could stand there afterward, looking so cool and gorgeous after a kiss that quaked her knees, was beyond Hailey. She might have quailed at so much poise in such a confident package if it weren't for the way he began anxiously toying with the cellophane.

"I don't know if my dad likes flowers," he said, plucking at the edges of the petals. "I've never asked him."

Partly to comfort him and partly to save the carnations from further damage, she slipped her fingers through his. Her small, unremarkable hand with its jagged nails and chipped polish felt insignificant against his massive, powerful one, but she could hear him letting out a breath of relief.

"They'll cheer up his room at any rate," she said. "I was either going with these or a pair of Cole Bennett socks to keep his feet warm. People in hospitals always have cold feet."

"There's no such thing as Cole Bennett socks," he protested.

"Um, yes there are. There's a local woman on Etsy who knits them. They have your little face on the toes."

Cole's demand to see a picture of the socks carried them through the hospital doors and past the reception desk. His incredulity at how inaccurate they were got them up the elevator. And Hailey's blushing confession that she had not just one but two pairs in her sock drawer had him laughing by the time they reached the nurses' station.

"If someone had told me I'd one day become a knitwear sensation,

I wouldn't have believed them," he said, barely noticing that they'd arrived at his father's door. "People should be ashamed of themselves."

She reached up and brushed imaginary dust from his shoulders and adjusted the perfectly straight collar of his pullover. The actions seemed to bring him comfort, though she wasn't sure why *he* was so nervous. She was the one crashing a family hospital room without an invitation.

Before she had time to check her own shoulders and collar, the door swung open. Mia rocketed out of the room and latched herself onto Cole's and Hailey's legs without hesitation.

"Uncle Cole!" she cried. "Puppy lady!"

And just like that, Cole regained his confidence. "Favorite niece!" he cried in the same excited tone. He planted a kiss on her forehead. "And before you ask, no, Miss Hailey isn't going to give you her phone so you can watch her puppies."

The girl's face fell in a comical frown.

"Because I'm going to give you mine." He drove his hand into his pocket and pulled out his cell phone. In a short space of time, he'd pulled up a full-color video of a very large and very well-lit living room. It was expensively furnished, although the puppy toys scattered around and the corner of a pristine white couch that had been eaten down to the stuffing displayed evidence of wear and tear. "You'll notice that the person watching Philip this evening is your nanny. She charges inordinate rates, by the way. I had no idea you were so expensive."

"She's not." Regina appeared at the doorway with a tight smile for Cole and a friendly nod for Hailey. "I told Velma to charge you double. She has a master's degree in child psychology, Cole, and it took me months to find her. I forbid you from turning her into a glorified dog walker."

"Desperate times call for desperate measures," Cole replied easily. He made a move as if to enter the hospital room, but Regina barred the door with her body.

"What are you doing here?" she asked, her voice dropped to a low whisper. "Have you lost your mind?"

"Hailey wants to see Dad."

Regina cast one look at Hailey and shook her head. "She does not. You dragged her here as a pretext."

"True, but now that she's come all this way, can you really slam the door in her face?"

Hailey had no qualms about what was expected of her. Cole's sister was right about her being used as a pretext, and if any other man had pulled this kind of stunt, Hailey would have supported Regina to the end of the world and back again. But Cole had asked her to come because she had experience with this, because he couldn't face it alone.

She knew that feeling too well to let him down now.

"We won't stay long," she promised. "We'll be in and out before any damage can be done."

"He's not supposed to be here." Regina glanced down at her daughter, who was fully absorbed in the live puppy feed, before crossing her arms and adopting a much firmer tone. "We talked about this, Cole. We agreed."

"I don't remember agreeing to anything." Cole's stance matched his sister's. They were a formidable pair, tall and gorgeous and built like twin stone parapets. "He's my dad, too, Reg. You can't keep me out forever."

"It's not forever. It's just until all this nonsense about the Kickoff Cup is done."

"The nonsense about the Kickoff Cup will *never* be done. You know that better than anyone."

Something about Cole's tone, which was veering on the edge, caused Hailey to step up. "You might as well give in," she said. Recalling Garrett's words from that day in her office, she added, "I don't know if you've noticed, but Cole can be a bit of a drama queen when he doesn't get his way."

Next to her, Cole choked on what was either outrage or a laugh.

"Of course, you could leave us standing in the hallway, but I should warn you that there were a whole gaggle of people pretending not to wait for us when we got off the elevator. If you don't let him in, he's likely to have the whole hospital shuffling by. They'll want pictures. Autographs. *Conversations.*"

She had no idea if it was the mention of Cole's dramatic tendencies or the adoring fans that worked, but Regina relented with a sigh.

"Fine. You can go in." She held up a finger in warning. "But make it a short visit, and don't do anything to increase his blood pressure. I mean it, Cole. He's not as strong as he looks."

"Are any of us?" Cole returned.

It must have been a rhetorical question, because he waited just long enough to nudge Hailey before stepping through the door.

The first thing Hailey noticed was that her floral display wasn't going to be noticeable among the many recovery gifts that had already been sent to Julian Bennett. Flowers, stuffed animals, balloons, and cards covered every bit of available space, turning an ordinarily dull room into what looked like a child's birthday party. Even the blankets covering the bed were festive, with a colorful quilt that looked to be handmade spread over the top.

Hailey's heart gave a lurch to see such an affectionate outpouring. Her own father hadn't survived the ambulance ride, but she had vivid memories of sitting alone in an empty hallway, holding a cup of vending-machine coffee that had long grown cold. Every footstep down that hall had sounded like it echoed from miles away, every fluorescent bulb highlighting the stark white of her surroundings.

This was much better.

"Don't say it," Cole said as he stepped in to greet his parents. As if sensing Hailey's hesitance, he put a hand on the small of her back and propelled her forward. "I know I'm not supposed to be here, but I came anyway. And I brought a present."

Hailey held out the flowers, thinking it was just like a man to take credit for something he didn't buy, when his mom opened her arms and pulled her in for a crushing hug. *Crushing* was the only way to describe it, since both Hailey and the flowers were pressed so hard against Paula's chest that neither of them survived the encounter. The flowers, because they lost almost their petals, and Hailey, because she couldn't remember a time in her life when a woman had held her like that.

Like the room, like this whole family, it felt so warm and so right that it was all Hailey could do not to cry.

"She's perfect," Paula said and with such sincerity that Hailey believed her. "We need a fresh face after the parade of gloomy doctors and relatives shuffling through here. We only just got rid of Julian's mother, and the Wegmores have been haunting us all week. Wouldn't you know it? They booked a trip to France in April. That's what we need—all those croissants and cassoulets added to the mix. I swear on everything I love, if Gertie takes to wearing a beret after this, I'm crossing her off next year's Christmas list."

Hailey gave a watery giggle, grateful that the older woman's chatter gave her a moment to compose herself. It was ridiculous for her to be the one bursting into tears—it wasn't her father lying in that bed, and it wasn't her life that would forever be changed by his condition—but that didn't seem to stop her.

"Stop hovering over the poor girl," Julian called from the bed. Despite the various machines and tubes attached to him, he looked remarkably robust, as though he might jump up and start giving her football pointers at any second. "Come over here and tell me what you thought about Cole attempting to run the ball from the fifty-yard line on Sunday."

"I'm standing right here, Dad."

"Hubris, I call it. He's never been light on his feet."

"I can hear every word you're saying."

"Then again, they did get a first down. Sometimes hubris has a place."

Hailey laughed to see the expression on Cole's face, but she also felt a pang of pity. If he'd come here hoping for a quiet, personal chat with his father, it was obvious he wasn't going to get it.

She, however, was. Cole's dad indicated the chair next to him, and this time with enough authority that she complied. He accepted the crushed flowers with a sniff, but it was a *pleased* sniff, so she was glad she'd brought them.

"Whatever it is you're doing to break that curse, keep it up," he said with a nod across the room at Cole. "We're so close to the Kickoff Cup that I can taste it. What's your secret? Chanting? Sage? Promises of your firstborn child?"

Hailey smiled and shook her head. "It has nothing to do with me, I'm afraid. I'm only a spectator, like you."

"Bullshit."

Cole's mom overheard this last part. "Julian, *language*."

Julian shot Hailey a conspiratorial smile. "Bullshit," he said, quieter this time. "Is it those dogs of yours? Regina told me you gave one to Garrett Smith this morning. If you're handing out lucky puppies, you might want to add Byrd to the list. His defensive tackles could use some work."

She couldn't resist. "Actually, there is a sweet little beagle who could use a place to stay for the next few weeks—"

"Hailey, I absolutely forbid you from giving my parents a puppy."

She sneaked a quick peek up at Cole. Although he still looked like a little boy who was afraid his parents were about to send him to his room, the lines on his face had relaxed. It was as if just walking into the room—seeing for himself that his father was sitting up and talking and well on his way to recovery—had calmed him.

Which, if his family had any sense, they would have realized last week. Hailey could think of fewer fates worse than to be shut out at a time like this. These people were obviously everything to Cole, and he was obviously everything to them.

Didn't they realize how precious that was? How rare?

"I wouldn't be *giving* her to them," she protested. "It's only temporary. And it doesn't seem fair that all your puppies get to enjoy rich, cushy homes before the big game while my puppies suffer deprivation and despair."

"A beagle?" Cole's mom pursed her lips thoughtfully. "They are awfully cute, Julian. And you know what the doctor said about you getting more exercise as soon as we get you home. You could take her for walks."

"Don't fall for it, Mom."

Both of Cole's parents ignored him. "It *would* be one of the lucky ones, right?" Julian eyed Hailey askance. "Not a knockoff?"

Hailey soothed her conscience with the thought that she wouldn't even *be* in this situation in the first place if Cole hadn't asked it of her. Besides, a cuddly beagle was just the thing a man recovering from a heart attack needed. Unconditional puppy love healed everything.

Well, almost everything.

"Absolutely," she promised. "A bona fide Puppy Cup puppy, and I'll even deliver her to your door myself—including all the supplies you'll need to take care of her."

She could see them relenting and was toying with the idea of seeing how Cole's grandmother and the Wegmores felt about temporary puppy custodianship when they heard a light knock on the door. It was followed by the entrance of a lab-coated woman in a bright-purple headscarf.

"Ghastly of me, I know, but I've come to see if I might borrow your visitor for a few minutes." The woman, whose name tag proclaimed her as Dr. Shad, spoke with a cultured British accent. "Actually, that's a lie. It never takes a few minutes, does it?"

Considering how hard Cole had fought to get into this room

in the first place, Hailey was afraid he would take the interruption badly. At sight of the woman, however, he broke into his signature dimpled grin.

"And here I thought I might be able to slip in and out unseen." He shook his head and heaved a mock sigh. "I should have known better."

Dr. Shad looked immediately contrite, her exquisite brows drawing together in the center of her forehead. "Oh no. Do you want me to pretend I didn't see you? I can, you know. I didn't tell any of them you were here."

"Them?" Hailey echoed.

"Children's ward," Regina supplied as she and Mia slipped into the room behind the doctor. She didn't quite meet her brother's eyes. "I meant to tell you, Cole, but for some reason or other, it kept slipping my mind. Amara wanted to know if you'd be available to make a round during one of your visits."

Hailey didn't believe that for a second, and one glance at Cole's face convinced her that he felt the same. But a man who spent as much time with a camera trained on him as this one didn't have to be told how to hide his emotions.

"Then it's a good thing I'm here now, isn't it?" Cole said lightly. He nodded at the doctor. "Of course I'll swing by."

Dr. Shad's face broke out in a bright smile. "You're sure you don't mind? I know your schedule is busy right now, and I'm sure you have a hundred other places to be, but—"

"I don't have anywhere else to be," Cole assured her. Hailey thought she detected a flat note in his voice, but it could have been her imagination. "I'm yours for as long as you need me. Hailey?"

"Of course." Hailey moved her hands in a sweeping gesture. "Go do your thing. I'll, uh, visit with your parents for a bit longer and then hang out in the cafeteria or something until you're done. I don't mind."

Dr. Shad clucked her tongue. "Don't be silly. You're more than welcome to tag along. You're that puppy woman from the news, aren't you? The one who's going to break the you-know-what? The kids will get a huge kick out of that. They love animals."

Hailey wasn't sure she liked this new reputation of hers, but there was little she could do about it now. Besides, that was the deal, right? Break the curse, save the puppies. All the rest of this stuff—Cole and his family and friendly doctors knowing her on sight—were just temporary perks. Emphasis on *temporary*.

"Come with me," Cole said, adding his fuel to the fire. "Please?"

She felt a little weird about it and might have protested further, but the thought of sitting and chatting with Cole's parents for the next hour was worse than following him around the hospital. Not because she felt unwelcome but because she had no doubt that they'd happily keep her company the entire time.

If she thought it was difficult not getting attached to the dogs she fostered, then not getting attached to this good-natured family was a hundred times worse.

"I'd love to," she said, giving in. Since she still had some dignity left, however, she turned to Julian and Paula and added, "But think about what I said regarding that beagle. The offer is an open one."

———

"He's something else, isn't he?" Dr. Shad—Amara, as she'd insisted Hailey call her—leaned on the wall next to her. It was brightly painted with underwater sea creatures and mermaids, all of which were frolicking down the hallway and through the nurses' station. "He comes down every few months to check on them."

"Yeah, he's something, all right," Hailey agreed, stifling her sigh.

It wasn't extraordinary for a man like Cole to include charitable hospital visits in his regular lineup of duties. Football players did it all the time—usually for publicity or as part of a Make-A-Wish promise—bringing a small bit of joy into the lives of kids who needed it the most.

But why did he have to be so good at it? There wasn't a camera or journalist in sight, and she doubted the Make-A-Wish Foundation ran to playing checkers with every child on the entire floor. Yet that was what Cole was doing, treating each game as a precious opportunity to hone his skills—and to lose in a spectacularly hilarious fashion.

He just *had* to be great with kids on top of everything else, didn't he?

"It's a nice thing you're doing, by the way," Amara said.

"Oh, um." Hailey was startled into a blush, fearful that her uncharitable thoughts were showing. "I don't mind…not really. They obviously adore him, and I'm not busy."

"Not the kids." Amara pushed off the wall and turned to face her. "The you-know-what."

Hailey couldn't pretend not to know what she was talking about. *The curse.*

"To be honest, I'm doing it more for the puppies than the Lumberjacks," she confessed. "We're expecting record numbers of viewers this year. My boss is over the moon."

"I'll bet." Amara pointed up at a nearby television. "It's all they've been talking about on the news."

Although Hailey would have gladly ignored the images moving across the screen, the alternative was to watch as Cole showed a child hooked up to an oxygen tank how to throw a football using a teddy bear as a prop. At least the news had the sound turned all the way down. She could pretend the newscaster was making sensible remarks about the lowering annual rates of puppy adoption and how viewers could make a difference.

"Here," Amara said, squashing Hailey's plans by pulling a remote from out of her pocket. "You probably want to hear what they're saying."

The newscaster paused on an image of Cole and Hailey

standing close to each other in front of the puppy drafting board, both of them laughing at something Penny had said. From the way their bodies were angled, they gave the appearance of holding hands. For a brief, shining moment, she hoped it was just her imagination, but Amara finished switching off the mute function.

"…which begs the real question: Just how far is Cole Bennett willing to go to break the curse?" asked the female anchor, whose blond bob cut across her shoulders like a scythe.

The male anchor chuckled. "It looks to me like he's willing to go all the way, Karen."

Hailey felt her cheeks burn. "Oh dear. I didn't know word would get out so quickly."

Amara laughed. "You didn't think you could keep this sort of thing a secret for long, did you? He's Cole Bennett, darling. The only thing the fans care about more than his game play is his love life."

"It's not like that—" she began, but she stopped herself short. Technically, it *was* like that. That night on her couch was burned into her memory, tingling in places better left unmentioned while in the presence of so many children. So was the fact that Cole showed every intention of wishing to repeat his performance, kissing her in full view of the world and bringing her to the hospital to visit his father. Sometime in the past week, their relationship had officially become a thing.

The idea of their entanglement was reinforced when Cole glanced up from the child's bedside and caught her eye. The smile he gave her—that deep, dimpled, *devastating* smile—was impossible to ignore and even more impossible not to return.

So she did.

Amara saw it, of course. The doctor sighed as though she'd made the match herself. "I can't wait to tell my husband," she said. "He was heartbroken when the Lumberjacks lost to the Timberwolves last year. Whatever you're doing, keep it up. I haven't seen Cole like this in a long time."

"Like what?" Hailey couldn't help asking.

"Not as stiff in his movements. Not as worried about his shoulder. We noticed it in the game last Sunday, but I chalked it up to the new pain meds his doctors switched him to." She beamed at Hailey. "I'd much rather it be this. I worry about him."

"Worry about him?" she echoed.

"Of course. Don't you?"

Hailey didn't have a chance to follow up before the man in question finished his last game of checkers and came up to join them.

"Well, I think that's all of them." Cole bore the self-satisfied look of a man who'd just made two dozen children deliriously happy—and enjoyed himself in the process. "Now they're pumped up and likely to keep your nurses awake all night. You're welcome."

Amara chuckled but showed no signs of dismay as she accompanied them down the hallway. Hailey wished she could say the same. Dismay was all over her—in the careful way she took each step, in the way her head whirled, in how her heart wouldn't stop pounding.

"Thank you for playing along," he said, the words low and next to her ear. "I know this wasn't how you planned to spend your evening, but they're good kids."

"Of course," she murmured back but without fully registering his words. She was too busy trying to make sense of this new information.

Cole was stiff? There was something wrong with his shoulder? *I'm supposed to be worried about him?*

"Was that our faces I saw on the news just now or another pair of puppy-drafting professionals?" he asked, louder this time.

Amara answered for her. "I was telling Hailey that you two have been the highlight all week. Everyone is sure that this year's Kickoff Cup will be the one to end all Kickoff Cups."

"Excellent," he said, more to himself than to either of them. "That's exactly what we were hoping for."

Hailey stepped back as Cole and Amara made plans for a future visit to the hospital as soon as the Kickoff Cup was over and Cole's schedule returned to normal. It was a perfectly ordinary conversation, and nothing about it should have upset her, but her stomach felt tight at every word.

"What's wrong?" Cole asked as soon as Amara walked away and the two of them were left alone next to a waiting room filled with half-finished puzzles and several battered board-game boxes. "What did Amara tell you to make you look like that? Whatever it was, she was lying."

Hailey smiled but didn't allow herself to be charmed. "She sang your praises, naturally. What else could she do? You're really good with those children."

"I like kids. I always have." He gave a half shrug, dismissing his generosity as easily as if it were a pair of socks with his face knitted into the toes. "Well, what's next? A cup of coffee and a snack cake in the cafeteria? Some of those strange vending-machine french fries that only seem to exist in hospitals? I brought you all this way. The least I can do is feed you."

She could appreciate what he was trying to do, but she'd never been any good at pretense, and she wasn't likely to start now. There was no way she could eat vending-machine fries without giving everything away.

"I think I'd like to go home, if that's all right with you," she said. "It's been a long day, and if there are going to be reporters showing up at my house demanding that I throw dice or nail horseshoes over my doorstep, I need to start preparing now."

Cole laughed but didn't press her. "Just open the door and let them get a glimpse of your living room," he said. "If that doesn't convince them you mean business, I don't know what will."

chapter
15

THERE WERE TIMES WHEN HAILEY WISHED SHE HAD A BIGGER house so she could have a roommate—not just someone to split the bills with but someone to split her time with, someone to make the place less lonely on cold, gray winter nights when the whole world seemed to be asleep.

This was not one of those times.

"It's a good thing I tried—and failed—to take up knitting last year," she said to the puppy she held cradled in the crook of one arm. Rufus had just finished a very satisfactory bottle and emitted a sleepy yawn. "This red yarn adds a touch of pizzazz to the whole thing, don't you think?"

Now that he was sated and cozy, the puppy answered by drifting off to sleep. Which was for the best, really. Even a three-week-old runt of the litter would find it easy to judge her for this latest exploit.

She stepped back and viewed her handiwork.

If she were to die right here and now, her body found on the living room floor after being eaten by puppies, the world would assume she was the stalkeriest stalker in the history of stalkerdom—and with good reason. The wall in front of her was a collage of Cole Bennett images and articles she'd printed out, along with various stat sheets and injury reports. It covered the past six years of Lumberjack football highlights, including a breakdown of the plays in every single Kickoff Cup playoff game to date.

It also included a complete medical history of labral shoulder tears, surgeries, and recovery rates.

"I can't believe I didn't see it before," Hailey said as she absorbed the whole. She'd always been a visual learner. Seeing the timeline laid out like this, the cause and effect attached with red yarn that was, okay, possibly a little over the top, had a way of clarifying her thoughts into one cohesive whole.

Cole Bennett had been on a steady decline ever since his shoulder injury. It was such a mild rate of deterioration, disguised by the regular ups and downs of a six-month season, that it had gone unnoticed by the public.

And by her.

"If he continues like this, he has one, *maybe* two more years in him," she said to the sleeping puppy. "But they won't be his best ones. No wonder he's been taking all those unnecessary hits. His time to throw is almost double what it used to be."

She lowered herself to her couch and fell back against the cushions, seeing but no longer seeing the facts laid out in front of her. Everything was starting to make a dizzying amount of sense.

The way Cole had been so stiff after wrenching open those elevator doors, the things Amara had said at the hospital...*what he's doing with me in the first place.* She wasn't just some good-luck token to break the curse; she was a piece in a much bigger, much more final puzzle.

This was probably Cole's last chance at a Kickoff Cup.

Her phone rang with such portentous timing that Hailey was almost startled into dropping Rufus. Fumbling to reach into her back pocket without disturbing the puppy, she was too breathless and distracted to take note of who was calling her.

And by the time she said "hello," hanging up was no longer an option.

"Oh good! You're up. I was afraid it might be too late to come over. It's not too late to come over?" The female voice on the other end of the line laughed and added, "I should probably add that I'm literally standing on your doorstep. I brought bubble bath. And wine."

Hailey bit back a groan. Although part of her was elated that Penny had followed up on her promise to visit for a long soak in her bathtub, a much larger part realized that there was no way she could hide all this evidence in time. Even if she tore it down and shoved it into the fireplace, evidence littered her living room.

"You're not saying anything. Is Cole there? Sigh once for yes and twice for no. I can leave the wine and go."

"I'm alone," Hailey said, and since there was no use trying to pretend she was the calm, cool, and collected woman she'd always aspired to be, she went to answer the door.

As promised, Penny held a bottle of wine in one hand and a bottle of bath soap in the other. She was also wearing a long coat thrown over a pair of sweatpants, her hair up in a sloppy bun. It was the first time Hailey had ever seen her look anything but perfectly dressed and coiffed.

"I know." Penny glanced down at herself with a grimace. "But I have terrible cramps and couldn't face the prospect of wallowing in bed with a heating pad by myself. It's really okay? You can say no."

This burst of sentiment—one Hailey had often felt herself—caused her to pull the door the rest of the way open. So many times, she'd wished for something exactly like this. A kind smile to allay the symptoms of PMS. Someone to share a bad night in comfy clothes with.

A friend.

"It's really okay," Hailey said. "To be honest, I could use the company. It's been a day."

She was rewarded with Penny's bright smile. "You're telling me.

I'm always exhausted after eight hours of chasing down all those puppies. I don't know how you do it, day in and day…" Penny's voice trailed off as she reached the living room, the bottles she carried falling heavily to her sides. She spent a long moment absorbing the charts and images, the red string that crisscrossed everywhere.

It was on the tip of Hailey's tongue to defend herself, but Penny spoke up before she could formulate a reasonable excuse.

"Oh my," she murmured. "If I go in the bathroom, am I going to find a dead body?"

Hailey couldn't help a giggle from escaping. Given the mayhem all around them, it wasn't an unreasonable question.

Encouraged, Penny shot a smile at Hailey over her shoulder. "I'll help you bury him, of course, but it's not going to be easy. He must weigh at least two hundred pounds."

"Two twenty-one, actually," Hailey said and immediately clamped her lips shut. That kind of detailed information wasn't going to help her look *less* like a murderer.

Penny, however, only laughed. "You are, without a doubt, my favorite person in the world. Here. Trade me the puppy for the wine. I think you should crack this bottle immediately."

Hailey did as she asked, but not without first saying, "I thought you came to use my bathtub."

"I did. But this looks much more important."

A strange torrent of emotions moved through her as she took the bottle of wine to the kitchen and poured them each a full glass, careful not to wake Bess and her sleeping litter as she did. She should have been ashamed of what was happening in the other room—of having a living, breathing person witness the inner chaos of her mind—but she wasn't. She was a little embarrassed, yes, and would probably never live it down, but the feeling foremost in her heart was relief. She wanted to talk to someone else about this. She *needed* it.

It had been too long since she'd allowed herself that liberty—of needing another person, of putting herself in their hands and trusting that she'd be safe there.

Nine years too long, in fact.

"Here." Hailey returned and handed Penny the glass of wine. The other woman was standing in front of the poster board, rocking back and forth in an effort to keep Rufus asleep. "There's also some ibuprofen and a heating pad in the medicine cabinet. Help yourself to anything you need."

Penny nodded her thanks but didn't make a move to grab either item. She sipped her wine and kept staring at Hailey's handiwork instead.

"He's hurt, isn't he?" she asked. "That's what this is. You mapped his injuries."

Hailey nodded, surprised that Penny was so quick to pick up on the trend of her thoughts. "It's not inju*ries* so much as inju*ry*, but yes." She pointed at a red dot on her timeline. "This is when he hurt his shoulder in the game against Atlanta. He was only out for a few weeks, but everyone knew he wouldn't be back up to full strength without surgery."

"That was the year they missed the Kickoff Cup by a field goal, right? The same year we moved to the new warehouse for filming."

"Yeah." Hailey took a long, fortifying sip from her own glass. She didn't know enough about wine to recognize the type or the quality, but it tasted dark and sweet. "That's also when everyone started getting fixated on the curse. It was always whispered about before, but things really took off after that. Poor Cole."

Penny murmured her agreement, but Hailey doubted whether her friend understood the extent of the burden that must have been put on him after that. She doubted whether *anyone* did. Even she treated the curse more like a joke than an actual problem, a sort of mystical punchline to explain away every loss and every bad play, but Cole must have felt the pinch of it every time it was mentioned.

He already took so much on himself—made himself responsible for his team and his family, adopting puppies when she asked and showing up when he was needed—that this additional burden must be crushing him.

"So what does this all mean?" Penny waved her wineglass in a vague gesture over the living room. "Why are you awake at ten o'clock and channeling your inner Dana Scully?"

Hailey laughed, but it was a short-lived sentiment. "Cole took me to visit his dad at the hospital today."

"Oh wow." Penny paused. Hailey assumed she was going to say something about what a coup that was for the status of her relationship, that things between them must be getting serious, but what came out of the other woman's mouth surprised her. "Was that hard? After losing your own father the way you did?"

Hailey could only stare at her. She didn't recall ever telling Penny—or, indeed, anyone at the office—about her personal history. It wasn't the sort of thing that came up in the natural course of conversation, and it had never occurred to her to volunteer the information over the water cooler. Not about her father and *definitely* not about her life before that.

"Don't look so surprised. I know a lot more about you than you realize." Penny nuzzled the puppy in her arms. "I mean, I don't know your exact weight or have a collage of your career highlights, but you can't work next to a person for six years without figuring a few things out. You're not a difficult person to read."

"One-forty," Hailey replied, somewhat dazed. "And the only career highlight I have is this one."

Cole Bennett. With the Kickoff Cup Curse. In her living room.

"Well, there you go. Now I know everything." Penny bumped her with her hip. "Except what happened at the hospital today."

To be honest, Hailey wasn't too sure about that herself. Cole hadn't seemed either surprised or upset when she didn't invite him over afterward, but that was likely because he was exhausted. After a full day of practice, a visit to the Puppy Cup warehouse, and the emotional upheaval of visiting with his parents and all those kids, it was a wonder he had the energy to keep standing.

But he did. He always did.

"Nothing happened," Hailey said, more to herself than to Penny. "In fact, he was peak Cole Bennett—the perfect son, a smiling football player, a generous brother."

"But?" Penny prompted.

"But I'm starting to think that I'm not going to be able to break this curse after all." Hailey stared at the board in front of her, her heart sinking. She was no statistician, and there was always a chance she'd miscalculated, but she hadn't been wrong about Cole Bennett yet.

For six years, she'd watched him play football as a way to stay connected to her dad. For six years, she'd counted on him to carry her fantasy team to success. For six years, she'd seen that dimpled, smiling face on television and felt that a world where he existed couldn't be such a bad place.

He'd given her so much for so long and without even being aware of it. And now that he needed something from her—a boost of luck, a little confidence, a chance to take that one final step to victory—she wasn't sure she could return the favor.

"I'm starting to think that all the puppies in the world won't be enough."

chapter
16

"HOW SOON IS TOO SOON AFTER SEX TO ASK FOR A FAVOR?"

Cole lay on his back in Hailey's bed, watching the rise and fall of her head where it lay on his chest. His fingers toyed with the peaked tip of her nipple, his touch teasing and light. He would have liked to stroke her back to arousal for another round, but he didn't think he *could*. There was physical exhaustion, which he knew well, and then there was physical-sexual-emotional-existential exhaustion, which was what being with Hailey seemed to elicit.

Sex with her wasn't just sex. It was hot as all hell, yes, but it was also a reminder that there was more to the deed than friction and a few well-timed thrusts. Friction and well-timed thrusts could get the job done, obviously, but only if the goal was to get off.

Cole didn't want off. He wanted to be on and under and below. He wanted to be *in*.

"Is that favor opening up the bedroom door and letting Philip in?" Hailey asked without opening her eyes. She arched her back into his touch, the jut of her breasts so enticing that his exhausted cock gave a twitch. "Because if so, then it's definitely too soon. I love puppies, Cole, I really do, but this is one place I refuse to let them in. I don't care how many sad eyes you give me."

Cole sighed, but only because *his* eyes weren't the ones that had looked so sad. From the way Philip had watched the pair of them shut the bedroom door, clutching his battered football as they left him not-alone with Bess and Rufus and five other adoring playmates, you'd have thought they were locking him up and swallowing the key.

"There are some places a cold, wet nose should never go," Hailey said. She smiled and added, "You were just in most of them."

"I still think you were unnecessarily cruel to shut the door on the poor guy, but no, that's not the favor." Cole shifted so he was propped up on Hailey's padded gray headboard. Of all the rooms in her house, this one felt the most like her. There was no sports memorabilia and no puppy gear, but the two of them lay sprawled on a large bed piled high with plush blankets. Oversized abstract paintings and more pillows than any human being needed added to the appeal, as did the bright-yellow vase full of daisies.

It was comfortable. Cozy. The sort of place you could stay for hours.

The sort of place they *had* stayed for hours. Cole was already late for the team shuttle to the airport. He'd have to hightail it directly there or miss the charter plane to Los Angeles.

"Would you be willing to watch the game with my parents this weekend?" he asked. His hand dropped from her breast to the soft undulation of her stomach, his fingers now circling her belly button instead of her nipple. "My dad's home and doing well so far, but I'm worried about how he's going to handle it. This is the closest the Lumberjacks have come in a long time, and if anything should happen—"

Hailey stilled the movements of his finger by placing her hand flat on top of his. They'd enjoyed this once already, with her hand guiding his between her legs, and the results had been enough to send him off in a spiral of lust and longing that hadn't been sated until he was deep inside her. This time, however, there was nothing playful about her touch.

"Nothing is going to happen," she said, her words heavy with emphasis. "You're going to play football the same as you always do."

"Yes, but—"

"You might win," she continued. "Or you might lose. Either way, it's still just a game."

"I know, but—"

"Cole." She struggled to a sitting position, her hair breaking around her shoulders as she looked down at him. He wanted to reach up and play with the tumbling locks, to trace the pattern of freckles he was coming to know so well, but that would be more of the same. Her breasts, her belly, the silken strands of her soft brown hair—they were distractions. They were *pleasant* distractions, and he'd have appreciated more time to indulge in each one, but Hailey would never let him get away with it. *He* might be willing to cast his career and all its obligations to the wind for a chance to be near her, but she was a lot less needy than him.

It was a lowering reflection, but what could he do? He needed. He wanted. He yearned.

Fuck. He couldn't remember the last time he'd yearned for anything as much as he yearned for this woman.

"You know it's not going to be the end of the world if you guys don't make it, right?" She sounded an awful lot like a teacher talking to a particularly obtuse student. He knew, because he'd *been* a particularly obtuse student. "It'll be disappointing, obviously, but nothing will have changed. You'll still be you. I'll still be me. And your father will handle the disappointment and move on with his life."

Cole had to bite back a snort at that last bit. He and Hailey might not undergo an irrevocable change if the Lumberjacks lost, but he'd never hear the end of it from his dad. *If* his dad survived long enough to deliver his lecture, that was.

"You can take your beagle over when you go," he said, knowing that of all the arguments he might make on his own behalf, none of them would have as much impact as this one. "Hell, take two beagles. Take a whole litter."

She remained unconvinced. Naked and sitting cross-legged among the piles of blankets and pillows, so appealing that his chest and cock ached as one, she was nonetheless immovable.

"It's not that I mind spending time with your parents," she said, softening as she reached for his hand. She twined her fingers through his. "In fact, I kind of adore them. But what good can I do? I'm not his doctor. I'm not his daughter. I'm just some random woman he met less than a month ago."

Cole didn't know how to explain that her presence had a way of bringing out the best in people—including the irascible, inflexible man who'd turned his only son into a football star through sheer force of will. She was kind and warm and giving. She didn't make any demands that weren't related to puppies. She'd charmed both his parents and the entire city of Seattle, making them believe she had the power to change a twenty-year curse using nothing but her heart.

"You're not a random woman," he protested. "You're the good-luck charm, remember? If you're there, he might be able to keep his stress levels in check."

A grimace flashed over her face before being replaced by a much firmer set of the mouth. He knew that look, knew even more that it presaged her refusal to be budged and/or charmed, but he tried anyway. Lifting her hand, he turned it over and pressed a kiss directly in the center of her palm. She tasted of salt and sex, of the hours they'd spent in each other's arms.

"Please, Hailey?" he asked. "I've done nothing but take from you since we met, I know, but—"

"Fine," she said. "I'll go. It's fine."

Nothing had ever sounded less fine unless he counted the time he'd thrown a football at his mother's favorite sea-glass vase when he was five years old and shattered it to pieces. Only the fact that his aim had been dead-on had saved him from the grounding to end all groundings.

"This will all be over soon, and then we can take a break from football and family and everything attached to them," he said. "Maybe we can even take that trip to Ibiza. It's beautiful this time of year, remember?"

She gave a slight smile at the memory of that first conversation in her office, when he'd been so sure that all it would take was his fame and a little charisma to get his way, but it didn't reach her eyes. "That sounds nice."

"I mean it, Hailey." He put his hand under her chin and tilted her face up, his voice thick with sincerity. "There's more to me than football, I swear. In the off-season, I'm a totally normal guy. I go to movies and eat cheeseburgers and take Mia to story time at the library. I throw barbecues for my friends. Sometimes, I even…"

He let his voice trail off, uncertain whether or not this was the right time to reveal his deepest, darkest secret. *Sometimes, I pretend that life can always be like that. Sometimes, I imagine a world where story time with Mia is enough.*

"Sometimes…?" she prodded.

He bit back a sigh. Although he liked to think that Hailey saw him as more than Cole Bennett, quarterback extraordinaire, they probably weren't there yet. In this oasis of her bedroom, where there was nothing related to football on the walls and they were just two naked and sated people sharing a bed, it was easy to ignore the rest of the world. But as soon as he opened that door, he'd be surrounded by reality once again.

Lumberjacks. Regina. His parents. Football.

"Sometimes, I even whisk beautiful women away on vacation against their will," he said, planting a kiss on her lips. "Consider yourself warned."

Although Hailey accepted the kiss readily enough, her mouth

as soft and willing as it always was, there was a wariness in her expression that indicated how little she believed him.

"I'll send Reggie to pick you up on Sunday," he promised. "She was planning on coming to the game with the team, but she thinks it'll be better if she stays home. Between the two of you, you should be able to keep my dad calm. And, Hailey?"

The wariness in her expression traveled over the rest of her body, transforming her from warm, postcoital pliability to a woman leery of being asked for yet another favor.

So he didn't ask one.

"Thank you."

———————

"Um, this is *your* house."

Regina pulled her car—a luxury hybrid as expensive and decadent as Cole's—into the driveway of her Queen Anne home. "Yes, it is," she agreed. She pointed over her left shoulder. "And that one belongs to my parents. Don't say it… I know. A grown woman living next door to her mom and dad is pathetic on so many levels."

Hailey paused in the act of exiting the car, but not for long. The soft-eyed beagle she held on her lap tumbled out and began tugging excitedly on the end of her leash. Unlike Philip, who cowered in fear at everything that moved, and Cleopatra, who was on a mission to cover as much ground as possible at all times, Nala had no personality quirks that made her ill-suited for life in an animal shelter.

She was, however, one more mouth to feed and one more kennel to clean. The man who ran the shelter where Nala had been housed was sad to see her go but also grateful. There were already twelve more dogs on the waiting list ready to take her spot.

"That's so nice for Mia," Hailey said as she tugged Nala toward the house in question. It was just as large and just as expensive as

Regina's, but there were fewer kids' toys and more carefully tended rosebushes in the backyard. "And for you. It must be wonderful to be able to pop over and see them anytime."

Regina glanced at her over the top of the vehicle, amusement pulling her bright-red lips into a pursed half smile. "'Wonderful' is one word for it."

Wonderful was the *only* word for it, but Hailey knew better than to attempt an explanation. She'd tried with Cole the other day and had failed miserably. If there was an easy way to tell a gorgeous, naked man that she was in danger not just of falling in love with him but with his whole family, she hadn't yet come across it.

The smart thing to do would have been to dig her heels in, refuse to watch the game with them, partition her life and her heart to keep them safe.

Yet here she was, her heart fully exposed. *Again.*

"Cole and I didn't grow up here, if that makes a difference," Regina added. "He bought our parents this house with his signing bonus. He bought my house when Mia was born. I'm terrified of what will happen if anything else goes up for sale on the block. It'll be a full Bennett takeover."

Hailey's chest clenched at the image this conjured up. Not of all those millions of dollars invested in real estate but of a family so tied together in affection that their lives were completely entwined.

"I know… Talk about champagne problems," Regina said. "I'm well aware of how it sounds, but I don't know how else to explain our family. From the moment Cole was born, everything my parents have and are has been tied up in him. His practices and his games, his training and his career… We used to go on vacation every year to whatever football camp he got accepted into. One of them was a stone's throw from Disneyland. I could practically see the castle from the field."

"You didn't get to go?"

"Oh, I went. One of the other moms took a bunch of the siblings one day." Regina sighed. "Want to guess how many of them grew up to become managers, agents, coaches, and football support staff? Actually…no. Don't. It'll just depress you."

Hailey cast a sharp sideways glance at Regina, but the other woman's concentration was fixed on her house. "You don't like being Cole's manager?"

"Of course I like it. He's my brother. I wouldn't have anything if it weren't for him. None of us would."

Regina didn't sound sad or upset; her voice carried more resignation than anything else.

"Come on in," she added with a gesture toward her parents' house. "It'll just be the two of them this time, I promise. No extended family bombarding you with boring stories and nosy questions."

Hailey knew that was supposed to reassure her, but there was something a lot more personal about her descent upon the Bennetts this time.

"Mom?" Regina opened a side door painted to look like a gingerbread cookie. "Dad? Where are you? Hailey's here with your new puppy. She's a looker, so be careful."

Nala *was* a looker, and Hailey had no doubt that she'd be one of the first puppies adopted after the show aired, but she was also in a new place with hundreds of exciting smells. Her keen ability to sniff out dropped pieces of food kicked in before they'd made it all the way through a neatly organized mudroom to the kitchen beyond. With a nose pressed firmly to the floor and her tail stiff with excitement, she took off in pursuit of her quarry—*any* quarry.

"Oh dear." The leash fell from Hailey's clasp, and the puppy took off. From the looks of it, this was a very clean and well-run home. The Bennetts might not take Nala's sure-footed enthusiasm very well. "Reggie, will you see if you can grab hold—"

She didn't have an opportunity to finish. No sooner had she

crossed the threshold into the kitchen than she was being pulled into yet another hug.

Cole's mom held the embrace much longer than most people could get away with, heedless of the puppy snuffling around her kitchen floor. There was nothing awkward or strange about it, nothing that made Hailey feel as though she was anything but welcome.

"Thank you for coming," Paula said, the words muffled by the press of her mouth against the top of Hailey's head. "I feel so much better having you here today. We all do."

"Would you like to meet Nala?" Hailey asked as soon as she was released and once again gained control of her crushed lungs. Her color felt heightened, but for once in her life, it wasn't because of embarrassment. This flush was nothing but pleasure. "She's a little hyped up right now, but that's because of the drive. She'll settle down once she has a chance to gain her bearings."

"Of course she will," Paula said with nothing but earnest reassurance.

Regina finished removing her outerwear and entered the kitchen with a purpose in her step. "Hey, Mom." She kissed both of her mother's cheeks in greeting. "Is Mia upstairs?"

"In the playroom watching cartoons, I believe." Paula bent down and patted Nala, who found much to interest her in the flour-covered apron placed at nose level. The puppy wriggled and licked and used her big brown eyes to her advantage. "What a darling she is. Julian can take her for a walk after the game. He'll hate it, but it'll be good for him."

"What's that?" came a shouted reply from the next room.

"It'll be good for you to walk the dog!" Cole's mom shouted back. She shook her head. "He can hear me just fine, but I'm being punished for the egg-white omelets we had for breakfast. Head in there, hon, and take him these carrot sticks."

A plate of immaculately cut carrots was placed in Hailey's hand.

She felt a little overwhelmed by all the warmth and noise of this house, but Cole's mom winked and gave her a light push. "Go on. He won't throw the carrots at *your* head." She laughed and pursed her lips before adding, "Well, he might, but you won't mind that. It means you're one of us."

"Thank you." Hailey got up on tiptoes to press a kiss on Cole's mother's cheek, unable to resist the impulse. The older woman smelled of roses and sandalwood. "I appreciate this more than you realize."

Cole's mom laughed and returned the kiss. "Well, aren't you the sweetest thing to ever walk through my door. It's only a puppy."

She wasn't thanking her for Nala, but explanations were impossible.

"I hope I'm not intruding," Hailey said as she entered the next room, which looked to be some kind of television room and den rolled into one. "I brought you a...snack?"

Cole's dad glanced up from the recliner chair he was seated in, an exact facsimile of the one he'd been in at Regina's house. He smiled when he saw Hailey and frowned as soon as he noticed the plate in her hand. "Drat that woman," he muttered, but he gave an impatient wave until Hailey handed him the plate. "Does this look like food to you?"

"Carrots are very good for your cholesterol."

"Bah." His grunt of displeasure said everything, but Hailey noticed that he picked one up and ate it. He also patted the recliner next to her, accepting her presence here with the same ease and friendliness that his wife had. "Come and sit with me. Tell me what you think of this next play."

Hailey sat on the arm of the chair rather than the seat, but her attention was soon sucked into the television. Even though it was far too early for the Lumberjacks' game to start, the screen depicted—what else?—football. The reception wasn't great, and there was a grainy quality to the footage that made her think it wasn't of recent origin.

As she watched the crimson-colored jerseys move around the field, she found that age didn't much matter. It was a good game—a great one, if that throw from the quarterback was any indication—and she found herself getting sucked in.

"Holy crap," she said as the spiraling throw shot down the field like a bullet. It landed in the hands of a waiting wide receiver with so much strength that the receiver gave a slight start before catching himself and hurtling toward the end zone. "That was like nothing I've ever seen before. These are the Mountain Lions, right? From Pullman? College ball?"

"They sure are." Julian cackled. He held out a carrot for Hailey, who took it and crunched down before she realized what she was doing. "You've got a good eye."

She did have a good eye, and there was something about the way the quarterback—number eight—moved to accept his team's enthusiasm that gave her a start. Cole had played for the Mountain Lions during his college career, but that couldn't be him. The images were too old, the helmets too outdated. In fact, they looked like they probably used a similar football to the one encased in glass on her mantel.

Hailey popped the rest of the carrot in her mouth and leaned closer to the television, her eyes narrowed as she watched the next few plays. Everything about number eight looked and felt like Cole. The way he moved and the way he threw, even the way he did a little victory dance when he made a good play.

She wasn't sure when it clicked, but she whipped her gaze from the television to the man next to her, her eyes wide. "That's you," she said, no hint of a question in her voice. "You played for the Mountain Lions. You were better than Cole."

Julian's deep, cackling laugh confirmed her suspicion and made her realize what she'd just said. Her color rose, but she didn't—as she might have in the past—cover her mouth or backtrack in the name of embarrassment.

"I know I shouldn't say that, but it's true." She shook her head as she took in the man next to her, his large frame at one with the chair. "You were amazing. Did you go pro?"

"I told Paula there was a reason I liked you," he said, chuckling again. "And it's not because you're eating these damned carrots for me. Keep watching."

Wordlessly, Hailey took another of the carrot sticks held out to her and returned her attention to the screen. She was no stranger to old, outdated games, since her dad had enjoyed replaying football footage from the seventies and eighties almost as much as he liked watching it live. In addition to going by an entirely different rulebook, the players weren't as big or as fast—a thing that might have given them a disadvantage in modern ball but that made for a much more interesting game.

However, size and speed weren't an issue here. Julian Bennett—how had she never heard that name before?—was both big and fast, and he handled the ball with an ease that looked ingrained. Hailey could feel herself straining as he prepared a trick play that would either end in an incredible score or disaster for the team.

The disaster won out in more ways than one.

"Good God!" She leapt from her seat and held a hand to her mouth as Julian took a blunt-force tackle from the side. The visuals weren't so detailed that she could see the bones breaking in his body, but there was no doubt in her mind that something had been shattered.

Something *had* been shattered, she realized—and not just in a physical sense. That looked like the end of a dream.

"I'm so sorry," she murmured. "That looked awful."

"It was. I sprained both knees and damaged my back so that it never worked the same again." Cole's dad spoke without emotion as he lifted the remote and switched the television off. "A damn shame, really, but what can you do?"

Hailey didn't have an answer for that, so it was for the best that the skitter of puppy claws on hardwood provided a distraction. Nala darted into the room with a speed that made Hailey feel incredibly smug for having chosen this puppy for her own team. The beagle might be small, but she was fast and she was sneaky. Hailey could respect those qualities.

"You little monster." She scooped Nala up before the puppy could make a leap for the carrot sticks. "You're not supposed to misbehave until after I leave. That way, they won't give you back."

"Give her *back*?" Cole's dad made a grunting sound and extended his arms for the puppy. "Why would we do a thing like that?"

Because puppies were a lot of work. Because their cute little faces lost some of their appeal after the tenth late-night bathroom howl. Because Hailey had no real right to ask anything of these people.

"Oh dear." Paula came in, wiping her hands on a dishrag. "That's one fast doggy."

"I'm sorry." Hailey winced. "If she's too much work, I can—"

"Nonsense." Paula came forward and handed the rag to her husband, who laid it out on his lap like a bed. "We meant it when we said we'd be happy to do anything you need. If you think that animal is quick on its feet, you should have seen Cole at that age."

"He was fast," Julian said with a nod at the black screen of the television. "Not as fast as me, obviously, but we knew he had something special."

Paula gave a cluck of her tongue. "Have you been showing her old footage of your glory days?" She turned her attention to Hailey. "Don't pay any heed to it. To hear him tell the tale, he was the greatest quarterback to touch a football. Balderdash, I call it, when Cole outstripped your yardage by the time he was eighteen."

"They measured things differently back then."

"A yard has always been a yard."

Julian pointed a finger at his wife in warning, but his expression was one of affection. "Woman, don't contradict me when I'm trying to show off for a pretty girl."

Hailey's blush started to mount. "Oh, you don't have to—"

"I was good," Cole's dad said with a nod. "Probably one of the best. I was devastated when I took that hit, but if there's one thing all those months of convalescence were good for, it was to lay me flat on my back. There's no better position for—"

Paula swatted at him. "Julian! Don't you dare."

He dared. With a wink, he turned to Hailey and said, "That boy being born saved my life in more ways than one. He's everything I was—and more, because he doesn't quit when he's down."

"Oh geez. Are you talking about Cole again?" Regina appeared in the doorway, her daughter on her hip. As soon as Mia saw the puppy, she dashed into the room with a squeal of excitement. "You've got them started now. You'll never hear the end of it. Mia, love, you have to be gentle."

"I *am* being gentle," Mia said as she settled herself into a comfortable position on the floor and began twirling her fingers at the puppy. "Ask the puppy lady."

The puppy lady watched Nala and Mia closely and, finding nothing amiss with the way the girl handled the animal, nodded her approval. "She has a very natural way with dogs."

Regina rolled her eyes in Hailey's direction with a warning glance. "Don't start. I cannot and will not add a puppy into the mayhem that is my house."

"That's not what I meant."

"That little puppy you have earmarked for Mia is cute, but we're a strictly dog-free house."

"Of course you are. I won't mention it again." Hailey made the motion of a zipper over her mouth.

"After seeing all the trouble Garrett has gone through to tame that giant beast you saddled him with, you can hardly expect me to open my arms and my home."

Hailey couldn't help but laugh. "Cleopatra is a bit of a handful. I hope he's not too upset with me."

"He's not. I was over at his house a couple of nights ago, and he was training the animal to run on his treadmill. I couldn't tell which of them was enjoying it more."

Hailey's interest perked. She didn't know this woman well and knew Garrett Smith even less, but something about the casual mention of being at his house struck her. She was struggling to come up with the most tactful way to ask about their exact relationship when Julian told them both to quiet down.

"Those puppies of yours are on the TV," he said, pointing. Sure enough, he'd turned on the pregame show, where scenes from the Lumberjacks locker room showed Philip and Cleopatra sitting alongside their temporary masters. Philip's teal bow tie was askew, as it almost always was, and Cleopatra was tugging on the hem of Garrett's jersey, but the image was a powerful one.

"There are a lot of these little guys waiting for good homes," Cole said as he lifted Philip to his cheek. As if aware that he was being watched by millions of people around the world, Philip lolled out his tongue and gave Cole a shameless kiss. "Not just the puppies appearing at the Puppy Cup in a few short weeks but in shelters across the country. Even if you can't open your home to one of them, you can open your wallet. Every little bit helps."

Hailey felt every part of her heart swell. Cole was plugging her puppies on live television. Cole was plugging her puppies on live television without being asked.

And oh, he looked good doing it—smiling and slightly disheveled, his uniform stretching tight across his thighs. It was bizarre to think that she'd had those thighs intertwined with her own, more bizarre still to accept that she was sitting in his parents' house and getting ready to watch him play.

"Well," Paula said, summing up Hailey's feelings. "If that doesn't get you a place for every puppy in the country, dear, I don't know what else will."

————————————

It was, without a doubt, the greatest game Cole Bennett had ever played.

That was the consensus of the room where Hailey watched, anyway, and it could be argued that she was sitting among the country's leading experts. She'd always had a critical eye where he was concerned, but it was nothing compared to the running dialogue his dad made the entire time.

Every play was analyzed from start to finish. Every decision was run through an internal checklist. Even the smallest feint was ranked according to ones made in the twenty-odd years that Cole had been training.

"Did you see that, Hailey?" Julian demanded when Cole performed a seven-step drop back that resulted in a forty-yard gain. "Not a single stumble. Not a moment's hesitation."

"Yes, I saw," Hailey soothed. It had only taken her a few minutes to realize that her role today was to calmly agree with everything Julian said. She *could* have argued with several of his points, especially the ones regarding Cole's tendency to resort to an unbalanced T-spread under pressure, but she kept her lips sealed. She'd promised to do her best to keep this man relaxed and alive, and she intended to uphold her end of the bargain.

After what Cole had done for the Puppy Cup—and for her career—it was the least she could do. There were no fewer than fifteen excited texts on her phone from Jasmine and the rest of the office. Apparently, the phones were ringing off the hook.

"You did this," Julian said, turning to her with a beaming smile. Nala had long since fallen asleep on his lap, and despite his occasional outburst and jerk of excitement, she seemed content to remain there. "You and the puppy. You and *all* the puppies."

"We're only up by three points," Hailey pointed out. "And it's not even halftime yet. Let's just wait and see how things roll out, shall we?"

"Why?" Julian asked sharply. "What do you know? What do you see?"

Across the room, Regina caught Hailey's gaze and rolled her eyes. Sometime in the hour since kickoff, both of Cole's parents had decided that Hailey's supposed luck extended to clairvoyance. They kept peppering her with questions about the game's outcome. No matter how many times she disclaimed such a power, they remained steadfast in their beliefs.

"I don't see anything," Hailey said. "But I don't like the way the referee is so quick to call an interception."

"Yes, that's true. Isn't it true, Julian?"

"I never liked that guy. I don't trust his face."

Confident that she'd bought Cole—and his dad—a little wiggle room, Hailey sat back in her chair and fixed her eyes on the screen. She'd never admit it to anyone in this family, but she was watching Cole's movements much more keenly than she had in games past. Now that she knew the exact scope of his shoulder problems, she could see it in every move he made and every play he called. To outward appearances, he was as much in control of himself as he always was—precise and powerful, making the most of his team and their cohesiveness.

But there was a hesitation to his movements that she hadn't noticed before. He guarded his right side with more care than usual. It was a feeling she knew well. He was protecting himself.

"Take the opening, boy!" Julian jumped up from his chair as one of the offensive tackles from the other team stumbled and left a huge gap. "This is your chance!"

Hailey also leapt up, but only so she could catch Nala, who was understandably alarmed by this sudden movement. Her attention was so taken up with making sure the puppy didn't fall to the floor that she missed the crash.

She heard it, though. Not the literal blow but the effect it had on all those who were watching. Julian, Paula, Regina…even the announcers on the television audibly winced. Hailey couldn't bring herself to look at the screen, so she looked at the faces of Cole's loved ones instead.

It was a mistake. Bodily impact was a physical thing—a tangible thing. Hailey had spent far too many years watching football to be squeamish about a blow or two. The things those men went through on the field were sometimes akin to battle, but she was inured to it by now. The expressions of mingled dismay and despair, the way Mia's face scrunched up and tears—lots of them—began to fall, was a much more difficult thing to witness.

"Is Uncle Cole okay?" the girl asked, her voice small but unmistakable in the horrified silence of the room. "How come he's not getting up?"

"He'll get up," Julian said, his mouth a grim line. "Give him a second."

"He always gets up," Paula agreed. Her mouth wasn't grim or a line. It wobbled, and in such a way that Hailey's blood turned cold. She had yet to see this woman anything but cheerful and resolute, even when standing over her husband's hospital bed.

Inadvertently, Hailey looked to Regina. Of all the people in this room, Cole's sister was the one who was closest to him. She was his manager and his friend, the person he turned to first when things went wrong.

What she saw in the other woman's face didn't just turn her blood cold. It froze it in her veins.

He's not getting up.

Hailey clutched the puppy in her arms and forced herself to look at the television. By now, the announcers had managed to control their first outbursts of emotion, all three of them starting to speculate on what they'd witnessed and the likelihood of Cole pulling himself together again. She tuned out their voices and focused on the image of Cole instead. He was moving, which was good, but not in a vertical direction. He thrashed and shifted, his right arm hanging limp at his side.

Having so recently watched the footage of Julian Bennett's career ending before her eyes, Hailey had no difficulty identifying what she was witnessing right now. A few days ago, she might have joined this family in willing Cole to his feet, in hoping that he'd rise up to the challenge and see this game through to the end, but she knew better now.

There would be no more games after this. Oh, he might try another surgery or a long rehabilitation, but there were limits to what the human body could endure—limits to what it *should* endure.

"I'm going to make some tea," Hailey announced. No one in this room wanted tea, but it was the only thing she could think of to offer. "Mia, do you think you could show me where it is?"

Regina picked up on Hailey's meaning right away. "What a good idea," she said. "Mia, love, could you help Hailey in the kitchen? You know where Grandma keeps the tea stuff, right?"

Mia nodded, her eyes still stricken and wide, but she took the hand Hailey offered. Nala wriggled to be let down, but the puppy would serve as a good distraction if the girl started to feel overwhelmed. Taking a page from Cole's book, Hailey tucked the puppy under her arm in a football hold. She wasn't nearly as strong as Cole, but the puppy instantly calmed down.

In the manner of all four-year-old children, Mia was easily distracted by the task of locating and making the tea. Hailey had to fight every instinct she had not to peek at her phone or switch on the television mounted next to the refrigerator, but she managed it. There were already enough people in this house doing their best to turn the accident into a tragedy.

"You're very good at this," Hailey noted as Mia set about arranging plates and spoons on a tray. "You must have a lot of tea parties."

The girl nodded as she reverently placed a bowl of sugar in the center. "Uncle Cole likes tea. We drink it this way." She went through the motions of sipping from one of the porcelain cups, her pinkie finger held exaggeratedly in the air. She only got about halfway through before her eyes started filling with tears. "Did he have a heart 'tack? Like Grandpa?"

Hailey wasn't sure to what extent she was licensed to console a child who wasn't her own, but she took the initiative anyway. "No. He hurt his shoulder, that's all. He might not be able to play football for a while, but he'll be okay."

This served to calm Mia's fears, but that obviously wasn't the case when they returned to the other room. Regina stood off to one side, her phone pressed against her ear and a low-voiced, urgent conversation taking place. Paula was wringing her hands and watching Regina talk, lines of anxiety around her mouth. And Julian was staring fixedly at the television as though he could will his son into wellness.

Hailey felt like shaking these people. Okay, so it was bad. Cole wasn't going to finish the game. The Lumberjacks could very well lose the game. The curse had struck and struck hard, and Hailey was likely to bear the brunt of the blame.

But he was *fine*. He hadn't suffered a concussion, and from the sound of it, the only thing the announcers were worried about was the likelihood that he'd be able to finish out the season.

"Give me that lucky puppy," Julian demanded, holding out his arms. "Marshall is going to have to pull this game out of his ass if we're going to break the blasted curse. Lord knows he's no Cole."

Hailey wasn't sure about handing over a soft, delicate creature when Julian was obviously so upset, but at a nod from Paula, she gave in. The puppy seemed to soothe the older man, calming him down as he ranted and fumed at the television screen. Nala also seemed to exert a beneficial influence on the Lumberjacks as they sent their backup quarterback in. Tucker Marshall was no Cole Bennett, it was true, but he was a perfectly good football player in his own right. He was young and untried, but he was also hungry. How could he be anything else? For the past few years, he'd been relegated to the role of Cole's much-less-exalted shadow.

The rest of the game passed in something of a blur. Hailey drank tea with Mia and took Nala out for regular bathroom breaks. She made sandwiches for Cole's parents and listened as Regina tried to find out what was happening in the X-ray room.

No one asked her how she felt, and no one solicited her opinion on Cole's condition. No one commiserated with her unenviable position as the woman whose luck had caused the Lumberjacks' star quarterback to get hit so hard that his shoulder dislocated during the final playoff game. In fact, by the time the Lumberjacks scored a touchdown in the final minute—six points that not just broke the curse but shattered it in a blaze of last-minute glory—it was almost as though she wasn't in the room at all.

And that was fine with her. Julian was anxious but alive. Against all odds, the Lumberjacks had won the game and were officially in the Kickoff Cup. Cole might not play football again, but he was going to be okay.

In her world, that counted as a pretty good day.

"He'll be back," Julian said as Hailey discreetly made arrangements for an Uber to pick her up and take her home. She had the feeling this family was going to need some time to reconcile themselves to their new future. "A week of rest, another to regain his strength, and he'll be ready for the Kickoff Cup."

Hailey could only stare at him, so painfully optimistic, so unwilling to accept the evidence before his eyes, but he wasn't finished yet.

"Just you wait, Hailey," he said reassuringly. "Nothing keeps a Bennett down for long."

chapter
17

"IF YOU LOVE ME, LOCK THE DOOR." COLE DIDN'T WAIT FOR HIS sister to make it all the way inside his condo before issuing orders. "Put up a Do Not Disturb sign. Tell Mom and Dad that I'm asleep and likely to stay that way until next year."

Regina clicked the door behind her. She *didn't* lock it, but her next words allayed his fears. "Relax. I left them at home. Lucky for you, the doctor told Dad he needed to take it easy for the next few days. Mom is standing guard over him as we speak."

"I guess doctors do have their occasional uses," Cole said with a rueful glance at his arm. The sling he wore was a pain in the ass but a lot less invasive than he'd feared. Regina tossed him a paper-wrapped sandwich, at which point he grinned and added, "So do sisters. Thank you. I'm starving."

"Yeah, well. Eat it fast. Dr. Hampton wants to see you."

He was in the middle of biting into a giant turkey sandwich—which, he noted, had been deliberately garnished with kale—so he had to respond by shaking his head and swallowing.

"No can do," he said when all Regina did was stand and stare menacingly down at him. He pulled a piece of turkey from his sandwich and tossed it to Philip, who sat ready and waiting at his feet. "My better half and I are needed at the Puppy Cup set this afternoon. Hailey's orders."

"Cole."

"Reggie."

"He's your team doctor. You can't avoid him forever."

"I made a commitment to Hailey. I can't avoid her, either. Not when the appearance of luck is more important than ever. We're going to have to transition hard if we want to convince the team—and Seattle—that she still has the power to break the curse."

Regina showed signs of glaring at him for as long as it took for him to give in—a thing she had done in the past and could very well do again—but he ignored her. Okay, so he should *probably* make an appearance at the Lumberjack medical offices, and he was sure Coach and Aiko had a whole list of inspirational pep talks ready to go, but that was too bad. Marshall could handle things on the quarterback front for a day or two. Cole had puppies to coach.

"She'll be here to pick me up any minute, so you'd better wrap up whatever this is." Using his left hand, he twirled a finger in his sister's general direction. "You might be able to intimidate me into doing what you want, but you won't be able to move her. She'll somehow end up getting her way *and* giving you a puppy, and then where will you be?"

Regina didn't, as he'd hoped, take offense at his words and storm off in irritation. Instead, her expression grew somber, and she lowered herself to the couch next to him, careful to avoid the spot that Philip had eaten through.

"What are you doing, Cole?" she asked. "What is this really about?"

He wasn't sure which *this* she was referring to, but he suspected it had less to do with football and more to do with Hailey. He also knew that once Regina started in on this topic, it wouldn't end well for either of them. They'd had their fair share of squabbles over the years—in their profession and with their family history, how could they not?—but the one thing they'd always avoided was giving each other relationship advice. If Regina thought his choice of supermodels in the past was somewhat questionable, she kept it to herself. When she'd had a one-night stand with a stranger and ended up pregnant with Mia, he'd tactfully refrained from reproach and thrown himself into helping raise his niece instead.

"You're veering on dangerous ground, Reg," he said, surprised at the note in his voice. Even Philip seemed to pick up on it, his recognition of that tone causing his ears to come up and his stance to drop.

"I'm just saying. Mom and Dad are starting to wonder. All this puppy stuff will be over in a few weeks, and then what?"

He didn't have an answer for that, just like he didn't have an answer for what was going to happen when all this football stuff was over in a few weeks, either. At this point, all he could do was take one day, one hour, one minute at a time.

In this particular minute, he was getting very tired of his sister.

"Unless you have something other than sandwiches to contribute, I won't keep you," he said. "I don't think they need you at the set today."

She didn't take the hint.

"It's not a big deal, and it won't take long," she persisted. "You can go with Hailey afterward. It's just a follow-up X-ray, a few tests to make sure you'll be recovered enough to play in the Kickoff Cup. Dr. Hampton is really optimistic about your chances."

The sandwich turned to dust in Cole's mouth, and it wasn't because of the kale. He tossed the entire thing to Philip, who lost no time in carrying his precious scrap to the farthest corner of the living room lest one of them decide to take it back. The food would probably slow the puppy down and make him useless in the game this afternoon, but Cole couldn't find it in him to care. As if his team had ever had a chance against Hailey's in the first place.

He didn't know the first thing about puppy football. All he knew was the human variety, for all the good that was going to do him now.

"Knock-knock!" Hailey poked her head in the front door, a welcome distraction in a day—a week, a year—that was starting to look decidedly shitty.

Cole could barely remember a time when he could look at her and find her merely cute. Those adorable freckles, the tinge of color on her cheeks, the worn red shoes—they weren't the sort of qualities he'd sought in the past, but he'd have been damned if he could go without them now. When he'd been carried off the football field, knowing the tackle that had dislocated his shoulder was the end of the line for him, the only thing he could think of was that he wished Hailey were there with him.

She was a comfort and a delight to his soul. She was sexually responsive in ways that most men only dreamed of. She represented a world where laughter and puppies and her no-nonsense practicality made everything else in his life feel like an overblown, ridiculous sham.

He loved her.

The thought struck like a blow almost as hard as the one that had felled him on the field. His head spun, and his chest contracted so tightly that he couldn't speak right away. All he could do was watch as Hailey glanced back and forth between him and Regina, her cheeks starting to redden.

"Oh dear," she murmured. "Is this a bad time? I can come back. There's a coffee shop down the street—"

"Don't be silly," Regina said, her words terse enough to make Hailey wince. "Cole has clearly made his decision. I can tell when I'm in the way."

"You're not in the…" Hailey's voice trailed off as she caught sight of Cole. He wanted to move his facial muscles into the shape of a smile, to reassure Hailey that he wanted nothing more than to pull her into his arms and show his appreciation the best way he knew how, but although he *might* be able to manage the smile, there would be no suave embraces. His shoulder fucking hurt.

"I can be ready in five minutes," he promised as he rose to his feet. Both Regina and Hailey made a move as if to help him, but he wasn't an invalid. He could stand without toppling over. "Reggie was just going."

She did go, but not very happily. "I can put them off for *maybe* a day, but you have to head in tomorrow. They need to update the injury report, and there are all kinds of interviews lined up—"

"I know, Reggie."

"I'm just saying. The Puppy Cup will buy you a little time, but not much." Regina glanced at Hailey and held back a sigh. "Make sure you use it wisely."

Hailey tactfully busied herself with greeting Philip and thus avoided any kind of conflict with Cole's sister. He was more grateful for that than he could say. For the past three days, his life had been a barrage of excessive emotion. His parents, his coaches, the press, even the doorman in his condo building—everyone was demanding to know what his plans were and how likely he was to fulfill all their hopes and dreams for the Kickoff Cup.

He was tired and he was sore. He just wanted to play with his puppy and his woman. Why was that so hard for everyone to understand?

"I told you this was a bad idea," Hailey said as soon as Regina disappeared out the door and they were left to the peace and quiet of his condo. It was the first time Hailey had been here, but she showed no surprise at the surroundings. Or awe. She proved it by taking a quick glance around and wrinkling her nose. "This isn't a very puppy-friendly place to live, is it? I should have asked before I gave you Philip. I hope Garrett's house is less...pristine."

Cole laughed for the first time in days. Of course Hailey would be just as unimpressed by the expensive and overdone furnishings in his home as she was about his career. She saw everything through the lens of her puppies. If it couldn't feed them, house them, or play fetch with them long into the night, it was essentially valueless.

God, he loved that about her. He loved *everything* about her.

"My cleaning woman threatened to leave me about six times, but she brings in home-baked doggy treats for Philip, so I suspect she's mostly talk." Unable to resist the urge any longer, Cole strode across the living room and planted himself in front of Hailey, pulling her into a one-armed hug.

She smelled, as she always did, like lavender and puppy formula. Since he couldn't greet her in the suave, debonair way he wanted, he buried his face in the top of her hair and inhaled instead.

"What are you doing?" she asked, her voice muffled by where it was pressed in his chest.

"Smelling you. Do you know it's the one thing that's been keeping me sane?"

"The way my hair smells?"

"The way your hair smells. The way your hair feels. The way your hair tickles my lips and my nose and makes me want to kiss every part of you."

"Well, then." She put her arms around his waist and hugged him back. "I'm glad I buy the expensive shampoo."

He laughed again, their bodies shaking as one. Even so slight a movement as laughter caused his shoulder to twinge, and although he quickly subdued his reaction, she noticed.

"Oh God. I'm sorry." She stepped back, taking her delicious scent and the warmth of her body with her. "How is it?"

He'd only had an opportunity to chat with her briefly on the phone since the accident, but he had no doubts that Hailey knew down to his blood pressure and oxygen levels how he was doing. Not only did she have a direct pipeline to his parents, but she would have made it a point to read the stats and articles, to listen to the news reports and assess his condition from a distance.

Which was why he lied. He didn't want to talk about stats and articles. He didn't want to discuss his condition. He wanted to kiss her and film a bunch of puppies *not* playing football. In that order.

"Not bad, actually. A little sore, but that's only to be expected. Dr. Hampton thinks I'll be as good as new in no time."

She didn't draw close enough for him to kiss, and Philip, finishing his sandwich, demanded immediate attention. She gave it to him, which only served to put yet another barrier between them. Lifting the puppy and curling him to her chest, she planted a kiss on his head and examined Cole as though he was wearing his skin inside out.

"How is it really?"

He shrugged, using his right shoulder to prove that things weren't as dire as they looked. The truth of the matter was, they *weren't* as dire as they looked. It had only been a partial dislocation, and—miracle of all miracles—his labrum hadn't torn. The scar tissue and the surgery had done their job, holding him together even when he'd been hit from the side at full speed by a three-hundred-pound man intent on bringing him down.

From a medical standpoint, he'd be fine in about six weeks. In any other man, the injury would be a minor nuisance, an irritation in an otherwise full life. In *this* man, it meant he was probably never going to play pro ball again.

"I'm giving it a few days to rest and heal, and then we'll see," he said. "It's too early to tell. My dad and Dr. Hampton are sure I'll be fine for the Kickoff Cup."

He was no longer able or willing to accept the puppy barrier that Hailey had placed between them. Philip or no Philip, he was going in for his kiss. Since his arms were only half-functional and Hailey's were holding a dog, he had to go in face-first. It wasn't a play he was used to running, which was what he blamed for the quick way Hailey turned her head at the last second.

His kiss went awry, hitting the side of her mouth, but it was enough. He wanted to taste her. He wanted to feel her. He wanted to forget, for one goddamned minute, that—

"I know about your shoulder, Cole," she said, turning her head again. This time, his kiss landed somewhere near her ear. Never in his life had he felt—or acted—so awkward.

He was Cole Bennett, dammit. His kisses went exactly where he wanted them to. He swept women off their feet and made them whimper with desire. He'd held *this* woman in his arms and devoured her moans as she came time and time again beneath him.

"Would you stop wriggling?" he asked. "I'm trying to kiss you."

"I know you are," she replied without smiling. "But I think we should talk."

His heart gave an erratic, heavy thump, but he strove to keep things light—to pretend that this was an ordinary day in the ordinary course of an ordinary relationship.

"Oh yeah?" he said. "About what?"

"I know about your shoulder, Cole," she repeated. Even though this was one of the topics she normally thrived on—football—there was no sign of a metallic spark in her eyes, no playful challenge in the way she looked at him. She set Philip down and didn't speak again until she'd regained her stance. "How you've struggled since your surgery, how hard you've worked to hide that it's weakening. How this was your last chance at a Kickoff Cup, and now your career is most likely over for good."

Cole had very recently been thrown to the turf and piled on by more men than anyone should feel on top of him at one time, but that was nothing compared to the impact of Hailey's words.

She knows. She sees.

Thank holy fuck. I don't have to pretend anymore.

"It's bad, isn't it?" she persisted with a nod at his sling. "Worse than the news is saying?"

He nodded, not yet trusting himself to speak.

"They have you down as questionable on the injury report, but there's nothing questionable about it." This time, she wasn't asking. "It's over. For good."

"There's always a chance things could miraculously turn

around, but yeah." It was the first time he'd said the words aloud, and it felt amazing. He was free. "There's no way I can finish the season like this."

"And next year?" she persisted.

Since he'd already come this far, he decided to take it all the way. "I'm done, Hailey. I've been done for quite some time. I just wasn't ready to admit it out loud."

She smiled with her eyes before her lips—a thing Cole didn't know was possible but that instantly lightened the load on his heart. For the first time in thirty-two years, he didn't feel as though losing football would be the end of something. With Hailey in his life and by his side, it could be the start of something instead.

It could be real life. *Finally.*

"I'm sorry," she said, the words simple and all the more meaningful because of it. She *was* sorry, he knew, but she would also be the first to tell him that there were far worse fates in life—most of which were currently being lived out by the thousands of puppies waiting for their forever homes.

But then she ruined it.

"How are your parents taking the news? I haven't talked to them since Monday. Your father must be devastated."

He shook his head, as much to warn her off the subject as to relate the information that his father's feelings on the subject were the exact opposite of devastation. His dad was resolute and determined and cheerful. He was sure that nothing—no act of God and no man-made disaster—would stand between him and the thing he desired most.

In his mind, his precious quarterback son would soon rise again to bring honor to the family name, and that was all that mattered.

"I'd be happy to go over sometime this week and hang out if you think it would help distract them," Hailey offered. "Someone from the production office has been picking up and dropping off Nala, but I could easily do it instead."

"No. Don't do that."

His words came out harsher than he intended, causing the color to immediately blanch from Hailey's face. It was the opposite of her delightful blushes but just as telling.

"I'm sorry," he was quick to add. "It's nice of you to offer, but I haven't talked to them about it yet."

Philip came trotting up with his well-worn plush football in his mouth. Dropping it at Cole's feet, he waited patiently for the game of fetch that was sure to follow.

"Not now, buddy," he said. To Hailey, he added, "I'm waiting for the perfect time."

"The perfect time?" she echoed, her brows knit. "As in... tomorrow?"

"Sure. Maybe. If it feels right."

"If it feels right? Are you serious?"

Now she drew close enough for him to kiss, but it was obvious from her expression that she was in no mood for romance. "They should hear it from you instead of a press release," she said. "And the sooner, the better. You're only building up false hopes by pretending you can recover from this. It took *me* several days to get over the shock, and I'm not personally invested in your career. I can't imagine what it's going to do to them."

Cole could. He could picture the exact look on his dad's face— disappointment and dismay, the crushing loss of everything he'd worked toward. His mom would try to hide it, but that would be worse. She'd smile and make everyone dinner and tactfully refrain from mentioning football for the rest of her life.

And Regina, well. Regina would start making plans. Marketing plans and financial plans. Lists of sponsors who might be interested in an overpriced former football star. Ways he could eke out his fame so that the light stayed bright and focused overhead, so that the name Cole Bennett *meant* something.

Until she realized that his name was useless and she stopped.

Even though he knew this day had been coming—had wished for it, even—he wasn't sure he had it in him to crush his entire family's dreams.

What kind of man did? What kind of *son*?

"You have to tell them, Cole," Hailey said when he hesitated too long over his response. She tilted her face up to his, her eyes narrowed as she took in each exhausted line, every strained nerve. "I know it's going to be awful, but they're your parents."

That truth—so simply uttered and so much more direct than any of the other criticisms Hailey had leveled at him—hit Cole much harder than he'd expected.

"Awful" didn't even begin to cover it. Didn't she realize? She could critique his game play and laugh at his faults for an eternity without hurting him, but this was the one thing that had the power to *truly* break him.

"Exactly," he said, feeling the cold sensation of dread and a deep, abiding fear clamp on his heart. "They're my parents. Not yours."

She blinked, clearly taken aback by his response. So was Philip, who renewed his bid for attention. He pawed at Cole's leg and nudged the football closer.

"Not *now*, Philip."

"Don't take your bad mood out on your puppy." Hailey picked up Philip's football and tossed it across the white marbled floor. Her aim sucked and her technique was deplorable, but that didn't stop the puppy from bounding happily after it. She took one look at Cole's expression and added, "And don't take it out on me either. I get it… It sucks to get pulled from the roster this close to the Kickoff Cup. It's not how you'd have chosen to end your career. You wanted to go out in a blaze of glory. But it's not as if you didn't know this was coming. It's not as if you thought you could keep this up forever."

Everything Hailey said was absolutely true. It *did* suck not to finish the season out, and he would have preferred to retire on his own terms. He wanted to play in a Kickoff Cup game and—yes—maybe even win it. And this career always had an expiration date—that was a thing every football player knew, or if they didn't, they learned it as soon as that first concussion hit.

But if she thought for one second that it was the *glory* he was pining for, if his hesitation came from not getting to ride on the shoulders of the adoring crowds any longer, then she didn't know him at all.

"This has nothing to do with the Kickoff Cup," he said.

Her look of disbelief spoke volumes.

"Okay, maybe a little of it does," he admitted. Even in his present state, his stomach in knots and his heart heavy, he could recognize just how far he'd gone in the name of the sport. The puppies, the press, the fact that Hailey was in his life at all... Why had he done any of it if not for his team? "But that's not the real reason I don't want to talk to my parents. You've seen them, Hailey. You've spent time with them. Don't you know by now that this news is going to kill them?"

"Your dad will be fine." She reached out and touched his arm. It was just a light press of her fingers, but he felt as though he was being held down by a rock. "I know you worry about him, but he has your mom and sister to help look after him, and the doctors—"

"You don't understand," Cole protested. "Everything he has, everything he is, is wrapped up in my football career. He and my mom both, not to mention Regina and Mia. This doesn't just mean the end for me. It's the end for all of us."

She offered him a wry smile and took her hand back. She placed it on Philip's head instead, running her finger up and down the velvety length of his nose. "I think you'll survive. No offense, but if the five of you have blown through your entire salary already, you need to rethink your long-term financial plans."

"*Money*?" The word came out in a rush of breath and bitter laughter. "You think this is about money?"

"Isn't it?"

It wasn't. Not even remotely. He'd give up every penny he had if it meant he could avoid the heartache—the absolute upending of everything he knew to be true—that this news would cause his family.

"My dad has been molding me into a football player since the moment I was born," he said. He barely recognized the sound of his own voice, but he pushed on anyway. He needed to say this. He needed for someone else to *know*. "Everything I ate and played and did was to make me a better quarterback. Nothing was too good for me, nothing too much—provided, of course, that it pushed me closer to the end zone. The cookies my mom baked had protein powder ground into them. They tasted like paste, but that was too bad. My development came first.

"I only got football gear for every single birthday and Christmas, no matter how much I wanted a remote-controlled car or a puppy. I didn't have friends; I had teammates. Even my own sister wasn't allowed to play with me—not in any way that counted. We didn't fight over Monopoly or take turns playing *Super Mario*. She fetched the footballs I threw through a tire in the backyard, ran me through sprinting drills and timed my progress."

"Poor Reggie," Hailey murmured.

"Yes," Cole agreed, jumping at this opportunity. "It *was* hard on her—harder, probably, than it was on me. She didn't get a childhood of her own, was never given a chance to be anything other than my manager. My dad is a quarterback's father. My mom is a quarterback's mother. Regina is a quarterback's sister. And me, well, I'm a quarterback. Period. Full stop."

"That's not true, Cole, and if you'd just—"

Cole didn't let her finish. "It's all any of us ever were. It's all any of us will ever be. Don't you get it? When I leave the Lumberjacks, I'm not just ending a job. I'm ending an entire way of life. I'm ending my family. Without football to bind us, I don't know what we're supposed to be. I don't know what we'll have."

"I do," Hailey said without hesitation. "You'll have each other."

He didn't know what it was about Hailey's answer that caused such a visceral reaction. Maybe it was the confidence with which she uttered it, the way it didn't even occur to her to question the strained relationship between him and his parents, between him and his sister. It could have been how earnest she was, how much she truly believed in what she was saying. Either way, he couldn't stop the words that came out of his mouth next.

"Sorry, but I don't think you're in a position to lecture me about my family."

She balked at his words but didn't stop. "They love you, Cole. Anyone who's spent five minutes in their company can see that. You don't want to disappoint them, I know, but they're not going to strip you of your name because you're injured." She laughed, as though such a thing was so preposterous that it couldn't even be considered. "They'll keep loving you. They'll help you figure out what you want to do next. They'll support you every step of the way. Believe me, Cole Bennett is going to land on his feet."

She didn't get it. She didn't understand. The one person he wanted—no, *needed*—on his side was just as wrong as everyone else. She looked at him and saw not a man, not someone who was terrified of what the future held and in desperate need of a friend, but Cole Bennett.

The myth. The millionaire. The motherfucking quarterback.

"You only say that because you haven't had to answer to anyone but yourself for nine years," he said, bitter and hurt rendering his voice hoarse. Somewhere in the back of his mind, he knew he was taking his frustration out on the wrong person—that Hailey was the closest thing to an ally he had in this—but something had broken inside him, the floodgates thrown open so far there was no way to close them again. "There's no one whose entire sense of self and happiness is wrapped up in what you do or don't accomplish on any given day. There's no one who counts on you for every single thing they are. You're alone."

All the color drained from Hailey face. A hole inside Cole's chest cracked to see it, but it was too late. He'd already committed himself to this, spoken the words out loud, and there was no taking them back now. As if sensing it, Philip gave an eager whine—a sound Hailey immediately latched onto. She latched onto the puppy, too, holding him as though he were the only thing keeping her standing.

"I'm not alone," she said, her voice cold. "In case you forgot, there are seven dogs currently living in my house, depending on me for survival. Eight, if you keep yelling at Philip."

Cole had never yelled at Philip—not when he ate the cushion off his couch, not when he demanded bathroom breaks at two o'clock in the morning, and not when he almost got himself kicked off the team plane for trying to storm the cockpit. In fact, he couldn't even imagine a world where yelling at Philip would be a choice. He adored that little dog, with his nervous qualms and his inability to keep his bow tie straight, the ratty football he carried around like it was the light of his life.

That Hailey couldn't see how much he loved and needed that puppy—how much he loved and needed *her*—was the final straw. Since the moment he'd met this woman, he'd pushed and pulled and done everything he could think of to reach her.

None of it had worked. She'd given him her body, yes, and maybe even her affection, but she'd not once let him near her heart.

"You mean the dogs you're too scared to keep for longer than a few weeks at a time?" he asked without waiting for an answer. "The dogs you refuse to adopt because it's too hard to let anyone in your life on a permanent basis? You can't even commit to a pet, Hailey. Don't tell me what it means to have a family."

He knew at once that he'd gone too far. The white pallor of her cheeks went instantly hot and red, her whole stance crumbling like stone cracked from the center.

"I think Philip and I should go," she said, her voice shaking so much that his heart gave an answering stutter. "I'll let the production office know that you're not feeling up to being filmed today. In light of your injury, I'm sure they'll understand. We can get a few shots of you playing with the puppies later this week."

"Hailey, wait—" he began.

"Don't." The warning in her voice was impossible to ignore. "I know you could easily go over my head, call Jasmine, and take over the entire Puppy Cup, but I'm asking you not to. You already have everything. You said it yourself… All I have are my dogs, and they don't even count. The least you can do is give me this."

"Hailey—" he tried again, but it was too late. She was already clipping Philip to his leash, already talking to him in a low, soothing tone meant to bring him comfort. It wasn't working, and had she asked, Cole could have told her that Philip needed his football and at least five treats before he was willing to leave the comfort of his home.

But she didn't ask. She didn't ask, and she didn't stick around to hear his apology. In fact, she didn't even hesitate as she walked out the door and out of his life without a single backward glance.

chapter
18

"HOW ABOUT GARRETT SMITH? I COULD PROBABLY GET YOU Garrett Smith. People love Garrett Smith."

Jasmine sat at the far end of the conference table, so far removed from Hailey that she was having a difficult time making out her boss's expression. Not that she needed to see Jasmine's face to know what she was thinking. Her posture—rigid and unyielding—and the fact that she'd returned to the white pant-suits told Hailey everything she needed to know.

"I don't want Garrett Smith. I want Cole Bennett. Cole Bennett is on the billboards. Cole Bennett is in the ad spots." Jasmine cleared her throat. "Because *you* put him there, if you'll recall."

"Then what about Tucker Marshall?" It was a long shot, but she had to try. Even if it meant she'd lose her job and have to sell her house and live in a kennel with Bess and Philip and all six of the puppies, there was no way she was going back to Cole on bended knee. "Since he's replacing Cole in the Kickoff Cup, it makes sense. You'll still have your Lumberjacks quarterback. Just not the one you started with."

Jasmine sighed and got up from the table. Her movements always looked so calm, but she somehow crossed the room and joined Hailey before she finished untangling Philip's leash from where it had wrapped around the table leg.

Hailey braced herself for the lecture she knew was coming. Jasmine certainly had her choice of topics. It had been unprofessional to sleep with Cole. She needed to stop bringing puppies to the office. Heartbreak wasn't a good enough reason to cancel a show they'd spent an entire year working on.

Which was why she was so surprised when Jasmine dropped a hand to her shoulder. It was surprisingly warm. And comforting.

"I'm sorry," Jasmine said. "I know it isn't ideal, but we don't have any other choice. It's too late to make these kinds of changes, or I'd do my best to accommodate you."

Hailey was too surprised by the kindness in her voice to do more than stare—a feeling that multiplied when Jasmine crouched down and extended a tentative hand toward Philip.

"So this is the little guy he abandoned, huh?" She made a tsking sound as Philip sniffed at her fingers. "He must be a real jerk to abandon a puppy like this."

Hailey felt a bizarre urge to rise to Cole's defense. "Technically, he didn't *abandon* the puppy. I sort of…walked off with him in my arms."

Jasmine glanced up. "But he didn't try to stop you?"

"Well, no."

She nodded and rose to a standing position once again. "Then it amounts to the same thing. When you want someone in your life—really want them—you don't let them walk away like that."

Hailey didn't fail to understand what her boss was saying. If Cole wanted her in his life—really wanted her—he wouldn't have let her walk away, either. Jasmine's approach might not have been orthodox, but it was kind.

"If, for example, you tried quitting on me after this, I'd have something to say about it," Jasmine persisted. She even cracked a smile. "Do the best you can with what you've got, Hailey. That's all I ask. Find a way to make it work, and we'll get you that producer credit for real next year. We couldn't do this show without you."

With that, she walked away, her pristine white heels clicking in the distance. Hailey could only stare, unblinking, as she went. Even Philip seemed to sense that something monumental had just happened, because he looked a little less depressed than he had for the past couple of days.

"Ohmygod." Penny appeared in a doorway toward the back of the room just as Hailey staggered dazedly to her feet. "Did she really say what I just think she said?"

"How long were you listening?"

"She smiled at you. She was nice to you. She *likes* you."

"Isn't that a janitor's closet?"

Penny moved a finger across her lips in a gesture of silence. "I wanted to be on hand in case she fired you. I thought you could use the moral support."

"I'm glad you were," Hailey admitted. "I needed a witness to that. No one would believe me otherwise."

She and Penny shared a knowing look. For what was probably the thousandth time since Cole had said those terrible things to her, Hailey was grateful for the other woman's presence. Without fail, Penny had come over every single night to drink and commiserate and take long soaks in Hailey's bathtub. At this point, she'd seen Penny naked from every possible angle, but that was okay. She didn't think she'd be here, dressed and functional, if it weren't for her friend.

My friend.

It still felt strange to think about—even stranger to say—but there was no denying that Penny was exactly that. She was everything Hailey had ever wanted and hoped for in a female companion, and she'd been here this entire time.

All it had taken was for Cole Bennett to waltz into her life to give her that final push to make it happen. Even after everything he'd done, the way he'd rooted out her biggest source of emotional pain and squeezed it, she still had something to thank him for.

It was almost enough to make her scream. He even managed to make being an asshole a way to shine.

"What are you going to do now?" Penny asked, voicing the exact question that had been pressing on Hailey's mind for days. "He's going to be at the warehouse for filming in less than an hour."

As if sensing that a reunion was imminent, Philip perked to a ridiculous degree. So did Hailey, which made her so annoyed that she responded with the only thing she could think of.

"The first thing I want is for you to do my hair," she said. "And if we have time, I think we should revisit the permanent marker too."

———

Cole wasn't at the warehouse when Hailey and Penny arrived. Hailey's hair looked incredible, pulled back in some kind of twisty cascade that made her feel like a goddess, and Penny had done things with the marker that were probably going to result in a staph infection—but that were worth it, because she looked freaking amazing.

The puppies, however, were present and accounted for. All fifty of them. No sooner had they walked in the door than Philip located his new friend Cleopatra and bounded off after her. Nala was there, too, lingering around craft services in hopes that someone would drop a platter of snacks while she was ready to catch them.

Big and small, well behaved and wound-up, exhausted and only recently awakening from their naps, puppies were everywhere.

Hailey normally loved days like this, where the chaos cast all other thoughts and considerations aside. No matter how empty her own house and life might be, moments like these made her feel like it was impossible to be alone. Today, however, she wasn't in the mood to look on the bright side.

"Well, I guess that solves one of your problems," Penny said. "If he's not here, you can hardly work with him. Not even Jasmine can expect you to manifest a football player out of thin air."

"Can't she?" Hailey sighed as she ran through a mental checklist of her options. They didn't have a formal contract with Cole, but he was on all the promo items and had verbally committed to seeing this project through. It would look very bad for him if he failed to show up now—worse, probably, than it would for her. He was still listed as questionable on the injury report, and rumors about whether or not he was going to play in the Kickoff Cup were pretty much all that anyone could talk about. If he bailed on the Puppy Cup now, people would be sure to assume he was in much worse condition than the Lumberjacks were letting on.

Which, Hailey knew, was the truth. Getting the great Cole Bennett to publicly admit it, however…

"I'll call Reggie," Hailey decided with a nod. "She's the one person who can get him to do things he doesn't want to."

Penny nudged Hailey with her hip and pointed to the opposite end of the warehouse, where a pair of double doors had been thrown open and light started streaming in. "The *only* one?" she asked.

Hailey's first instinct upon seeing those doors was to grab a headset and alert everyone on staff to make a dive for the nearest puppy. The last thing they needed right now was a stampede of canines making a break for it. All that stood outside the warehouse was an empty field, but it was a *muddy* empty field. She didn't even want to think about how many baths they'd have to give before the puppies would be fit for filming again.

Before she could do more than squawk a red alert, however, the open doors filled with shadows. *Massive* shadows, and a lot of them—all of them moving with a sense of purpose that couldn't be denied.

Penny was the first to figure out what they were looking at, and she clutched at Hailey as though her life were on the line. "Don't move," she said, only this time, her voice wasn't loud. It was barely above a whisper. "Don't blink. Don't even breathe."

Hailey didn't need the reminder. Moving and blinking and breathing were well outside her capabilities by this time.

Those were Lumberjacks. *All* the Lumberjacks.

It was around this time that the rest of the warehouse figured out what was happening—humans and canines alike. Most people were frozen into a kind of shocked immobility, but Philip showed nothing but joy. With a yap of pleasure that echoed through the sudden silence, he darted toward the figure leading the pack.

Cole. Dressed to kill in yet another too-tight shirt, his arm sling nowhere in sight, looking as though nothing could touch him. He was gorgeous and confident, and all Hailey longed to do was kick him.

"Are you kidding me right now?" She stormed across the empty space to where he'd fallen into a squat, accepting Philip's enthusiastic greeting like a man coming home from war. "What are you doing here?"

"Upholding my end of the bargain," he said, his face unreadable. He moved a little stiffly, his right arm held against his side in a way that was unmistakable, but showed no other signs of distress. "Hailey, I'd like to introduce you to the team. Team, this is the woman I was telling you about."

It was, without a doubt, a dream come true. As Hailey stood there, bemused and bewildered, she found herself surrounded by thirty huge men, all of whom she knew by name and reputation and face. There was Johnson, the kicker. Marshall, the backup quarterback. Washington and Byrd and Aarons. Juarez and Evans and Hodges. Even Garrett Smith was there, looking apologetic and wearing a rueful smile.

She was taken by surprise when Garrett greeted her with a kiss on the cheek. "Take it easy on him, will you?" he said, his voice a low whisper next to her ear. "He's had a rough couple of days."

A snort escaped her before she could stop it. Garrett heard it, of course, but that was too bad. Let him know how incredulous she felt. Let them all know. She didn't care how rough Cole's days had been or what he was attempting to do here today. She had a show to film, and every Lumberjack in the world couldn't stop her.

Well, technically, they could very easily stop her. There was enough manpower surrounding her right now to overthrow a small country, but that wasn't the point. This wasn't Cole Bennett's show. It had never been Cole Bennett's show.

He'd taken her heart and her dignity. He'd stolen the affection of her puppies and her coworkers. He wasn't taking the Puppy Cup, too.

"Okay, listen up," she called, clapping her hands once to pull the attention of the entire football team—not to mention the crowd of crewmembers who were rapidly gathering around them. "I don't mind if you stay to watch the taping, but you have to stand out of the way of the cameras and the crew. And keep the activity to a minimum, if you please. The puppies are already overly excited. We don't want them getting fatigued before we're even halfway through."

"Bennett wasn't kidding about this one, was he?" she heard a male voice murmur. "She's scary."

Hailey felt the color starting to mount to her cheeks, but she ignored it. Cole had obviously been telling his teammates all kinds of lies about her in an attempt to gain the upper hand, but she wasn't going to let that derail her. Jasmine trusted her to make this work, and that was exactly what she was going to do.

"Is it true you know all our stats by heart?" asked another voice. Hailey turned to see that it belonged to Jamal Hodges, a tight end who'd been on the team for almost as long as Cole and Garrett. "And you can tell us exactly what we did wrong in every game?"

Hailey cast Cole a fulminating glare, but he was impervious to it. He was too busy basking in Philip's love and watching as Hailey faced down thirty men who clearly had been prepped ahead of time. He wanted them to embarrass her and throw her off her game. She wasn't sure if it was a tactic to win the Puppy Cup—or if he just wasn't done humiliating her yet—but she wasn't going down without a fight.

"You're a hell of a blocker, Hodges, and you can bulldoze your way through a crowd of hundreds, but until the day you learn to catch anything on the outlet pass route, you'll never amount to much."

The roar of appreciation that this commentary elicited caused Hailey to flame up. It also gave her the courage to keep going.

"Johnson, you tend to show off too much when the kick is within field-goal range. Byrd, you can hold a point of attack better than anyone, but you have a blind spot when it comes to the middle line of scrimmage. And don't even get me started on Juarez's inability to defend a deep pass if he has to play close to the line."

None of the men seemed to take her criticism amiss. If anything, she seemed to grow in their estimation with each word. By the time she'd run out of things to say—and the breath with which to say them—the entire Lumberjacks team was laughing so much that she couldn't help smiling with them.

"I'm sorry," she said. "But you did ask."

"And that, guys, is exactly what I was talking about," Cole said, drawing forward. He looked as though he wanted to take Hailey's hand, but she was careful to keep herself out of his reach. She didn't want him to touch her. She didn't want to be charmed. He could do both of those things and cause all her defenses to crumble away in an instant, but she *needed* them.

She had no way to fight him otherwise. No way to protect herself. No way to survive.

"Well," he said as though there was nothing else to say. "Where do you want us?"

Hailey looked to Penny for support, but all her friend did was shrug. She looked even more lost than Hailey felt.

"Us?" Hailey echoed. "I can't film your whole team. You wouldn't fit on the turf."

"Oh, they're not here for the show," Cole assured her. He turned to the men and added in a slightly louder tone, "The puppies in blue bandannas are mine. Hailey's are in red. This little guy here is already spoken for, and I doubt Garrett will give up Cleopatra without a fight, but the rest are up for grabs. The more of you who adopt a puppy, the more our luck increases."

He lifted a brow at Hailey. "Unless you've started adopting them out already?"

Understanding was beginning to dawn—and with it, an anger unlike any she'd felt before.

"What do you think you're doing?" she hissed.

"This is what you wanted, isn't it? For the puppies to find good homes?" He gestured at his team members, who were starting to disperse in pursuit of the various animals running around the warehouse. "They won't find better homes than these."

"You can't bring a bunch of men in here and start handing out puppies. That's not how any of this works."

Some of the confidence started leaking out of his expression. "They'll go through all the regular channels, of course. Fill out the forms, pay the fees, whatever." He tried for a grin, but it fell wide of its mark. "You once said that the puppies don't do teams or competitions, either, but we've come this far without a hitch."

Without a hitch? Was he serious? She'd spent the past three nights sleeping on her floor because she couldn't stomach the idea of lying in the bed or on the couch where they'd once shared so much. Philip spent all his waking and sleeping hours curled up next to Rufus by the front door, certain that Cole would walk through it any minute.

Worst of all were the half-dozen messages on her phone from

Cole's parents. They were worried about her and how she was handling the press. Mia wanted a playdate with Rufus, if it wasn't too inconvenient. They wanted to know if she could come over for dinner on Friday and were terribly sorry but the Wegmores would be there, so could she please bring some kind of French wine to shut them up?

She'd finally called Paula back over that last one with a pathetic excuse about nonexistent preexisting plans—and even that had been a disaster. No sooner had Cole's mom offered to reschedule the entire dinner for Saturday than Hailey had to feign a disconnection or risk sobbing the whole story into the phone.

"You coward," she said, the words shooting out before she could stop them.

He started, obviously expecting a different response. "I don't think you understand. The puppies will have homes now. Not temporary ones but real ones. Forever ones. I only brought the guys who were willing to go all the way in. Even Garrett says he'll have a hard time giving Cleopatra back after this."

As if just remembering that Garrett wasn't the only football player who had recently become a foster parent to a four-legged friend, Cole reached down and gave Philip a loving pat. "I was hoping he could come home with me today." Quieter this time, he added, "I was hoping you both could."

"Coward," she repeated, mostly for the strength it gave her. She wanted so badly to fall under his spell again, to let him lull her with his strength and his goodness and his wonderful, beautiful family, but she held herself firm. "I'm not going anywhere with you, and neither is Philip. In fact, none of these puppies are leaving this warehouse with anyone except their handlers, so you might as well call your team off."

"But…" He lifted his good hand toward her and dropped it again, devastation in every line of his bearing. "You love these puppies. Everything you do is for them."

"That's because they're all I have, remember?" she asked, hands on her hips. If his wince was any indication, her words hit home, but she wasn't done. "I'm all alone in the world except for them. Or—wait—that wasn't quite it, was it? I don't have a family, but I also don't have a *real* dog either. I can't commit to one."

"You're twisting my words," Cole protested. "I know I said… I'm aware that I acted… *Dammit*, Hailey. I'm trying to do the right thing here."

She knew he was, which was why her chest hurt so much. He was operating at peak Cole Bennett, swooping in with a grand gesture to make her heart go *pitter-pat*. He'd save her puppies. He'd save her show. He'd smile and get his way, and everything would fall exactly where he wanted it to.

And it might work—for a little while, anyway—and they could even find some happiness together. But Hailey had learned a long time ago that big words and big gestures weren't what made the most impact. She didn't need a Kickoff Cup win or a huge puppy-adopting coup. She didn't need a professional quarterback with million-dollar hands and a billion-dollar smile.

Those things were nice, obviously, but more than that, she needed someone to sit patiently in front of a television with her, teaching her the rules of football because it was the only thing he could think of to bring her out of her shell. She needed someone to make her pancakes every Sunday morning—Lumberjacks-shaped or not—and talk to her about her day as though it were the most important thing in the world. She needed someone to hold her tight and kiss her forehead and tell her that she was worth being loved.

Because she was worth being loved. She *was*.

"Do you want to know the real reason why I don't adopt any of the dogs I foster, Cole?" she asked, tears pricking at her eyes. The last thing she wanted to do was cry at work—and with an audience of thirty pro football players, no less—but she was going to anyway. She always did. "Do you know why I'm so determined to see these little guys placed somewhere safe?"

"Tell me," he said, his voice hoarse.

So she did.

"You know that my dad died when I was nineteen, right?" She didn't wait for him to nod. If she stopped, if she let the thick feeling of oppression in her throat take over, she'd never get the rest out. "Well, the part you don't know is that he wasn't my dad until I was twelve years old. Legally, he wasn't my dad until I was thirteen, but we always celebrated the day he became my foster parent, not my legal guardian."

Cole's look of surprise was very real—and all the more difficult to see because of it. "Hailey, I didn't—"

She held up a hand to stop him. "You didn't know. I'm aware of that. No one does. It's not something I talk about very often, but I'm telling you now. I never knew my birth parents. I entered the system before my first birthday and stayed there for twelve long years. I lived in foster homes and group homes, grew up alongside dozens of kids whose lives were just like mine. Sometimes, I liked where I lived. Other times, I didn't. There was this one house, though, that I can remember from really early on. It was before I started school, so I must have been about Mia's age at the time."

Cole winced, and Hailey could tell that the reference to his niece hit home.

"Yeah. It's a rough life for a kid that age. But that particular home was nice—*really* nice, and I thought for a while that I might get to stay there forever." She shrugged. "But the mom, a doctor, got relocated to another state, so that was the end of it. I still think about them, though. How nice they were, how loving, and for no reason other than because it was the right thing to do. It's one of the only memories I have of a woman hugging me. Can you believe that? People don't really think about it, but that's the one thing kids in the system miss the most. Touch. Hugs. Affection."

She really was crying now, and she was pretty sure that she was speaking loud enough for several of the people around them to overhear, but she didn't care. She was tired of trying to be someone she wasn't, of being ashamed of the emotions that rose—literally—to the surface. Penny seemed to like her for who she was. Jasmine, too. Not to mention her dad.

If you want something, Hailstorm, go after it.

Well, she was going to. She wanted to say this, so she would.

"I went several years without feeling that again. My dad hugged me, and for a long time, it fixed something broken inside of me, but it wasn't until I met your mother that another woman held me in her arms." Drawing closer, she tilted her red, streaming face toward Cole's. He was starting to look seriously alarmed, but that didn't stop her. "She's *amazing*, Cole. Your whole family is. In the short time I've known them, they've hugged me and accepted me and treated me like I was one of them. It doesn't even occur to them to question their right to love and be loved. Just like it doesn't occur to you to do the same."

"Hailey…"

"No." Anger was winning now, and in a big way. Her sad tears mixed with furious ones, but she made no move to dash them away. "You think I'm the lucky one, but you're an idiot if you can't see what you have. I get it—they push too hard and want too much, and letting them down feels like the end of the world—but I can guarantee that your mom will still open her arms to you. You get to keep hugging her, Cole. You get to keep being hugged. For all the thousands of children who will never have someone like her, who will never know that kind of love and affection, stop being such a stupid, selfish chickenshit and *talk* to her."

Philip was the first to break the silence that followed this outburst. He gave a small whine and pushed his head underneath Hailey's hand, licking liberally at any part of her skin that he could reach. It was as if he, too, finally heard her—finally understood.

As much as he might love Cole and long to be with him, he and Hailey were the same.

"Er, if I might add a small caveat, it'd be best for us if you'd talk to her *after* we finish today's filming." Nelson drew forward with an apologetic grimace and a gesture at his wrist. The PA didn't wear a watch, but his meaning was clear. "Sorry, Hailey, but we're already way behind today."

She drew a deep breath and nodded, more grateful for this interruption than her tear-streaked cheeks might lead her coworkers to believe. She swiped at them with the back of her hand. "Of course. Try, if you can, to clear out the football players, although feel free to hand out the adoption forms if they're serious. Cole, you'll want to check in with hair and makeup first, but they probably won't do much. The handlers will have your team ready for you on the sidelines, and we'll aim for cameras rolling in...ten minutes?"

She lifted a finger to her eye to check the state of her own makeup and was grateful to find that Penny's permanent marker was holding fast. That woman deserved a bathtub of her own after this.

"Ten," she repeated with a nod. Cole had yet to move and was staring at her as though she'd pulled her still-beating heart out of her chest for him to inspect, but that was only to be expected. That was pretty much what had just happened.

For once, however, she didn't mind. Her public confession was embarrassing and unprofessional and exactly the sort of thing she always did.

And she'd do it again in a fully visible heartbeat.

"I'll see you on the field, Mr. Bennett," she said. "I hope you're ready for this. Our adoring public awaits."

chapter

19

"OH, FOR THE LOVE OF EVERYTHING." REGINA STARED AT Cole as though he wasn't the brother she'd known and taken care of for thirty-two years—the brother she'd known and *loved*. "Have you lost your mind? What did I tell you about adopting Hailey's puppies?"

"Why are you yelling at me?" Cole lowered himself to the kitchen chair nearest him. A tall glass of water and a bottle of painkillers were waiting there for him, but he reached for neither. Nothing could possibly hurt worse than the hole in his chest. "Did you not hear the part where I told you that she hates me?"

"Of course she hates you. *I* hate you. What were you thinking, taking the entire team over there like that?"

"She loves those puppies. I thought she'd be happy to see them all in good homes."

Regina threw up her hands. Her kitchen was always immaculate, thanks to the same fleet of cleaners who kept his home in such a good state, but she was attempting some kind of baking project, so flour was everywhere. "I said it from the start, but you didn't listen. You *never* listen. Adopting that woman's puppies won't make her like you."

"That's not helpful right now, Reg."

"Well, you asked my opinion. That's my opinion." She peered

closer at the cookbook that was open on a stand in front of her. "What even is cream of tartar? Do you think I can skip it?"

"Hell if I know." Cole began toying with the glass of water. He'd come over here at his sister's request—something about paperwork that needed to be signed—but he knew he wouldn't be leaving here until he told her the truth.

Hailey had been right about that. He was a coward and a chickenshit, and Regina deserved better. Hailey had been right about a lot of things, actually. *She* was the one who really deserved more.

"What are you baking, anyway?" he asked. He was going to broach the subject of his shoulder—he *was*—but he needed a minute to compose himself first. "And why?"

"I'm trying to make a lemon meringue pie, but none of this makes any sense. How can anything have this many eggs? And don't they have to be cooked to be safe?"

"Lemon meringue?" Cole ignored the bulk of his sister's commentary. Forget the pie—this whole situation didn't make sense. Regina didn't cook. Regina *never* cooked. Especially not a complicated dessert he couldn't recall ever eating before—but that happened to be a favorite of a certain wide receiver they both knew. "Reggie, who is this pie for?"

"I knew I should have just bought one and changed the pan out." She began searching through her cupboards in earnest—possibly in pursuit of the elusive cream of tartar but more likely to avoid looking at him. "This is what I get for trying to be creative."

"Reggie," he repeated, louder this time. Mia was next door at their parents' house, and Hailey had refused to let Philip come home with him, so he was at liberty to yell all he wanted. "Stop that and look at me. Are you making a pie for Garrett?"

"I don't think you want to start this game with me, Mister I-just-bribed-thirty-of-my-friends-to-try-and-win-a-woman-over. *And failed.*"

"It is, isn't it?" he demanded. "You're making him pie. You love him."

She snorted and gave up on her search. "Is that what you think this is? A love pie?"

"I didn't consider trying that. Do you think Hailey wants a pie?"

Regina threw up her hands. "You are quite possibly the dumbest man I've ever known, and I know some really stupid men."

"So that's a no on the pie?"

She released a shaky laugh and sat at the table next to him. He was glad that he'd managed to break through this strange domestic bubble she'd wrapped herself in, but the speed with which she grew serious took him by surprise. So did the way she reached across the glossy surface to take his hands. Despite their light dusting of flour, her hands easily clasped his, and Cole couldn't help remembering Hailey's words.

Regina thought nothing of reaching out and touching him. Physical affection was as natural to her as breathing. Even now—when she was obviously annoyed—it didn't occur to her that there was anything great or odd about it.

"I'm not dating Garrett, Cole," she said. "I'm signing him."

Cole was still lingering over the memory of his conversation with Hailey—that earth-shattering, devastating conversation—so it took a moment for those words to sink in. "Signing him?" he echoed.

"We wanted to tell you, but the negotiations to get out of his current management contract have been tough. We thought it would be best if we kept things quiet until we were sure."

"Signing him?" Cole echoed again. "As a client? You're his *manager*?"

He didn't wait for Regina to answer before he burst into laughter. It was an unnatural laughter, full of surprise and incredulity and an overwhelming sensation of relief.

Regina squeezed his hands. "It's a good thing for all of us. It'll mean I have less time for you, but you've said it yourself. With your shoulder the way it is, you're eventually going to have to think about retiring, and—"

At that, Cole only started to laugh harder. It wasn't quite such a foreign sound the second time around.

"What's so funny?" Regina demanded. "I'm good at my job. Mia is finally old enough for me to start taking on more clients. You were never going to play football forever, and there's no reason why I can't manage the extra workload. Dammit, Cole. Stop laughing. Hailey's boss even said she could get me a job in television if I wanted one. They've been really happy with my work on the Puppy Cup so far."

"You're right," Cole said as soon as he was able to regain some of his composure. That mention of Hailey helped, her name acting like a dash of cold water to the face. "You're absolutely right. You've been the best manager a man could ask for."

"Then stop looking at me like I just announced my candidacy for the presidency." She pulled her hands away and glanced at the baking mess with a frown. At least, he *thought* that was what she was looking at until she spoke again. "I know how much I'm in your debt, okay? My career, this house, Mia… You've been amazing to us, and I appreciate it, I really do. But I have to start forging my own path. Signing Garrett is just the start. What I'd like to do is build a whole roster. Bring on associates. Make a real go of things. I can, you know. Other people do it all the time."

"Hey, Reg. *Stop.*" Cole interrupted her before she started to work herself up any further. Everything she was saying was perfect—for her and for Mia, for the life they both deserved. The last thing he planned to do was stand in her way. "I'm sorry for laughing, but you have to admit it's funny."

She pursed her lips. "I don't have to do any such thing. My life isn't meant to be a source of amusement for you."

And here it was. The moment of truth. He picked up the bottle of painkillers and rolled it across the table at her.

"I'm not going to take these. Not now and not ever again." He nodded down at his shoulder which—yes—ached like the devil, but not as much as if he'd played real football. Running up and down a field all afternoon with puppies hadn't been physically taxing, but it had been a strain on an emotional level that he'd never experienced before. He'd happily be tackled a thousand times over if it meant he didn't have to stand there, pretending not to stare at Hailey as she pointedly ignored him.

"That's between you and Dr. Hampton," Regina said primly.

"No, it's not. He isn't going to be my doctor much longer." He paused. "I'm not going back."

A flicker of emotion crossed her face. "What do you mean, you're not going back? Like...this week? You're out until next year? They're pulling you?"

"*I'm* pulling me," he said, finding more comfort in those words than he thought possible. "I could probably piece myself together enough to play next Sunday, do my year of penance of rehabilitation, maybe even try another surgery to strengthen things, but what's the point? My heart's not in it anymore. It hasn't been for a while now."

"Cole, you don't mean it. I know it's been a rough couple of months and that you've been struggling lately, but—"

He sighed. "If I can't convince you how serious I am, I don't know how I'm going to convince the rest of the world. I'm retiring, Reggie. I'm closing this chapter of my life. I don't know what I'm going to do next or what your role in it is going to look like, but I need this. *Please.*"

The plea at the end seemed to check her. "Are you asking for my permission?"

"Yes. No. I don't know." He pushed back from the table and rose to his feet, unable to continue this while sitting on his ass. If Hailey could stand in front of him and reveal the deepest, darkest parts of her, tears streaming down her cheeks but her posture proud and tall, then he could have one honest conversation with his sister. He took a deep breath and tried again. "No, I'm not asking. I'm telling.

I'd like you set up a meeting with the coaches and the owners and my agent and anyone else who's required to be present when I hand in my resignation. I know it's going to be a hot mess in terms of press, and I'd like to do whatever I can to reduce the impact it will have on the Puppy Cup and Hailey, but—"

"Okay."

Cole checked in the middle of his sentence, unsure if he heard her correctly. "Okay?"

"Okay," she repeated with a nod. She also got up and began moving around the kitchen, though most of that was to start tossing half-full pots and pans into the sink. "You're right that it's going to be messy, and I have my work cut out for me, but when has that ever slowed me down?"

"Really? Just like that? After banning me from Dad's hospital room and 'forgetting' Amara's request for me to visit the kids and acting as though I'm basically holding my finger over the button that holds our father's life in the balance?"

She winced. "Yeah, that was a shitty thing to do."

"Agreed."

Her wince turned into a grimace. "You don't have to be so smug about it. It was an impossible position. It's *always* been an impossible position, trying to be your manager and your sister at the same time. A good manager wouldn't have let you get anywhere near that hospital while the playoffs hung in the balance."

"A good sister would have been the first to let me in."

Not surprisingly, this criticism had a way of causing Regina to flare up in her own defense. She was always quick to rise to temper, especially where he was concerned. "It's not always easy, you know. To find where the line is. To walk it by myself."

He knew how she felt. Keeping to that line hadn't been easy for either of them. He was looking forward to erasing it.

"For what it's worth, I'm sorry about it now," Regina added. She spoke more gently this time, as if she, too, was envisioning a world where they could just be siblings. "And I wouldn't have kept you out if he'd been in any real danger. You have to know that. The second he took a turn for the worse, I would have called you. Even if it was in the middle of a game."

Cole thought about holding on to his resentment a little longer, but there was no point. If they could go back and change things… what? Would he have refused to pick up a football the first time it was offered? Would she have renounced the family name and baked pies for a living instead of becoming his manager? The idea of Regina lovingly rolling out crusts in a frilly pink apron was enough to have him forgiving everything. She'd have been awful at it.

"Have you talked to them about this yet, by the way?" Regina asked suddenly. "Mom and Dad, I mean."

"No, but I'm going to head over there next." He sighed and rubbed a hand over his mouth. "They aren't going to be happy."

"No, they're not."

"You're not happy about it, either, are you?"

"What I feel doesn't matter. Is it going to be harder for me to build my client list if I lose the great Cole Bennett? Yes, obviously. Am I going to miss my ten percent of all your earnings?" Regina grinned. "Heck yeah. But with any luck, I'll convince all your big sponsors to transfer your contracts over to Garrett. You won't miss them. What's a few million dollars to someone as obscenely wealthy as you?"

He couldn't help laughing. That sounded more like the Regina he knew.

"And it won't change things between us, right?" he asked. This was the last and most important consideration—the thing that was weighing heaviest on his heart. "I mean, things will be different, but not a lot, right? You and me… *Mia* and me…"

Anything the least bit managerial or laser-shark-like about Regina disappeared in a flash. For the first time in a long time, she was just his sister.

"Nothing will change between you and Mia," she said, her reaction vehement to the point of caustic. "I mean that. You are the most important man in her life, and I hope you always will be. I know you'll probably have a family of your own someday, and you won't be able to give her as much of your time, but—"

"Never," he promised. Honesty compelled him to add, "Well, that's not true. I want to have tons of kids, but Mia will like that. She can order them around the way you used to do with me."

"Tons of kids?" Regina echoed. "Really? That's your dream of the future?"

He only shook his head, unable and unwilling to give voice to all the things he wanted. None of them mattered if he couldn't have Hailey. Every time he tried to picture what happened once football no longer took up the majority of his time, all he could see was her. Her house full of sports memorabilia and puppies. Her naked body poised unabashedly on top of his. Her freckles. Her smile. The way her hair never quite stayed where she put it and how quickly and easily she'd seen through all the bullshit that was the life of a professional quarterback.

The look on her face as he'd ruined all his chances with her not just once but twice.

"She doesn't really hate you," Regina said as if reading his mind. "I only said that because you're a moron."

"She might not hate me, but she doesn't like me very much."

"Yeah, well. Neither do I. But we're family, and that's all that matters."

———

If Cole thought his conversation with Regina was difficult, it was nothing compared to the one he had with his parents.

His mom cried. His dad *didn't* cry, but only because anger took over long before sadness had a chance.

"After everything we've done for you, all the sacrifices we made."

"How I would have loved an opportunity like the one you've been given. And you're throwing it away like yesterday's garbage."

"It's fine. Don't worry about me. I'll just die full of shame for the son who wasted his talent. Give me a moment. I'm sure the Grim Reaper will be here any minute."

Cole sat and took it—much longer than he thought he could and much more calmly than he might have had he not had Regina's blessing and Hailey's words to support him.

I can guarantee that your mom will still open her arms to you. You get to keep hugging her, Cole. You get to keep being hugged.

A few months ago, he wouldn't have believed that. The look on his mom's face was so shocked and so hurt that it was hard to imagine she could ever forgive him—for what he was doing to his father, for what he was doing to his family. Today, however, he knew it to be the truth. It might take months—years, even— before his parents could fully wrap their heads around his decision, but he knew without a doubt that his mom would end this day with a hug. Not because she understood how difficult this was for him, and not because she approved of what he was doing, but because that was what she did.

She was his mom. She hugged him. She hugged a lot of people, actually, and in a way that had been highly embarrassing during his teenage years, but that didn't matter. He'd never realized before what it meant to be offered physical affection for no reason other than the ties of family.

He realized now. It meant everything.

"I left Regina on the phone with the team," Cole said as soon as his father stopped railing at him to draw a much-needed breath. "They'll probably just list me as injured for the Kickoff Cup next weekend so the team doesn't completely freak out, but my retirement will be announced not long after that."

"If modern medicine had been in my time what it is today, I'd still be playing football myself," his father announced with a firm set of his jaw. "You don't know how lucky you have it."

At mention of that word—*lucky*—Cole couldn't help but smile.

"That's funny to you, is it?" his father demanded. "My back broken and my knees blown, everything I was put into your training..."

"Julian, *please*," his mom begged. "At least sit down if you're going to start yelling again."

"No, Dad. I don't think your injuries are funny—and I don't think mine are, either—but 'luck' is a funny word to use in this instance."

For some reason, this caused his dad to perk up. "*Luck*. That's it, isn't it? This is nothing more than the curse at work, the only way fate can stop an unstoppable force like you. Hailey failed."

"Don't." For the first time since this conversation started, Cole spoke with hard authority. His parents responded to it almost immediately, both of them turning to him with interest. "Don't try to blame this on Hailey. She didn't fail. She doesn't even believe in the stupid curse—and neither, might I remind you, do you. She only did all this because I asked her to, because I was too much of a coward to tell you to your face what I was feeling."

"As well you should have," his dad grumbled.

Although Hailey had taken Philip from him, Nala was still residing with his parents until the Puppy Cup aired. The beagle entered the room just then and, with one look at the tense faces of the three people in it, darted for his dad's side. Unthinking, his dad sat in his favorite recliner before patting his lap, at which point the beagle jumped up and immediately settled in for a nap. He had no idea that he'd done it—sat down and relaxed, his anger ebbing away with each brush of his hand over the puppy's fur—but Cole and his mom shared a knowing look.

"Does this mean she's coming over for dinner on Friday?" his mom asked, tacitly accepting the truce brought by the puppy. Cole knew it would be a while before any of them could talk about football without tempers flaring, but he was willing to accept his end of the olive branch. "I tried inviting her, but we got cut off before I could get a firm answer."

"You asked her to dinner?"

"The Wegmores are coming, and she handled them so well last time that I thought she might do the trick a second time. The poor thing. She doesn't have much family of her own, does she?" His mom clucked and shook her head. "Well, the Wegmores aren't much of a consolation prize, but what can you do? They're what we have to offer."

"You asked her to dinner?"

His mom looked at him with an odd light in her eyes. "Yes, dear. I already said that. Are you sure you didn't hit your head as well as your shoulder?"

"She won't come," he said, ignoring the question. "I'm sorry, Mom. I ruined it."

Cole wasn't sure what he said or did next, but he was in his mom's arms before he knew what was happening. In his lifetime, he'd been tackled and hit from every angle. He'd taken physical blows that would fell a tree and stood up to coaches shouting at him with so much violence that they'd actually spit in his face. He'd listened to his father shout him through football drills when he was barely old enough to walk and stood watching as Hailey showed him the inner workings of her heart.

This, however, was his breaking point.

"Cole, love, don't worry." His mom was tall and strong but not as tall or as strong as him. That didn't seem to matter as she continued holding him, her arms not quite reaching around his torso. "We'll pick another date, one that works for her. You know Gertie will do anything for a free dinner."

He gave a watery chuckle, but his mom didn't release him. It was as though she knew that she was the only thing holding him together, that the moment she let go, he'd fall to pieces.

"It's not the date," he said, his voice shaking. "It's me. I wrecked it. She's the best thing that's ever happened, and I blew my chance."

"Well, really. *Do* something, Julian."

"What do you want me to do?" came the irritable reply. "He won't listen to reason about football. What makes you think he'd take my advice about women?"

Cole couldn't help but be intrigued by those words. He pulled out of his mother's grasp and glanced at his father, who sat regally on his throne, petting his fast-sleeping puppy. "Do you *have* advice about women?" he asked.

His dad snorted his indignation. "I've been married to the love of my life for thirty-five years. I might be an old, doddering fool whose only son betrayed him, but if there's one thing I know, it's that."

chapter
20

H AILEY HAD NEVER BEEN SO NERVOUS IN HER LIFE. THE Puppy Cup was set to air any minute, the huge screen at the front of the restaurant switched away from the halftime show to the much-less-expensive cable channel they aired on. The entire crew and their respective families were sitting with her and waiting for it to start.

They'd all seen it about twelve times already, the edited footage completed and packaged days ago, but that didn't seem to lessen the excitement any. It helped that this particular restaurant had been more than happy to open the doors to both humans and canines, so in addition to the Puppy Cup production team, which was rapidly becoming drunk, there were several puppies and adult dogs running around underfoot. Hailey had been so confident in Bess and her pack of babies that even they were in attendance, albeit in a quiet corner where they could rest and nurse, should the need arise.

So far, resting was all they'd had an opportunity to do, since Philip stood guard over the pack. Rufus was finally starting to gain enough strength to hold his own against his brothers and sisters, and Philip was determined to see that he got his fair share.

"Okay, everyone, quiet down," Hailey called, raising her hand to try to stem the enthusiasm long enough to get a speech in. Against all odds and the devastating news that Cole Bennett wouldn't be playing in the Kickoff Cup, the Lumberjacks were up by seven points. Everyone was understandably elated—especially since there were so many Lumberjack ties to the Puppy Cup. If their luck held, there was a good chance that every puppy in the country would be adopted after this.

"It'll never work." Penny sidled up next to Hailey and passed over a glass of sparkling wine. Their doubled budget had allowed them to throw this party, but real champagne was still out of the question. "Everyone is already drunk. You'll have to flip on the karaoke machine and sing if you want to get anyone's attention."

"I'm not that desperate."

"I was afraid of that." Penny put a finger in either side of her mouth and released an ear-splitting whistle. Almost immediately, the movements and conversations in the room stilled. Even the puppies seemed to sense that quiet was called for. "There you go. The crowd is yours."

Hailey swallowed. Public speaking had never been her forte for obvious reasons. Even if she wrote everything out ahead of time and practiced it painstakingly in front of the mirror, she would inevitably stammer and blush the moment all eyes were turned her way.

In this instance, she hadn't written or practiced anything. The past week and a half had been a blur of puppies and filming and long hours at the editors' desks. She'd gone to bed exhausted every night and woke far too early every morning, determined that work, at least, would go well.

Her personal life might be a disaster, but that wasn't anything new. She also didn't have any family here to support her big day, and no one would be waiting for her when she got home, but that wasn't new, either.

She'd come into this world alone and would probably leave it that way, too. Some people were born lucky, and some weren't.

That was just the way the world worked, and if she'd thought for a few brief Cole-Bennett-fueled minutes that things could be different, that was on her.

"Um, first of all, I want to thank everyone for all their hard work these past few months," she said, her voice sounding small even with the hush in the room. "I know it's been—"

The doors to the restaurant whooshed open. She didn't want to hope and *really* didn't want to look, but the low murmur of surprise made it impossible for her to resist.

He's here. He came. He...sent his mother?

"Oops, sorry." Paula Bennett, decked out from head to toe in Lumberjacks teal, entered the room with all the confidence of a six-foot woman who had never felt the urge to make herself smaller. She waved a hand at Hailey, half in greeting and half in an effort to apologize. "Hello, dear. Ignore us. We'll slide in the back. Pretend we're not here."

The request was a ridiculous one considering how much noise Paula's arrival elicited. If she'd come alone, she might have gotten away with a discreet entrance, but she'd brought her entire family with her.

Well, most of her family.

Cole's dad was beside her, wearing funereal black instead of his usual Lumberjacks jersey. Regina was there, too, doing her best to balance Mia and Nala at the same time. Hailey's jaw dropped as she also recognized Cole's grandmother tottering toward the open bar, the Wegmores, and even Sam and her wife with their two kids in tow. It was the entirety of Cole's family, all of them large and noisy and beaming at her.

But not Cole.

"Go on, then," Paula said when Hailey made no move to speak. "Get on with the speech. You won't hear another peep out of us."

"Peep!" Mia called as she managed to get out of her mother's arms and make a mad dash toward the puppies in the corner.

I'm sorry, Regina mouthed. *We're the worst.*

It was that last unspoken bit that finally dislodged Hailey from her stupor. These people weren't the worst—not even close. They were noisy and unapologetically themselves. They lived and loved large. And for reasons she couldn't even begin to understand, they were here to support her in her moment of glory.

Her heart, as soft and vulnerable and exposed as always, swelled.

This time, she let it.

"Now that we're all here, I'd like to take a moment to thank everyone for all their hard work these past few months," she said. Her voice started out wavering, her suddenly blurred eyes making it difficult to see more than a few feet in front of her face, but the Puppy Cup logo flashed on the screen, forcing her to focus. "Oops… It looks like I'm going to have to make this fast, so I will. Six years ago, I came on this project as a production assistant in hopes that I might make a small difference in the lives of a few puppies. Thanks to Cole Bennett, Jasmine Jones, and the entire Lumberjacks team, we're expecting twenty million viewers this year. So sit back, relax, and enjoy the fruits of your hard work," she called and, unable to help herself, "Go Lumberjacks!"

Everyone toasted to that, and Hailey found her glass filled several times as she pushed through the crowd to where Cole's family had found an empty table. She'd had very little to eat for the past week, so she was understandably tipsy by the time she arrived. Her head swam, and she was vaguely aware of the vision of her and Cole squaring off over their puppies on the screen overhead, but that didn't stop her.

At this point, she doubted anything could.

"You guys came," she said, sniffling as Paula sprang to her feet and pulled her into a warm embrace. "That's so nice of you. I'm sure you must have front-row Kickoff Cup tickets that are going to waste right now."

"Box seats, actually," Sam said, taking her turn embracing Hailey as soon as Paula was done. "But this is better. We didn't want to miss your big moment."

This was a complete and utter lie, but Hailey was too overwhelmed to do more than murmur a feeble protest.

"Cole told us that you probably wouldn't have anyone here to support you, so we invited ourselves." Sam's wife wasn't as effusive as the Bennetts-by-blood, but she did offer a smile and a warm handshake. "I hope you don't mind."

At the mention of Cole, Hailey stiffened. As if by tacit—or possibly well-rehearsed—agreement, no one had mentioned him.

"I don't mind," she said somewhat shyly. "It's…nice to have people. It's not something I'm used to."

"Well, get used to it," Julian grumbled. "If my wife has decided to take you under her wing, you can plan to be stuck there for a while. Breathe carefully."

Hailey couldn't help laughing as Cole's dad took his turn greeting her. In addition to a black suit, he was wearing a black tie, a black shirt, and had even managed to find a black pocket square.

"He's in mourning," Regina said as she watched Hailey take it all in. "For the death of Cole's career. He's had every mirror in the house covered."

"I guess he can always be a reality-television star," Julian muttered as he watched his son cavorting on screen with his team of puppies. It had taken quite a bit of editing to make it appear like Cole had won—Hailey's puppies had been far and away the clear winners in the footage—but they'd managed it. "What a triumph for us all."

"Then he told you," Hailey said, the wine making her feel giddy and indiscreet. Although that wasn't fair to the wine… She was *always* indiscreet. "You know the truth."

"We know," Regina agreed. "And as you can tell, we're all doing our best to cope."

A giggle escaped before Hailey could help it. There was nothing funny about the things that had passed between her and Cole—even less about how hard it must have been for him to talk to his parents—but the fact that Julian was here, scowling up at the television while holding a beagle puppy who'd been decked out in a black sweater for the occasion, was too much.

"I'm sorry," she managed. "You must be devastated."

Julian looked as though he had something to say about that, but one glare from Paula had him clamping his lips shut. "We're doing the best we can, given the circumstances," Paula said. "But we didn't come all this way to talk about Cole. We came to celebrate *you*. Tell me all about what happens next. Is it more puppies, or do you have a different project after this?"

Hailey had no idea how much any of the Bennetts or the Wegmores actually cared about her career, but they listened and asked questions and otherwise made her feel as though they were genuinely interested in what she had to say. It was such a new experience for her that she talked too much and too long, failing to notice when the Puppy Cup ended and the television switched back over to the Kickoff Cup. In fact, it wasn't until Julian elbowed her that she realized the game had begun once again.

"That Marshall kid," he said. "What do you think about his presnap cadence? It's different, but I like the way it gives the offense its momentum."

"She doesn't want to talk about football, Julian," Paula said with a tsk.

"Of course she wants to talk football. What the hell else is she going to do for the next two hours?" Julian stabbed a finger at the television. "He's good, right? I've been watching some of his college footage. He's not as strong as Cole, and he's uncertain of his place, but I like his energy. He *wants* it, you know?"

Hailey nodded her agreement. She hadn't had much time to develop a firm opinion on Marshall's game play yet, but this seemed as good a time as any to start. She settled into her seat to talk strategy and watch the game with Cole Bennett's family—a strange cap to a strange day and an even stranger past five weeks.

The seven-point lead dwindled to a one-point lead as the game wore on, and tensions were understandably high. Most of the puppies and children were exhausted by this time, but the fans were holding strong, all eyes glued to the screen.

"Oh shoot!" Regina jumped from her seat and stabbed a finger at the clock. "Mom, look. It's six thirty."

"What happens at six thirty?" Hailey asked, slightly bewildered as Paula also got to her feet with a nervous start. "We booked this place until midnight. You don't have to hurry away unless you have somewhere else to be."

At the look that passed between Regina and her mother, Hailey blushed and added, "Oh dear. You have somewhere else to be, don't you? And I've been keeping you all this time."

It was just like her to monopolize someone else's family for hours on end, to cling pathetically to the idea that she was the most important thing in the Bennetts' life—and on Kickoff Cup day of all days.

"He's probably jumped into the harbor by now," Regina said, ignoring her.

"Or ripped all his beautiful hair out," put in Sam.

"Nonsense. He'd never do anything to hurt his hair."

This last one came from Cole's mom, who grabbed Hailey by both hands and pulled her up. "I'm so sorry. We were supposed to tell you half an hour ago. Cole's waiting for you out in his car."

"What?" Hailey yanked her hands back as though they'd been touching fire rather than a kind woman's palms. "He's here? *Now?*"

"Well, unless he gave up in despair and drove off," Regina admitted. "We warned him we couldn't make any promises. Not after he pulled that ridiculous puppy stunt."

"His heart was in the right place, poor boy." Paula sighed. "He thought he needed to do something big. Don't tell him I said this, but he's always been a bit of a drama queen."

Hailey let out a squeak that was part laugh and part alarm and might have continued on in this vein if it weren't for Cole's dad. He took her by the arm and started to lead her toward the main doors of the restaurant. They had to maneuver around several puppies as they went, but he managed to make it seem like a completely normal occurrence.

"Don't worry. He's still out there," Julian said and in a way that reminded her so much of her own dad that something in her heart gave a painful lurch. "I imagine he'll be out there all night. You go on and talk to him if you want to, and if you don't, then he can sit there forever for all I care."

"He's been waiting for me?" Hailey swallowed heavily and tried not to peer out into the mizzling Seattle darkness. "This whole time?"

"Not the whole time. We told him to give us until six or so, since we wanted to make sure you had yourself a nice party first." He cast a satisfied look around the restaurant and nodded. "It *was* a nice party. Thank you for inviting us."

"I didn't invite you," she pointed out.

"No, and I've been meaning to have a talk with you about that." He leaned down—his large form so much like Cole's, his movements just as assured and athletic—and pressed a kiss on her cheek. "You invite us next time, okay? And the time after that, and the time after that. We don't care if you go out and make up with that useless son of ours, or if you kick him to the curb like he deserves, or if you forgive him and then decide you can do better in a week or two. We're *family* now, Hailey Lincoln. You got that? There's no one I'd rather watch football games with than you."

She promptly burst into tears. It would have been very easy to take Julian's offer as an old man's kindness, as a good person saying what he could to make a lonely woman feel better, but she believed him. He meant every word.

"Well, now." He appeared slightly startled. "That wasn't the reaction I was expecting."

It might not have been what he expected, but it was what he was going to get if he planned on keeping Hailey around.

"I always cry when I'm happy," she said as she returned his kiss with one of her own. His cheek was rough under her lips and his scent slightly woodsy. Both of those things felt like coming home. "Then again, I always cry when I'm sad, too."

"What do you do when the Lumberjacks win the Kickoff Cup?" he asked with a jerk of his thumb over his shoulder. "There are only two minutes left. If you go out there now, you're going to miss it."

"Then I guess I'll have to miss it," she said as she steeled herself to head out the door. Every part of her might be quaking at the thought of seeing Cole again, and she was terrified lest he might no longer be waiting for her, but she could do it. She *would* do it. If he was willing to loan her his family on a day like today, to let her bask in their love and support when he could probably use some of it himself, it was the least she could do in return. "I'll let you know about the tears later."

———

He hadn't driven his Lexus.

In true football-player style, he'd chosen something flashy and over-the-top instead—an attempt, she assumed, to make her feel even more unsteady than she already was.

"His Aston Martin," she muttered, spotting the steel-gray sports car that he'd been seen shilling in commercials across the United States for the past year. "Of course he'd bring his Aston Martin."

She was so annoyed by this that she marched across the street and yanked open the passenger door before he could make some kind of suave move to put her at further disadvantage.

"You have some nerve, coming to my party in a car like this," she announced as she slid into the seat. The interior smelled strange, like too much cologne and not enough oxygen, which was what she blamed for how long it took her to glance at the man in the driver's seat. "If you don't know by now that I'm not impressed by flashy, vain, useless attempts to—"

She noticed with a start that the man in the driver's seat was not Cole Bennett. He was relatively the same age and dressed in similar clothing, but his mustache and the fact that he weighed about half of what Cole did were dead giveaways.

"Oh God." She gave a startled glance out the window, where a tall, well-built man in a black peacoat with the collar turned up was approaching them. She wasn't sure, but she thought she could detect a smirk through the expensively tinted glass. "I'm so sorry. I'm in the wrong car."

"Flashy?" the man said, frowning so that the ends of his mustache drooped. "Vain?"

"It's a lovely car," she said quickly. The door pulled open and a much more pleasant scent—of rain and open fields, of the man she'd been obsessed with for the majority of her adult life—assailed her nostrils. "Very sleek. I'm sure it's worth every penny."

She didn't wait to hear how her compliments were received. Taking the hand that was being held out to her, she allowed herself to be whisked out of the car and to the safe—if wet—sidewalk instead.

Cole didn't release his grip on her hand, but he didn't make a move to pull her into his arms, either. He just stood looking down at her. He was damp from head to toe, his hair curling in wet locks around his head and rain dripping from his nose. He looked gorgeous and cold and so good that her heart ached.

"Why aren't you in your car?" she demanded. "You'll freeze to death out here."

"I couldn't sit still." He pointed over his shoulder at where an understated black SUV stood parked. "And I wasn't sure if you'd recognize my car. I should have known better. You have every single vehicle I own cataloged, don't you?"

"It's an obscene waste of money to own that many," she said irritably. "Not to mention a drain on our ever-dwindling natural resources. You and that strange man should be ashamed of yourselves."

Cole sucked in a sharp breath, his grip tightening. "God, I've missed you. Hailey—"

She pulled her hand away with a jerk. She wasn't dressed for the weather, her skirt too short and her jacket too light, so she wrapped her arms protectively around her midsection. Cole noticed and immediately shrugged himself out of his coat. He dangled it from one finger the same way he had that day in the elevator, giving it a shake when she refused to take it.

"I won't touch you," he promised. "And if you want me to go, I will—no questions asked. It's just… Can we…? Will you…? *Please.*"

She had no way of knowing what he was asking for, but it was impossible to ignore the desperation in that plea. Since it seemed important to him that she put on his coat, she did.

She knew it for the mistake it was almost immediately. The wool was heavy and expensive, soft with the warmth of his body. It was like being wrapped in his embrace.

"Thank you for sending your parents to my party," she said, since she had to say something or risk catapulting herself into his arms. "That was nice of you. It felt good to have someone there."

He gave a short laugh and ran a hand through his wet hair. "I had nothing to do with that."

She blinked a question up at him.

"Should I have lied and taken credit?" he asked and immediately shook his head. "It wouldn't have done any good. You'd know. You know me better than anyone."

It wasn't a compliment. She *did* know him—as a public figure and a private one, a football player and a man. The problem was, he knew her, too. She'd never been difficult to figure out, her every emotion on display for all the world to see, and he'd used that. He'd found her weakest, most vulnerable part and hit it as hard as he could.

"It was my dad's idea to come today. He thought you could use the moral support." He gave a short laugh at her start of surprise. "Don't look at me like that... It's your own fault. He likes you a lot more than he likes me right now. In fact, you've probably replaced me forever."

"He'll come around," Hailey said. "He's upset now, but he seems to really like the new quarterback. Invite Tucker over for dinner one night, and you'll see. You'll be the golden son once again."

"I don't care about being the golden son."

This was such a patent lie that Hailey couldn't help smiling. She toyed with the cuff of Cole's jacket, plucking at nonexistent strings and wishing she was better at this. "For what it's worth, I'm proud of you," she said. "It must have been hard to tell them the truth."

"Not nearly as hard as this is turning out to be." He reached for her and, remembering his promise, dropped his hands again. She almost took pity on him and reached back, but something prevented her.

Pride, probably. And hurt. And the knowledge that there were people inside that restaurant who genuinely cared for her. She'd forgotten how good it felt to have that—how strong it made her.

"I'm here, Cole, and I'm listening, but only because your parents asked me to. What do you want?"

"You."

The assured brevity of that reply almost sent her toppling backward.

"I had a whole speech planned, but I can't seem to remember any of the words," he added in a rush of breath. "I used to be good at this, saying what I'm supposed to and smiling at just the right moment, but it's never mattered like this before. It *matters*, Hailey. You matter. So much more than I thought possible."

"Cole—"

He held up a hand, stopping her short. "Please, just let me get this out. Then you can go back inside or get in that strange man's car or bury yourself under a pile of puppies, I promise. I know I don't deserve anything from you, but I don't think I can stand to go another day like this." He waited in that thoughtful way of his for her implied consent before continuing, his expression so earnest and terrified that she had no choice but to give in.

His relief when she did was a palpable thing.

"I wish more than anything else in the world that I could take back those things I said to you," he began, his voice unsteady. "I knew before I started talking that it was the wrong thing, the *worst* thing I could say, and I've regretted it every second of every day since. Not only did I hurt you—an unforgivable thing—but I was wrong."

He laughed, a short, bitter sound that matched the sudden shake of his head. "In fact, I've never been more wrong about anything. You *aren't* alone in the world, and you *do* understand my family—better than I ever have, that's for sure. They fell for you as quickly as I did, and I know exactly why."

She waited, her chest so tight that it felt full and empty at the same time.

"You're the bravest and best person I know," he said. "You were dealt a crappy hand in life, but you didn't let it break you. Instead, you turned it into a way to make the world a better place. Every dog you've housed, every puppy you've loved and nurtured, is the luckiest animal in existence—and I'm not using that word lightly. I'm lucky to know you, Hailey. My family is lucky to know you."

Hailey had come to loathe that word, but as it tripped off Cole's tongue, it lost some of its power. Not because he didn't mean what he was saying but because he *did*.

Cole Bennett had been born under a lucky star, it was true. He had money and love and looks and talent. He'd never know what it meant to sit alone in a cage or be tied to a tree or abandoned at a fire station before he knew his own name.

But she was lucky, too. It had taken twelve years before she'd been given a family, but it had been the best family in the world. And now she was being given another one all over again.

"They're yours if you want them," Cole said, confirming it. "With or without me, on any terms you'll have them. I've racked my brains trying to come up with something I can give you— something meaningful, something that matters—but it turns out that the only real thing of value I have is them."

Cole's shirt had grown fully damp by this time, the white fabric growing increasingly see-through the longer they stood there. He had to be freezing, standing half-dressed and soaked, but he didn't seem to notice. Hailey had the feeling that he'd continue standing there, developing pneumonia, until she finally spoke.

"You weren't entirely wrong," she said, her voice quiet but determined. "That day at your condo, I mean. You accused me of being too scared to keep my dogs for longer than a few weeks, said I was afraid to open my heart on a permanent basis."

"I was an idiot. An asshole. I took all my fear out on you because I knew, in that moment, that nothing scared me more than the thought of losing you." He drew a deep, shaking breath, and Hailey was surprised to find that his hands were shaking, too. "My whole life, I've been scared of what would happen if I no longer had football to fall back on. It's all I've been and all I've known. But then you came into my life, and I caught a glimpse of what existed on the other side. I saw a future that didn't just look appealing… It looked like everything I've ever wanted."

His beautifully striking blue eyes met hers. He must have seen something there that gave him courage, because the shaking finally stopped. "That future is you, Hailey Lincoln, and the life we could have—the two of us, together. The thought of missing out on that scared me a hell of a lot more than all the rest."

He looked so shaken and cold, so much like a puppy who'd been abandoned on a doorstep, that Hailey took pity on him. Since she knew that he wouldn't break his promise, wouldn't touch her unless she said it was okay, she flung herself into his arms.

"I'm scared, too," she admitted, her words muffled by the hard press of his chest. She could feel the beat of his heart, erratic but strong, and knew that there was nowhere else she would rather be. Especially when he wrapped both his arms around her. "Terrified, actually. I've been alone for most of my life, and I thought I could stay that way forever, but I can't anymore. I want to have dogs and friends and family. I want to watch football games and sit with Penny while she takes baths and throw parties for my coworkers. I want *you*, Cole Bennett. With your useless shoulder and your too-tight shirts and your big, generous, beautiful heart."

"You do? Even after what I said? Even after what I did?"

She had to smile at how uncertain he sounded, how incredulous. That lonely, despairing pang might be new to him, but she knew it well.

She also knew exactly how to fix it.

"Even after what you said," she agreed. "And even after what you did. You might not know this about me yet, Cole Bennett, but I'm a bit like a hailstorm. You never see me coming, but once I'm here, I'm not so easy to get rid of."

Cole didn't wait for her permission to kiss her this time. It might have been the fact that his body temperature was rapidly decreasing and he needed her to stay warm. Perhaps he heard the raucous cries from the restaurant signaling what must be a win for the Lumberjacks.

Or maybe, just maybe, he loved her as much as she loved him. Maybe, just maybe, she'd finally found where she belonged.

"Well, I'll be damned," Cole said as they stood breathless and panting in the rain, neither one willing to be the first to pull away. "My dad was right."

"About what?"

"About how I can put my months of convalescence to good use. Grab those puppies of ours and let's go. It's time you and I went home."

She blushed at the implication and the promise—and the fact that Cole had apparently discussed their sex life with his father—but held her head high. "*Which* puppies of ours?" she asked suspiciously.

"As many as we can hold," came his prompt reply. He grinned and gave her a meaningful squeeze. "I don't know if you know this, but I'm an unemployed millionaire with a bleeding heart for a girlfriend and a recent Puppy Cup win under my belt. There will be no stopping me now."

Epilogue

"I'M HAVING A HARD TIME DECIDING IF THIS IS A BLOCK PARTY OR a family reunion."

Cole flipped the cap off a bottle of beer and handed it to his sister. "Does it matter?"

Regina cast a look around the backyard of Cole and Hailey's new house, which abutted her own and was already scattered with more dog and children's toys than was seemly in a neighborhood like this. "People are going to start thinking there's something wrong with us. You aren't supposed to spend this much time with your relatives. It's weird."

"Tell that to Mia. She's having the time of her life."

It was true. Cole had spent the better part of the morning finishing the small wooden door that led through the hedge from Regina's yard to his own, and Mia was painstakingly teaching the dogs to use it. Nala and Rufus had picked up on the process right away, but Philip was showing a marked tendency to cower.

Regina paused a moment to watch her daughter before smiling. "You'll never get rid of her after this, you know. Kids can't resist secret doorways."

"It was either this or a tunnel from your basement to ours," Hailey said, coming up to join them. She was dressed simply but adorably in a yellow dress that made the most of the rare burst of sunlight. Fall in Seattle could be very touch-and-go in terms of weather, but the gods had smiled on them for their barbecue.

The gods had been smiling on them for quite a while now, actually. Hailey liked to say that all their good fortune came from his side of the family, but he knew better. The day he'd walked into her office had been the luckiest day of his life.

"I was only just able to talk Cole out of it," Hailey added. "He had an excavator picked out and everything."

"Don't even think about it. The day you touch my foundation with an excavator is the day I pack up and move away forever." Regina spoke with all the vehemence of an older sister who was putting her foot down, but Cole and Hailey only laughed. She'd been more excited than the rest of them when the house next door to hers had gone up for sale. She'd had her real estate agent on the phone before Cole could blink. "But I'm serious. If she gets to be too much, let me know and I'll—"

Hailey touched her arm. "She's not too much. We love having her around."

Regina nodded once, and that was the end of it. Cole could have pointed out to both women that if *he* had been the one to make that statement, there'd have been arguments and insults and a determination to have the last word no matter what the cost, but there was no point. Since the day Hailey had finally agreed to move in with him, his family had taken her side in everything.

Even after all these months, they liked her better than him, but that was okay. He liked her better, too.

They stood and watched as Mia coaxed Philip in an attempt to get him through the door. The pit bull had grown considerably since his formal adoption after the Puppy Cup, but he would always be a little on the small side. Rufus was well on his way to outstripping him, and even Nala, who his parents overfed to a ridiculous decree, was growing by leaps and bounds.

"The only way he's going through that door is if you lead by example," Hailey said after a few minutes. She landed a playful slap on his ass. "Down, boy, and show him how it's done."

Cole was only too happy to comply. To some men, crawling around on all fours might not seem like a step up from a glorious football career, but he knew better. He'd achieved quite a lot in his lifetime, but he'd never been as happy as he was these past few months. He played with the dogs and with Hailey, took Mia to all the library story times her heart could handle, and made the occasional commercial appearance courtesy of Regina's continued hard work on his behalf.

He and Hailey had also started filling out the paperwork to become foster parents, but they weren't publicizing it yet. It was a long and difficult process, and they were taking their time so they could do it right.

As if sharing his thoughts, Hailey glanced over and smiled, her expression somewhat misty. The journey had been understandably emotional for her, but she was facing it with the same bravery she showed in the face of every challenge. She produced television shows and personally adopted out hundreds of dogs to anyone willing to take one. She sat for hours watching old football footage with his dad and offered critiques to any of his old teammates who wanted them.

She was everything to him, and now she was giving him his tons of kids, too.

"*Olá!*" a friendly voice called. Regina didn't manage to subdue her groan in time, but Hailey expressed nothing but delight at the sight of the Wegmores escaping his parents and heading straight for them. "*Como você está?* Would you believe it? We've already booked our next trip. You'll never guess where we're going this time."

Cole made good his escape before he could hear the answer, scampering off after Mia with his pockets full of dog treats. Leaving Hailey to the mercy of his relatives might have been the cowardly thing to do, but he knew it was what she wanted most of all.

Because he loved her. Because she loved him.

Because she was family.

Enjoy a sneak peek at this unforgettably funny enemies-to-lovers rom-com about a grumpy dog show judge, a determined former beauty queen, and the golden retriever more interested in stealing bacon than winning Best in Show.

I HATE YOU MORE

by Lucy Gilmore

Coming November 2, 2021

THAT IS, WITHOUT QUESTION, THE MOST BEAUTIFUL creature I've ever seen."

Ruby gave a start of surprise at the unexpected voice so close behind her and jerked the leash in her hand. Predictably, the dog on the other end—a poodle shaved and trimmed into a series of white puffs like a Q-tip—didn't move. Ruby had been holding on to her for over five minutes, and she had yet to see the dog do anything but blink. Her owner had commanded her to stay, so stay was what she intended to do.

"I shouldn't say that," the voice continued in a low, flirtatious rumble. Its owner, a tall, well-built stranger with shoulders like a linebacker, smiled as he stepped close. "I'm not supposed to play favorites, but you've obviously put a lot of time and effort into this dog. What's his name?"

"Her," she said. "It's a girl dog."

"Well, she's got something special, that's for sure." The man extended a hand, his eyes smiling down into hers. They were gorgeous eyes, so dark they were almost black and ringed with the kind of long, curling eyelashes that Ruby had regularly pasted on when she was kid. "I'm Spencer Wilson, by the way. In case you can't tell, I'm one of the judges."

In studded jeans and a faded T-shirt that stretched a little too tight for Ruby's tastes, he didn't *look* like much of a dog-show judge, but she knew better than to be deceived by appearances.

"Ruby," she said, shaking his hand. "Ruby Taylor. Only there's been a mistake. I'm not—"

At the sound of her voice, the only other dog in the room sent up a howl of dismay. They were in a hallway of sorts, waiting to submit their entry to the West Coast Canine Classic, and the golden retriever wasn't happy with the delay. He wasn't happy about *anything*, especially the fact that Ruby was giving all her attention to the perfectly poised poodle that had been left in her care. The poodle's owner had forgotten some papers in the car and dashed out to grab them, begging Ruby to keep an eye on her precious darling in the meantime.

Unfortunately, Wheezy wasn't a dog who shared. Wheezy wasn't a dog who did much of anything except make Ruby's life difficult.

"Yikes," the man—Spencer—said as he took in Ruby's *actual* charge. It didn't help that Wheezy had met with an accident on the way in, which mostly involved the discovery of a mud puddle and a determined effort to reach the bottom of it. "What happened to him?"

"It rained this morning," Ruby said, feeling defensive. Okay, so Wheezy didn't look his best right *now*, but the competition hadn't technically started. They were just here to drop off their paperwork and pay the entrance fee. There were still a good two months until the actual dog show. "There are puddles all over the parking lot."

"And yet you managed to get your dog inside without falling into any." Spencer grinned at her. It was a *good* grin, the kind that started in his eyes and crinkled into laugh lines around his mouth, but something about it felt off. Probably because the man was mocking poor Wheezy before they'd even managed to get a foot in the door. That didn't seem like very professional dog-show-judge behavior to her. "I'm sure I don't have to tell you how many of these we get every year."

"How many *whats* you get?" Ruby asked, suspicious.

He heaved a mock sigh. "Everyone with a beloved family pet seems to think they can just roll up here and enter the show. No training, no grooming, no pedigree… I mean, come on. Would *you* bring an animal like that to the most prestigious dog show on this side of the country? To compete against a gorgeous girl like this one?"

Spencer placed a reverential hand on the poodle's head, but his gaze wasn't focused on the dog. Instead, his wide, obvious smile took Ruby in from top to bottom.

She pretended not to understand him.

"He's not *that* bad," she said with a nod at Wheezy, who'd given up howling to scratch at an itch on his neck. Enthusiastic flecks of mud splattered all over the white linoleum. "A little rough around the edges, maybe, but he has something this poodle doesn't."

"Fleas?" Spencer suggested with a laugh.

Ruby wasn't impressed. "I was thinking more along the lines of personality."

To be fair, the man wasn't entirely wrong. Wheezy—a golden retriever of questionable parentage, zero formal training, and the personality of a slug—was the last animal on earth who should be entering *any* dog show, let alone the West Coast Canine Classic.

Yet here they were, doing it anyway.

"Why, dear—don't you think you can help Wheezy win?" Wheezy's owner had asked. Mrs. Orson, who weighed all of a hundred pounds soaking wet, had been in bed at the time, which was Ruby's excuse for giving in so easily. Mrs. Orson always looked her most frail while she was lying down. And she knew it, too, the old sneak. Of all the residents at the retirement community where Ruby worked in the nursing home, Mrs. Orson was the wiliest. *"I was so sure you could manage, with all your experience in pageants…*

No matter. It's only a dying woman's last wish. I'll ask Harry if he can do this one small thing for me instead."

Harry, who'd never set foot on a pageant stage in his life. *Harry*, who'd once thrown Mrs. Dewan's Maltese into the community pool after Ruby had spent two painstaking hours combing the tangles out of its hair. *Harry*, who'd gladly let Ruby do every bit of work around the nursing home and then proceed to take credit for it.

If Ruby had stopped to think for five seconds, she'd have seen Mrs. Orson's tactics for what they were. The older woman had been threatening to die for as long as Ruby had known her, and always rallied the moment she got her way. But Ruby, with her pride on the line and the image of Harry Gunderson in her stead, had ruffled up, hotly defended her ability to claim any crown no matter the odds, and accepted the task set before her: to bring home a dog-show trophy for the world's most useless animal.

In theory, putting Ruby in charge of a golden retriever's show-dog debut was a sound plan. For the first eighteen years of her life, she'd been a show dog herself. Okay, she'd technically been a show *human*, but the idea was the same. She'd been primped and curled and trained to jump through the right hoops. She'd spent hours every day on grooming and deportment. She'd gazed longingly out the window at the other children chasing balls and going for walks.

She'd won, too. Her childhood bedroom—untouched by time or her mother's hands—was a testament to all she'd once been and would ever be. The walls were lined with obscenely large tiaras, stacked and organized by size and weight. Should the Big Quake ever hit Seattle and raze it to the ground, no one standing inside that room would survive. They'd be buried under a mountain of Ruby's gilded—and wasted—potential.

"Where's his owner, anyway?" Spencer asked with a glance at his watch. "It's past ten. The show's probably closed to new entries by now."

"*Probably*?" Ruby echoed. "Shouldn't you know? I thought you were one of the judges."

"I am," Spencer was quick to say—almost too quick, if you asked her. "Which is why you're in luck. For the small price of dinner with me, I'd be willing to fudge the time stamp in your favor."

Every part of Ruby recoiled. Like most women who'd grown up on the stage, she was well aware of the image she presented to the world. Her hair was a tangle of golden-blond curls that she tamed into submission every morning, her eyes a rich brown that she made of the most of with carefully winged eyeliner. Add her mother's fantastic bone structure and years of good skincare into the bargain, and Ruby had all the traditional Eurocentric beauty standards checked.

None of that made interactions like these more palatable. Getting chatted up by strangers was nothing new, but she didn't take well to such heavy-handed tactics. It was nice when a man at least pretended to be attracted to her personality first.

Before she could tell Spencer what she thought of his methods, the poodle's owner appeared in the doorway, breathless but holding the requisite forms. As Ruby knew from the stack in her own bag, there were *a lot* of them. You could buy a house with less.

"Thank goodness," the woman said. "I hope I'm not too late. Muffin would be devastated to miss the deadline."

Muffin looked as though she'd never suffered a disappointment in her life, much less a devastation, but the poodle sniffed happily as her owner drew near.

"Muffin?" Spencer asked with a laugh. "Did you name him that because he ate too many of them?"

Ruby stiffened. While there was no denying the golden retriever was somewhat…portly, she didn't appreciate jokes being made at Wheezy's expense. It was hardly his fault that he was carrying a few extra pounds around the middle. Life as the pampered darling of a dozen elderly ladies would do that to a dog.

"Oh dear," The woman took the leash from Ruby's hand and cast an anxious eye over her poodle. "Do you think she's put on too much weight? We switched to organic chicken breast recently, but I didn't think—"

"Wait." Spencer reared back with a start. He glanced back and forth between the two women and then the two dogs, confusion lowering his brow. "This poodle belongs to *you*?"

"We've been looking forward to this all year, haven't we, Muffin?" the woman cooed. She swelled with maternal pride. "Muffin comes from a long line of show dogs. Her mother took Best of Breed at the national dog show three years ago."

"Come, Wheezy," Ruby said, hoping to put Spencer in his place. It didn't work. Wheezy showed as little interest in her as he did the air around him. He heaved a sigh and dropped to his belly instead.

"We're still working on that one," she explained. They were still working on *all* of them, but she wasn't about to admit that out loud.

The poodle owner spoke up. "We're not too late to enter, are we? We were both here in plenty of time, I promise. It was only that I left the silly papers in the car, and this woman very nicely offered to wait for me before heading in."

"Weren't you just saying you'd be willing to change the time stamp for me?" Ruby asked, sensing an opportunity. "It's only fair that you'd offer the same to my friend and her poodle."

Hope lit Spencer's eyes. "Does that mean you'll go out with me?"

"Of course not. But I'm sure the AKC would love to hear about how you use dog-show extortion to trap women into dating you."

For the longest moment, Ruby was afraid she'd pushed too far. It was obvious that this Spencer guy was used to getting his way—and even more obvious that he felt no remorse at breaking the rules to do it—but she'd stopped using her physical charms to win pageant judges' approval years ago.

Ten years ago, in fact. And she wasn't about to change that now.

With a good-natured laugh, Spencer threw his hands up in the air. "Fine. You win. I can't resist a gorgeous woman making threats. Welcome, both of you, to the West Coast Canine Classic."

The poodle owner let out a long, relieved sigh, but Ruby wasn't buying it. "Don't you need to look over our applications first?"

"Caleb!" Another sharper male voice interrupted before the man could answer. "What are you doing here?"

Ruby turned to find herself facing another version of Spencer. A *literal* version of Spencer that made her swivel her head in a double take. Instead of facing one finely sculpted paragon of masculinity with eyelashes painted by the hands of a master, she was facing two of them. The newcomer was built just as powerfully as the first, but he was dressed more formally in a button-down shirt and well-pressed slacks. He wore his dark hair neater and cropped closer to the head, and his movements were more rigidly controlled, but they were otherwise as identical as, well, twins.

"Spencer!" Spencer said—only…wait. That couldn't be right. "Just the man to help us out of this fix."

The newcomer strode forward, his mouth set in a firm line. "Caleb, I don't know what you're doing or how you got here, but you need to get home." He glanced at a clock on the wall and added, "*Now.*"

"Don't worry," the man said. "I have a half hour until the next bus comes, so I thought I'd pop in and see how things are going."

By this time, the poodle owner looked as perplexed as Ruby felt. "I'm sorry…" She glanced back and forth between the two men. "Which one of you should I turn the application in to? Muffin and I are anxious to get everything squared away."

Muffin didn't look the least bit anxious, but Wheezy was starting to show serious signs of *something*. He strained and pulled in an attempt to get closer to the newcomer, a low whine escaping his lips. In all the time Ruby had known this dog, she'd only ever seen him this animated about pork products.

"To neither of us, I'm afraid," the newcomer said. He stabbed a finger at the wall. "The entry cutoff was at ten. You missed it."

At this, Wheezy let out a bark of protest. Ruby wasn't slow to follow. "But this man—Spencer, Caleb, whatever—said we could still enter."

"*I'm* Spencer," the newcomer said. "And I'm in charge of the dog show. I don't know what my brother told you, but rules are rules."

Wheezy showed exactly what he thought about that. With a yelp, he flung himself at the real Spencer and did his best imitation of a dog who'd never known the comfort of a human's touch. To his credit, Spencer immediately squatted down to Wheezy's level and extended a calming hand. Instead of accepting it, Wheezy began enthusiastically licking the man's face.

"I don't understand," the poodle owner said.

Ruby did. She cast a sideways look at the first brother—Caleb—at which he promptly winked. "Can you blame me?" he asked, laughing. "I'd have lied and pretended to be Prince Harry if it meant I'd get a chance to talk to you."

"Prince Harry would never do anything so underhanded," Ruby retorted. "Prince Harry is a *gentleman*."

By now, the rest of the party had caught up on the lie. The poodle owner looked flustered, Caleb looked amused, and Spencer looked extremely displeased.

Ruby could hardly blame him for it. She was leaning that way herself.

"Let's try this again, shall we?" Ruby said, forcing her irritation down. "My name is Ruby Taylor. I'm here to enter this golden retriever in the dog show." She turned to Spencer. "And you must be the *real* judge. Where would you like us to drop off the forms?"

Instead of ameliorating the man, his displeasure seemed to grow. "I'm sorry, but I can't allow you to enter." He glanced at the poodle owner with a touch of actual regret. "It sounds harsh, I know, but we have to stick to strict guidelines. In the name of fairness."

At that, Ruby's competitive instincts sat up and took notice. It seemed this new Spencer wasn't going to be nearly as easy as the first—and she loved a challenge.

"If it's *fairness* we're talking about, then you should let both these dogs in," she said. "Your brother already said we could enter. It's only right that you honor his promise."

"But Caleb isn't—" Spencer drew a deep breath and tried again. "Despite what he may have told you, my brother doesn't have anything to do with the show. Not officially. He's a dog trainer, not a judge."

"And yet promises were made. How are this woman and I to know which of you is which? Is it our fault we were misled about your identity?"

"It's not—" Spencer was cut off as Caleb released a low chuckle.

"I think you should give in," Caleb said. "I already tried to get the better of her, and it didn't work."

A spark of something combative flashed in Spencer's eyes. All at once, Ruby was struck with how much better that spark suited those long lashes than Caleb's insouciance. Eyes like that were meant to be taken seriously. Eyes like that were meant to carry fire.

"Fine." Spencer stood up and took a step back. "Show him to me."

"Um…" Ruby waved her hand in Wheezy's general direction. "He's right there."

"No, I mean *show* him. Put him through his paces. Let me see what he can do."

Ruby hesitated as she ran through her list of options. It wasn't a long one. Wheezy's skills included very little outside of eating and napping. Putting him in the spotlight—and with that dratted poodle looking on—wasn't going to end well for any of them.

Except maybe the poodle.

"Wheezy, sit," she said.

Wheezy didn't sit.

She went for an easier one. "Wheezy, stay."

In a move of pure perversity, the golden retriever heaved himself up and started wandering down the hallway. A sound halfway between a laugh and a snort escaped Spencer's mouth. That did more to set Ruby's hackles up than all the rest combined. No man laugh-snorted at her and got away with it. At least, not unless she *wanted* him to.

"Wheezy, you stubborn beast, make us both look like fools," she said.

This time, Wheezy happily complied. Discovering a half-open garbage can, he got up on his hind legs and started to explore its contents.

"Oh, for the love of Pete." Ruby took off after the dog. She grabbed hold of his collar and tugged, but it was no use. It took a lot to get Wheezy animated, but once you did, he was a force to be reckoned with. Wheezy had discovered something delicious inside the garbage and had every intention of digging his way through until he found it.

To her surprise, a solid male form came up behind her. She didn't need to look to know it was Spencer. The ease with which he extracted the golden retriever from the garbage can was clear proof of that.

"You can't seriously plan to enter this dog in the West Coast Canine Classic," he said. The hand he laid on Wheezy's head was gentle even as he squared off against Ruby.

"Oh, I don't," Ruby replied, turning to meet him head on.

Relief started to touch Spencer's lips, but Ruby stopped it short. "Wheezy isn't just going to *enter* the dog show. He's going to win. Can't you tell a pedigree champion when you're looking at one?"

Apparently, he could. "This dog is overweight."

"Don't be rude. Beauty comes in all shapes and sizes."

"He isn't properly trained."

"That's not true," Ruby protested. "He knows all the commands. He just doesn't always feel like listening to them."

"He doesn't look like a purebred."

Ruby had no response for that one. Mrs. Orson swore up and down that Wheezy was as much a pedigreed golden retriever as his papers claimed, but Ruby was pretty sure she'd had them forged. For such a sweet old lady, Mrs. Orson had some pretty shady connections.

"I have his paperwork." Ruby crossed her arms defensively. "And the full entrance fee. He deserves his chance as much as any other dog."

"Let me see his papers."

Ruby blinked. Spencer might be in charge, but she'd never responded well to demands—particularly when they were uttered by people in positions of authority. Police officers, bosses, teachers…the more power they had to shape her life, the less likely she was to fall in line.

She was a lot like Wheezy that way. She knew all the commands. She just didn't always feel like doing them.

"Why?" she asked. "What are you going to do?"

About the Author

Lucy Gilmore is a contemporary romance author with a love of puppies, rainbows, and happily ever afters. She began her reading (and writing) career as an English literature major and ended as a die-hard fan of romance in all forms. When she's not rolling around with her two Akitas, she can be found hiking, biking, or with her nose buried in a book. Visit her online at lucygilmore.com.